River is a heartbreaking journey of loss, love, and healing. It is a work not to be devoured, but savored for its quiet nature. It is a love song to the river and to those that pass away too quickly. River is truly a fantastic way to lose yourself and find peace."

Katie Glasgow
Book Buyer, Mitchell Books
Fort Wayne, IN

"Many reviewers will write that this or that book is so compelling "I could not put it down" or "I was up all night reading." Lowen Clausen's *River* is not that book. It should be slowly enjoyed like the long, solo kayak trip that is experienced within its pages. It is a tale to be savored for the bittersweet tale that unfolds, the heartbreaking humanity of the main character but most especially for the lovely descriptions of the natural beauty and power of the rivers on which he paddles."

Sue Zumberge
Manager, Garrison Keillor's Common Good Books
St. Paul, MN

"Lowen Clausen has written an exquisitely heart-breaking novel, with a soul as big as the eponymous River. After the death of his son, a father takes the river voyage he has always dreamed of. Starting out from his family farm on the headwaters in the Sandhills of Nebraska, his inner voyage takes him to new acceptance of the son he never said goodbye to in life, while he faces the solitude and challenges of the river itself. The land plays as large a part of the story as do the people on the river."

Tammy Domike
Manager, Seattle Mystery Bookshop
Seattle, WA

River is a restrained but heartfelt tale of repentance and redemption, following in the wake of Huckleberry Finn's raft—swift, honest, sometimes scary—as a man leaves behind the successes and tragedies of his life to live out a last promise to himself."

Nick DiMartino
Book Buyer, University Book Store
Seattle, WA

"While most of his readers will never undertake the kind of journey that Clausen describes in *River*, in one way or another, readers will find parts of themselves and their own life journeys in this story and enjoy traveling with the narrator on the river."

Carolyn Statler
Manager, Three Sisters Books & Gifts
Shelbyville, IN

River is a magical Thoresque, picaresque journey beginning in Nebraska and ending nearly 2,000 miles away and, in many ways, years away in experiences.

Clausen obviously has drawn from many personal experiences and writes with an easy lilt, with almost poetic descriptions. From Wamaduze Creek, the Loup, Platte, Missouri and Mississippi Rivers the story wends its way through beautiful scenes and carries the author and reader through the riverside and a personal journey of discovery at the same time.

Jim McKee
Owner, Lee Booksellers
Lincoln, NE

RIVER

LOWEN CLAUSEN

~~~

SILO PRESS

St. Paul, Nebraska/Seattle, Washington

Also by Lowen Clausen:

First Avenue
Second Watch
Third & Forever

dedicated to the memory of my mother, Emma Caspersen,
and my father, Haakon Clausen,
who lie buried in the Nebraska prairie
but are not forgotten

SILO PRESS
St. Paul, Nebraska/Seattle, Washington

SILO PRESS
PO Box 326
St. Paul, Nebraska 68873

Jacket Photograph by Steven Brumbaugh
Book Design by Constance Bollen

Published in the United States by Silo Press.
Printed in the U.S.A.

10 9 8 7 6 5 4 3 2 1

Library of Congress Catalog Card Number: 2007902732
ISBN 978-0-9725811-2-7

RIVER

~ ~ ~

The sunrise is long in coming. First there is a softening of the darkness, a gray tinge that dims the stars above the eastern horizon, then a pink glow that seeps through. It turns into a swath of yellow as if the sun will fill the whole sky, but it doesn't. It concentrates into a sphere of gold that rises above the sandhills and hurts my eyes.

Weariness weighs down my body as I get up from the riverbank and drag the kayak closer to the water. Her name is Gloria, and the idea of a journey with her has gotten me through one day after another. For months I've been planning this trip, buying equipment and supplies and storing them in the barn beside Gloria. Now that the day is here, the anticipation of leaving is gone and I feel empty.

Once more I look across the river into the hills as if I won't see them again. The coarse grasses along the banks of the river are green, but the rolling sandhills hold the dead brown of last year's growth. There are no trees on the hills and few even beside the river except at this place where the creek wanders down from the beaver dam to join it. Here willows cling to the bank and cottonwood trees have rooted in the low spots behind them. The willows are beginning to form new leaves, but the cottonwoods wait for more certain weather.

I push Gloria into the water and draw her close to the bank. The current pulls impatiently.

—Not yet, river. Wait for me.

While grasping the raised cockpit combing with both hands, I place my right foot inside her hull. Getting into Gloria was easy when I practiced on land, but now she shifts precariously in the water. It would be simpler to stand in the river and straddle her, but I don't want to get my feet wet. Again I feel the pull of the current. A few more seconds won't matter, but impatient it is and now is the time. In a single motion I lift my left foot from solid ground and slide awkwardly into the cockpit. Gloria lurches forward, and I feel the weightless suspension of water. The suspension is short-lived as the kayak rolls onto her side and dumps me into the river. I try to right Gloria and me by shoving off from the sandy bottom, but the current drags us downstream and prevents me from gaining any leverage. Finally, in disgust, I give up and push myself out. Without me to disturb her balance, Gloria rolls neatly upright.

The paddle floats away, and I slosh ahead to retrieve it. Farther downstream my hat is sailing lightly along, twirling around in the current like a boat without a rudder. I've had that hat a long time, and I consider trying to catch up with it. Instead Gloria catches up with me, bangs into my legs, and nearly knocks me down. Pushing her away, I grab the handle at her stern and let the river have the hat. The cockpit is half full of water and Gloria feels heavy and clumsy, just as I do. I'm glad no one else is here to see this.

After I drag Gloria back onto the bank, I dump out the river water, kneel beside her, and sponge out what remains in the cockpit. For the last several months as I glued together and coated epoxy onto the thin strips of marine plywood from which Gloria is made, I tried to imagine the feel of the river beneath me, the freedom of floating, the possibility of seeing the river and even myself in a new way, and now I've seen us.

Freed of the concern for dry feet, I push Gloria back into the river, straddle the cockpit, and lower myself into it. This time I raise both feet out of the water simultaneously, press them firmly against the foot braces mounted inside the hull, and begin stretching the waist skirt over the combing as Gloria floats away. The waist skirt is a silly-looking contrivance that is supposed to keep the water out of the cockpit, and it's difficult to manipulate into place. We float sideways for some distance before the elastic cord is secured completely around the lip. Gloria, I decide, is like a young mare being ridden the first time. A foolish rider ends up on the ground, but one with patience and a little humility can climb into the saddle without being thrown. Accepting my humbled presence she turns her bow downriver.

I've thought about this moment a long time, maybe all my life. The first memory I have is of carefully placing sticks into this river and watching them float away. Later my best friend Joe and I made toy rafts by tying the sticks together with willow branches. We wondered how far our rafts would go or could go with the right water and solemnly vowed to each other that one day we would build a bigger raft and follow them, a sort of religious ceremony that I've practiced with less devotion in other waters.

This small river, the north branch of the Loup, is fed by spring water that has gathered for millions of years in the great Ogallala Aquifer, which stretches through the heart of this country from the Dakotas in the north to Texas in the south. From the river's origin in a low-lying marsh some thirty miles to the east—thirty by the direct flight of the prairie hawk—it has widened to twenty-five feet by the time it reaches our ranch and might be three or four feet deep in its deepest places after a rain. But it seldom rains, and I have never seen the prairie hawk fly straight. It circles effortlessly high above on wind currents that are swifter by far than any in the water.

From long observation I've noted that there are usually two channels in the river that flow beside each bank. One of them is wider and deeper, but Gloria doesn't require much of either—a few feet of width, a few inches of depth—so there is little need to choose one over the other. Nevertheless a sandbar creeps toward us and pushes Gloria closer and closer to the bank until the sand scrapes the bottom of her hull and brings her to a stop. Even from my low elevation I can see that the current is deeper and faster on the other side. There is nothing to do but get out and pull Gloria to deeper water.

Without my weight she frees herself from the sand, and I don't have to pull her anywhere. I have to hold her back, which I do by grabbing a rope that I've tied to the stern. While I wade behind her, Gloria crosses the shallows at the far reach of the sandbar and enters deeper water. Having learned my lesson, I straddle the cockpit and drop down into her with my feet on both sides of her hull. The current pulls us away before I can bring them inside, and there is another moment of awkwardness as I lift my legs out of the water. This time we stay upright.

The paddle with double blades, which I've never used before, requires an unnatural contortion of the wrists in order for it to enter the water properly. Too often I strike Gloria's unscathed wooden bow. Sorry, I mutter to her as I used to mutter to the young mare before understanding her idiosyncrasies.

–Sorry.

So completely do I focus on the condition of the water, on the mechanics of the paddle, on the balance of the boat that I seldom look beyond the immediate stretch of river before us. What does that ripple mean? Is there a log buried in the sand? Is the water darker and deeper here or over there? The primary channel, small as it is, sweeps back and forth across the river, and at every crossing the water spreads out into many small fingers until it gathers and reforms on the opposite side. Sometimes we become stuck in the sand so close to the channel that I rest the paddle on Gloria's deck and push crablike with my hands on the sandy bottom until we reach deeper water. Sometimes it's too far and I have to get out. Before long I realize the futility of the waist skirt, take it off, and fasten it behind the cockpit beneath elastic shock cords that hold the life jacket and a clothing bag that wouldn't fit inside the storage hatches. It's getting crowded under those cords.

Through the morning I have a feeling that someone is watching, but I see no one. Perhaps it's only myself who is watching, or the little boy who placed sticks into the water and watched them float away from the spot just ahead where the cottonwood trees line the bank below the home place. The tall white barn my grandfather built farther up the hill comes into view as the river turns toward it. Through the large sliding door below the roof peak my grandfather and his five sons loaded in hay with horses and rope and pulley. The last time they filled the haymow was more than fifty years ago, but some of that hay is still up there.

After the Sunday noon dinners that my grandmother always made, my brother and I would become bored with grown-ups and their never-ending talk. We would walk down to the barn, climb up the ladder to the haymow, and slide open the door so that we could see the river as we played basketball on the rough floorboards. On that floor neither of us ever became good dribblers. We could shoot, however. The peaked ceiling of the haymow was so high that it permitted the highest arching shot either of us ever made at the netless hoop, which had been mounted there by one of our uncles when he was a boy. In the winter we might keep the door closed to hold out the wind. Then the pungent perfume of old hay permeated our play. The basketball hoop is still there. No one uses it anymore.

The uncertainty of rain was the reason my grandfather settled along the river. He intended to raise a mix of beef and dairy cattle and concluded that there would always be water for them from the spring-fed river and always hay in the low-lying meadows. The dairy half of his idea was not well-suited to the region, which was sparsely populated and too far from potential markets. He eventually abandoned the milking business except for a few Jersey cows that he kept to supply his growing family with milk and cream. When my grandfather came to this country, I don't believe he could understand the distances of the sandhill prairie. He could see it, surely, but his mind-set was formed on the small island in Denmark where he grew up. The island was smaller than the eventual size of our ranch.

My grandfather built the large elegant barn not long after he took possession of the land and some years before he replaced the one-room house, which my grandmother described, in her always blunt description of how she saw the world, as not being fit for the pigs. By the time I came along, it had become the residence of the less discriminating chickens.

When my father, the only son who remained on the ranch, bought his own land adjacent to my grandfather's, he should have been able to see clearly what my grandfather could not, for he grew up on this land. Surely it was cheaper and more efficient to buy milk from the store in town than to milk his own cows. But like his father he kept a few milk cows that bound my brother and me to the morning and evening chores we learned to hate. When I left home at eighteen, two days after graduating from high school— my brother left before me—I vowed never to milk a cow again. My father sold the milk cows after I left.

I thought I would never come back, not to live anyway, but I've come to believe that life is a sort of regression into our earliest ideas. Which is another way of saying that it plays tricks upon you, giving and taking so that you don't know which is which. When I returned, it was for my brother's funeral. He was killed in a jungle in Viet Nam that must have been as different from these sandhills as is possible on this planet. He didn't want to fight anybody, but no one listens to the young. My plan was to stay a month through Christmas so that my mother and father, especially my mother, would not be alone. I was the one who found Grandfather dead on the big hill north of the house on the morning after the longest night of the year. Joe, Annie, and I had been with him that night, and I believe he walked up there to watch the sunrise. I have always wondered if he saw it.

He left me his land along the river and Serafina, the Jersey cow he kept and milked by hand until the last day of his life. I never understood why my grandfather didn't leave the ranch to my father or my father's brothers, or to all of them. He divided up the rest of his possessions, but the land he left to me. He must have known I wouldn't sell it or the cow, and each morning and each night I followed the routine of my grandfather, sometimes grieving and sometimes cursing and sometimes both at the same time while I sat on my grandfather's worn one-legged milking stool and milked Serafina until she finally died of old age. A one-legged stool requires a special sense of balance.

The expansion of his small ranch and the business enterprise that followed would have confounded my grandfather, just as the distances of the vast prairie confounded him when he arrived in this country. If I had grown up on a small island, I might have shared his perspective. When he first saw the river, he imagined a steady source of water for his cattle. I saw it and imagined something much different—a mysterious passage through these hills that would take me all the way to the ocean if I ever wanted to leave— a journey that has to begin in the imagination of a child.

Without grounding us in the sand, the river carries Gloria and me past my grandfather's barn, the house he eventually built for his bride from Denmark, and the bigger house I built for Annie—or claimed I built for her—and all the corrals and machinery and animals that I'm leaving behind, as if it understands that we have to get by this place without stopping. I could have carried Gloria down from the barn and begun here, but I had to start upriver at the creek to make the journey complete.

An hour before dark I reach the barbed wire fence that stretches across the river and marks the eastern boundary of the ranch. Leaning back on the deck of the kayak I slip under the single strand of wire. It has taken all day to reach this point, all day to pass through the ranch where my grandfather settled nearly a hundred years ago, where my mother and father lived and died, and to which I added section by section of land until it became so large that it required many families to keep it going. I am wrong to think that it has taken only a day. It has taken much longer. Was it worth it—this accumulation of land, friends and enemies, families, memories? I don't know the answer or even if it is the right question to ask.

Now, before it's too late, before I lose the will to do anything, I am leaving this land to follow the sticks I placed into the river so long ago. I have built a raft unlike any that Joe and I ever made or imagined. When you don't know what is most important and you lose it, you have to do something; you have to find something that you believe in or at least pretend that you do. I am going back to the river.

The river is up in the spring, and I'm hoping there will be enough water to carry us farther east where it becomes deeper. Of this I am not certain. More water is being taken from it every year. I've taken my share and more. Even the great Ogallala Aquifer is being used up and is shrinking from its farthest reaches and deepest depths. But here in the rolling mostly unpeopled sandhills of northwestern Nebraska where spring water rises to the surface and makes a river, the aquifer is deepest and purest—as deep and pure as it may ever be until everything begins again.

~ ~ ~

The campfire is the only man-made light I see, in all likelihood the only one for miles around. Overhead the stars are brilliant in the moonless crisp air of April spring—the Milky Way a wide streak of frost on the window of the prairie sky. I note Polaris in the north, the traveler's star.

From the six-liter plastic container I pour water into the smaller of two titanium pots from the cooking set and place it at the edge of the fire. When the water is warm, I make a cup of instant coffee. I'm not hungry enough to cook anything. All around me are yellow waterproof bags that I have pulled out of the kayak. My unused stove and fuel are in one bag. Lying on top of the axe is the book I might read. Beside the book is my soap and toothbrush. In the morning I'll get better organized. I should have marked the bags so that I would know what is inside them, and I should have packed them so that I wouldn't have to empty the entire kayak to pitch a tent and make a cup of coffee.

A noise draws my attention to the brush behind me, and I see a flashlight coming my way. It must be my neighbor on whose property I'm camped. I don't want to explain to him what I'm doing. Maybe he already knows. There are few secrets in this valley. Then I remember. I don't have a neighbor anymore.

"So this is how far you got."

It is not my neighbor who is no longer my neighbor. Juan switches off the flashlight, squats down beside the fire, and tosses a piece of wood onto the flame. Although he is older than I, his knees are more flexible. I have to sit on the ground with my back resting against Gloria. He places a gunnysack beside me.

"Consuelo made you tamales. She would have made *chiles rellenos* if she knew you were leaving this morning."

"I couldn't sleep last night so I decided I might as well get started."

From the gunnysack I pull out a paper bag. Inside the bag are a dozen or more tamales wrapped in newspaper to keep them warm.

"I found your truck at the creek," Juan says. "I had one of the hombres drive it back to the house."

"I figured you would."

"You didn't tell us goodbye."

"I've been saying goodbye all winter."

"It's not the same."

"I know I didn't know how to say it."

"That's all right then."

Juan and I have been friends a long time. Twenty-five years ago I started out as the boss, but that changed early on. Juan and I have been changing from the first day I met him. The work I hired him to do was supposed to be temporary: to fix the fences that my hired man disliked fixing. There were a lot of things the hired man disliked fixing. Juan offered to do that work and any other that I had for him on his days off from the meat packing plant in Lexington. A man who wanted to work on his days off was the kind of man you didn't have to watch very much. The hired man didn't like him, which was also in his favor.

"Have you been watching me today?"

"Now and then. I didn't want to disturb you, but Consuelo would be unhappy if I didn't bring you these tamales. And I brought you a bottle of my hot sauce. You will need it for whatever is in those aluminum bags you bought. There can't be food in them that tastes like anything."

I remove one of the tamales and hand the paper bag to Juan so that he will join me. After unwrapping the newspaper and the foil beneath it, I carefully drip Juan's hot sauce onto the corn breading.

"Delicious. Please thank Consuelo for me."

I'm hungry after all.

Juan opens a foil packet of sliced limes that he retrieves from the bag of tamales.

"There is tequila in the sack also, in case you need a little. My brother-in-law bought it in Durango last year and smuggled it across the border. Tastes better that way."

I reach inside the gunnysack for the tequila bottle and hand it to Juan. He pulls out the cork and hands it back.

"You first," he says.

"*Salud.*"

After taking a swig I pass the bottle to Juan and reach for a slice of lime from the crumpled aluminum foil lying before the fire. Consuelo has sent the limes to squeeze on her tamales, but she probably knows that we will use them for the tequila, too.

"*Salud,*" Juan replies.

He drinks from the bottle and takes a bite of lime. Then he settles onto the ground beside me, using Gloria for a backrest as I have done, two no-longer-young men who find the ground harder than it used to be. He points to Gloria's name shining in the firelight.

"My cousin tells me it is a dangerous business to give a woman's name to a boat. If you give it the wrong name, your woman will be jealous. But if the boat is no good, you still have the woman. Where does this Gloria come from?"

"I got it from a book."

"Nobody you know?"

"No."

"Maybe it's better that way. If she sinks, you won't feel like you are losing a woman that you love. It could happen, you know."

"I know."

"But you don't know any Gloria, so you can let her go."

I don't think I could let her go even if her name is from a book. Her name and the need for it came to me gradually as the kayak began to take shape. Maybe it was the way Juan's grandchildren touched her when he brought them to see it, or the way I did. Sometimes in the middle of the night I walked down to the abandoned milking room in the barn just to look at her. I didn't expect to name the kayak because I have been a failure with names. But I gave her a name anyway and drew letters in pencil on her bow and filled them with gold paint. Now the name is varnished over and permanent.

"*Salud.*"

I toast Juan again and raise the bottle to my lips. His deep wrinkles are highlighted by the shadows created from our fire.

"Anything you need?" Juan asks. "Anything else I can bring you?"

"What size hat do you wear?"

"I don't know. The size that fits my head. What happened to yours?"

"It's floating down the river."

"How did that happen? Wind?"

"Water. I got into the boat the wrong way and she turned over."

"You see? You should have let my cousin build you a boat. I told you, he built fishing boats in Mexico. He would make one that wouldn't turn over when you got into it or break apart on the first rock it finds like this one will."

Juan has a cousin, a brother, a daughter, or a sister's son for every purpose, and he has made me richer than I would ever have made myself. Maybe it can be said the other way, too, although I never intended for that to happen. It seems that you get started one way and if you don't hit a rock, you just keep going. First it was Juan. Then he brought Consuelo, who brought Rosario and her two younger brothers. Then came Juan's brother who lived with them for a time all cramped in the trailer where the hired man had lived alone. Then we bought a ranch north of us, and Juan and Consuelo moved into that house and took the trailer with them for his brother and the brother's wife and child. And so it went with the trailer moving from one place to another until it became too dilapidated to live in except for a month at the spring calving pasture.

The arrival of the Mexicans was not generally welcomed by those who had been here before. I could have stopped it, I suppose, somewhere, anywhere along the line, but I didn't. I didn't want to. Or maybe the notion that I had any control was wrong from the start. It's even beyond Juan's control now, and sometimes he sounds like one of the old ranchers complaining about the young hombres who don't want to work anymore.

"I'll try to miss the rocks."

"This Gloria is too skinny. That's why she tips over. My cousin would have made it bigger on the bottom."

"A man from Harvard University designed this kayak with a computer. She's made to sail in the ocean. I think she will be all right."

"Don't be so sure," Juan said. "You're not in the ocean yet, you know. And maybe they don't learn much at that university, not like the one in Chicago where Rosario went."

Juan has great respect for everything from Chicago ever since Rosario, his oldest child, went to school there. He lived there once himself and didn't like it at the time, but the city has risen in his estimation since Rosario was there.

"Maybe I should have had Rosario design the boat."

"Maybe. She doesn't come to see what you are doing," Juan says.

"She knows what I'm doing."

"I know, but she didn't come to see how the pieces of this boat fit together. It is quite something really, I admit that. If you had built this boat only to look at, I would say it is a fine thing. But you didn't build this boat to look at."

"No."

"How far is it from here to the ocean?" he asks.

"I'm not sure. About two thousand miles, I guess."

"God in heaven! Two thousand miles! How can you go that far in this boat with no motor?"

"It's all downhill. I can just sit in the kayak and let the current do the work."

"How fast is this current?" Juan asks me, gesturing toward the river that we know is there but can no longer see. His question is simple and basic and is the logistical key to my journey. Juan always asks the key question.

"I don't know."

He looks at me with new apprehension. I have listened to him for so many years that I can hear his voice even when it stays within him.

"The current seems to change a lot. One of these days I'll dig out the GPS I bought. It's supposed to tell me where I am and how fast I'm going."

"Oh, my friend," he says with despair in his voice. "You don't know how fast the current is or how long it will take to get to the end of this river, and you don't know what you will do when you get there. I don't think you should take this trip. What if you get lost?"

"You can't get lost on a river."

"If you do, you can call me and tell me where that machine says you are. Then I will come in the pickup to get you and your boat. It doesn't matter where you are. You understand? It doesn't matter where you are."

"I understand."

"Maybe you will decide tomorrow that you have gone far enough."

"Maybe."

"But that won't happen."

"No."

"I don't know why you want to do this," he says. "You have spent your whole life here, your father and your grandfather before you. You have worked hard, and you have thought hard, too, and you have this fine place with everything you need, and more. You have friends here—we are like your family—and now you want to get into this river and see where it goes. You don't tell me what you will do when you find out, but you are putting everything into this new corporation that I don't understand, and you want Consuelo and me to move into the big house. We don't want to move. We want everything to stay as it is."

"Nothing ever stays the way it is, but you will run the ranch just as you have all these years, and Rosario will take care of the other things in Omaha. You already own part of the ranch. You will just own more, and so will the others. And there will be money for the children if they want to go to college like Rosario. Someday she will need help, too."

"If all the children go off to college, who will be here to cut the hay, or plant the corn on the farms up north, or fix the fences? Who will look after the cattle if we have deep snow in May like we did that first year?"

"I'll come back and help then. That year we did it all by ourselves—you and I."

"And Annie," he corrects me. "In that snowstorm she worked as hard as any man." It is the highest compliment Juan can give. "Don't forget that."

"I won't forget."

"We will keep your grandfather's house for you. We'll keep it just as it is except that we will make it better. We will begin working on it tomorrow. You will keep the house so that you have a place to come back to."

"I can stay with you in the big house."

"No. You will have your own house. And the river. This river will stay yours, too. Have Joe put that into the papers, or I won't sign any more of them."

"The river is public domain. It doesn't belong to anybody. He can't change that."

"That's all right, then," Juan says. "Nobody owns the river, but you put into the papers about your grandfather's house or I won't sign any more."

There was nothing left to sign concerning the transfer of ranch assets, but if one more paper will give Juan peace, we can sign one more—a short addendum to the long complicated set of papers that say that this ranch was once mine and Annie's, but I don't want it anymore. She never did.

"You should give it more time," Juan says. "It hurts bad now, but time will heal any wound."

"I have given it time. Some wounds won't heal and some shouldn't."

This is as close to talking about him as we have been able to come for a long time, but still we can't say his name out loud, the unspeakable name that smothers the ranch and everyone on it like the unexpected and dangerous snow that fell in May the first year Juan was here and changed everything.

~ ~ ~

Outside the tent I cinch the string of Juan's old black hat under my chin and stretch my back in all directions to get it into some tolerable configuration. The sleeping pad I bought is supposed to be the top of the line, but I must have awakened a dozen times during the night to blow into the tube or let air out. It didn't do any good. My back is stiff and sore, and my left shoulder feels as if it has been jammed into the ground all night.

The waterproof bags are lying about in the same places they were when Juan left. I pack my cup into the bag with the cooking set and place my book, which I have not yet opened, into the bag that has one of the three flashlights I brought along. I'm not sure where the other two are. As I pack the kayak, I find there is now room for the clothing bag that I had to strap on the deck the first day. The other bags must have compacted during the night.

I kick sand into the hole I dug for the fire. The grass is pressed down where the tent has been, but already some of the shoots are beginning to point upright. In a few hours there will be no sign that I have been here.

From the low bank I push Gloria into the river and let the current pull her bow forward. Like a cocoon I have everything I need to survive inside the kayak—today, tomorrow, and for many days—everything I need.

The kayak groans to a stop, and I look up and see that the channel has switched to the other side. There is no obvious reason for the change, but it has and we're stuck. The current rotates the stern forward until we are sideways in the river. Although I try to push Gloria free with my hands, she is firmly stuck in the sand, and I have to get out of the cocoon and pull Gloria to the other side of the river. When we reach deeper water, I get back in.

—We could use a little more water here.

I must be talking to Gloria.

Some say we are in the fifth year of drought, others that it is the sixth. We had a good rain a week ago, and it was early for such a rain. I suggested to Juan then that the drought might be ending.

"We need more than one good rain to get out of this," Juan said.

But it might be the beginning of the end. Every drought has to end.

Even if the drought has not ended, I had hoped that there would be enough water left from the last rain to carry me downriver. There is enough water, but sometimes it spreads out too much. If it would just stay together, I would have all the water I needed.

When I was building the kayak, Juan felt that it was his duty to keep me informed about the water level of the Platte River that I will reach in another two hundred miles. His nephew drove a truck route on Interstate 80 from North Platte to Omaha and crossed the Platte several times on his route. Juan reminded me that the Platte River had completely dried up west of Grand Island the summer before.

"There's some water there now," Juan said. "They have those birds there that need it, so they can't take all the water away. But you better get there before the birds leave."

He was talking about the sandhill cranes, and already they are leaving. Their plaintive primeval call spreads across the valley as they fly overhead so high that their V-formation is barely visible against the depth of the blue sky.

"There is water in the Loup," I told Juan after one of his reports. "There is always water in the Loup. Maybe the Loup will put enough water into the Platte to get me down. I need only five or six inches."

My grandfather told me that even during the drought of the '30s, there was water in the Loup from the underground springs that did not depend upon the fickle cycles of rain.

"The Platte is a mile wide and an inch deep," Juan said. "That's what they say about that river."

That's what they said about the Platte when it ran freely. Now there are dams in the west that capture the snow runoff from the mountains and deep irrigation wells that pump water from the underground river that follows the wide and shallow Platte, leaving even less water to flow on the surface. Now there is a drought that dries the reservoirs behind the dams and forces the wells deeper. Here the river is small and narrow, and still we get stuck in the sand. What will happen on the Platte, a mile wide and an inch deep? One inch is not enough. But why do I think about the Platte when I have two hundred miles to go before I reach it?

Two Canadian geese take flight over the bow of the kayak and practically knock me over with the sudden beating of their wings. I shouldn't be surprised. Pairs have been nesting in the tall grass all along the river, just not as close as these. The geese alight downriver, honking with alarm, intending to draw Gloria and me away from their nest. When we are no longer a danger, they circle behind us and return to their eggs. It's a process that is repeated again and again with the geese performing their part of the play, and Gloria and I ours.

When the sun is about as high as it's going to get, I paddle to the bank where a stand of cottonwood trees has taken root and pull Gloria out of the water. With my back against the largest tree I listen to the dry brittle sound of last year's leaves rattle in the breeze as I open the gunny sack that holds the food bag Juan brought me last night. I peel away the newspaper insulation and aluminum foil from one of Consuelo's tamales and drip Juan's hot sauce over it. There are a half-dozen left, so I won't have to cook tonight either. After eating two tamales, I remove Juan's hat, rest my head against the tree, and close my eyes. Consuelo's food has made me sleepy. If I don't get up, I will fall asleep.

So what if I do.

When I wake I discover that ants have found the open foil wrappers. A parade of them is carrying away crumbs that are bigger than they are. I dump the remaining crumbs onto the ground so that the ants can continue their parade after I leave.

We have good water when we return to the river, which is how I think of it when it forms a channel deep enough that I don't have to get out of Gloria. Maybe it will last, I think to myself, but don't say so out loud. You don't want to say these things out loud.

The river of good water cuts through the side of a tall hill, and Gloria drifts over to the bank. A willow has sprouted on a ledge, and I grab it and pull Gloria tight against it. She is impatient with any delay now that we have found good water. Above the ledge is a black layer of peat, what Joe and I used to call dead man's back when we stepped on it in the river. In the sandstone below the peat, a stream of water trickles through the porous stone. A jagged edge provides a lip from which some of the water drops. Beneath the lip I make a cup with my hand and drink the water. It tastes fresh and sweet. I dump out my water bottle and hold its mouth beneath the rock lip. It will take awhile to fill, and Gloria is eager to get away.

–Patience, Gloria. This might be our last chance to fill up with good water.

I often thought we should bottle this spring water and sell it. If people would pay a dollar or more for a bottle of water from France, what would they pay for pure water from Ogallala Springs—the name I conceived for the spring water from the aquifer? After telling Juan and Rosario about my idea, Rosario was interested. But that was another life. Another life, I remind myself. Now I want just one bottle of water, and Gloria will have to wait while I get it.

Our good water lasts until we come to a flat meadow where the river spreads out in search of a passage. I trudge through the shallows, paddle, trudge again. When finally we reach the end of these shallows, I see a pickup truck parked on a bluff above the river. A nice herd of young Angus bulls is feeding from a bunker close to the truck. I know where I am, whose bulls they are. A young woman in blue jeans followed by her two children walks down the bluff to the river to meet me. The current, what little there is, flows down the middle of the river, but I guide Gloria toward the north bank. We get stuck before reaching it. I get out and pull Gloria behind me. I haul her up onto the sandy bank and leave her there while I walk toward the washout in the bluff where the woman is waiting.

"Hello, Rebecca. Nice group of young bulls you got up there."

"We're getting them ready for the spring sale. I heard you were coming this way."

She lifts her head so that her cowboy hat lets the sun reach her eyes. Then she folds her arms across her chest and pulls them into herself as if in pain. The pain is clearly written in her face. It's a look I've seen too often the last few months.

"Is it true that you're going to the ocean?"

"I guess so, if I can find enough water."

"What kind of boat is that?" her son asks. He's about ten years old and finds Gloria to be more interesting than I am.

"It's a kayak."

"Like the Eskimos have?" he asks.

"That's right. You can sit inside her if you want."

He looks up to get his mother's approval.

"Your boots are dirty, Blayne."

I raise my shoes from the sand so she will see them. Today I'm wearing long waterproof socks that I've pulled over the top of waterproof pants, but it still feels like the water is seeping through.

"It doesn't matter."

"All right, but don't break anything."

"Can I, too, Momma?" her daughter asks. She's a year or two younger than her brother.

Rebecca nods and the girl follows her brother down to the kayak.

"The water gets deeper a little farther down," Rebecca says. "In about a mile there is even a small rapids, if you can call it that. You should watch out for the rocks."

"I will."

Now her eyes cloud with tears that don't drop, and I know what's coming.

"You weren't at the service so I never had a chance to tell you. But I'm really sorry about your son. I just want you to know that. We're all sorry."

"Thanks. I decided it was best if I just stayed away. I've never been much for church services like that."

"I know."

Her son is sitting in the kayak and has picked up the paddle from the sand. The girl is bent over the cockpit and is looking inside.

"I've forgotten your daughter's name?"

"Augusta. But she doesn't like it, so we call her Gussie."

"My son never liked his name either. We should just call them you until they get old enough to pick their own names. Then they would have to live with their own choices."

Rebecca smiles. So we've gotten through the worst of it. There is always the part in the beginning that's hard, but we're through it now. I walk down to the kayak and squat in the sand beside the girl.

"Do you want to sit inside, Augusta?"

She looks at me after I say the name she doesn't like. I like her name. She might, too, someday, but today she doesn't. She might have corrected me about the name, but she wants to take her brother's place inside the kayak and needs my help to get there.

"Let's give your sister a chance."

Blayne makes one more sweep with the paddle before crawling out of the cockpit. Augusta takes his place and reaches for the paddle that Blayne is holding. He gives it up reluctantly.

"How do you steer this boat?" Augusta asks.

"It kind of steers itself from what I can tell, or you can turn it with the paddle. I'm sort of learning as I go."

"How old are you?" Blayne asks. He's standing up straight and looking at me carefully.

"I'm almost fifty."

"Are you sure you should be taking this trip by yourself?"

"Blayne," his mother says with a sharp point to her voice, a warning for him to mind his manners. But I'm laughing. I can still remember when I thought fifty-year-old people were so old that it would hardly be worth it for them to get up in the morning, and I'm glad Blayne has said so. His words are better to hear than any words of sorrow from an adult.

"Maybe you should go with me and show me how to do it."

"Me, too," Augusta says.

"You bet. You, too. But I think your mom has other ideas."

Both children look at their mother who has other ideas.

"We'd better get back to the house," she says to the children. "You're welcome to join us for supper," she says to me. "And we've got an extra bed. They say it might storm tonight."

The sky is clear blue, marked only by the lingering contrail of a jet airplane.

"More rain would be good. Might get rid of this drought yet. Thanks for the invitation, but I think I'll paddle a little farther and take advantage of this good weather."

"It is a beautiful day," Rebecca says. "Almost like summer, except there aren't any bugs."

"Even better, then."

"Even better."

I wait until Rebecca and her children have walked back up the washout to the truck before I remove the paddle Augusta had carefully stored inside the cockpit. Then I drag Gloria back out into the current and settle down where the children had been. It feels better now that they have been here.

The rapids Rebecca warned me about are little more than a few riffles in the water with a half dozen large rocks sticking up, but the riverbed is hard and ungiving when my paddle hits it, not sandy as it has been before. I thought I knew this river, this part of it anyway where I grew up, but it is already different from anything I expected.

Over the rapids I carry Rebecca's grief, and mine, freshened by the memory of a son who didn't like his name either. It was one of the reasons I decided to leave, to spare these people and me the grief that they have to share, the gut-tightening pauses when meeting someone I haven't seen for a while who needs to tell me how sorry she is. I could get used to it, I suppose, if he hadn't hated the name I gave him, and the work, and the stories that went with the work. Sometimes he even hated the place, this beautiful fragile place with hills of sand with a little dirt on top. They are stable now but will begin to move again if the drought lasts too long. The drought would have to last a long time to kill the drought resistant grasses and plants that hold the hills, but it's happened before. This place was once a desert. It had once been the bottom of a shallow sea. It had once been a home, too, but it doesn't do any good to think about that now.

~ ~ ~

Clouds are bunching up in the west where the sun will set in another hour. It might rain after all. I am pulling Gloria through shallow water where the terrain has flattened again. If I'm oriented correctly, I have come to McDonald Flats. And if this is McDonald Flats, Wolf Creek is where the trees follow the valley up into the hills. Juan and I once looked at land there.

Gloria floats freely again, and I sit in the cockpit with my feet dangling in the water while she carries me along in the current until we reach the mouth of Wolf Creek. There I get out of Gloria, grab her bow handle, and pull her out of the water over the two-foot high bank. She groans a little from the weight of the supplies.

There are names like Wolf Creek that become so common that we don't think about them. I never knew and never thought about where the name of this river came from until Joe wrote me about it. It was after he moved to

Omaha, when we wrote to each other every week. "Listen to this. The Loup got its name from the prairie wolf." He had found the information from a book in his school library. We had twenty or thirty books in our library and none about the Loup River or the wolf. Joe had discovered that the French trappers who came to this country in the 1700s named the river the Loup after the Skidi tribe of the Pawnee, Chaticks-si-Chaticks, men-of-men, who had settled along its banks farther east. The Skidi had taken their name from the prairie wolf that followed the bison herds on their migrations, and loup was wolf in French. We didn't have anybody in the valley who spoke French. I wrote back and asked Joe what the Pawnee called the river, but he could never find that information, not even in the thousands and thousands of library books in Omaha.

The creek wedges into the river through a stand of naked trees and exposes parallel layers of sandstone, each layer a slightly different color. A large bone projects from a layer close to the top, and I climb up the steep bank to inspect the bone. When I brush sand away to expose more of it, an arrowhead tumbles down to my feet. I reach down and pick it up. The point and edges are still sharp.

When Joe and I were boys, we often looked for arrowheads along the river. Once we found a hill that no one knew about where there were hundreds of arrowheads along with pieces of broken pottery. Joe insisted that the hill was sacred and that it would bring us bad luck if we took anything from it. He knew more about Indians and sacred hills than I did even before he moved to Omaha. I couldn't imagine why one hill was sacred and another was not. Nevertheless, we told no one about the sacred hill and left all the arrowheads behind. He must have been right, because our luck was almost always good.

Joe would know which tribe had made the arrowhead I rub now between my fingers. This was disputed land. The Ogallala Sioux sometimes raided south into the Pawnee hunting grounds. The site would be a good place to camp—fresh water, trees, shelter from a storm. The buffalo needed water, too, and might gather at the river to drink. Or they would graze in the hills with the prairie wolves that gave their name to this creek and to the river it feeds, circling and preying upon the stragglers. At night the call of the wolves would echo through the valley. I stick the arrowhead back into the bank of the creek. For all I know, this place might be sacred, too.

I stake out the floor of the tent on a high spot close to the creek. The tent dome is four feet high at the highest point on the curve. A separate rain flap goes over the top and extends beyond the tent to protect it from driving rains. In case Rebecca is right about the storm, I tie additional ropes to the frame and anchor the ropes into the ground with stakes. And she might be. Thunderheads, like those that usually wait until summer, are boiling up in the west.

After digging a shallow fire pit in the sand, I arrange kindling on the bottom and stand thicker wood around it. My long-barrel lighter is not in the bag with the shovel where I thought I had stored it. It's not in the next likely bag either, the one that has the cooking set. But there is a canister of matches, and I use them to light the fire. Tomorrow, I'll get organized.

I take off my clothes, lay them on top of the tent, and wade into the river with a bar of soap and a washcloth. The water is warm for this time of year, and I sit down in it. A flash of lightning pierces through the red and white thunderheads on the horizon. There is no thunder, indicating that the lightning is a long distance away.

At the campfire I turn naked circles until I have dried. Then I put on my clothes and sit down beside the fire. The sun has disappeared behind the clouds, and as a faint sound of thunder rumbles through the valley I eat the last four of Consuelo's tamales. Tomorrow I'll have to dig in the food bag for a package of freeze-dried food. The food bag is somewhere among the jumble of bags around the kayak.

Darkness comes early with the dark clouds in the west covering the sunset. Lightning flashes brighter and thunder rumbles louder as I pack the bags in the kayak, fasten down the hatches, and tie the bow rope to a tree. Along with the life jacket that I have yet to use and the spray skirt that I used once, I place the two separated sections of paddle inside the cockpit and stretch the cover over the combing. To make sure that nothing is left out, I shine the light from my flashlight around the tent and over the ground. Before crawling into the tent, I kick sand on top of the coals to smother them. It is warm for April, too warm for so early in the year.

The wind is getting stronger, and I hear it blowing through the naked trees as I lie in the unzipped sleeping bag. The tent will either stand or it won't. It's an expensive tent, and I think it will stand. Rain strikes with force as the leading edge of the weather front moves through. I turn on the weather radio and listen to the computer voice advising me to take shelter. If I am in the open, says the mechanical voice, I should find a ditch or a low-lying place and lie down in it. If I could, I would laugh at such advice. I wonder how high the river and the creek will rise. Will the rain wash away the arrowhead?

The wind increases again and howls through the trees like the wolves that once roamed this ground. Unlike the buffalo, none of the prairie wolves survived. They're gone forever, and their ghosts howl on the prairie as the storm passes over and my eyes close in the darkness of the tent.

Joe runs from the river toward the solitary hill and I am behind him. He has tied a shoestring around his head and has stuck a feather in it, but the feather keeps floating away. Leave it alone, I tell him, but he stops to pick it up. The wolves are behind us, so why is he laughing? I throw rocks to keep them away while he sticks the feather back into his headband. We climb the hill together and below us the wolves howl as they circle the hill. A wolf breaks from the pack, charges toward us, but retreats when it reaches the hill. Another wolf charges and comes part way up before we frighten it away. I pull the shoestring from Joe's head and fasten it to a bow. I pick up an arrow from the hill and aim at the third wolf coming toward us. This is a sacred hill, Joe says. The wolf won't hurt us. I pull the bowstring taut and aim the arrow. Don't shoot! Joe is shouting now. The wolf is nearly upon us and I can see its fangs and laughing mouth. Do I release the arrow or believe in Joe's sacred hill? A feather floats to the ground at my feet. Joe is gone and I'm alone and the wolf is coming up the hill.

~ ~ ~

The river and creek have risen during the night, and the wet line on the creek bank shows how high the water has reached. Branches lie on the ground, evidence of the wind that blew through the camp. I look for animal tracks in the sand. There are only mine, and they have been leveled by the rain.

To the Sioux and Pawnee who hunted here, the wolf was a brother who cleaned the prairie of buffalo carcasses and culled the herds, leaving the herds stronger. This I know from books, only from books. Nevertheless the howls I heard last night seemed more real than a dream, more real than my imagination could make them.

Digging through the bags, I find the stove that I lit once before to test it. After I spread out its spindly wire legs, it looks like a giant spider clinging to the sand. Instead of taking down the tent while waiting for the water to boil, which is what I would do if I were trying to be efficient, I prop myself against a tree trunk and watch the blue flame flash up the side of the pot. After the water begins boiling, I pour half of it into my cup to which I add instant coffee. Into the remaining water I dump a package of instant oatmeal and stir it.

As I sip the tasteless coffee, I remember the morning my son told me we should bring back the wolves. I had made him get out of bed because there was work to do, and I was waiting for him at the kitchen table, enjoying the first cup of coffee before breakfast. It was something he had read the night before in a magazine from New York. The magazine announced where it was from right on the cover. The writer proposed that the whole region of what he called unproductive land, which stretched through the high plains and sandhills, should be turned into a nature preserve so that tourists could come here for safaris like they do in Africa. Tear down the fences, he wrote, return the land to the buffalo and Indians, and bring back the wolves. It wasn't so much the writer's fantasy or his ignorance that made me angry—it was my son's delight in repeating it.

Maybe, I told my son, he could get up in the morning on his own when there was work to do if he didn't spend the whole night reading magazines. His delight in the story disappeared, as his delight disappeared every morning when there was work to do.

When I was his age, I didn't like being told what to do any more than he did or having to do work that I had no voice in. But I didn't tell my father or grandfather that their lives had been a waste of time, which was what I thought my son was telling me when he repeated the writer's nonsense. I just left. My son did, too, a few years later: off to college, not to come back, I thought, except for obligatory appearances. But I was wrong about him, just as I was wrong about myself. Neither of us could stay away. I wish one of us had.

Why do I bother with this tasteless coffee? The spring water would taste better by itself. I dump what's left onto the ground.

When the kayak is packed and I'm ready to leave the camp, I bring out the GPS for the first time from the low-profile deck bag where it's been stored with the binoculars, hand wipes, and toilet paper. I turn on the battery-powered device and place it beneath the first shock cord that stretches across the deck in front of the cockpit. It tells me that it is searching for satellites. After a few seconds it claims to pinpoint our location within an accuracy of thirty feet. A moment later it refines the accuracy to twelve feet. On its tiny screen a winding river appears with an even tinier arrow pointing south, the same direction as the compass on the bow of the kayak. I look up to the invisible satellites in the sky and wonder what kind of black magic this is. The device is supposed to give me an assortment of other information, too, if I press the right sequence of buttons. But that will wait for another time. It's time to get back on the river.

What had been a two-foot high bank the night before is six inches now. Gloria slides easily from the sand into the high water. I slide less easily into the cockpit. Immediately the high water sweeps us away before I have time to look back. Soon we're in a narrow section of river that is full, bank to bank, and I check the GPS to see how fast we're going. It reads eight miles an hour.

Compared to yesterday, we're flying. The water is turbulent where the current is digging at the sand. Gloria slices through the turbulence as if she knows what to do. The river is deep enough that we pass over the sandbars that would have stopped us yesterday. This high water is what I have been wishing for. If it holds I'll reach the Platte much faster than I expected and finally leave these fragile hills behind.

There is a flash of reflected light downriver. Before I can make out what it is, we enter a sharp curve where the centrifugal force of the current sweeps

Gloria toward the outside bank. I duck to avoid the willows overhanging the river, but the branches tangle us up anyway. Gloria feels like she's slipping away from me, and I grab a willow for support. The current is pulling her downstream even as I'm tangled in the branches. Her stern breaks out of the willows first, and we're swept backward down the river. I try to turn her around, but the current is too strong to overcome with a paddle. Before I know it, the force of the next curve throws us into the willows on the opposite bank. This is not what I expected, not what I'm prepared for. But I better prepare soon or Gloria is going to take this trip without me. This time she is facing downstream after she breaks free.

There is another sharp curve coming and I get ready. So does Gloria. She turns her bow away from the approaching bank, and I paddle as hard as I can toward the center of the river as the current pushes us toward the edge. We come round the corner unscathed, and I feel like cheering.

The fast high water of this new river is exhilarating and manageable now that I am becoming used to it. I only have to anticipate what is ahead, prepare for the curves, and paddle hard. Even if I'm no longer a young man, I can still paddle hard.

The air smells washed and clean after the rain, the sunshine is warm on my face, and the river is deep enough to carry us without getting stuck in the sand. And I'm doing something I've thought about all my life. I should have done it sooner, much sooner, but I'm doing it now. For the first time in months I feel alive. Maybe this feeling won't last, most likely it won't. Maybe it's only this river, the speed that doesn't allow me to think of anything else, but that's enough for now..

Gloria feels more stable than during the first two days. I'm able to let her lean to one side or the other without worrying about flipping over. If she leans one way, I lean the other. The river requires my attention, but even so I look away into the hills, which like the air have been washed clean by the spring rain.

Downstream there is the flash of light again. It must be sunlight glancing off the water, for when I look intently there is nothing else. Then I see something far ahead that is too solid to be a reflection. A low bridge emerges as we get closer, concrete instead of wood, twenty or thirty feet across. Before the bridge the riverbank is lined with rock so that the water funnels toward the center. The current picks up speed. Two concrete pilings support the bridge, offering three narrow passages between them. I choose the center passage and line up to pass through the center of the center. Just as we are about to pass beneath the bridge, I sneak a peek at the GPS. Instead of a number on the tiny screen I see a concrete beam ahead that protrudes from the bridge column and is nearly submerged in the water. I flail the paddle to turn away from it, but the current smashes us into the beam. A gut-wrenching thud shudders through Gloria as she flips over. I expect to hit something myself and bring my arms in front of my face to protect me. Nothing hits me except the water, which is all around me. But not for long. I kick free of the cockpit and lunge for the surface. Gloria is floating upside down beside me, and I grab on to her. The current has washed a deep hole in the river beyond the bridge, and my feet don't touch bottom for a long time. Or maybe time only seems long when you've lost control.

When the river becomes shallow enough so that my feet find the bottom once again, I drag Gloria to shore. Her cockpit is full of water, and the water bag behind the seatback is floating freely. Everything else seems to be in its place—life jacket, waist skirt, deck bag. Juan's hat is still on my head thanks to the cinch string, and the extra paddle is still fastened beneath the shock cords behind the cockpit. But the paddle I'm supposed to be holding is nowhere to be seen. You are supposed to hold onto the paddle no matter what happens, I read in the instructions, but how can you hold onto anything when all of a sudden you're under water? The paddle is light enough to float, and it has to be floating downstream ahead of us. As fast as I can I dump the water out of the cockpit, unstrap the spare paddle from the rear deck, and take off after the paddle I lost.

How long did it take me to get back into the river? Fifteen minutes? I should be able to make up fifteen minutes. I paddle hard to catch up with it, and I continue paddling hard long after I know it's futile. When I finally slow down and take stock of what happened, I see that the GPS is gone, too. Eight hundred dollars of equipment floating down the river. It serves me right for paying attention to a machine instead of focusing on the water. Now I'm down to one paddle, and I'd better not let go of this one. I hear the voice of the boy back upriver asking me if I should be taking this trip by myself. At the time I thought it was funny.

As the day wears on and my strength wears down, I continue to look for the paddle, hoping that it has become lodged in the willows and deadfalls along the banks where this fast current still wants to take us. It is becoming more difficult not to let it. This high water has worn out its welcome.

A herd of deer is grazing on tall grass that grows among a stand of cedar trees. It is a place of refuge that draws me toward it. The deer bound away when they see this strange man and apparatus approaching them. The current would carry us past this ground, but I turn Gloria against it and paddle to the bank. I slip out of the cockpit into waist-deep water and climb up the bank with Gloria in tow. The bank is high enough that even if it rains again the river won't reach us.

When I unload the kayak, I discover that the back hatch is half full of water. On the bottom the wood is punctured, and it looks as if something has struck the hull with a hammer. The hammer, I'm sure, was concrete. After the collision with the bridge I was too intent on catching up with the paddle to notice the damage on the bottom. It's hard to believe that I could have missed it.

Everything that was packed in the hatch is wet, including the gear in the dry bags. I drape the tent and sleeping bag over small cedar trees, separate the contents of the bags, and spread them out to dry in the grass.

At least I had enough sense to bring repair supplies with me. With the butt of the hatchet I tap the damaged wood back into its original shape as well as I can. With duct tape I create a seal from the inside, then turn Gloria over and repair her damaged hull with fiberglass tape and epoxy. The repair stands out like an ugly scar on her beautiful skin.

It's dark by the time the tent and sleeping bag are dry, and I set up the tent by flashlight. The stove got wet and won't light, so I crawl into the sleeping bag and eat peanuts and raisins and sip from the half-empty bottle of tequila that Juan left me in case I needed a little reinforcement.

Deer return to their sanctuary among the trees. The soft splashing of their footsteps comes closer until they reach the bank. I hope my scent doesn't frighten them away. It's their ground, not mine, and tomorrow I'll be gone. A few feet beyond the tent the river hums with the unexpected delight of its temporary rise, reminding me that it will not stop just because I do. Somewhere downstream are my paddle and the GPS. Maybe they'll arrive at the ocean ahead of me—if I make it. That seems less certain now, although I've finally gotten the high water that I wished for.

~ ~ ~

*S*he is smiling on top of me. Her hair touches my face, and I force myself not to brush it away. I don't close my eyes when her lips touch mine—soft lips that send a chill through my spine, or maybe the chill is from the winter still captured in the sand. The day has been warm, the first warm day of spring, but the sand holds the memory of winter as does the water from the river. The river is here. I hear it. She is saying something to me, but I can't hear what she is saying. I can hear only the river. I feel her lips pulling away from me, her body lifting from mine. It is cold without her.

Annie, I hear myself saying.

For a moment I don't know where I am. My eyes are open, but it's so dark that they might as well be closed. Then I remember the dream. It is a consequence of age that once my eyes open, I can't drift off to sleep again. I pull the unzipped flap of the sleeping bag over my shoulders. The cold is from the night air, not from my dream. I raise my left hand in front of my eyes and see the glow of numbers on my watch. It's nearly four o'clock.

Every night there is something to think about. On this river I want to work hard enough so that I will sleep deeply through the night. If I don't accomplish anything else, that will be enough.

I should have known Annie would come to me sooner or later. In the sand beside the river she traced the words that she was afraid to say out loud—words that I should have been afraid to say, too. That was the trouble back then. I wasn't afraid of anything.

I unzip the sleeping bag all the way down to my feet and sit up inside the tent. The flashlight is where I left it beside the sleeping bag, and I switch on the light. Then I pull my pants over my long underwear that is made of some miracle fabric that will keep me warm even when wet. It has already failed the first test.

Outside the tent there is enough light from the stars to see the faint outline of the river, and I turn off the flashlight. I walk past Gloria through the wet grass and sit beside the river. In the northern sky I search for familiar constellations. When I was a boy I knew many of their names, but I've lost touch with the sky. The last phase of the old moon is rising in the east ahead of the first light from the sun. My hand brushes the sand beside me as if I am erasing the words Annie wrote long ago, but there are no words in the sand now.

When there is enough light to see, I take down the tent and pack away the gear. The patch on Gloria's hull has hardened overnight, and I think it will hold. There is only one way to find out. The river has gone down during the night, but the current is still strong. Nevertheless I don't have to paddle quite as hard to keep away from the banks, or maybe I'm getting used to the high water.

Everything in these hills is familiar to me, but not from the angle the river gives. Two whitetail deer watch from a bluff, then bound away with their tails in the air. A curlew with long legs and a long curved beak stands in the shallows along the shore, its attention focused on the water at its feet. Killdeer scurry on the flats where sandbars have survived the high water, unconcerned by our passing. Horses, always curious, run in pastures alongside us, but soon determine that we offer no competition. Slender green shoots of grass are emerging from the hills and shade the winter's dead brown with the first seductive hint of spring. Cottonwood trees stand on the horizon, gangly isolated giants in the immense panorama. When I was a boy, I foolishly thought this land was monotonous and unchanging. Whenever I leave it now, I long for it like an old man remembering the beauty of his first love.

How does Annie survive in the city where tall buildings surround her and she can't see the horizon anymore? Has she forgotten our honeymoon trip to the mountains where we camped in a forest? The forest was beautiful—so lush and green. We walked on a trail through dense trees, and she took my hand. I felt her reluctance to follow the path, but I ignored her silent message and pulled her along. Finally she stopped and would go no farther. The trees were too close upon her, she said. She couldn't see anything; she couldn't breathe. How could anyone be afraid of trees? Her fear didn't leave her until we got back to the campsite where there was a stream and an opening to the sky where she could breathe again. Before we made love that night in our tent, I promised I would never again take her to a place she didn't want to go.

She got over her fear of the forest, and the open vistas of the ranch became the place where she couldn't breathe. The world was too small here, she said—too narrow and too confining. All this sky, all this open land, and still she couldn't breathe.

A silence comes over the land and me like the departure of a woman's soft voice. Hush, she·says before she leaves, and all is quiet. Then I realize that the wind has quieted down. For the last week it has come from the south, bringing warm air, rain, and the hope of spring. Now it's gone. I look to the willows along the river for confirmation. They stand perfectly still.

We have wind so constantly in these hills that we say that it has changed direction, or picked up, or quieted down as if it lives among us. It seldom leaves altogether and never for long. On days without wind we know something is missing, but sometimes we don't recognize what it is. Annie began to hate the wind. It should have given her more air to breathe, not less, but to her the wind took her breath away.

The water slows, spreads, and becomes deeper. Ahead lies the straight concrete line of a solid structure. Whatever it is, I approach it cautiously and paddle toward the bank long before I reach it. I don't want to repeat yesterday's folly with the bridge.

It's an irrigation dam, the first of several I am expecting. The water sounds ominously threatening as it rushes over the steel sluice gates that control the river's flow. No water is being diverted into the irrigation canal; it's too early in the season. In a few months the gates to the irrigation canal will open and the sluice gates on the dam will rise and that's why I'm here now—to get down this river before too much water is siphoned off. That's how I explained the early start to Juan. Water and no mosquitoes, and I want to get south before it's too hot. I have explained everything.

There are no warning signs on the river for this dam, only on land where people are anticipated. If somebody—I, for instance—went over the sluice gates, he'd be in trouble. The water drops eight or ten feet over the gates into a swirling boiling cauldron. Get into that and I might not come out. I'm not getting into it.

Returning to Gloria I load all my gear into two large portage bags that I bought for this purpose and carry the gear a hundred yards beyond the dam. Then I return for Gloria, hoist her over my shoulder, and carry her past the cauldron. It's slow work and tiring, and it won't be the last portage on the Loup.

The epoxy patch has held up well. No water has gotten into the rear hatch since leaving the camp, and the patch feels as hard as the rest of the hull. I have enough epoxy for one more patch, but I don't intend to use it.

–Do you hear that Gloria? No more patches.

When I begin paddling again, a light breeze from the north touches my cheek. It feels noticeably cooler, and becomes more than a light touch. If I know anything about this country, it means that the weather is about to change. It hasn't changed yet, but it's coming.

Late in the afternoon I reach another dam. This one is new, the concrete still a light gray. Once again I leave Gloria upstream and walk downriver to take a look. At this dam some of the river water is being diverted into a canal heading north, which surprises me. I didn't think water would be taken out so early. What is left of the river runs over a steel gate just as it did at the dam upstream. The river beyond the dam is shallower, and there are sandbars again in the middle of the channel.

The shortest portage is from the south side where the water has backed up into a marsh behind the dam. I return to Gloria and paddle to the south bank. While standing in water up to my waist I unpack the hatches and place all the gear onto broken chunks of concrete that cover the embankment. From there I carry the portage bags up the rocks, over the dam, and deposit them beside the river on the other side. The wind feels particularly cold on top of the dam. While I'm carrying Gloria up the rocks, a man drives by in a pickup truck on the road above and parks beside the small control building. He waits outside his truck as I approach him with Gloria over my shoulder.

"Afternoon," he says.

· He's wearing a new cap with a smooth uncreased bill and a heavy work coat.

"Afternoon."

"You canoeing down the river?"

"Trying to. I thought I'd get ahead of you guys. I didn't think you'd be drawing out water so early."

"We get ours early while there's enough to keep up the flow."

"Where does it go?"

"Calamus Dam."

"How much are you taking out?"

"About a third, I guess."

"Looks like more than a third to me."

"I'll bet it does. Water is getting more valuable every year. Nobody wants to see it wasted."

"Are they taking water out anywhere else?"

"I don't know. I just started working here last fall. Had a farm south of here but sold out last year. This is a lot easier. How far you going?"

"I'm not sure. Until I run out of river, I guess."

"Supposed to get cold tonight. They say it might even snow. You need a ride into town?"

"No thanks."

"Well, you have a good day. I better check my gauges."

A gust of wind catches Gloria and turns her sideways on my shoulder. She feels heavier than at the first dam. The wind feels colder, too, after the dam tender's mention of snow.

When I deposit Gloria beside the other gear, I find the bag where I keep the weather radio and cell phone. The radio reception is poor beside the depleted river where I'm shielded by the hills, and I'll have to climb to higher ground if I want to hear the forecast. The wind is much stronger when I reach the top of the hill. A distinct dark line like the straight edge of the dam is drawn across the north horizon. I sit down in the grass and turn my back to the wind.

The computer voice on the radio says that the wind will reach thirty miles an hour by midnight. Lows tonight will be in the twenties. Snow is likely across the panhandle of Nebraska east to Valentine and is possible as far east as Burwell.

A single bar rises on the indicator of the cell phone when I turn it on. I lift the phone above my head and turn it in all directions until I find another bar off to the east. The screen displays that I've missed four calls. The first is from Joe, two are from Juan, and the last is from Rosario. Of the four calls, there are three messages. I want to hear their voices, but then again I don't. I don't want to hear about problems on the ranch or answer any questions. Only a few days have passed since I left, but I have been leaving much longer than that.

Joe's is the first message. He gives some details about the change that Juan wanted to the sale agreement; then he asks, "Where are you? What's the river like? Call me if you need anything." Next is the message from Juan. I'm sure that he called and hung up the first time when he got my recorded message. Now he tries to talk to me through the machine, but he doesn't like to talk one-way. He has heard the forecast for snow. He can come for me in the pickup wherever I am. If I don't want to return to the ranch, he can take me to a motel where I can wait for better weather. It will be cold tonight, he warns. It is cold already as I sit with my back to the wind. The wind penetrates the paddle jacket, and I need to put on more clothes. The final message is from Rosario. She, too, has heard about the snow. "I hope you find a warm place," she says. "I hope this river of yours is bringing you peace."

From the top of the hill I look down at this river of mine as Rosario calls it and see the dam that takes away too much of the water. It's a small dam on a small river and it's not mine.

If I call Juan I'll have to sound stronger than I feel right now. And if I give in to his practical advice, I might never come back to this river. How often do you get more than one chance?

Despite my fear I call the ranch, hoping almost that Juan won't be there and no one will answer. Consuelo doesn't like to talk on the telephone, and Juan doesn't have a machine to answer his calls. He picks up on the second ring. Yes, he has been waiting for my call. He has the map spread out on the kitchen table.

"Where are you?"

"Don't worry about me. I'm fine."

"But what about the snow?"

"It has snowed before. Snow will be good for the pastures. First the rain, now the snow; the pastures will get a good start this year."

"But where are you?" he asks. "Have you passed any towns?"

"I'm not sure. Can you see any towns from the river?"

"How should I know? Don't you have the machine that tells you where you are?"

"I lost it. It fell off the kayak. Can you believe that? I don't want you to come, Juan. You and I have worked in the snow many times. This will be nothing. Don't you remember that first year when we worked all night in the snow?"

"That was a long time ago. We were younger then, and Annie was with us."

So now we are older and Annie is not with us. Does that mean I cannot spend the night in the snow? He has never understood why she left, why I let her go, why I never went after her. I believe that he would give up his position on the ranch, all his hard work, his success, if we could go back to that time when Annie was with us. I try not to think that way. It does no good.

"Are you still there?" he asks.

Juan doesn't trust my cell phone. He can't adapt to the delay in the way it transmits and receives voices. When he says something, he wants it to be heard right away. Rosario gave him a cell phone to carry in his pickup in case he ever needed help. He tossed it into the glove box, and it has long since been covered by pliers and fence cutters. The first and only charge of its battery dissipated long ago.

"I'm here. You'll have to check if there are any calves tonight. There shouldn't be any this early, but you never know. I'll be in a warm sleeping bag, but they'll get dropped onto the cold ground."

"We'll check them," he says.

"Tell Joe and Rosario that I got their messages and I'm fine."

"We didn't lose any calves that night, did we?"

"Not a single one."

"It was a good night even if it snowed."

"It was a good night."

"Take care, amigo."

"Good-bye, my friend."

To end the call I touch the red button on the cell phone. Will our words float endlessly into space? I have heard that happens. A million years from now a being from another universe might hear my instructions to Juan to check for early spring calves. Will he understand what I meant?

After all the talk about snow I decide to make camp here at the dam before the storm arrives. There is level ground beside the river, and the hills will shield me from the wind. When I stake out the corners of the tent, I position it so that the strongest side of the tent is facing north and make sure that every Velcro strap of the heavier rainfly is secure. As a precaution I anchor the tent with extra rope and stakes. Lastly I turn Gloria upside down and tie her bow and stern ropes to a tree.

Inside the tent I take off my wet shoes and prop them up against the tent wall. I put on two pair of dry socks, two pair of long underwear, a fleece jacket, and a stocking cap. With the tent door unzipped and tied open, I assemble the stove on the ground outside so that I can reach it from within. I set a pot of water on the stove and warm my hands over the flame. Tomorrow I will have to refill the water bottles.

Annie always made clam chowder when it snowed, but I don't have any packages of freeze-dried chowder. Instead I dig through the food bag until I find a package of chili con carne, which is what Consuelo made when it snowed. I wish I had asked Juan if Consuelo were making chili tonight. Juan adds his hot sauce with the claim that it prevents colds and chills and all maladies of cold weather. When the water boils, I pour two cups of it into the aluminum foil bag of freeze-dried chili, add a dozen drops of Juan's hot sauce, and seal the top of the bag to retain the heat and all the value of Juan's cold remedy. The printed instructions on the bag say I must wait ten minutes before eating.

While I wait, I disconnect the fuel tank from the stove and store the tank. The stove cools quickly and I store it, too. A few flakes of snow float past me toward the river. I lean out of the tent and look at the sky. The dark line of the weather front is nearly overhead, and it is eerily straight. The sun is setting in a line that follows the river. I am somewhere between them, suspended like the first flakes of snow that can't decide where to land.

I close up the tent and wrap the sleeping bag around me and eat the chili that is mediocre even with Juan's hot sauce. When I finish, I arrange the tent so that I will know where everything is. I am sure that I put my headlamp in the bag where I keep the book that I planned to read at night. On the ranch I always read to fall asleep. It makes sense—book, headlamp, reading to fall asleep. In the book bag I find a small spiral notebook, two pens, maps for the Mississippi rolled together and secured with rubber bands, and extra batteries. I also find another flashlight, the batteries for the headlamp, but no headlamp.

Giving up, I crawl into my sleeping bag and reach for *Huckleberry Finn*. I haven't read the book since I was a boy, and yet I am sure that it is in some way responsible for this trip. How many boys have dreamed about Huckleberry's raft? Would girls dream about it, too? I don't think Annie ever had such dreams, but I wonder about Juan's granddaughters now that they've seen Gloria. She is long and slender compared to the raft Jim and Huckleberry found, and I am almost ashamed to think about the thousands of dollars worth of gear stuffed into her. We all build our rafts differently, but maybe the idea is the same.

It is awkward to hold the book in one hand and the flashlight in the other, and I have to switch the hands holding the book and light, and switch again. Perhaps if I tie the flashlight onto the tent loops at the ceiling, I won't have to hold the light. That doesn't work, so I try propping the flashlight on the tent floor so that it will shine up on my book. That doesn't work either. Finally I determine that the odd shape of the flashlight barrel could be useful. It is flat on two sides where the batteries fit, and I balance the flat barrel on my forehead. As long as I don't move my head, I can achieve the correct angle of light.

Outside the wind has picked up, and I unzip the tent door and the heavier weather flap and shine the light into the night. Snowflakes still float in the air without landing, but there are more of them—many more. I turn on the weather radio and try to hear the weather voice through the static.

Now and then a word comes through the garble, but not enough words to make any sense.

After turning off the radio, I try to read more of Huckleberry's story. But my mind drifts away to the first calving season with Juan. He had volunteered to stay through the night in the hired man's trailer so that the hired man could go into town for a dance. The hired man had been talking about that dance for a month, and I let him go because I was tired of his complaints. Annie loved to dance, but I didn't want to leave Juan alone on the ranch. She understood, but she loved to dance. A winter storm was supposed to stay well to the north where winter belonged that time of year, but something changed, some anomaly in the atmosphere. The storm came hard and fast despite the contrary prediction. Sometime after dark Juan knocked at the kitchen door as I was putting on my insulated overalls. I let him in.

"Bad storm," he says. "Bad time for it, too."

He's right. The new-born calves will have a tough time if this weather keeps up.

"I've saddled old Hershey. My idea is that we'll hitch up the horse trailer and you drive the pickup and bring in the ones that are having trouble. I'll stay out there with the rest of them."

Annie walks into the kitchen as Juan is presenting his idea.

"I'll drive the pickup," Annie says. She is dressed in so many clothes that I can't make out the shape of her small body. She walks out to the porch and lifts her work coat off the hook. She knows how important these calves are to us. I've stretched us so thin expanding the herd and the ranch that we can't afford to lose any. Annie couldn't bear to lose them even if there was no stretching.

"I'll saddle Geronimo, too," Juan says.

Geronimo is the huge bay gelding that I ride when there is no fooling around. Geronimo knows how to work better than any of us.

The three of us ride in the cab together to the heifer pen—Annie is in the middle, I'm driving, Geronimo and Hershey are in the horse trailer. The temperature now is well below freezing. Most of the heifers are bunched together against the wind, but with the headlights of the pickup we spot several that have separated from the herd. Two have new babies. Juan and I lift the calves into the horse trailer, and Juan rides with them to the barn where he will spread hay on the floor so that they can stay warm. I stay with the heifers until Juan and Annie return.

The main herd is in a sheltered pasture along the river a mile from the house and barn. Juan and I ride side-by-side on Geronimo and Hershey on the rutted trail, and Annie drives behind us in low gear. The snow isn't deep yet, but drifts are beginning to fill the trail. The wind-driven snow is hard and biting as it hits our faces. Geronimo plods ahead without nonsense. Alone, Hershey would have been eyeing the trail back, but he knows there is no use looking back with Geronimo there.

There are five hundred and eleven cows in this herd. Juan tells me that he had counted eighty-three calves that afternoon. The herd is in a tight group in a ravine close to the river where we feed them. They're not alarmed as Juan and I ride through the center looking for calves that are having trouble. Each time we see a calf on the ground, we walk up to it. If it doesn't get up on its own, Juan picks it up and we drape it across my knees on top of Geronimo. I take it up to the trail where Annie waits in the trailer. In an hour the horse trailer is full.

While she drives back to the barn, Juan and I begin looking for cows that have wandered off by themselves. I have a flashlight with me, but I don't use it until Geronimo sniffs out a cow. The first one we find is still in labor. He finds another, and the calf is fresh. The cow is still licking the afterbirth. Geronimo moves between the cow and calf as I lift the calf onto the saddle and climb up behind it. Geronimo lowers his head toward the cow and blows a warning through his nose. The cow stands off but follows us back to the herd. The lights of the pickup are coming toward us through the blowing snow.

When Annie sees the wet calf I have brought, she opens the pickup door and points to the seat. I lift the calf into the heated cab and point Geronimo back into the wind. We work through the night. On the last trip back to the barn before daylight, the pickup gets stuck in the snow. Juan and I tie ropes onto the front bumper, and the horses pull it out of the drift. I have trouble bending my fingers, and I no longer feel anything on my face. But I don't say anything. Nor does Juan. Hershey is eager to get back to the barn, but Geronimo is the same as when we started. He will work as long as there is work to do. I would be a rich man if I had a dozen like him. I would be richer still if I hadn't gelded him as a colt. That is a mistake I often regret.

When we get back to the ranch, Annie makes coffee. The three of us sit in the kitchen and try to warm up. The hired man still hasn't returned. Juan thinks he should check on the heifers again, but I tell him that we will warm up first. I am more grateful to him than I know how to say. I am grateful to Annie, too. Juan praises her coffee, but he is trying to tell her something more, that he thinks she is some woman. He doesn't know how to say it, but at least he says something.

"I'm going to fire him when he comes back," I say.

"Maybe something happened," Juan says. "You should wait and hear what he says."

"It doesn't matter what he says. It's snowing in town, too. You've got a job here permanently if you want it."

"We could use more help," Juan says. "If you want, I will call my brother. He is good with cattle and he's not afraid to work and he won't leave when a storm is coming. I promise you that."

I didn't know then but do now that Juan would never make a promise he couldn't keep.

The wind picks up outside, and I wonder if I'm asleep or awake. It seems that we are still at the kitchen table, and Annie's face is red and glowing from the wind and the cold and from a night when we all worked well together. I have never seen her face more beautiful.

~ ~ ~

Through the plastic window of the rainfly, I see a dazzling blue sky. Inside the tent the warm air of my breath condenses in the cold. I unzip the tent door and rainfly and peek outside. Snow covers the ground and a two-foot drift has built up on the protected south side of the tent. I'm warm inside the sleeping bag. Why shouldn't I stay where I'm warm?

It was a fast-moving storm, but most are in this country. When we joke that there is only one tree between us and the Canadian border to protect us from the north winds, we are only half-joking. My grandfather liked to tell a story about one day in October when the temperature reached 110 and before sunrise of the next day it was 10 below zero.

That was in the '30s when the weather tested the tolerance of even tolerant people like my grandfather. The dust storms then were worse than any spring snowstorm. A snow of dirt covered the buildings, the clean wash on the line, the grass on the hills. Dust sifted into the house like the flour my grandmother sifted into her bread bowl. She would have left this country if she could. By the time I came along there were no more thoughts of leaving, but there was always a trace of bitterness in her voice when she talked about those early years. This country was always too much of something—too big, too hot or too cold, too violent and harsh.

I like the size of this country, this bigness that bothered my grandmother. Perversely perhaps I even like the extremes of weather: the heat in August, the cold in January, snow late in spring or early in fall. But maybe I wouldn't like it if I had never sat on the wood box next to the cook stove in my grandmother's kitchen, sipping coffee even when I was a child, eating her *kringle* cookies or freshly baked rye bread. I can still smell the wood burning in the stove, still see the gleam of the polished chrome railing, feel the warmth of the stove and her coffee and her voice offering another cookie. After she died, my grandfather and I would sit in the living room instead of the kitchen. In the evening I would find him on his reading couch, and I would pull a chair over to it. Within the glow of the single bulb from the lamp on his desk we talked about things—about books and ideas or the country he had left or the country he had found—his voice so soft that it wouldn't reach the empty kitchen where the cook stove no longer gleamed.

I missed my grandmother, too, but I had no idea then of how my grandfather felt, thinking back over a life and knowing there were things he would do differently. He wished he had spoken a gentle word more often to his wife and sons. His words were always gentle to me, and it wasn't possible for me to imagine them otherwise.

The cold makes me linger inside the warm bag but I have to pee badly enough that there is no choice but to get up. The body always fails us in the end.

My shoes are frozen stiff; so are the socks that have been mislabeled waterproof. The socks let water in slowly and just as slowly let it out. If I had been thinking ahead as I lay in the sleeping bag instead of thinking back, I would have stuffed the socks and shoes beneath the bag and thawed them out. Now I have to force the frozen fabric onto my feet over insulated socks and feel the cold overcome the insulation.

Once I am on the river the sun feels warm on my face. The water is warm to my hands, and not even my feet are cold. Snow drops from the cedar trees along the river and sparkles in the fresh light. The land looks perfect and unspoiled beneath the layer of untouched snow. And so the morning is beautiful after all—so quiet after the wind, so bright after the dark clouds.

Often after a new snow I have ridden out into the pastures where everything looks unspoiled, but it's not. I spoil it as I go with my intentions and with the tracks of the horse. Here on the river I change nothing. When I paddle, the water regains its form immediately after I pass. And when I float with the current there is not even the temporary disruption of the paddle. To float with the river, to leave no mark on water or land is something I have not done before. Already the snow is melting, and small rivulets of pure ice-cold water are entering the river.

Many small streams make a great river—an old Danish proverb from my grandfather. It seems to be a day for old words.

Gloria grinds to a stop in this not yet great river. There are signs of high water from the heavy rain a few days earlier when even the diversion dam couldn't take enough. The grass is bent down on the sandbars and debris hangs from the bare lower branches of a bush. But the high water is gone, and I get out of Gloria and pull her to the next channel.

The river bottom is less predictable than before, and it wasn't predictable before. There are holes where I don't expect them and shallow water where I expect it to be deep. In one spot my leg sinks into the sand all the way up to my crotch, and I grab Gloria to keep from sinking any farther. The sudden high water has just as suddenly receded and made a mess of the bottom.

There hasn't been time for the sand to settle down. Old stories of quicksand swallowing horse and rider slide into my memory. A horse would be too smart to get stuck in this sand.

Gloria wants to turn away from the bank and head toward the other side. I see where she wants to go. The channel has formed over there, but the crossing doesn't look promising. With the paddle I keep her close to the left bank. On my right is the edge of a sandbar; ahead are ripples where the shallow water is disturbed by the sand beneath; farther down is the darker color of deeper water. Sand scrapes the bottom of the kayak, and I feel the sand bulge beneath my seat and take its final grip.

I try to push her over the shallow spot while staying in the cockpit. My fingers are getting sore from the abrasion of the sand, and my arms and shoulders are getting tired from lifting and pushing, and we don't move. So I get out and stumble as Gloria swivels about in the current and takes off without me, forcing me to grab her bowline and hold her back.

–Just wait a damn second.

My legs are getting tired, too.

We have good water after that. Maybe Gloria heard me or else the river did, for we sail along with ease. Perhaps the river has adjusted to the greed of the dam. It is no dishonor to adjust, I wish to tell it, and I promise to leave no mark if you let us pass.

There are marks from others on the river, however—deep gouges where the bank has been dug away to accommodate irrigation pipes. Set back from the bank are diesel engines that drive pumps that will take more water from the river. The engines are resting quietly now, but in the summer they will come to life. Nobody wants to waste this water, the man said back at the dam.

Houses and yards replace fields and pastures. A bridge crosses the river, and the water tower of a town rises above the hills. As I float beneath the low bridge, a vehicle passes overhead. The noise of its passing is so loud that I recoil from the sound as if the bridge is about to fall on top of me.

The river loops north where it receives the water of the Calamus River— the water, at least, that is released from the dam that blocks that river, too. Water from the last dam was diverted into the Calamus Reservoir, and now it comes back down. There must be a logical explanation, but I don't know what it is. From the juncture with the Calamus, the river turns decidedly south toward the town. Then it widens and deepens behind another dam.

Maybe it's because I'm getting used to the sluice gates or maybe it's because I don't want to carry stuff any farther than I have to, but I stop closer to this dam than the others. I lift myself out of the cockpit, grab the bow handle, and pull Gloria up the embankment. She feels unaccountably heavy, and I gasp for air. When I was paddling I didn't feel this tired, but my legs are trembling as they support me on dry ground.

I've landed in a deserted park close to a baseball field that is covered with snow. When I was a boy, I played ball here. Once I get around the dam, it is not far to the highway bridge, and from the bridge it is not far to a motel where I've stayed before. I need drinking water; a hot shower and a warm bed wouldn't do any harm. Neither would a good meal and a stiff drink, maybe two.

Gloria has gained weight on the river, or I've lost some. I stop and cinch my belt a little tighter so that my pants won't ride down on my waist as I lug her around the dam. When I begin walking again, I step into a depression filled with snow. Gloria and I fall hard to the ground, and I twist my knee in the process. It's a tough haul for both of us.

The paddle to the bridge takes only a few minutes, and it is as far as I'm going to paddle today. I drag Gloria out of the water again, catch my breath, and drag her farther up the incline into a clump of bushes. Kneeling down in the snow I open the rear hatch where I have stored my clothes. In addition to a hot shower, I am hoping for a washing machine at the motel, and I will turn the heat in the room on high. In the book I'm reading I can't recall one time that *Huckleberry Finn* looked forward to four walls and civilization. But it is warmer in his story, and he is younger and more resilient.

Among the confusing jumble of yellow waterproof bags inside the hatches I find the two clothes bags, one in each hatch, and continue to dig through the mess until I find the bag that has my razor and toothbrush. I stuff all three inside the large portage bag, together with the empty water bottles, and sling the strap over my shoulder. After climbing up the steep embankment to the highway I head for town. A muddy pickup slows down as it approaches. I wouldn't mind a ride, even if I have to explain to the rancher or farmer what I'm doing on this road and listen to his response when I tell him. I know what his response will be; I know what it will be before he even says a word. The pickup continues to slow until the farmer is almost upon me; then it picks up speed and continues without stopping.

As he passes, I see his face. It is a face I might recognize among the men who come into town and talk about cattle prices, or the cost of fuel and fertilizer, or the crazy neighbor who is trying something different. But he doesn't recognize me. I haven't shaved for days; my black paddle pants are covered with mud; and I'm wearing a strange-looking yellow jacket. To him I could be a bum who is passing through town. If I were wearing my blue jeans, he might have stopped. The jeans are in one of the bags in the portage bag that is hanging from my shoulder. I've been on the river less than a week, but already I've become a stranger in this town. The town is just ahead, and I know it well enough even if it doesn't know me.

In the parking lot of the motel, I take off my paddle jacket and stuff it into the bag that I leave outside the motel office. Now I am less strange, although strange enough that the man who comes to the check-in counter doesn't quite know what to make of me. He ought to recognize my hat. It's a cowboy hat any one of us might be wearing, but the check-in man looks at me warily. He's wearing a western shirt and bolero tie like a rancher on a Sunday afternoon, but his shirt is stretched too tightly in the front to be a rancher. It eases him some when I put a credit card on the counter.

"Here for the horse sale?" he asks as I write my address on his check-in form.

"No. Just passing through."

I push the completed form back to him.

"We got people coming here from all over the state. I don't have any rooms tomorrow."

"I'll be gone tomorrow."

"Put your license number there."

He points to the blank space on his form. Briefly I consider telling him about the vehicle I came in but decide it's not worth the trouble.

"I can never remember it."

"What are you driving?"

"A Ford pickup."

My description satisfies the man on the other side of the counter, and he hands me a room key.

I stand for a long time in the shower and shave by feel as the hot water cascades over me. My hands hurt as they warm up. There are large cracks beside the fingernails, and they are raw from being wet too long. From several of the cracks I squeeze yellow pus.

A woman has taken over the check-in counter, the man's wife I presume, and she trades my dollar bill for quarters to use in the washing machine that's in the utility room off the lobby. Without my asking for it, she gives me laundry detergent and tells me to use as much as I need. I appreciate her domestic kindness and consider telling her about the kayak I left down at the river. But once such stories begin, how do you ever end them? And why would you start?

When my laundry is dry, I walk down to the main business district, which is four blocks of old buildings around a town square of other old buildings. At the grocery store I select hand lotion that the label says is good for fishermen's chapped hands, a jar of peanut butter, saltine crackers, and a dozen cans of smoked oysters and sardines. In the section where there are school supplies, I find a black magic marker that I can use to label my storage bags. As I walk up and down the aisles scanning the shelves for useful products, I pass a young woman pushing a shopping cart with a little boy about three years old in the seat. We are both scouting the store from west to east, but we begin each aisle from opposite ends. The little boy points continuously at the shelves, and the mother alternates between ignoring him and giving in to his persistent whining. When we meet in the final aisle, her cart is heaped full. I haven't found anything since the magic marker. There is only one check-out person working, and I walk with deliberate speed to make certain that I reach the check-out line ahead of the young woman and child.

After leaving the store I find a restaurant across the street and walk into the bar. I order a rib steak, the biggest they have, and a double scotch and water. A baseball game from Kansas City is on the television. The other team is from Texas. Texas is a big place for one team to claim. During the commercial pretty blond women in tiny tight dresses try to persuade me to switch to beer. Maybe if they were in the bar and not on the televisions set, I would be persuaded. The other two men and one woman on barstools on either side of me are not persuaded either.

I find that eating with people who talk about the weather outside over the noise of a baseball game and commercials and between deep draws on cigarettes is an experience more jarring than the sudden change of weather they're discussing. At a table behind me several men are talking about the horse sale. Without committing myself I lean toward that conversation. The men mention horses' names that I recognize, names that retain the name of the mare or stallion or both with the expectation that their value will be enhanced by what they are called. Then I hear a name that sucks the wind out of me as if I were hit in the gut, and I recoil from their conversation. I finish the scotch with one gulp and drop my paper napkin over the unfinished steak.

"Another scotch?" the bartender asks.

"No. I've had enough."

Outside I fill my lungs as deeply as I can after the smoke and stale air in the bar. I can't seem to get enough air. Two men in fancy new cowboy hats and sharp-toed boots pass me on the sidewalk on their way into the restaurant. They greet me with low voices and deferential nods as if they know I belong here, but I don't belong here anymore.

Carrying the plastic grocery bag I walk back to the motel where I lie in the warm bed and look out the window to the lights that illuminate the highway. *Huckleberry Finn* lies on the cigarette-scarred bed stand, but I don't turn on the bedside light to read. Nor do I turn on the television to see who won the baseball game.

I breathe slowly and deeply and stare at the black ceiling. Through the grogginess that comes with sleep, I hear a familiar sound outside on the highway. What would a horse be doing on the highway this time of night?

The black horse stands beside the river, beautiful in the new snow. With the vanity of royalty he dismisses me with a shake of his head as I approach on foot. He is the horse of my dreams, the horse from the books I read as a child. I carry a rope in my shaking hand, but I know any rope will be futile with this horse. He lowers his majestic head and paws the new snow with his front hoof. Unlike any horse I've ever known, he stares straight into my eyes. I reach out to touch him, but he rears on his hind legs to warn me that I have come close enough. Then he spins around and gallops across the river where I cannot follow him. On the fresh fallen snow there are no marks except my footprints. Across the river the black horse has vanished as if he were never there. And yet his tracks remain in the water where no tracks ever linger.

~ ~ ~

At daybreak I leave the motel room carrying the portage bag now heavy with full water bottles. I am wearing the bright yellow paddle jacket and muddy pants that look strange to the people who pass me in their cars and pickup trucks, but I don't look back at them. At the bridge I retrace my footsteps in the snow toward the camouflage of bare trees and shrubs where I hid Gloria. More snow has melted during the night, including all the snow in a straight line beneath Gloria's keel.

I pack my gear into the hatches, drag Gloria down the bank to the river, and ease her into the water. Unlike the morning before when I was content to float with the current, I pull the paddle forcefully through the water until the bridge is well behind me.

The morning turns warm, and briefly I have the illusion that my speed has something to do with the warmth, but it doesn't. The weather is coming to me much faster than I am going to it. I take off my jacket and slip it under the elastic cords on the deck. An hour later I take off my sweatshirt, leaving exposed a long-sleeve shirt that is supposed to repel mosquitoes through twenty washings. The shirt has now gone through one. With or without the repellant, it is too early in the year for mosquitoes.

For some time I have been aware of the difference in topography, but until I see the forged black spikes of an old cast iron cemetery fence rising from the top of a snow-covered hill, I don't focus my attention sufficiently to know what it is. The cemetery provides the focus. Below the old fence deep gullies are carved into the face of the hill. The sun has melted the snow on the north side of the gullies, revealing layers of clay, each descending layer darker than the previous. I have left the sandhills behind.

My family lived in those hills a hundred years, three generations. It is an insignificant blink of the eye in the geological time etched in the layers of clay, but it is all that we have in this country. Whatever the measurement, I have left it behind. All that is left of us now are the graves that lie side-by-side beneath modest headstones like those on top of the clay hill. We are not a family who erect large monuments to death. On each gravestone are the names of those lying below them and the dates of birth and death. What else is there to say?

I was once certain that my gravestone would stand there, too, close to my mother and father, grandmother and grandfather, close to my brother, close to Annie or her close to me. But all that changed when Annie scattered our son's ashes in the calm water behind the beaver dam on Wamaduze Creek—her idea, not mine, because I wasn't there.

By then I had left the ranch with the black horse trailered behind the pickup to take him back to the wild horse range in Wyoming where I should have taken long before. But no one was supposed to ride that horse except George or me. No one.

I told Juan that I wasn't going to stay there and listen to that dried-up old priest's empty prayers and lies. Maybe I had to do that when it was someone else's son, but I didn't have to do it when it was mine. It hurt Juan when I said that, and even as I said it I knew it wasn't the reason I left. I couldn't bear to see the way Annie would look at me when she returned to the ranch from her apartment in the city, or the way I would see myself reflected in her eyes.

"I wish you had come back. It wasn't as hard as I thought it would be," she wrote to me after she left the ranch again and I finally did come back. We could still write words on paper that we could no longer say to each other. "It was one of those strange warm days in January that happen now and then and the creek was flowing. Juan and Consuelo went with me, and George. I think it was harder on him than for the rest of us. He blames himself for what happened, like you do. It just happened. No one is to blame. Our son never fit in there, and I didn't want to bury him in that ground where he didn't belong. He's free now. The beaver dam was his favorite place on the ranch. Do you remember that?"

I remembered.

The beaver dam was a point of contention between my neighbor and me for some years. Long before either of us was born the ranchers along the creek cooperatively deepened and straightened the creek so that it would drain the valley better in wet years. The trouble came during the dry years, which came more often than the wet ones. Then the creek drained the land too well and dried the hay meadows too early in the year. When the beaver built the dam, I thought we should leave it alone. My neighbor thought we should blow it up. Once you let beaver get started in a place they're hard to get rid of, he said. If he had voiced a strong opinion, I wouldn't have continued to object, but he didn't and the dam stayed. It turned out to be our son's favorite place on the ranch, maybe the only place he liked. Even if he didn't see them, for beaver stay out of sight most of the time, he knew they were there. He liked the idea that the beaver didn't have to ask permission from the long-legged men who thought they owned the ground.

"I'm going to build my house there when I grow up," I remember him saying.

He is setting the table for supper, and Annie is standing beside the stove whisking flour into the pan for gravy. I am at the table thinking about my meeting that afternoon with the banker who told me that there was talk about the Mexicans working on the ranch—talk that the other ranchers won't buy my bulls or sell me any more land. 'It's a big country,' I told him and devised a scheme in his office to buy his damn bank someday. 'If I could find a half dozen ranch hands who work as hard as the Mexicans, I would hire them.'

"I'll help you," Annie says. She stops whisking the flour and smiles at her son's dream. "And your father will help, too."

"I'm going to build it on the other side so that there has to be a bridge to get there," he says. He is placing the fork beside my plate on the left side as Annie has taught him.

"You mean the west side," I say. "That's not our property, and Jim Grant wants to blow up the dam so that the creek will drain better. I might have to let him do it."

The little boy lays the fork carefully beside my plate. I see his small fingers as they leave the table, I hear Annie scolding me, and I should be able to see his eyes as he looks up to me so that he will know that I'm only kidding.

But my memory stops with his fingers leaving the table, and now as the river carries us past the cemetery on top of the clay hill, I wonder why I didn't tell him what I really thought—that the beaver dam was useful, the way it collected and calmed the water before letting it pass downstream. And it held the water only a short time, not like those we've passed that take it away forever. If Jim Grant wanted to blow up a dam, there were plenty of others that he could start with.

We shouldn't be surprised when a child dies. Among the earliest gravestones in the cemetery back in the sandhills are children—more children than old people buried back then. We should be prepared for the death of a child, but we're not. Or at least not for the emptiness that comes knowing that he was small enough I could have picked him up and put him on my lap and begun laying out the design right there on the kitchen table with the silverware as the beaver dam and the dinner plate as his house and the salt and pepper shakers for trees. What is the harm of a child's dream? Had I forgotten how many I had that never amounted to anything?

Now I'm on this river following an old dream, following my son's ashes. What are the chances that I'll catch up with either?

Once again I see the reflection of light from some object floating far ahead on the river. It disappears around the curve just as I spot it. I dip the paddle deeper into the water, set my feet against the foot braces, and pull harder through the strokes. When I round the curve, I lift the sunglasses from my eyes and squint ahead. There is nothing, only the marsh grass in the shallows where the water runs slowly, only the clay hills beyond the river, covered with melting snow, rising into the painfully bright blue sky.

~~~

I have lost track of the days since starting at Wamaduze Creek. Since the snowfall, each day has been warmer so that now there is no trace of snow even in the shaded spots along the river. The country is greener, too, and there are more trees along the banks—tall cottonwoods sprouting light green leaves, and pines and cedars with new growth. Maple and oak trees stand beside the river now, but they're still bare from winter. Corn planting is underway in the ever-widening valley, and the soil is rich and dark with moisture where the corn planters have disturbed the ground.

Two carpenters stand upright from the sloping plywood roof of a new home they are building beside the river, and one waves as if he knows me. His hair is blond like my brother's hair, which unlike mine never darkened or grayed, never had the time to change. I return the carpenter's friendly wave, the first contact I've had with anyone since leaving the motel.

Beneath a highway bridge are hundreds of mud and straw swallow nests, but it's too early in the season for swallows. As we pass through the shadow of the bridge, Gloria turns sharply and decisively toward the other bank. Maybe I'll follow her lead for once. She can't do any worse than I.

Resting my paddle on her bow, I let her go and wait for the outcome. It doesn't look good. She skims the downstream side of a sandbar and is headed for shallow water. Although the channel is re-forming, I don't think she'll make it. Just as she is about to ground on sand that is easy enough for me to see from my higher elevation, she slips sideways a little and noses through a slight opening that is just wide enough and deep enough for us to pass.

Was it luck or better instinct? When riding Geronimo or the black horse home at night, I often gave them the lead because they had better eyesight than I. But how can you say that about a boat? Maybe I'm making it too complicated. Her keel floats within the current, and where the current flows so does she. But it's only one successful crossing, and anybody or anything can get lucky once.

Ahead is a tree-covered island that divides the river, and I let Gloria choose which side she wants. She crosses to the southern side. Beyond the island the river opens into a wide confluence where it joins the rest of the Loup.

The Loup River has three branches, all beginning in the sandhills within fifty miles of each other. The northern branch flows through our ranch and has carried Gloria and me nearly two hundred miles to the forks where the North Loup meets the already combined southern branches of the river. I was hoping that when the branches formed a single river there would be ample water to carry us, but the riverbed widens and the river remains as shallow as before. It must fill up now and then, or it wouldn't be so wide. But it's not full now, and as it waits for water the river shrinks into a single primary channel that is now on one side and now on the other. I let Gloria choose the way here, too, and use the paddle to push us forward but not to disrupt her. It amazes me how well she does. I should have followed her lead from the beginning.

But even with her acute sense of the current, she can do nothing when there isn't enough water. Sometimes we make it across without touching bottom; sometimes we don't. If we are close to the re-formed channel, I try to sneak over the final barrier by leaning back so that I will raise her bow just enough to escape the sand's grip. Sometimes I wiggle the bottom of the kayak with my knees braced against the hull and slither through like a snake in the sand. Other times I push crablike with my arms over the last few feet before the channel. I even learn how to help Gloria choose the crossing instead of working against her. Sometimes her momentum carries her farther than she wants to go, and I use the paddle to work back against it. When Gloria can't find enough water to get us through in any fashion, I get out of the cockpit and pull her to the channel. It gives me a chance to survey the water from a higher altitude. What I see is that the water is too shallow—everywhere.

Some distance down from the forks I spot a fisherman on the bank who is watching his line floating downriver and doesn't see us until we are nearly upon him. His expression tells me that Gloria and I are like some strange creature that he's never seen before.

"Hey! Where are you going?" he asks, recovering from his surprise.

"New Orleans."

I don't know why I said that—maybe to explain our strange appearance, maybe to seem more important than we are. He's a young man, and I expect him to laugh or shout some joke. Instead he drops his fishing pole on the ground and runs along the bank to catch up with us. He has to fend off the willows that get in his way.

"There's a diversion dam up ahead," he shouts. "Keep out of that canal. It goes underground."

"Thanks. I'll watch out for it."

To slow our passing I paddle backward against the current.

"There's not much water after the dam."

He is close enough now that he no longer shouts.

"There's not much now."

"I can give you a ride around the canal. Save you a little time. Won't be much fun carrying that boat to the Platte."

He has gone as far as he can. A creek entering the river blocks him from following us any farther. An airboat is tied up in the mouth of the creek, and I suspect it's his. I paddle backward a little harder, and Gloria turns sideways in the current. Even so we will soon leave him behind.

"How far is it to the Platte?"

"Twenty, thirty miles, I guess. Won't take any time at all in my boat, but you got yourself a job in yours. You're gonna be walking a lot. I live in Columbus, and I've been up and down this river more times than I can count. I don't think you can make it."

I'm tired of walking and thus inclined to believe him. There isn't time to equivocate.

"I wouldn't want to ruin your fishing."

"Oh hell, no fish anyway. I just got my line in the water as an excuse. Pull in there." He points to the calm water beside his boat. "I'll get my pole and be right back." He heads back through the willows, slapping them out of the way in the same manner as when he came.

Gloria is already turned toward the bank, and I paddle toward the airboat. Once I reach the mouth of the creek, the water eddies around a point and provides an easy approach. I paddle around his boat and land on a muddy bank. My feet sink into the mud as I get out.

The young man returns with his fishing pole. He's sweating a little around the tight band of his cap, and the sweat trickles down his round friendly face. He reaches out to shake my hand and introduces himself.

"Bob Morrison," he says.

I'm a little amazed by how quickly things change. A few minutes ago I was wondering when this river would ever get deep enough to carry us, and now I'm wondering how we'll ever get Gloria on top of his boat. There isn't much room there—two seats in front of an enormous engine and an airplane propeller. The propeller is encased in a steel mesh box so that it won't rip off an arm or a head, but it still looks dangerous so close to the seats.

"You sure you want to try this? You might be getting a heavier load than you expected."

"No problem," he says. "This son-of-a-bitch will haul us over anything. I'll drop you off on the Platte after the canal comes back into the river. Plenty of water there. Unless you want me to take you farther?"

"That's far enough. I don't know how to thank you."

"Don't mention it," and his hand brushes away any words I might think about mentioning just as he brushed away the willows that were in his path.

The muddy water is up to my waist as I help Bob Morrison slide Gloria over the flat deck of his boat. There is just enough room for her on the passenger's side. I don't mind standing in water; I've been standing in it plenty. Bob looks like he's a little past the prime condition of youth, still with strong shoulders but also with a substantial belly from which he grunts as he lifts Gloria's heavy bow.

"Shit," he says from way down in his gut. "I guess you are going to New Orleans."

We tie Gloria down with the ropes I've attached to her bow and stern. She sticks out over the front and back and looks sleek and beautiful beside the huge engine and propeller. Bob hands me a pair of ear protectors and starts the engine. We sit on the front seats like spectators at a sporting event. He lets the boat float out into the current before engaging the propeller.

He is right about his boat. The son-of-a-bitch will go over anything as long as it is reasonably flat, including the sandbar that he roars over to escape the low-water dam that diverts water into the Loup Power Diversion Canal. I doubt I would have seen the dam in time to get to shore before tumbling over the spillway and dropping five feet into the swirling water below. From upriver the water looked perfectly flat. Bob shakes his head and grins as if he knows what I'm thinking.

"Genoa up there!" he shouts into my ear protector as we pass under a bridge. "Nice little town. Used to have an Indian school."

Genoa up there, Columbus ahead. Must have been Italians who gave the towns these names.

"I didn't know there were so many Italians around here."

"What?" He cups his hand over his ear protector. "Indians?"

"Italians!"

He nods his head and grins, but I'm not sure he understood me or maybe I didn't understand him. The engine and propeller are so loud that it is point-less to talk, and maybe that's why he hasn't asked me to explain what I'm doing or why I'm doing it. Instead of talking we bounce our way down the river, over the sandbars and the willows that grow on them, covering the distance in an hour that would take me all day pulling Gloria. I sit back in the seat and watch. It's a fine warm day and it would be a pleasant ride, except his boat makes the loudest noise I've ever heard.

"Just about there!" Bob shouts.

We pass under a railroad bridge, then under power lines spanning the river, by a road, houses, a public park, a highway bridge, and the park again—Pawnee Park in Columbus, Nebraska, I read from the sign as we pass.

A few minutes later we reach the confluence of the Loup and the Platte, both rivers more sandbar than river, but an incredibly wide river neverthe-less. I look over my shoulder at the great Platte River—a mile wide and an inch deep as someone once said. When I was looking at maps during the winter, plotting my route and thinking I could get a sense of what was to come from lines and names on a sheet of paper, I was pretty sure that I would make a camp at this confluence. Certainly there is ample dry ground for a camp. Instead I watch it disappear behind us with little regret.

"On the Platte now!"

Bob points over his shoulder with his thumb in the motion of a hitch-hiker, except I'm the hitchhiker. Finally we come to the water from the Loup Power Diversion Canal where it spills over a gate and makes a real river of it after all. Bob shuts off the engine and rams his boat up on top of a sandbar. For a moment I don't realize that he has shut off the engine. The noise seems trapped inside my head by the ear protectors.

"So here you are!" he shouts. It takes a moment for him to adjust, too.

"I think you saved my life."

"I saved you a little time and a lot of work, that's all. It gets deeper now. How long do you figure it will take you to get down there to New Orleans?"

"I don't know. I've given up even trying to guess."

"You got anybody who's meeting you along the way?"

"No."

"Well, maybe that's the way to do it. Get yourself a little boat and float along like Tom Sawyer or somebody like that. Don't pay any attention to time. Just float along and see what happens. I could see myself doing that."

"I'll bet you can."

"Have yourself a good trip," he says as we shake hands. "Call me if you get stuck somewhere. I'm in the phone book."

"Hope you catch some fish."

"Done fishing for the day."

Standing on the sandbar with Gloria beside me I watch Bob head back up the Platte in his airboat. The noise diminishes to a dull drone after he leaves my sight, and finally the noise disappears completely. Although I didn't get here quite like I thought I would, I made it. I didn't think I'd care to have company either, but you reach a confluence of two rivers and it's nice to have someone to share it with. Always when I thought about it before, I was sure it would be Joe who would be with me if anybody was. But we don't always get to pick our companions, and Bob Morrison was a fine companion whether I picked him or not.

"Hey," Joe answers, surprising me that I don't get connected to his voice-mail. "Where are you?"

"Just past Columbus on the Platte."

"So you made it."

"Yeah. I was beginning to wish we had grown up on a deeper river."

"I'll bet you were, but you'll be close to Omaha any day now. Maybe Rose and I could meet you somewhere. Have a picnic or something. I have to go New York tomorrow, but I'll be back in a few days."

"A picnic? When was the last time you went on a picnic?"

"About a million years ago."

"You wouldn't even know what to bring."

"Beer. What else is there?"

"Nothing. Maybe I'll give you a call when I get close. Is everything going okay?"

"You mean at work? Sure. You want to come in and check on Rose?"

"No."

"Annie wants to start an education foundation for the Mexican kids and name it after Amleth."

"She can do whatever she wants."

"She knows that. She still wanted me to ask you," he says.

"I don't know why she would want to use that name. Amleth hated it."

"Maybe you want to call her yourself."

"I don't think so. You call her back, will you?"

"Sure. No problem."

"It was my great grandfather's name. Did you know that?"

"No."

"And it was the name of the character in an old Danish legend that Shakespeare stole for his Hamlet story. My grandfather told me that, and I looked it up. I thought Amleth would learn to like it over time, but he never did. He told me once that I gave him that name because I expected something from him. I don't know. Maybe I did. You were my lawyer back then, too. Why didn't you tell me to name him Bob or Bill?"

"Or John?"

"Can you imagine what he would have said about that?"

"No."

"You were smart not to have any kids."

"Didn't have anything to do with being smart. Leslie and I weren't married long enough to have any."

"Same thing."

"We never know, do we?" Joe asks. "Is it going the way you thought it would—the trip, I mean? Is it going okay?"

"Does anything ever go the way we think it will?"

"Never does for me."

~ ~ ~

The Platte River is like a braided rope that is repeatedly pulled apart and cinched tight again. More of it flows beneath than above the surface of the sand and gravel bottom that Gloria scrapes with dismaying frequency. There is water here and water there and water around that island and this one and in the strand that I didn't take that has now disappeared into the trees.

Some of the water is from snow that has melted on the eastern slopes of the Rocky Mountains in Wyoming and has blended with the water from the aquifer and from the rain and snow that fell in the sandhills and collected in the branches of the Loup, but I can't tell the difference. It feels the same as it squishes in my shoes, which let the water in and out as the water wills.

Before this trip I read that the leg muscles of kayakers atrophy while the shoulders grow strong. The writers were not writing about kayaking the Loup or the Platte. My leg muscles are getting stronger and more tired as I trudge through the water, as I lift my feet from the sucking sand. It brings to mind once again the old cowboy movies of men disappearing into quicksand until only an outstretched hand is above the water. Sometimes the hand disappears, too.

When I find enough water to float Gloria, I sit in her with my legs dangling over the sides so that I can easily get out. Without the support of the foot braces my paddle stroke is feeble, but feeble paddling is pleasant compared to walking through sand and water.

I try not to think of the water that flows in the Missouri up ahead, but I have to think of something. How easy it will be once I reach that deep water, how pleasant it will be to float along and not worry about grounding in the sand. Sometimes I concentrate so thoroughly on the deep water farther down or the shallow water of the river just before me that I don't think about anything else.

But it doesn't last, and Amleth who hated his name and the black horse that we couldn't find a name for seep into my thoughts the way the river seeps into my shoes. If Amleth had listened to me, I wouldn't be here. I'd still be back in the sandhills. Sometimes I want to shout as loud as I can, "Leave that horse alone!" as if he will hear me. But there is no one to hear except me, and it's too late for me.

I wonder if the black horse survived the winter. He must have because I can't imagine him dead. When Juan and I first saw him, he was greater than our imagination—wild but not mean, so fast and agile that he could change himself before your eyes could see the change. At the wild horse auction the farmer who bought him was in way over his head. He couldn't load the black horse into his trailer even with the help of three government workers. I wanted that horse, had wanted him the moment I saw him moving among the herd with the rare authority that you seldom see in any horse or any living thing. Our lottery number was too far down to choose the black horse, but I wanted him anyway.

We were there because I had an idea how we could use wild mustangs to sell tame cattle. That the idea was completely illogical had no bearing upon whether it would work or not. What did a mustang have to do with a car? Nothing. It was only the image, and the less the buyer knew about internal combustion engines, the better the image worked. A wild mustang rounding up cattle that fed on natural grass was an image that would help us sell those cows. That we never used the black in a roundup didn't matter. The less the buyer knew, the better it would work.

The farmer couldn't get him into his trailer. The more he forced the black horse, the more the horse resisted. After a few hours the farmer was ready to sell. I paid him the auction price of seventy-five dollars and a bit extra for his trouble.

Juan and I never looked at the black horse or tried to move him. Instead we moved the steel fence panels that surrounded him and our horse trailer, a foot at a time, encouraging him but not forcing him to join the mare we had bought with our auction number. She was a fine young mare and didn't resist the halter or rope that held her in the trailer. The black horse stayed away from us, stayed close to the mare and the trailer as we moved and removed the fence panels until there was as much room in the trailer as in the fenced area around him. Juan placed a bucket of grain beside the mare, and the black horse stepped in quietly beside her. He sniffed the bucket, pushed away the mare's head, and tasted the grain. It was sweet from the molasses Juan had added.

In the wild horse preserve in Wyoming where the snow melts from the mountains and feeds the Platte, I cut the fence and led him through. There is nobody to give him sweet molasses anymore. I doubt it matters to the black horse, but still I wonder. He was the only horse I ever had that could look straight through me. I had the rifle in my hand, but if I had to shoot something, it wouldn't be the horse.

Walk, float, walk and pull the kayak. Wish for rain, wish for sun, wish for deep water. Try to forget, remember, forget again. Focus on the water. Forget who I am and where I'm going. And so the day passes; so every day passes.

At the west end of an island a ten-foot bluff is crumbling into the river. Beyond the bluff the ground slopes gently downward toward the flow of the current from the snow water of Wyoming and the springs of the aquifer. Trees are thick on the gentle slope, but on the east end tall grass grows on a level plain. Beside the trees stands an abandoned duck blind with white goose decoys stacked beside it on the ground. The duck blind draws me to it for my legs are too tired to go any farther.

While I wait for the water to boil so I can make my supper, I walk through the grass to the river's edge and watch the sun drop below the band of clouds that stretches across the western horizon. The clouds turn gold at the top and red below. I have seen more beautiful sunsets than I can remember, but this may be the most beautiful of all—the wide shallow river before me, the trees reaching up from this island with the early green hope of spring, the golden fleece of the clouds, and the red fire of the sun. Someone with a camera might try to capture this wild beauty in a picture. I don't have a camera, and it is just as well.

~ ~ ~

During the night I hear cautious movement in the water. The sound mixes into a dream in which the black horse is returning to find me, but I wake and realize that deer are crossing the river from the south bank that is closest to the island. They pause in the water when my scent reaches them and flee the danger they sense from me. Later there is more splashing, but the sound is too distinct, too heavy for the light cautious tread of deer. I unzip the tent door and look out. Fog covers the river and diffuses the beam from a flashlight that shines on the tent. Two men are pulling a flat-bottom boat loaded with white decoys. So the hunting blind isn't abandoned after all.

"Morning."

One of the two men answers my call with a duplicate greeting.

While they pull their boat up to the blind, I put on pants and shirt and sit in the tent door with my feet outside. There I pull on the socks and shoes that I've left out to dry. Neither has.

"I didn't think the duck blind was being used. What hunting season is going on now?"

"Spring goose season," the taller of the two men says. He was also the one who had answered my greeting. "That's why we left our decoys out here. How far have you come in that?" he asks.

He doesn't know what to call Gloria, or what to think of us. He's not friendly, but not unfriendly either.

"From out in the sandhills. Started on the Loup."

"Nobody shoot at you last night?" the other man asks. He is dressed in green camouflage from top to bottom. Even his boots are camouflaged.

"No. Maybe they could see I wasn't a goose."

"Wouldn't matter to some of these guys. They drive out from Omaha and pay a lot of money to hunt here. They wouldn't be happy if you ruined their hunting by floating through their decoys."

I don't like his tone or his camouflaged swagger.

"There weren't any decoys out there. And some asshole shoots at me, he had better hit me the first time."

As when the black lowers his ears at another horse who crowds him, my threat shuts up the second man whose swagger I don't like.

"It's Tuesday, Hank," the tall man says. "Those guys were back in Omaha last night."

"Maybe," Hank says grudgingly.

"But Hank's right," the tall man says. "You might want to wait with us a few hours before taking off. There are goose blinds every couple hundred yards for the next fifty miles. Nobody will care if you go by during daylight, but sunrise and sunset are the best times for hunting. Course with this fog, we might not have much of a sunrise."

While the two men anchor the goose decoys in the river around the island, I take down the tent and pull Gloria into the trees so that the geese won't see her. Then I join Hank and Walt in their blind to wait for the sunrise. They have thermoses of hot coffee and freshly baked cinnamon rolls and a flask of whiskey, and they share everything with me. I am ashamed now that I lowered my ears and say so in so many words without saying so. And Hank is sorry that he suggested anyone would shoot at me without saying so and passes me the flask.

"Last summer was so dry out west," Hank says, "that you could drive on the riverbed from Columbus to Kearney."

"Farther than that," Walt adds.

"You're right," Hank says. "We're lucky. The Loup always has water, so we always have water here. You should have seen it last October. They had four inches of rain out west, and when the water got here it was as green as can be from the grass and willows that grew up in the riverbed. I never saw anything like it before."

Now and then Hank or Walt gets up from the stools they have brought to the blind and checks on the thickness of the fog through the framed opening that faces the river to the east. In my bright yellow jacket I remain sitting on the ground and rest my back against a canvas bag of decoys. I can't see the river, and it can't see me.

"I'm curious about these islands. How do you decide who owns them?"

"Our property goes to the middle of the channel," Hank says. He and Walt are brothers. I've learned that with the passing of the whiskey flask.

"But I thought the channel was to the south of this island."

"It didn't use to be," Walt says, "and it might change again in another month. There are channels all over this river. We staked our claim here a long time ago. Nobody bothers us about it."

I doubt that anyone owns the islands, but I don't say so. We are past that now. When the sun finally burns off the last of the fog, it's too late for good hunting. Not a single goose has flown into the range of Walt and Hank's shotguns or even within their range of sight, and the two men pull in the decoys and stack them up again beside the blind. There hasn't been a goose call, real or artificial, or a gunshot all morning. Walt and Hank pack up their boat and pull it back across the channel, and I return with Gloria to the river where no one can stake a claim.

If the brothers are correct about the ownership of the islands, it means that I have the right to paddle down the river but not to land anywhere except on public rights-of-way below bridges and at public parks. Their determination to claim their island, their small piece of useless land, seems absurd, except that it reminds me of the dispute my father and a neighbor had about the boundary line of their land. The line wasn't in dispute; it was the straightening of it that caused the problem.

A fence, which marked the boundary of the two properties, ran north from the county road, over a hill, down through a hay meadow and on up the opposite hill. If you looked carefully from the top of the first hill, and I finally did, you could see that the fence veered off toward the neighbor's property at a slight angle on the other side of the meadow. By the time it reached the far hill it encroached ten or fifteen feet upon our neighbor's land.

The encroaching fence line ground on the neighbor the way he ground his teeth down over the years. My father felt it was foolish to do all the work that was necessary to move the fence for a few feet of ground. The fence had been there since the neighbor's father owned the land and long before my father ever bought it. Nevertheless our neighbor's agitation seemed to magnify when he turned sixty.

My father told the neighbor that he wouldn't object if the neighbor moved the fence, or he would give him a few bales of hay each year to compensate for the loss of land in the hay meadow. Our neighbor maintained that correcting the error wasn't his responsibility. And he didn't want any hay. He had plenty of hay. It was the principle that mattered.

When I was thirteen my father accepted my neighbor's principle and assigned me the job of straightening the fence. It was late in May, the first week after school let out for the summer. The barbed wire was so rusty and brittle that the wire needed to be replaced anyway, and most of the fence posts were rotten. In addition to that and most importantly, my time wasn't worth worrying about.

When our neighbor saw that I had been assigned to correct the error, he felt sorry for me and embarrassed for himself, and he came every day to help. I had to listen to his stories about the hard times in the '30s, listen to him grind his teeth and cuss at the weather and the price of cattle and the idiots who were so blind that they couldn't see a straight line if it was right in front of their faces. My father laughed every night at supper when I described my progress. Maybe he could have my brother help, I suggested, or maybe come out himself and tell the neighbor I could handle it on my own. My father was sure that I could handle it. I was doing a fine job already. He never went out to look at the new fence until the job was done.

Eventually I bought the neighbor's land. By then it was owned by his son who lived in Los Angeles and didn't care about any of the fences. The fence I had straightened was a nuisance every time we put up hay in the meadow, and I assigned Amleth the job of removing it. He was about the same age as I was when I had to move it. I told Amleth my story about straightening the fence, thinking it would make the chore easier for him. It had the opposite effect. Amleth seemed to hate every minute that he was out in the hay meadow removing the fence the neighbor and I had strung. If he had not made me angry with his sullen resistance to work, I would have helped him. My father never even came out to check on me. I told Amleth this, too, as I stood beside him on a morning when the meadowlarks were singing a spring song that was as beautiful as any he played from the music books on top of his piano. Amleth never looked up from the hole he was filling. I had come to help, but he wouldn't look at me. So I left him to finish the work alone.

Far down the river the sun reflects off something on the water. If it is a goose decoy, I intend to circle it widely despite my unspoken claim to Walt and Hank that I have as much right to this river as anybody. All morning I have seen blinds along the shore and on the islands, but no hunters and no decoys on the water.

I have often thought about that morning—how Amleth's stubbornness prevented me from staying and helping. Now, for the first time, I realize that it wouldn't have hurt me any to stay with him even if he wouldn't look up. I could have gone down to the next post, dug it out, filled in the hole. He would have had to walk past me to get to the next one, and I would have had to walk past him for the one after that. Upon one of the passings he might have said something, and I might have said something in return, and before we knew it we might have talked to each other like father and son. There was nothing I had to do that morning, nothing that couldn't wait until another morning. Then in the afternoon I could have handed him a beer as we sat on the tailgate of the pickup the way my neighbor handed one to me the day we finished the job.

"Don't tell your father," he said.

—Don't tell your mother, or we'll both be in trouble.

He would have said what I said, what every boy would say.

"I won't."

~~~

On the river "a mile or two" is open to considerable interpretation. When Rosario called an hour ago, she said she had found a park beside the river a mile or two south of the bridge at Venice and was waiting for me there. I have been looking for her since reaching the bridge. From the highway map I can guess the distance, but I can't guess if the channel will hold or if the water will disappear into the sand. Still I hope this channel will hold a little longer because I'm eager to see her. Since she first called last night and said she was coming, I have been hearing the voice that I heard when she was a girl.

"It's not how you said it."

It's as if she is straddling the kayak behind me the way she used to straddle the fence in the corral while she watched Juan and me working with the colts, only this time she is in the kitchen sitting beside Annie at the table where my grandparents and their sons used to sit. Annie reads the sentence in the storybook again, pointing to each word as she pronounces it. Rosario's finger replaces Annie's, and she repeats the words.

"Very good," Annie says.

"It's not how you said it."

Every afternoon after school Rosario studies at the table with a half dozen of her sisters and cousins. Rosario is the oldest and has been at the table longest. She helps the younger children with their homework or with the work Annie gives them. Annie is a natural teacher. She should have taught the country school but some of the neighbors who made up the school board feared that she would spend too much time with the Mexican children. Most of the Mexican kids, the neighbors complained, couldn't even speak good English. Most of the neighbors, Annie snapped back, couldn't either.

At the kitchen table Annie teaches them more than they ever learn in school. Rosario is her first pupil and her best. When Rosario came to the ranch, she knew four words of English. Yes, no, horse, cow. She was eleven years old. Along with new English words, Annie taught her the numbers one through ten, and what she could do with those numbers. Now Rosario can do more with those numbers than Annie or any of us ever expected.

Annie reads the sentence a third time, and Rosario watches her mouth and works her lips and tongue silently with Annie. Rosario repeats the sentence to Annie without looking at the words in the book and shakes her head in frustration.

"But Rosario," Annie says, "that was perfect."

"It's not how you said it."

Annie and I begin to speak our words more distinctly around Rosario. Neither of us wishes to be the one who teaches this child searching for perfection an improper pronunciation. When alone, Annie and I question each other, "Is that the way you say it?" and laughing, we retreat to the dictionary for confirmation. Rosario's English improves faster than Annie's Spanish, but both improve at an amazing pace. I even learn a few words of Spanish, more than a few, but nothing like Annie.

Juan believes that Rosario should spend less time in Annie's kitchen and more in her own helping Consuelo, but that kitchen belongs to Consuelo and she will determine who is needed and who is not. And so Rosario continues her lessons and soaks up everything Annie teaches.

In the winter of Rosario's eighth and final grade at the country school, I place a huge blue book on the kitchen table. Rosario and the younger children watch in silence as I flip to a page that I once often visited. I read out loud:

> To be, or not to be: that is the question:
> Whether 'tis nobler in the mind to suffer
> The slings and arrows of outrageous fortune,
> Or to take arms against a sea of troubles,
> And by opposing end them?

I look up from the book and recite from memory. I spent hours once learning this soliloquy, hours and hours, and I am surprised how much I remember.

> To die: to sleep;
> No more; and by a sleep to say we end
> The heart-ache and the thousand natural shocks
> That flesh is heir to, 'tis a consummation
> Devoutly to be wish'd. To die, to sleep;
> To sleep: perchance to dream: ay, there's the rub;
> For in that sleep of death what dreams may come

I am showing off a little, I suppose, and Annie frowns at me from the stove. She had gotten up to check on a pot of winter soup, and I had slipped into her chair. Amleth is in the living room, plunking away at the piano. Annie divides her time now between the kitchen table and the piano.

When I finish, none of the children says a word. Perhaps they don't know I am done. I push the *Complete Works of William Shakespeare* across the table to Rosario.

"Is this English?" she asks.

She is looking at the page, one of a thousand pages; each covered with two columns of small print and bound into the large blue book I bought in college. The corners of the book are bent and frayed.

"Yes, it is English. It is the greatest speech in the English language."

Full of self-importance now, I am quite proud that I remember so many of the words.

"But what does it mean?" Rosario asks.

There is a troubled look on her face, and I begin to wonder if my intrusion is such a good idea. I intended to show her what is possible with language, but it is clear that this language only confuses her.

"The speaker is wondering if life is worth living, but he fears what happens with death. Death, he says, is the undiscovered country from which we never return. But it is how he says what he says as much as what he says that makes all the difference."

Rosario turns one page after another of the *Complete Works*. Now and then she pauses, and I see that she is trying to read a passage, a line, a few words. Her troubled face does not clear with the words she reads, nor does Annie's. Only the young children sit passively with untroubled faces. Rosario's lips begin to quiver within the hard line she has set them, and I fear that she is going to cry. She runs away instead. She runs out the back door without stopping for her coat while I sit, stunned, at the table.

"Way to go," Annie says.

When she looks at me like that, there is no use explaining what I intended, and I walk out the door where Rosario has run and look for her on the road. It isn't cold. A warm wind has come from the southwest with the first false promise of spring. Rosario is not on the road that leads to her place two miles east of ours. I don't see her anywhere.

She must have run into the barn. The black horse and the large white stables built for him are yet to come. I walk to the barn my grandfather built before I was born and hear a shovel scraping the concrete floor. Juan assigned the chore of cleaning the horse stalls to the children, but they are supposed to do it on Saturday mornings.

From the walkway that separates the horse stalls from the calf weaning pen that we no longer use, I watch Rosario through the wood slats of Geronimo's stall. I don't know if she sees me, but she doesn't stop scraping the manure into the trough that runs the length of the barn. Geronimo stands at the outside door and mutters the low contented greeting he gives when he thinks a bucket of grain is coming.

"What's the matter, Rosario?"

She shakes her head and continues scraping. Some of the manure is frozen to the gutter, some is not. It gives off a sweet pungent smell that is not offensive, unlike the manure of the dairy cows that I had to clean here and in the barn on my father's place.

I walk into the stall with her and sit down on the edge of the manger box. She is done with this stall and will have to move to another if she intends to keep working.

"That book," she says. "It's as big as the Bible. I didn't know there were other books that big."

She scrapes a little more into the gutter. The stall is already clean enough.

"It has everything in it that Shakespeare ever wrote. That's why it's so big."

"I'll never learn all that. I can't even understand the one page you read. Annie never told me about this book."

"Come here and sit down."

I place my hand on the heavy boards of the manger. Rosario drags the shovel behind her and sits down beside me. I have not imagined her beyond the precocious child who amuses Annie and me, who is dearer because she does not recognize her own precociousness. But now in her eyes I see the first signs of the woman she will become—the anger, frustration, and fear when a man places a huge book in front of her and recites from memory a dozen or more lines that she has never heard before and doesn't understand.

"Have you read the whole Bible?"

"Not yet," she says. "I'm trying to read it in English, but I have to stop all the time and look up words. And I don't understand why it goes on and on about the burning of meat for this offering or that. There are so many pages of it that I don't know where I've stopped and where I should begin again."

"Maybe you should just skip over the burning stuff."

"I don't want to miss anything."

Her "I's" still hold the hint of the Mexican form that she is working so hard to overcome.

"It took me years to read the Shakespeare book. Years, Rosario. I had to stop and look up words all the time just like you. Now I can't remember what half the plays are about. I knew that would happen even when I was reading it."

"Then what's the point in reading the whole book?"

"I didn't want to miss anything."

She understands that I am repeating her words, but she doesn't understand that repeating the words is all I'm doing, just like the words I repeated from the Shakespeare book.

"You know his whole speech by heart. You didn't have to read it from the book. I don't even know what the words mean. I can never remember them."

"To be or not to be."

I gesture for her to repeat the words. She is reluctant at first, but finally repeats them and the next words I say. Then we repeat them again and again until she knows the first ten lines by heart. I tell her what the lines mean as well as I understand them. It is more than living that Hamlet questions. He is not saying 'to live or not to live' but rather 'to be.' He is questioning how we live and why and what it means to be and what it will mean if we end it.

I see in her eyes the transition from girl to woman and wonder why I have never seen that before. We hear the other children running from the house, shouting to each other in Spanish now that they are free. I take the shovel from Rosario. It is time for her to go home.

"To sleep," she says, "ay, there's the rub; For in that sleep of death what dreams may come."

The first ten lines were not enough for Rosario. Within a week she had learned and memorized the entire soliloquy from the book she borrowed from me. She asked me what some words meant. She had looked them up in the dictionary, but some she couldn't find and some didn't make sense even when she did find them. And some, I had to admit, I didn't know either.

She rose to the top of her class in the public school. When she gave her speech as the high school valedictorian, there was only the slightest hint of an accent left in her words. There was resentment from a few of the other parents that this Mexican girl won the award, but her speech was perfect. Everyone could hear that. At the university in Lincoln she studied business, and it was Annie's idea to send her to the university in Chicago. When Rosario told Juan and me that we could sell our beef for a higher price in specialty markets if we made a few changes in the way we raised the cattle, we smiled to each other as old cowhands listening to a tall tale—until we heard how much more they would pay. Then we stopped smiling and began listening to her.

I see Rosario waving to me from the green grass among the green trees beside the less green river. Her bright red blouse would be impossible to miss even if her arms weren't moving. Fortunately the current has decided to stay above the sand and pass close to the bank where she is standing.

Rosario treads carefully down to the waterline as Gloria's bow wedges into the bank. She squats beside the kayak and grips the hull over the gold-painted letters. Her new blue jeans have a pressed crease running straight down her legs to the small polished black shoes on her feet. I lift my feet out of the kayak and plant them in the shallow water. Gloria swivels with the current as Rosario holds her bow and I wade ashore.

"Did you think I would never get here?"

"I knew you would. How are you?"

"I'm fine."

She stretches her face toward me, and I bend down and kiss her cheek. Her earrings glitter in the sunshine. With Rosario it is always the small touches that tell the story. When she meets our customers, they see a beautiful woman with a refined taste for clothes, but if they look closely, they will also see golden earrings of wheat dangling from her ears. I am from the land, she says through her earrings. In fact we raise no wheat on the ranch. I once told Rosario that she should buy earrings with corn or cows, but she wouldn't do it. And she was right. Ears of corn would never be as beautiful as these.

"You've lost weight," she says.

She is looking into my eyes, but they can't be any thinner than before.

"Exercise and healthy living."

"How did you get that hat away from my father?"

"He gave it to me. Mine floated away the first day on the river. You didn't see it while you were waiting here, did you?"

"No. Only a few sticks and water. Lots of water."

"I'm glad you came, Charo."

Her eyes mist with the name that I haven't called her for such a long time. I picked it up from Juan when she used to ride between us in the pickup in the early years when he and I were the only crew on the ranch. Juan would tell her that she should go back to the house and help her mother, but I said, "Let her come."

It has been a difficult time for us since Amleth's death. We have each been walking within our own circles of responsibility as if the two circles did not meet, but they are often the same circles. We have just been moving at different speeds. Today I moved slowly enough that anyone could find me.

I pull Gloria out of the water and into the tall grass and follow Rosario to the picnic table that she has covered with a yellow vinyl tablecloth. There are two wine glasses on the table.

"Wow! Look at this."

"After I talked to you last night, Joe called from New York. He said to make sure that I brought plenty of beer. So there's beer if you'd rather have that."

"Wine sounds good to me."

"He's not happy to be missing out on this picnic. It was his idea, he said, and he'll be back tomorrow. We could have another picnic then, or you could come back to Omaha with me this afternoon. Maybe you would like a day off to rest up and do some laundry."

She is looking at my shirt. It was clean this morning, the last clean shirt I had, but now the sleeves are stained by the muddy water that drips from the paddle on every stroke. I had made some effort to be presentable, bathing and shaving at a public campground beside the river last night and putting on clean clothes this morning. But whiskers grow and the water is muddy, so what can you do?

"This shirt was clean this morning."

She looks down from the false smile I show her and begins pulling food out of the picnic basket. There are sandwiches from a delicatessen in the Old Market, and sliced carrots, broccoli, and red peppers, cheese and soda crackers, and chocolates in shiny gold paper.

I eat and drink everything in front of me, but Rosario takes only a few bites of her sandwich and a few sips of wine. There was a time when our conversation would be filled with all matters of business, but there isn't business to fill it anymore. Its absence creates an awkward silence between us.

"Are you still angry with me for dumping it all on you?"

She looks at the sandwich that she isn't going to finish and wraps it carefully back into the aluminum foil with the old frugality of her mother and father. She doesn't look at me until she places the foil package onto the table.

"I have never been angry," she says.

She moves the bottle of wine out of the way as if that is all that separates us.

"You'll be fine without me. You know everything about our business."

"How do you know how I will be?"

"Don't do it if you don't want to. Hire someone else."

"There is no one else. You know that. You're the one who taught me about this business. I can't leave."

"I think we learned it together."

"No. You taught me what I know, you and Annie."

"Annie was a better teacher than I was."

"No, she wasn't."

"He wouldn't agree with you."

I don't have to tell her who I'm talking about.

"I don't understand what good it does to leave. You won't bring him back, and you won't forget him."

"I'm not trying to forget. I'm trying to remember where it was I lost him."

"Maybe he lost himself."

"What do you mean?"

"When he was at the ranch, he wanted to be someplace else. But when he was away, he wanted to come back. And everybody knew that they were not to ride that black horse. If I wanted to ride a horse, I would never even think about taking that black one. We all knew that."

"Everyone is different."

"Yes. Everyone is different. And you think you will change how you feel by leaving us behind, but it won't change anything. Come back with me to Omaha. Joe will be coming home tomorrow. We could do something together. Sooner or later you will have to stop this. Why not sooner?"

The appeal in her eyes has always been hard to resist. Even when she was a girl, I would tell her father, "Let her come." How many times had I wished Amleth would look at me like that, to be like this girl? There's the rub, as the book would say.

"You might be right, Charo, but I can't stop now. It's not much farther to the Missouri, and I want to feel what it's like to be on a big river. I want to just paddle along and not get stuck on a sandbar, to do something as simple as that and nothing else. It might not change anything, but I'm going to try. I have to. I felt like I was dying back there."

"Then I will pray that you make it to wherever you are going. You don't want me to pray for you, but I will pray every morning and every night. What else can I do? I will pray that you come back."

I am startled by the intensity of her voice. All morning I have been thinking about the little girl who rode between her father and me in the pickup, but her voice is not the voice of that child. She is a mature woman now with a voice that I hardly recognize, and I must have gotten older, too. How this happens, I don't know.

~ ~ ~

As Rosario observed I have lost the softness around my belly. When I cinch the belt around my waist, the strap left over is longer than when I began the trip. And I don't feel the weather as acutely in my bones. It is not only that the weather has changed and gotten warmer; something has changed in me. I no longer shiver in the cool mornings as I put on the shirt I wore the day before and no longer dread the pulling on of wet socks and wet shoes. I've become used to them. The cracked cuticles of my fingers are beginning to heal, and they don't hurt anymore when I roll up the tent and brush away the coarse sand from the smooth nylon groundcover.

Despite the warning of the goose hunters, despite the invitation from Rosario to go with her to Omaha, I am on the river early, for if I have luck with the water today, I will reach the Missouri before dark. I am ready to finish these shallow rivers where the sand fills my shoes and crowds my toes. I am ready for the deep water of the Missouri.

When I stop on a sandbar mid-day to eat—crackers, cheese, chocolates, and vegetables that Rosario left with me—I watch the water flow by. I recognize a log with a distinctive white metal band encircling it that I caught up to and passed earlier in the morning, and I hate to see it go by. It's absurd to care about such things. Nevertheless I eat faster, get back into the kayak, and paddle to catch up again. 'Why are you doing this?' I ask myself as if this 'you' is another self. I want to get to deep water. When I reach the Missouri, there will be no sandbars to slow me down. In deep water any channel will do.

There is more to it than that. On this final great curve of the Platte, I am traversing an arc that remains a half hour from Omaha by car no matter where I am on it. The compass on Gloria's bow gives minute readings of our changing directions, but its general progress is from south to east. Like the arrow on the second hand of a clock, I follow it around, except this second hand is going backward, and the seconds are hours, and in these hours I push through the water as if I'm afraid that something will catch up with me and pull me back.

The aroma of barbecue drifts across the river with the smoke from the fires of The Three Pigs Restaurant. Joe, Rosario, and I often drove here for barbecue when I was in Omaha, especially in the summer when we could sit outside and watch the water of the Platte pass beneath the bridge on its last stretch to the Missouri. My mouth waters from the smell of the barbecue. A dozen cars are parked in the dirt lot. Another car is bouncing down the rutted driveway.

If I pulled Gloria off the river at a sandy landing beneath the bridge, I could walk up to the restaurant. And then if I call Joe and Rosario, they will come and meet me. Rosario said they would. It's five o'clock and the traffic will be heavy out of Omaha, but they will come anyway. I have followed this river across Nebraska, and all that I've accomplished is to keep ahead of water that always catches up and passes me by sooner or later. *'Why not sooner?'* I hear Rosario whisper. *'Why not sooner?'*

I let Gloria decide because I can't. The current edges away from the sandy bank beneath the bridge, and Gloria follows it across to the opposite side where we disrupt the solitude of a single blue heron. The heron squawks its displeasure and takes flight. It alights a hundred yards down the river. We come upon it again, and it repeats the cycle, drawing us away.

The river turns south and gains momentum. Quite suddenly there are no sandbars as the Platte narrows and pushes against rock and broken concrete that have been dumped along the north bank. A south wind kicks up waves that wash back against the current. Ahead of us is the deep water of the Missouri.

—Whoa. We're not ready for this.

The life jacket and waist skirt are still strapped to the deck behind the cockpit, but there is no way now that I can stop and put them on.

We cross beyond the rocky and artificial separation of the two rivers into the Missouri. Gloria feels unsteady beneath me. I'm not sure why. It's only water beneath us, the same as before, although this water is dark and muddy compared to the Platte, which looks green as it flows side by side with the water of the Missouri.

I take a deep breath to steady myself as I look back at the confluence. Three hundred miles ago the river was no wider than a county road and seldom deeper than a few feet. Since then I have passed through land so flat that the river spreads for a mile or more into its many channels, and now I've reached a river that has already traveled a thousand miles to get here. It's a big river now, and it sounds like a big river. The Loup and Platte had soft ethereal voices, but this river has a powerful force within it and a much deeper sound. Maybe it's the sound that makes me uneasy.

I look downriver for the source of the sound. A green buoy is lunging toward us in the current, and the sound I hear is the current dividing around it. We're too close to that buoy, way too close. With my head down, I dig the paddle into the water and bull ahead as hard as I can. It's not hard enough. The current is stronger than I, and the buoy catches the side of the kayak and holds us momentarily. I slam the paddle into the buoy to push away. The paddle snaps in half, and the river spins Gloria around the buoy and flips us over. For a moment I'm too stunned to react as I float upside down inside Gloria. Then I hear the massive flow of water. It's a frightening sound when you're in it.

Pushing and kicking, I escape the cockpit and come to the surface beside Gloria. One piece of the paddle is in my right hand; the other piece is floating beside us. I grab it with my left hand, and now my hands are full. The water rushes us toward another buoy, and I see no way to avoid it. I let go of both halves of the paddle, although I have no other, and thrash and kick in the water to move away from the buoy. It's the current and not my thrashing that washes me away along with Gloria. I reach over her, turn her upright, and hold on. One section of the paddle is right beside us. I grab it and stuff it into the cockpit. The other section is a little behind. Sliding back along Gloria I grab it and stuff it into the cockpit, too. Now all that I can think about is getting to land.

With my left hand holding the stern handle on Gloria's deck, I begin swimming with my right arm as hard as I can toward the nearest bank. There's a rock jetty up ahead, and it looks like we'll crash into it. The jetty gathers the current and flings Gloria and me back toward the center of the river. The water is alluringly quiet behind the jetty, but we can't get there. Another jetty is waiting ahead, and I swim hard with Gloria in tow toward the bank. Again we are swept out toward the center.

The exertion is making me breathe hard—or maybe it's fear. There is fear in this river, too. The water is colder than the Platte, and I'm beginning to shiver. I can lower my head and bull forward as hard as I want, but it won't get us to the bank. There's another jetty ahead, and it's going to throw us away from the bank just like the others. Maybe I'll have to let Gloria go.

Or maybe I'll have to use my head for a change and work with the current instead of against it. Instead of swimming toward land I pull Gloria farther out into the river so that we are beyond the reach of the jetty. When we float past it, I swim one-handed and two-legged toward the bank as hard as I can with Gloria behind me. This time we enter the quiet water behind the jetty, but I don't stop swimming even when my hand scrapes the muddy bottom. Two more strokes and my knees touch the bottom. For a moment I let them sink into the mud as I gather enough strength to stand.

The cockpit is full of water, and Gloria is so heavy that I can pull only her bow onto the bank. I turn her over and empty out most of the water. A waterproof bag holding my cell phone and extra batteries floats out with the water, but it's easy to retrieve. After careful inspection I find one small smudge of green paint on Gloria's hull, hardly noticeable among the scrapes and scratches she has received from the sandbars and submerged logs on the Platte and Loup. So it could have been worse.

The sun won't last much longer, and I need to get out of these wet clothes because I'm beginning to shiver again. Behind the jetty the bank is muddy and slippery and it's an ugly place, but on the other side of the rocks there is a clearing of flat ground where I can set up the tent—if I decide to stay. I'm not sure what I want to do. I feel as if I've been tricked. Why would anyone put a buoy out there to knock you over? Who would build these jetties that throw you out into the current and trap dirty water behind them where pieces of wood, plastic oil containers, milk cartons, and other junk circles endlessly?

One way or another I'm going to have to paddle out of here. I've landed on a bank within a narrow band of trees that borders an enormous plowed field. The field is in a wide valley that stretches east across a flat plain for some miles. There are no roads in sight.

'Maybe you tricked yourself,' I say to the other self as I resume the conversation we had coming around the arc of the Platte. 'All you had to do was look downriver and you would have seen that buoy.'

I examine the two pieces of broken paddle at my feet, pick up one end, and feel the clean break through the carbon fiber.

'What were you thinking when you finally saw it?' the other self replies. 'You could have just straightened Gloria and slipped right by. The water would have pushed you away.'

One of us sees the stand of willow trees close to the river; the other finds the hand axe and cuts down a sapling. One of us, or maybe it's both now, strips the sapling with a sharp knife, rounds and forms the two-foot piece of wood so that half of it fits snugly into each end of the two pieces of broken paddle. After wrapping the paddle with duct tape outward from the center, I grip the paddle with both hands and flex it between them. The paddle is a little heavier but feels strong, and the extra grip of duct tape is comfortable in my hands.

'It's better than it was before,' I tell the other one.

Some miles to the west, smoke from the fires of The Three Pigs rises high enough into the blue sky that I can see it drifting off in the direction of Omaha. The sun is still shining on the tops of the hills that rise from the valley floor in the east, but here beside the river, the evening shadow has reached us.

'I got us to Iowa,' the other one says. 'Tomorrow you get us out of here.'

~ ~ ~

From a distance a big river looks like a monolithic force flowing evenly between its banks, but all around Gloria and me there is turbulence and turmoil. A whirlpool forms just ahead, and I hold my breath as Gloria slides past the vortex and is swept sideways before straightening herself on the opposite side. Suddenly the river rises beneath us, and its surface flattens out like an overturned saucer. The paddle loses its grip in the water, and the rapid motion of my suddenly unrestrained stroke nearly capsizes us. I regain my balance and cautiously insert the paddle on the other side of the bow. We float on this eerily smooth water for some distance before the water breaks and flows out into the current, carrying us with it.

The strength of the river beneath my outstretched legs forces me to think ahead, anticipate, and exert as much control as the river will allow. It is like the first time I rode the black horse out of the confinement of the corral into the wide-open hills. I didn't know what to expect from him and was conscious of every movement, of every signal he gave. It took me a long time to learn that I would never know what to expect.

I want to stay in the middle of the river to avoid the buoys—the red buoys shaped like cones and the green buoys shaped like barrels—but against my will Gloria edges closer to them. At first I don't understand why she won't just stay away from them, but after awhile I realize that there is a channel here, too. It is marked by floating debris and faster than the rest of the river and crosses and re-crosses from side to side just as it did in the Loup and Platte.

The buoys must mark something about the river, but what—go here, don't go there, watch out? I don't know, and there is no one to ask on this river. Not a soul. Maybe I should have learned a few practical details about river navigation before leaving, but the river I had imagined was the river of Huckleberry Finn and Jim; the river I had imagined was the river I knew as a child where a stick that I dropped into the Loup might find its way to the ocean. This river is not in my imagination. It is here beneath me, before me and behind, and it discomposes me as I had never imagined. You'll get used to it soon enough, I tell myself. Just give it a little time.

A gust of wind crosses Gloria's bow and disappears upriver, passing so quickly that I wonder if it was merely a rogue current that found its way to the river. Then another gust of wind leaves its track on the water, ripples that define and mark its arrival and departure. There are more ripples ahead.

The river has ventured farther from the Nebraska bluffs into a flat alluvial plain and is now turning south into a fresh warm wind. How clearly this wind marks the water. I feel it precisely when I cross the line it has drawn. The wind snatches at the paddle blade, and I tighten my grip on the taped shaft. The ripples, growing larger, lose their fanciful markings and wash against the hull. Gloria noses into the waves and ignores them, but I cannot, nor can I ignore the wind that howls in my ears until I turn my head away.

I brace my knees against the foam pads inside the hull, and my body tenses like an inexperienced rider. Maybe the middle of the river is not such a good place to be after all, but Gloria is finally content here and disinclined to move closer to the bank. Maybe, I think to myself, we should get off the river and wait for the wind to die down. She isn't inclined to do that either and she's right. We could wait a lifetime for that. On land this wind would be nothing, a nice breeze to cool the skin, but out here the river channels the wind between the banks and makes it stronger. The current pushes against the wind and the wind pushes back against the current, and waves wash over the hull and drain away from the deck. My knees begin to ache from bracing. Gloria is at home here, but I am a stranger on this river.

Just as I think that this wind and these waves will last all afternoon, the river turns away from it. The roar in my ears becomes fainter, the waves smaller, until once again the tiptoe steps of a pleasant breeze cross before us. Gingerly, one at a time, I pull a foot off the foot braces, stretch the leg straight into the forward end of the cockpit, and shake it to get the blood flowing.

When the river turns south again, I expect to see the wind returning to the water. But the south wind is gone, and the river is calm and flat as if a giant hand is pressing upon it. So peaceful has the river become that I think its peace has entered me, and I paddle slowly and carefully, not wanting to break the river's spell. When a small swirl catches Gloria's bow I let her go, and she straightens on her own.

A fisherman is sitting in a small open boat downriver at the mouth of a stream. His fishing pole is pointed up the stream, and he doesn't see us pass. This is the first boat, the first person I've seen on the Missouri. Not long after we pass him, I hear the outboard motor coming from behind us. The fisherman goes by with a friendly wave. A bit farther down he pulls into another backwater where he casts his line again. This time he notices me as I paddle past him, and again we wave to each other.

The tall columns of a bridge rise from the hills and trees on the right bank as the river turns left before them. It is the third bridge I've encountered today, and I don't like them. The noise the current makes as it builds up against the pilings is unsettling. The fisherman passes us a second time with his motor full-throttle. The bridge doesn't bother him at all. He glides beneath its span without slowing and turns toward the bank.

It's our turn to pass beneath the bridge, and I paddle with silent even strokes until we're beyond it. There is a small town on the right, but it is disappearing behind us. The current of this big river seems to have gained speed as I glide past *The Spirit of Brownville*, a large paddlewheel boat docked beyond the town. The fisherman is at a boat ramp that is nearly hidden behind *The Spirit*. He has backed a trailer attached to an old pickup truck down to the ramp and is winching his boat onto the trailer. It looks like there might be a campground just beyond the boat ramp. The fisherman waves to me again, and I take it as a sign of welcome. *The Spirit of Brownville* creates an eddy and calms the water, and Gloria glides easily up the boat ramp. The fisherman stops turning the trailer winch as Gloria's keel scrapes the concrete. The scraping makes me wince, and I back off a bit.

"Need a little help bringing her in?" he asks.

His voice is low and flat and reminds me of my great uncle—my grandmother's brother. This uncle didn't talk much, but I always felt better when he did. We all did.

"Sure."

The fisherman leaves the winch and steps over to Gloria where he grabs the bow handle and pulls us farther up the ramp. The bottom scrapes again on the concrete, but this time I don't wince.

"This here is a kayak, isn't she?"

"She is."

"Pretty," he says and rubs Gloria's smooth bow with a weathered hand. "Come far in her?"

I pull the elastic of the waist skirt off the cockpit combing and lift my feet out of the boat.

"I started out west in the sandhills. Came down the Loup and Platte."

"That's quite a trip. How far are you going?"

His face is lined with deep wrinkles from long hours in the sun.

"I'm not sure."

I stick the paddle into the cockpit and unzip the life jacket.

"I've fished upriver as far as Nebraska City," he says. "I thought that was a long way. Looks like you need a new paddle."

"Oh, this one is all right. A little banged up, that's all."

"Do you carry everything you need in there?" He points to the bow hatch where the straps hold the cover firmly in place.

"And here." I point to the second hatch at the stern. "Is that campground over there open to the public?"

"Sure, but they charge you seven dollars a night."

He sounds apologetic about the fee.

"That's pretty reasonable. How was the fishing today?"

"I caught a catfish and two nice bass. Say, you can have them if you want."

"Thanks, but I don't know how I would cook them. My frying pan is about the size of my hand."

"I have a skillet you can borrow," he says. "I always keep one in my truck with my gear. Course you might not like fish."

"I like fish. Do you want to join me for supper? I've got some food somewhere in those hatches that we could have with it."

The man extends his hand across Gloria. The cuffs on his red and black plaid shirt are frayed enough that the color there no longer shows through.

"Tom Reeves," he says, and we shake hands firmly. "I'll help you carry her up to the camping place."

To reduce the weight, I stuff most of the gear into the portage bags and loop the straps over my shoulders. Tom Reeves grabs the bow handle, I grab the stern, and we carry Gloria past several campsites that are close to the water. He points to a well-tended area where a small aluminum trailer is parked. There's no one around the trailer, and no vehicle parked beside it.

"These places are a little nicer for your seven bucks," he says, still apologetic about the cost of hospitality.

The grass has been mowed and raked, and there are neatly stacked piles of wood beside the fire pits in each campsite. Not far away is a concrete block building, which must be the toilets. I hope they have hot water and showers.

While Tom goes back to the ramp for his truck and boat, I look for dry kindling in the wood pile. I find better kindling in the untended ground at the edge of the campsite and build the fire within the three-sided concrete pit. When the fire is going strong, I roll out the tent and stake it to the ground. Tom is back by then and watches me snap the tent poles together.

"They think of everything, don't they?" he asks.

"They do."

Tom places his black skillet on the grate where the fire rises through the steel bars. I set up the camping stove on a picnic table and add water to the pot I place on it. Tom digs in the back of his truck, which is covered with a metal canopy, and produces two mismatched lawn chairs. He offers me the green chair, which is in better shape than the blue one.

Tom cleans his fish on a newspaper spread over the tailgate of his truck. Their dead mouths open involuntarily as he slits the bellies. Then he scrapes the intestines onto the paper with his fingers and cuts fillets from the three fish. His fingers are thick and strong. They are hands that are used to hard work.

I have no oil with me to fry the fish, but Tom has some in a cardboard box in the back of his truck. It seems he has about everything he needs there, including flour that he sprinkles onto the moist bass and catfish fillets. I don't even have salt and pepper in my cooking gear, and Tom returns to the cardboard box. By then I have found the hot sauce Juan gave me to spice up the bland food in the aluminum foil packets. Tom demurs from using it. Juan would have sprinkled a little on the fish in addition to the salt and pepper, but then Juan used his hot sauce on everything, including popcorn. When I was with him, I used it, too, but Tom Reeves is frying the fish and I put the hot sauce back into the waterproof bag.

The fish is delicious. The macaroni and cheese I found in the food bag could use a little hot sauce, but I satisfy myself with salt and pepper. Tom brings out a six-pack of beer—metal cans that are tied together with a plastic halter. One by one he pulls the beer cans free.

"Your trip got anything to do with that Lewis and Clark thing? You know the one they're doing for the two-hundred-year anniversary?"

"That was last year, wasn't it?"

"The keelboat came back down a couple weeks ago. I thought maybe you were following along behind it."

"I'm not any part of that. I'm just paddling down the river."

"To tell you the truth, I'm sort of glad to hear it," Tom said. "That keelboat was supposed to be just like the one Lewis and Clark had, but they put a motor on it. How can it be like their keelboat if it's got a motor? It stopped here to give some sort of demonstration. I didn't even come down to see it."

Tom trails his thick finger around the rim of his third can of beer and looks over the fire pit toward the river. There is a wistful look about his eyes.

"What I'd like to see is the way this river was before they started changing it. Sometimes late in the summer I think I know what it was like, but I still wish I could have seen how it was back then. You run into any of those piping plover birds along the way?"

"Don't think so."

"Too early, I guess," Tom says. "Not enough sandbars for them right now. You got them out where you come from?"

"A few, I guess."

"There used to be a lot of them, I hear. They make their nests on the sandbars after the spring runoff. But there isn't a spring runoff anymore like there used to be. They hold most of the water behind the dams up in the Dakotas. Now they're talking about letting more water out of the dams in the spring and drawing the river down in late summer so that it will be more like it used to be so that the plover can build its nests here again. They say it will be good for the sturgeon, too. Used to be a lot of them in this river, but they're about done in. It's got the barge companies all upset. They say it will put them out of business if the river is too shallow for them to operate all year long."

"What do you think will happen?" I ask.

"Did you notice all the rock the Army Corps of Engineers brought in to hold the banks, all the jetties they built, all those buoys they put out there?"

"Yes."

"Well, after they do all that, do you think that little bird has much of a chance?"

"Probably not."

"We got an Asian carp in the river now that will jump right into your boat. They brought them in to clean the catfish ponds down in Arkansas and Mississippi, but they got flooded out of the ponds in '93. Now they're destroying the river for the native fish: the catfish, bass, and sturgeon. Sturgeon has been here millions of years, but it's not going to last either. They're spending tons of money trying to restore their habitat, but it isn't going to work. The water runs too fast now. They're cutting side-channels into the bank so the fish got someplace to lay their eggs. Did you notice them when you were coming down?"

"I guess not."

"Well, it's a good idea, except they've dumped rock along the banks to keep them from eroding, and the rock leaches off minerals, and the fish won't lay their eggs there. And then they're dumping whole piles of rock out in the middle of the river to make a place for the fish to get out of the current. This time of year the river gets up just high enough so that you can't see them, but they'll rip the bottom out of your boat. You best watch out for them. They're going to kill somebody someday, and then they'll dig 'em all back out. Doesn't make any sense. Wish I could have seen it the way it used to be."

"So do I."

"Well, they're not going to pay any attention to a couple old river rats like us," Tom says.

He has finished his third beer as I have, and he wipes the grease from his frying pan with newspaper. He tosses the paper into the dying fire, which erupts with the quick-burning fuel of grease and paper.

"Need me to bring you anything from town?" he asks, after he puts the frying pan into the cardboard box in the back of his truck.

"No thanks. I have everything I need."

"This is a nice little town, but there ain't much here. We're getting a fancy new bookstore though. Got a Greek name I can't pronounce. It's mostly for the tourists, I guess. We get a lot of tourists here, being as it's the oldest river town in the state. Used to be a stop on the Underground Railroad, too. You've heard of that railroad, I suspect."

"I have."

"Missouri over there on the other side," Tom says, nodding toward the river. "Slave state back in the old days. So wasn't everything so perfect back then. I'm glad we never got that over here."

"Me, too."

The fire has consumed the newspaper and died back down. Tom stands beside Gloria and rubs his hand over her bow again.

"I've thought about doing something like what you're doing. I could probably fit everything into my johnboat and cover it up with some canvas.

Just head on down the river. I've thought about doing that someday. Good luck to you, sir," he says and holds out his hand for me to take.

"Good luck to you."

"And good luck to those little birds," he says. "They're going to need it more than you and me."

~ ~ ~

When I crawl out of the tent early in the morning, Tom Reeves is waiting a discreet distance away in his pickup. During the night he got to thinking that I might need help carrying the kayak back to the water. He has brought with him a thermos of hot coffee and doughnuts, and we sit in the old worn-out deck chairs that he fetches again from the back of his truck.

"Supposed to rain pretty hard today," he says. "If you got a little time, I could show you around and you could come up to the house tonight. Got an extra bed if you want it."

"Thanks, but I guess I'll keep going. I'm just beginning to get used to what this river is like."

"I understand," he says. "I'd feel that way, too."

"Maybe you can tell me what those red and green buoys are for. They don't make any sense to me."

I gesture toward the river, which looks quiet and peaceful from where we are, just a ripple here and there on the surface and a few logs floating by in a silent procession.

"To tell you the truth, I don't pay much attention to them. I guess they're supposed to mark the channel for the barges. That's about all I can tell you."

"That's more than I know."

"You get downriver a few miles you're going to come to the nuclear plant. You want to stay over on the left side to keep away from it. They use river water for cooling whatever it is they got to cool. You don't want to get yourself into that intake."

"That's for sure."

"I stay away from it myself. Fishing's no good down there."

As we carry the kayak back to the boat ramp, Tom has one of the portage bags slung over his shoulder and I have the other over mine. He watches with interest as I stuff the waterproof bags into the hatches, one after another. I have finally established an order for them, but it still takes some time to put everything away.

"Hard to believe you can fit all those bags in there," Tom says.

"It is, isn't it?"

Finally all the bags are stowed away, and I put on the waist skirt and life jacket. I ease Gloria into the water and lower myself into the cockpit. Tom bends down and holds the stern handle while I stretch the waist skirt over the combing. The elastic cord has to be secured in the back before working it forward, and I'm not very good at it yet. The cord keeps popping off the combing behind me before I can stretch it over the front. Finally it stays where it's supposed to, and I pick up the paddle.

"I guess I'm ready."

"You want me to give you a little push?"

"I'd appreciate it. Thanks for all the good food. It's been a pleasure meeting you."

"Same goes with you. And if you ever catch up with those Lewis and Clark fellas in the keelboat, tell them to leave the river alone."

He pushes Gloria gently away from the boat ramp, and the river takes hold of her and me and carries us toward the mock explorers who are pretending to travel down a river that doesn't exist anymore. I am used to thinking of the river as the water that rises up from the aquifer in the sandhills and flows through wet and dry years to find its way to the ocean. But now I wonder if the river is more than just the water. Is it also the piping plover that makes its nest on the sandbars and the sturgeon that has been in this water longer than any man? Could it be Tom Reeves and maybe even me, now that I'm here—Gloria and me?

I imagine Tom back at the campground rummaging through the cardboard box in the back of his pickup and thinking about what else he might need if he were to toss the box in his johnboat and follow me down the river. That's what he'd like to do. I saw it in his eyes—get into the river and see where it goes.

Far down a massive shadow clings to the bank. At first I think it might be the cloudbank that's building up in the southwest, but as I'm drawn closer the shadow becomes the concrete form of the cooling tower of the nuclear power plant. Just as Tom warned me, a sign directs boat traffic to stay away from the water intake. I cross to the opposite side and paddle close to the Missouri bank. The power plant is quiet as I pass, and I am quiet, too. Steam rises downstream where the discharge from the cooling tower returns to the river, and I stay away from the steam, although it's supposed to be harmless.

The gray mass of clouds stretches over us, and rain begins to fall. I cinch the Velcro strap of my paddle jacket tighter around my neck. Water puddles on the brim of Juan's hat and drops onto my back and shoulders and onto the waist skirt stretched tautly over the cockpit. Although my body is protected from the rain, the gloom of the sky and the rain chill me and make me feel even more isolated than before. Since leaving Tom, I haven't seen another person.

Beyond the trees on the west bank there is a paved road and a parking lot with one car in the lot facing the river. Maybe there's a building there where I can warm up. I paddle toward the bank and into a protected cove lined with trees whose gnarled roots hold on to each other above the ground. At a shallow landing, I release the waist skirt and stand out of the cockpit. Gloria drifts with the slow current of the cove when she is free of me, and I grab the bow handle. With it I pull her higher onto the bank.

A signboard in the parking lot lists the rules for Indian Caves State Park, and a laminated brochure attached to the sign gives a history of the caves, which can be reached by a staircase that scales the steep bluff on the other side of the road. The caves in the limestone walls of the bluff were used as temporary shelter for several thousand years among the tribes who lived here—the Otoe, the Pawnee, the Omaha. The caves are protected by wooden railings, but anyone could climb over them and many have. The soft limestone walls are covered with scratched graffiti, most of them professing some sort of affection; others have only a single name and date to announce their presence. There are older petroglyphs, too, among the recent scars. Among them are buffalo that the Indians carved into the walls and one that looks like a horse. In one of the caves water has eroded the limestone in such a fashion as to make a chimney, and beneath the chimney the cave walls are blackened from ancient smoke. The thought of fire makes me shiver again as the rain continues to fall.

I walk back down the stairway to the parking lot below and am hailed with a brusque wave from a man as he gets out of a pickup. It's not at all like the wave Tom gave me yesterday. The man places a beige hat on his head. His hat and green jacket give him the appearance of a forest ranger or at least a person of some authority. The truck verifies my impression. *State of Nebraska. Official use only.*

"Is this your car?" he asks, pointing to the only other vehicle in the lot.

"No."

"You need a sticker to come into a state park."

The ranger's face is red and splotchy, and his green jacket is tight around his belly. He looks like he spends more time in the truck than walking through the woods.

"I came in a kayak."

I point past the parking lot toward the river. He looks where I have pointed, but he can't see the kayak. Neither can I. It's hidden in the brush.

"So where did you park your vehicle?"

He must not have heard what I said.

"I don't have a vehicle. I'm paddling down the river in a kayak. My boat is in the bushes down there by those trees."

"You paddled here? What are you trying to do, kill yourself?"

"No."

"They're getting heavy rains north and west of us, and the river's going to come up fast. When that happens, that current won't be anything to fool with. If it was me I'd get out right here. How far do you figure on going?"

"I don't know. I just stopped to look for a warm building where I could get out of the rain for a while."

"You doing it for that Lewis and Clark thing? They didn't stop here, you know. There's nothing in their journals about these caves."

"I'm not part of the Lewis and Clark thing."

"There's a campground up the road a ways in the park, but you can't camp down here by the caves."

"I'm not camping here. I'm about ready to leave."

"Suit yourself. The closest campsite for Lewis and Clark is about five miles down the river. It's on the Missouri side. I think they got a sign set up there."

We seem to be talking in different languages. I thank him in the language I know, although I don't know what I'm thanking him for. If he were Tom, I could sit in his truck and warm up, but I don't think there's any way to get warm here.

When I'm with Gloria again, I sponge out the rainwater that has collected in the cockpit and ease her back into the river. I paddle steadily through the rain. As long as I keep paddling, my body stays warm. It's only when I stop that I get cold.

In the afternoon the clouds become so heavy and low that the gray river and gray sky become one. The steady rain turns into a downpour, and the surface of the river becomes white as millions of raindrops, billions I suppose, hit the water, bounce into the air, and land a second time. If I look carefully I can distinguish one raindrop from the billions. I stop paddling, reach out, and touch the ricocheting drops with my hand.

Toward evening the rain stops, and sunlight sneaks through the clouds. I look for a place to camp, first on one side of the river, then the other. There are no islands like those I found on the Loup or Platte, no sandbars in the rising river. I begin to look for irregularities in the riverbank, for sharp bends or projections of land where there might be slack water. Trees are thick along the bank, and there doesn't seem to be a piece of clear flat ground that is large enough even to pitch the tent. Soon it will be dark. Maybe I'm being too particular. Maybe I'll have to make my own clearing.

Ahead on the right bank is a spot where the ground levels out from the hills. The river turns slowly and widely around the level ground, and through an opening in the trees shines the golden light of sunset. The bank rises steeply from the water, but I find a shelf at the river's edge just wide enough and long enough for Gloria. There we land.

At the top of the bank the trees form a narrow wall beside the river. Beyond them is tall grass, and beyond the grass is an immense cornfield where the corn is just emerging from the rain-soaked soil. Here is more flat land than I will ever need.

I'm not sure where I am, somewhere close to the Nebraska/Kansas border unless the river has marooned a piece of Missouri on the right bank. Most likely I'm in Kansas.

The computer generated voice on the weather radio says that there have been heavy rains in central Nebraska, seven to ten inches in some places causing the Platte to flood. Ten inches of rain on the Platte. What would that be like? There would be no sandbars there either. I wonder if the goose blind survived. The Missouri River will rise during the night says the voice on the radio, and low-lying areas along the Kansas-Nebraska border will begin flooding by morning.

From the lower shelf beside the river I drag Gloria up to the higher ground where I've set up the tent and tie her bow line to one of the crossing tent poles. If the river rises this high, we'll float away together. I hang a flashlight from the tent ceiling and prop another between two bags on the floor so that it shines up while I eat the reconstituted freeze-dried food I've prepared, chicken teriyaki this time. The tent reminds me of the soot-blackened cave where I saw the drawing of the horse, except that my cave has no drawings on the wall. After finishing supper I lie in my sleeping bag, staring at the blank ceiling where the flashlight is making a circle of light. I could draw a horse of my own up there, but I don't need a drawing to remind me.

～～～

The Indian boy leads the black horse out of the cave beside the river and climbs onto its back. Without saddle or bridle he directs the horse by touching its flanks with his heels or his toes, each variation of pressure a different sign that the horse understands and accepts. The Indian boy jumps down, and I climb onto the horse. I grasp the mane, lean forward, and click with my tongue. The black horse explodes from the bank and jumps into the dark river. His movement in the water is so fluid that he becomes part of the river, and I flatten myself on top of the horse so that we are like one animal instead of two. Now there is no difference between the river and the horse, no difference between the horse and me.

I lie awake thinking about the Indian boy.

"Why would you hire this boy from the reservation?" Juan asked. "We don't know anything about him. When we bring somebody here, we know who they are—the father, the mother, the brothers, the sisters, cousins, everything. We have all these people making sure he will work, that he won't get into trouble. With this boy we have nothing, and now I have to tell Carlos, my own brother, that he won't train this horse. It's his job to train the horses. If you want to work with that black horse, that's all right. But how do I tell my brother about this Indian boy?"

"Tell him this horse is different from any horse we have."

"He's different all right," Juan said. "He's a wild son of a bitch, and you should get rid of him. Nothing good will come from that horse."

Juan was wrong and right at the same time. George, the Indian boy, saw what I saw and much more. I saw how we could use the image of this horse in our ranch business, but George saw the horse.

"I could train him for you," George said as he stood behind the tall steel railing of the corral where I was working with the black horse. "I know this horse."

How he got out to our ranch or why he came, I never found out. I was introducing the black to the snaffle bit, applying gentle pressure to his mouth. Everything had to be gentle with this horse. As soon as I pushed him too hard or too fast, he balked and threw off everything he had learned. Then I had to start over. I didn't want to start over again.

"He doesn't like the bit," George said to me through the steel railing.

"He's just getting used to it."

"He'll never get used to it," George said. "I'll make a halter for him. That's all he needs."

When George showed me the halter he had constructed, I got off the black horse and led him over to the fence to the Indian boy. The halter had a looping rein, and it began and ended with the same knot from a single length of worn rope. Over many years I tried to duplicate George's work with the rope, but I never figured it out. Carlos came close, but his halters never fit a horse the way George's did.

George removed the snaffle bit from the black's mouth and slipped on the halter. Then he took off his boots, unsaddled the black, and rode the horse bareback and barefoot in the corral. Carlos thought that George was only trying to show off. I thought that was possible until I rode the horse bareback and barefoot like George. Of course Carlos might still have been right. He could make this horse stand on his head, he told me later, if I gave him as much time with the horse as I allowed George.

The black horse did everything we asked of him. He was wonderful to ride—smart, intuitive, athletic. He was all the adjectives we could think of, or all that I could. George didn't use many adjectives. My vision for the horse grew, and I let George have as much time as he needed. We could bring buyers out to the ranch and let them see George and the mustang. We could print an image of the horse in our advertising brochures and maybe even use it for the name of the ranch. We didn't have a name for the ranch yet, but maybe this horse would give us the name we didn't have. There was nothing exotic about a bunch of cows, but a mustang, a wild horse, a wild horse with an Indian rider, that was as exotic as you could get. We might even be able to start our own breeding line with this horse. He was that good.

When I came back from the wild horse preserve in Wyoming, George was gone. He never told anybody where he was going. Wherever he is, he still limps from the broken leg he got when one of the black's colts ran him into the railing. Nearly all the black's colts were wonderful horses, but that one was too wild even for George.

A soft constant moan rises from the river as it pushes against the bank. Inside the tent it is so dark that I don't know if it is early morning or late night. I could find my watch, but it doesn't matter if it is early or late. They are the same to me now. Perhaps, like George, I am learning to cast away these adjectives that mean nothing.

At his first reining competition at the county fair, we decided that I would ride the black instead of George. George was the better rider, but we wanted to win, and we would have a better chance with me riding, someone the judges knew, rather than George. We modified an Australian saddle and shortened the stirrups so that I looked like a jockey on a race horse. The cowboys laughed at the whole affair—a rope halter with no bit, the Australian saddle with short stirrups and no horn, moccasins instead of boots. They had heard about the Indian boy and me and were eager to laugh.

When the black horse entered the arena, I dropped my feet from the stirrups, held the rope reins with the tips of my fingers, and never moved them during the entire routine. The black horse may have heard the laughter of the cowboys because he performed beautifully. I gave him signals with my feet just as George had taught us, but I don't believe the black needed any instruction from me. We won the competition and silenced the laughter.

Sometimes George rode in the arena during competitions and sometimes I did. We won more often when I rode. Sometimes George was disqualified because he refused to even touch the reins of the rope halter. The judges determined that the rider was exerting no control, although we explained that George gave the horse signals with his feet and voice. The black horse was sensational whether he won or not. We entered him in regional and national contests with the same rate of success. Sometimes we won and sometimes we didn't, but the black horse was always sensational. I can still feel him beneath me, the smooth stride that George would never describe. It is the horse, he would say.

What bothered the cowboys and the judges was that George didn't look like them. He wore buckskin pants, but no boots and no spurs. And he never wore a hat. I think that bothered them most of all. In only one competition did the black perform poorly. George finally led him out of the arena before finishing the routine. "The black didn't like these people," he said.

"This horse will have to run," George told me. "It is in every horse, but it is more in this horse than any I have known. Sometimes we have to let him go or he will forget who he is."

And so we let him go, and as I look up at the ceiling of the tent where I see nothing I can still feel the horse beneath me and remember what it was like in the sandhills with no fences in sight. Then even I would forget all the ideas I had for this horse and would just let him run.

It is morning after all, and daylight filters through the tent. Unlike the Indian caves upriver, this is a flimsy cave at best. I stuff my sleeping bag into its waterproof bag and toss the bag out the door. The sun is shining and I am hoping for good weather. The weather is good, I tell myself. Look to the east. See the sun. Feel it. Instead I look to the west where the clouds are building up once again. I chose to travel down the river in spring when the weather is least predictable. If I wanted predictable weather, I should have waited until fall. I could barely wait until spring.

The water has risen during the night, and the current is faster, stronger, and full of debris. Shredded cornstalks, tree branches, logs, plastic bottles, and softballs—white, green, and yellow softballs—form a parade in the current that we join. The softballs are a mystery.

Although the river is higher and faster than it was yesterday, it feels no different. I steer Gloria around the logs and debris, but since we're moving faster than the current there is no difficulty. The whirlpools behind the jetties are bigger than before, but we stay away from them. If the river rises above the jetties, the giant logjams of trapped debris will wash downstream. Some of the buoys have already reached the end of their chains and flail back and forth like half-submerged dying monsters.

There is an extraordinary racket ahead. At first I think we must be coming to a manufacturing plant, but far downriver I make out the shape of a barge creeping along the east bank. It's the first barge I've seen on the river. Uncertain what to expect but expecting the worst, I move away from it to the opposite side.

As we pass the barge, I discover what all the noise is about. A dredger is bringing up sand and mud from the river bottom and dumping it onto a conveyor belt, which in turn deposits it to a barge tied behind. A hill of sand and mud is forming on the barge and behind it is another barge and another hill. The dredger plods slowly upstream against the fast current, clearing a channel for shipping. But Gloria is the only other vessel on the river, and the river is already deep enough for her. Although the propeller on the towboat churns the water violently, the wake that reaches us is inconsequential and Gloria shrugs it off indifferently.

On the side of the river where the dredger passes, houses are tucked among the trees below the bluffs, and a long freight train roars by on a levy between the riverbank and the houses. Farther down a new gambling casino stands on flat ground and encroaches upon the river. Its parking lot swallows up acres of rich bottomland, but its yield per acre is likely more profitable than any cornfield. Another bend and the old town of St. Joseph creeps toward us, for it seems that we are still and the land is moving past us like the frames of an old movie—until I reach the railroad bridge.

The river makes a fearsome noise as the water backs up and divides around the enormous concrete pilings of the bridge. Now it is clear what is moving. We are moving with the river. Gloria is inclined to slip close to the concrete buttresses, but I steer her away. Still we pass closer than I wish or expect, close enough to feel and hear the power of the river. I should be used to these bridges by now.

Unlike the other river towns we have passed, St. Joseph comes right down to the edge of the water. Old brick buildings, warehouses, a cement plant, even a new park are built along the waterfront and on the hill rising from it. We pass beneath two more bridges, and beneath each I steer Gloria to the center of the widest span. As the river carries us away from the city, the buildings, homes, and vehicles along the left bank become farther apart until the bank is covered once again only with trees.

After St. Joseph the river crosses a wide valley before turning south again beneath the bluffs on the Kansas side. Here the river is straight for a long distance, and green grass meadows begin at the river's edge and run up the valleys into the hills. Black cows graze on the thick grass, reminding me of the hills that I have left.

–What do you think, Gloria? Don't you like a little grass now and then instead of all those trees?

Gloria turns toward the green meadows when I stop paddling. Together we float among the debris in the current. I talked to the black horse, too, especially when I rode him out into the hills away from the corral. He listened better than most people. But if I talked too long he would shake his head and stretch his neck against the halter. I had to let him go. When he ran, I nudged him a little one way or another—just a little. That was the deal we made. I could pretend to be in control so long as I didn't forget that I was pretending. When we came to the river, I stopped pretending and dropped the halter reins and let him pick his own course. Some days, hot days, he might walk for miles in the shallow water.

Although I never asked George what he did when he took the black out, I suspect it was a bit the same, but with one difference. With me there was always this business about who was in control. With George and the black horse I don't believe it ever entered their minds.

No one other than George or me was allowed to ride the black, or feed him, or have anything to do with him. We didn't want to confuse him with other riders and techniques, and I was afraid that another rider wouldn't understand the deal you had to make. George didn't have to make a deal. George should have been the only one who rode him. If I had not been so proud, so stubborn, the accident might never have happened and everything would be different.

–But goddamn it, Gloria, he was something to ride.

We float past the open meadows, and once again trees obscure our view of the hills. Rain begins to fall from the heavy clouds that now cover the sky, but I'm not thinking about rain. I dip the paddle into the water, and Gloria turns her bow downriver.

–He was something.

~~~

Numbers become tyrants. Since the first day on the Missouri I've been watching the mileage markers posted at one-mile intervals along the bank—blue signs with white numbers—and have deduced that the numbers represent the remaining miles to the Mississippi. Often the signs are fastened to trees, but sometimes to red and white or green and white geometric navigation signs that mean no more to me than the buoys out on the river. The first marker I saw this morning was 380 when I left the campground at Leavenworth, Kansas. The one I'm looking at now is 372.

The mileage markers allow me to calculate the speed of the current. It has changed every day. The first day when I was heading down to Brownville, the current was close to four miles an hour. By the second day the current had increased to five as the river rose from the heavy rains. It increased even more on the third day as I passed St. Joseph so that the current speed was close to six miles an hour. Now it's declining with the receding water. By paddling I add close to three miles an hour to the speed of the current—unless the wind is against us, which it seems to be most of the time.

I calculate seven miles an hour, fourteen hours of daylight, an hour to set up camp, an hour to take it down, an hour or two to rest. Maybe I'll stop a little early or get up a little late—nine hours of paddling, sixty miles a day, six more days to the Mississippi.

The trouble with numbers is that if one of them becomes fixed in your mind, it builds itself a throne. Often when I'm driving long distances in the car, I calculate when I will arrive at my destination, and often I arrive within minutes of my estimate. Am I that good at calculating time, or is it time that calculates me? What if I want to just float along for a day or find someplace where I want to stop? What happens to the number then? If I stop too long or too often, will I ever make it to the end? One way or another, I'm always asking this question, or one part of me is. Everyone must have these two questioners who argue between themselves. I know I do.

Today the wind is at my back. I have been wishing for a trailing wind ever since I reached the Missouri. Now I have it and Gloria won't go straight. She keeps turning sideways into the wind like the logs floating beside us. I correct her course with wide sweeps of the paddle. Often I correct too much and she turns the other direction. My shoulders are beginning to ache from the strain of correcting Gloria's course and correcting my over-corrections.

I am finished wishing for one wind or another. Better to have no wind at all than have a wind that holds you back or a wind that turns you around. If I had a rudder, I wouldn't have to do everything with the paddle. I shouldn't have believed the advertising that lied about how well this kayak would track. We're tracking all right; we're tracking all over the river. If the wind would just stay directly behind us it wouldn't matter, but it doesn't. It slips off a little to one side or the other, and Gloria turns toward it.

–Come on, Gloria, don't listen to that smooth-talking son-of-a-bitch.

But she turns to listen anyway. Maybe she's getting bored with me. Through the winter as I planned this trip I never imagined how slowly time would pass, paddling hour after hour, day after day, change coming so slowly that it doesn't seem to come at all. Most of the time I feel like I'm in a tunnel—water beneath me, trees on both sides obscuring what lies beyond the banks, sky overhead. And now the wind that I've wanted turning us around so that I don't want it anymore. My whole body hurts—shoulders, back, knees—rebelling against my demand to keep us straight, frustrating me even more. So to hell with it. I stop paddling. I refuse to do it. It makes no difference if I arrive at the Mississippi in six days or ten—no difference at all. I'll use the paddle to straighten the kayak now and then, but I refuse to paddle in any meaningful way. That will show them—the smooth-talking wind and the kayak designer who refused to include a rudder. I feel righteous with my boycott.

But I can't resist sneaking a glance at the mileage markers on the bank, and I discover that we are moving just as fast as when I paddled. It must be a temporary aberration of the current. As I continue my boycott, Gloria continues to travel the same speed. When I use the paddle to correct course, it feels so light in the water that I don't think it's meeting any resistance at all. But it does—just enough to keep us straight. After all this work I finally discover that I need only surrender to the wind to sail down the river with ease.

Just as I'm getting good at surrendering, I see the skyscrapers of Kansas City ahead. From here the river will run mostly east all the way across the state of Missouri until it reaches the Mississippi. My surrendering is over unless the wind changes.

The Kansas River joins the Missouri at the outskirts of the city and propels us east. Very suddenly we are in a much bigger river. I tighten my grip on the paddle because I don't know what to expect, except that now, finally, there will be boats and barges that I'll have to paddle around. Here I'll see the reason behind all the dredging, all the rock and concrete dumped on the banks, all the jetties that control the current.

There is a barge moored beside a mountain of scrap metal and another beside a cement plant farther down with a towboat idling behind it. Beyond them I have the river to myself again. Skyscrapers stand high on a bluff where thousands of people must work, but here beside the river are only train yards and industrial plants. There are no people—no one on the banks, no one on the river. It's as if I'm passing through a ghost town. The levy is high and forbidding, and I can't find a single place where I can stop. I am paddling through the heart of the city, but its heart is not here on this river.

One bridge follows another, and the high water rises even higher on the upriver side of the massive piers before cascading past. The noise is ominous beneath the bridges with the sound of the water rushing by the piers and the sound of the cars and trucks rushing overhead. There are too many of these bridges. Between them the water boils and swirls more violently than before. Gloria is twisted and jostled worse than in any wind, and I paddle hard to prevent us from turning over. There is no surrendering here. If I surrender, I'll be upside down in no time.

Finally at the outskirts of the city the river becomes calmer. High on the levy a park with newly planted trees evenly spaced in a single row stretches between two gambling casinos. The gamblers must be having good luck because not one of them is sitting on the benches that face the river. I would stop now if I could, but I'm afraid that the rocks on the bank below the park would tear Gloria apart. So I continue to paddle.

Through the afternoon I watch for the mileage signs as if there is nothing else to see. Even as I do, I know how foolish it is. The signs won't tell me anything that I need to know, and yet I watch for them, anticipate them, become irritated if they don't appear when I think they should.

Late in the day as I'm looking for the next blue marker, I see instead an old bridge that rises from the river on skinny rusty legs that appear as if they can't bear their own weight much less anything else. A large truck crosses over the bridge, and the bridge frame rattles all the way down to the water. I cringe beneath it. The bridge reminds me of how I feel. My feet have gone to sleep and I can't seem to rouse them, my knees hurt as I press them against Gloria's hull, and my back is stiff beyond my tolerance. But I've traveled seventy miles today.

Not far beyond the bridge there is a park along the river where a man and boy are unloading a boat from a trailer. The man is dressed in green and brown camouflage shirt and pants as if he's going hunting, but there is a fishing net sticking out over the side of the boat. I turn toward the bank and ease up onto the muddy ramp just beyond the boat. The boy is standing above the mud. He is wearing tennis shoes that make his feet look bigger than they are.

"Going fishing?" I ask the man who stops unwinding the winch on his trailer.

"Got lines down the river. Gonna check and see if they did us any good."

There is a southern twang to his words that makes me feel as if I've paddled a long way from Kansas City. The boy is silent.

"How do you set fish lines out in this river?"

"Plastic milk jugs. You just tie on an anchor. Anything heavy will do. Where you coming from?"

"Nebraska."

He looks at me with curiosity. Nearly everyone does.

"How far you going?"

His twang is infectious. I could give in to it and imitate it easily.

"I don't know."

"That's the way to do it," he says to me but mostly to the boy beside him. "Just get in a boat and go as far as you want. That's the way to do it."

I lift my legs out of the cockpit and find sturdy concrete beneath the mud on which to stand. At least I think it's sturdy. I won't know for sure until my feet wake up.

"This is a nice place. Where am I?"

"You got yourself to Lexington. Hold on to that rope, boy," the man says to his son.

I know it's his son because he wouldn't talk that way to anyone else.

The boy, who seems about thirteen years old and looks like he'd rather be anywhere than with his father at the river, takes hold of the rope tied to the bow of their small boat. The man unwinds the winch until the boat is floating freely. The boy pulls the boat toward the ramp on the side of the trailer opposite me until it scrapes bottom. He's done this many times, and he has no enthusiasm for it anymore.

"Is there a campground here?"

"I don't know. Never camped here," the man says. "We come down to use the boat ramp. There used to be an old ramp upriver a piece, but we got ourselves a fancy one now. They finished it last year just in time for that Lewis and Clark celebration. Sign up there tells you all about it."

He points to a new sign that stands above the ramp.

"If you're interested in the Civil War, there's a battlefield up on that bluff. Got a museum and everything. Course it wasn't much of a battle compared to the rest of them in that war. Yankees came to open up the river, and we wasn't going to let them have it. So there was a fight."

"Who won?"

"Yankees got the river. I guess that tells you. Don't let go of that rope, boy."

The man has some bitterness in his voice, and the boy receives the tail end of it.

The man returns to the cab of his pickup and drives the truck and trailer into the parking lot while I pull Gloria higher onto the ramp until her bow is out of the mud. If this place was good enough for Lewis and Clark and the Yankees, I guess it's good enough for me.

The man returns to the boat and starts the outboard with a single pull on the rope. The boy tosses the rope into the boat and climbs in after it. Then the man backs the boat into the river and turns it downstream. He stands at the stern with his feet widely spaced for balance, while the boy sits in the bow with slumped shoulders and holds on to the side.

As I pitch the tent on a grassy plane among the trees, I think about the boy out on the river and the other boy who seldom lets go of me. The tall grass reminds of the first time I put Amleth out in the hay meadow. He must have been ten or eleven, older than I was the first time I worked there. It was time he learned how to drive a tractor. Every boy wants to learn how to drive a tractor—every boy I knew. I took him out to the biggest hayfield we had. There was no way he could get in trouble there, especially since I started him in the middle of the field where there was flat ground, no fences, nothing that he could run into and ruin the mower. I intended to ride along with him on the tractor only long enough until he got the hang of it. He made two long sweeps through the field, lifting the mower from the hay when I told him to turn around and go back the other way. His line through the field wasn't straight, but it didn't matter and I told him so. That was when he smiled, and I decided to stay with him a little longer. I put one hand on his shoulder as I stood on the hitch behind him. It was the first cutting of the year, a beautiful afternoon. Nothing smells as good as freshly cut hay. Then there was a horrible cry that came from the ground, a sound like I'd never heard before, or if I had, never out in the hay meadow. I reached over Amleth and shut off the mower, but it was too late. The mower blades had run into a fawn that was lying in the tall grass, staying hidden like its mother had taught it. The mower had sheared off its back legs. Only then did it try to get away— pulling itself into the uncut grass with its two front legs. If I had a gun I would have shot it and put it out of its misery.

"It's not your fault," I told Amleth. "I didn't see it either."

Amleth stood in the swath of freshly cut hay and stared in horror at the stumps of legs and at the bloody streak that led into the tall grass. We couldn't see the fawn anymore, but we could see the grass moving and we could hear it—a shrill cry that pierced all the way into your gut. It didn't last long.

"Come on," I said. I tried to turn Amleth away from the trail of blood, but he wouldn't turn. "Let's go home. I'll come back and get the tractor later. It was just bad luck. It wasn't your fault."

Amleth wouldn't ride back to the house with me in the pickup. He walked the two miles across the meadow and down the road. I suppose he blamed me for what happened because I was the one who put him out in the hayfield, or maybe I blamed myself. I don't know why we do it, why we make them drive our tractors or ride in our boats and ruin whatever interest they might have in the land or in the river.

We never had a boat, I remind myself—not even a canoe. I wonder about that, too. The river was small enough up there that it would have been a good place for us to take a canoe trip. Everything else up there was big or got that way, but not the river. It was small enough and free enough that even Amleth liked going there.

~ ~ ~

In the morning when I paddle out from the Lexington boat ramp, I look for the plastic jugs that the fisherman and his son put out with their lines. I see plastic bottles floating with the current and more trapped behind the jetties, but none that are anchored to the bottom for fishing. Maybe the fisherman brought them in, he and his son. When they returned in the boat, my tent was too far away for me to see what they had.

The river moves away from the high bluffs that the Yankees wanted and off across the valley to the north. If I had never looked at a map, I might think that the river is going to take us back to Iowa. Eventually it turns and rubs against the southern edge of the valley once again as if it is trying to straighten itself from its northerly waywardness. From high overhead, and sometimes I feel that I am up there watching rather than down here on the water, a person could see the old course of the river by following the marooned oxbow lakes it left behind. At one time or another the river flowed over the entire valley, not just in this narrow confinement where it is now. If the Corps has its way, it will not spread out or straighten anymore. They have dumped tons of rock on every bank where the river might change its course, as if nobody or nothing should ever change its mind.

That no one should change was what I thought Annie meant when she told me that I had. Of course I changed, I told her. We all change. She was just lonely after Amleth left for college, I thought. Since I was flying to Boston with Rosario to meet a restaurant group of some sort, I invited her to come with me. We could take a few extra days and drive up to New England where the trees are supposed to be beautiful in the fall. I reminded her about our honeymoon in Colorado when she was afraid of the trees, but that was a mistake. She wasn't afraid anymore.

"All you think about is your business—how to make more money or borrow more money or make more money to pay for the money you borrow. This tangle of business and money is strangling us."

It wasn't the money that I was after. It was having an idea and doing something about it instead of talking it to death or letting someone else do it. It was telling buyers how much they had to pay instead of taking whatever price they favored us with, as my father and grandfather had been forced to do all their lives. And it was telling a banker whether I would accept his money or whether I would just make my own. I wasn't going to be like my father who bought one piece of ground and never changed it or increased its value so that my mother had the same rickety table in the kitchen from the time she was married until she died.

"And do you think you will change that by buying more land and making more money? That's just an excuse for what you're doing. I don't know you anymore."

Instead of going with me she went to Denver to visit her sister, and she was still there when I got back to the ranch a week later. I thought she was sending me a message that she had choices, too. I got the message. She didn't have to stay on the ranch or join me on business trips. She hated those trips.

From Denver it was a two-hour flight to Minneapolis where Amleth had gone off to college. It took her longer to drive into town from the ranch and get groceries than it did to get on the plane in Denver and visit Amleth. She was thinking about renting a small apartment and staying for a while. Why didn't I come to Denver and join her? She and her sister had gone to the symphony. They had seen a Broadway play about cats. They had been to an art museum where there were paintings from Picasso, Monet, and Frida Kahlo.

"Come to Denver," she said. "I'll take you to the museum."

"Who the hell is Frida Kahlo?"

I knew stubbornness could get in the way of a lot of things. On the ranch if you didn't adapt to new markets, you would end up with a product no one wanted. Why it was so hard to change with her? Maybe it was because I felt I could never quite measure up.

When she said that she didn't know me anymore, she probably didn't mean that she wanted to stop me from changing. Maybe she only meant that she didn't want to be left behind. But somehow her stay in Denver became a test of wills that I didn't want to lose, and it lasted long enough that I said words I wish I'd never said and heard words back that I wish I had never heard.

"Just so you understand," I said, "I'm not ready to dry up like one of those priests you and the Mexicans talk about."

"Just so you understand," she said, "I'm not either."

Amleth got caught between those words, and I had no doubt whose side he would take, which was why it surprised me so much when he came back to the ranch that last New Year after spending Christmas with her. Whatever happened between Annie and me had nothing to do with money, I told him.

—It was never the money.

I'm not sure when I began to speak out loud. I hear Annie's voice in the silent tomb of memory, but I speak my words as if she were here beside me or just ahead of me on the river. She isn't here. She never liked being on water, never learned to swim. She couldn't exhale under water without breathing the water in. It was the strangest thing. It was natural for me to wait until my head came up before breathing, but she would take a breath under water and come up sputtering every time. Annie would never choose to be here. I have brought her along against her will, and she has become silent again.

For a long time I stare into the muddy water where Annie would never choose to be. When I look up again, I see something far ahead in the instant before my eyes focus, but it's nothing more than a peculiarity of vision, a slowness of focus that comes with age. It could be a floating spot in my eye, or an image like the one that comes when you look at something intently and close your eyes, or like the springtime clouds we watched in the sandhills. I would look at a cloud and see a horse or a cow. Joe would look at the same cloud and see a map of Australia. Annie would look at it and say that it is only a cloud, but just once she wishes she could touch it.

Up ahead the river splits into two channels. The main channel, the wide one, flows off to the north, but the smaller channel cuts beneath tall trees that reach out from each bank and enclose the river. A heron squawks and takes flight from the head of the island, the first island I've seen on this regulated river. I'm tempted to take the smaller channel, but I don't want to waste my time heading down a dead end.

But the island is beautiful. Above the line of mud that fouls everything, the bank is clean and white with sand like an ocean beach. Small dunes have drifted into the trees. There has been nothing like it thus far. Gloria turns toward the beach as if she's seen it, too, and doesn't want to go any farther. There is enough daylight to paddle another three hours, another twenty miles before sunset, but here the sun is warm. It hasn't felt so warm all spring.

My landing frightens away a flock of killdeer that had gathered above the mud line. The mud and sand are crisscrossed with bird tracks, big and small. I lie down on the warm sand beside Gloria and close my eyes. First I hear the river dividing around the island. Then I hear a bird, now two, in the trees beyond the beach. They have a song of five notes that they repeat, first one, then the other with a slightly different tone—I'm here, where are you? I'm here, where are you? The flutter of large wings causes me to open my eyes. The heron is returning to its place at the head of the island. The killdeer land close by. They scurry across the sand in a stilt-legged dance. One by one they come closer. Sand fleas jump and scatter before them. I fear that if I move, everything around me will flee again. And so, for once, I remain still.

~ ~ ~

The valley narrows where the river cuts through layered limestone. Dark stains weep from the forested crest fifty feet or more above the river. It is seldom clear to me why the river changes direction. Here, if nowhere else, it ought to settle into a straight course, but instead it bounces back and forth between the sheer walls, invisibly eroding the stone. There is, I suppose, an underlying physical principle that explains everything, but it seems instead that the river changes direction because it wants to.

Gloria nudges a stick that is floating along with the current, and a water-logged spider tries to climb aboard. Gloria must look more promising than the stick of wood it's on, but the spider can't climb the angular slippery slope and thus clings to its small barge as I paddle by. Now that I notice one spider, I see more. Suddenly, all down the river, it's moving day for spiders. Filament strands float through the air with spiders clinging to them. The wind carries them to foreign territory like paratroopers landing behind enemy lines. But the river is wide, and many don't make it across. Those that don't cling to bits of wood or scurry across the water toward the kayak. Some are well adapted to water with balloon-like feet. Others, less opportunely appointed, are getting waterlogged fast.

If Amleth were with me, he would scoop up as many spiders as were within his reach. From the night Annie first read him *Charlotte's Web*, he never killed another spider. If there was one in his bedroom, he would leave it alone or capture it and release it outside. Annie had to clean around spider webs if Amleth were home. I can hear his child's voice behind me: *Why are they trying to get across this river? That one is sinking. Back up, Dad. It's not going to make it. Back up.*

And maybe I would. There is nothing else we have to do. We could spend the whole day crisscrossing the river, picking up spiders, and transporting them to solid ground. Tonight we could build a campfire and read *Charlotte's Web* instead of *Huckleberry Finn*.

A filament sails in front of me and lands on the bow of the kayak. The black spider hanging on to it remains immobile for a moment before cautiously edging toward me along the slippery varnished surface. Such excess. Send out thousands or millions of offspring. Some land on hospitable ground. Some land in the river. One in a million lands on Gloria's deck.

The spider is small, no bigger than a dime from toe to toe. Do spiders have toes? It watches me and retreats as I reach forward with the paddle and dip the blade into the water. Then it creeps toward me again, sensing somehow that the paddle is not dangerous in my hands. How would it know?

–It may be your lucky day, spider, but don't come too close.

There is an upwelling in the river that lifts us and carries us a distance before leveling out and discharging us in a wave that washes over the bow. Ah. So much for the spider. I can hear Amleth telling me to stop and pick it up, and I stop paddling and look at the water on either side.

–I'm afraid it's gone.

But it's not. It peers warily at me from the top of the deck bag where it blends into the black edges.

–Oh hell, it's time for a break anyway.

I paddle close to the bank looking for a suitable place to land and a suitable home for a spider. If I were a spider, where would I want to live? There are trees everywhere, but there were trees from where it came. Why didn't it just stay where it was? If the tree branch was crowded, it could have climbed a little higher. Why did it parachute into such dangerous territory?

The current carries us beneath a particularly fine-looking oak tree that stands apart from the others as if it has claimed its spot and doesn't want to share. It has branches that reach low and practically touch the water, and I take hold of one of the branches. From it I break off a twig that has mature and well-formed leaves. I coax the spider onto a leaf and carefully place the twig closer to the trunk in a notch where the branch has divided. Any sudden movement might alarm the spider and cause him to drop into the water. This has already been an effort that defies all common sense—saving one spider out of millions. It would probably not have enough sense to stay in the tree anyway. Amleth would make sure that it was safe before he left, but I can go only so far.

–From here on, spider, it's up to you.

When I release the branch, the current carries us away from the tree and the spider. I force myself to focus far enough downriver that I can't see the spiders landing beside me, for I can't bear to look at them any longer. It's not possible, however, to avoid seeing the gossamer strings that sail in front of me or feel the delicate threads that brush against my face.

Nevertheless, I keep paddling and don't even stop to appreciate the splendor of the gold-domed capital building in Jefferson City standing high on the western bluff. It's fenced off from the river anyway. A tall cyclone fence with barbed wire strung at the top separates the capital building and the railroad tracks that follow the river. It reminds me of the type of fence that surrounds the perimeter of a prison. It's not meant to be that, I'm sure, for on which side of the fence would the prisoners be?

Rivers and trains seem to go together, probably because the river has already done most of the engineering and the work of leveling a grade for the tracks. This is a busy section of railroad, and long freight trains roar past us frequently. The heavy screeching sound of steel on steel is in stark contrast to the silent sails of the spiders and Gloria's smooth passage though them. I like the sound of trains, always have, the Doppler effect of the lonely whistle, the last rumble of wheels telegraphed by the tracks. For better or worse, we're all following the river today.

As I seem to be doing more and more, I look over my shoulder and see a particularly handsome river entering the Missouri. A tree-covered promontory reaches out between the two rivers and shapes the confluence. It is a good-sized river, not as large as the Missouri but full-statured nevertheless. It has a peaceful aspect to it with the sun casting a shadow out into the water from the bluffs that rise behind it. I realize then that the railroad tracks have moved inland. Gloria turns with me against the current as if she is reading my thoughts.

The Missouri doesn't give much time for thinking, if what you are thinking is to see what another river is like. It is now or never. So it is now. I wouldn't have tried to go against this current five hundred miles back, but those miles have taught me to paddle in deep steady strokes with my whole body, not just my arms and shoulders. At first we seem to make no headway against the relentless counterforce of the current, but even that is progress. Sometime later, minutes probably but I'm not counting, we are close enough to the bank for me to see the clear line that marks the meeting of the two rivers. On one side is the fast muddy water of the Missouri, and on the other a clear peaceful green. The current is not strong once we cross over.

There is something about this river, this place that draws me into it. I'm not sure if it's because it reminds me of some other place or time or because it doesn't. When I look down past Gloria's hull, I see huge round boulders on the bottom of the river. I haven't seen the bottom of a river for a long time.

I paddle some distance up the clear river before stopping to make camp. The evening is warm and nowhere in the sky is there a hint of rain. So certain am I of good weather that I don't listen to the forecast on the radio and, for the first time, don't cover the tent with the rainfly.

Over on the other side the railroad tracks have rejoined the river, and colored boxcars pass through the trees every so often. Driftwood lies scattered around my tent on the sandy beach, but I don't feel like making a fire. Nor do I feel like crawling into the tent and reading *Huckleberry Finn*. I can't seem to read more than a page or two anyway before falling asleep. Huckleberry is still up in Hannibal trying to get away from his pap. Amleth never cared much for the story. I tried to read it to him when he was small. Given a choice between *Huckleberry Finn* and *Charlotte's Web*, he would have chosen the spider book every time. Tonight, I would, too.

～～～

The map that I dig out of the deck bag as I repack Gloria tells me that I have found the Osage River. I like the sound of its name. It starts at a lake in the Ozarks fifty miles to the southwest. I wonder how long it would take to reach the Ozarks if I went that way instead of heading back to the Missouri, which brings back the question Juan asked before I left. How do you know when you've gone far enough? When I get to the end of the river, I said. He understood my answer no more than I did. I never asked my grandfather how he knew when he had gone far enough. Why didn't he go on to one more valley, one more river? His decision held us, some of us at least, a hundred years. A hundred years is a long time for one decision to last; a hundred years is nothing.

Water distorts perception. What appears close is really farther away, but this water looks deep even with distortion as I peer at the giant boulders that have rolled down the steep limestone bluffs on the east side of the river and have become lodged in crevices in the bedrock. The same bedrock must lie beneath the Missouri River, only it can't be seen because of the muddy water.

Houses come into view as I paddle up the Osage. Smoke is rising from chimneys of small houses, and the sweet smell of burning wood settles upon the water. It's not hard to understand why some people would decide they had gone far enough. I'm thinking I'll go a little farther myself, on past the houses and on up toward the Ozarks for a while. There's nothing that says that I have to stay on one river.

A powerboat comes down the river toward me, roars by, and casts a steep wake. A teenage boy is at the wheel and two girls are beside him. The girls wave, but the boy does not. Nor do I. He doesn't wave because he's preoccupied with making a sharp turn while slowing as little as possible. Soon the boat is heading back up the river at full speed. I turn to face the first wake knowing that another will come from the other side. This time the girls do not wave as they pass. I hope he hits one of the rocks that jut into the river with his daddy's big boat. Ahead are the wakes of more powerboats, dulling the magic of this river a bit and telling me that I've gone far enough after all. Gloria rides over the first wake. The second wake catches up with us as we are heading back toward the muddy Missouri.

Midmorning the southerly breeze dies, and a stillness settles across the water that becomes as smooth and calm as a lake. By afternoon the sky and river are matching grays, with no break between the gray of the clouds and the gray of the water. Then I see the apparition that has taunted me since I began in the sandhills—a dark spot on the river that disappears just as I think I shall see it more clearly. I look away. By refusing to look I refuse to acknowledge its non-existence. But I have to look again sooner or later. There are two spots now, and they don't disappear. From the larger comes a flashing rhythmical movement, and I realize other paddlers are on the river.

Soon I catch up with a flotilla of canoes, rowboats, and kayaks, the first paddle-propelled boats that I have seen. Nobody is paddling very hard in this floating party. The current is doing most of the work. In the trailing rowboat a man is sitting in a lounge chair, drinking beer, and cooking on a grill that is mounted in the bow. He hands me a bottle of beer as I come alongside as if I'm part of the flotilla.

"Thanks."

"How about a bratwurst?"

"Sure."

He opens a package of hotdog buns at his feet and stabs a bratwurst with a long fork. He hands the bratwurst to me in a bun. I lay the unopened beer bottle on top of the spray skirt to accept it.

"What's going on?"

"Springfest," he says. "We do it every year. Where are you from?"

"Nebraska."

"No shit. Hey Chris!" he shouts to the closest boat. "This guy came from Nebraska."

"How far are you going?"

"Not sure. Might go down to New Orleans."

"Hey Chris! He's going to New Orleans. Here, you better have another beer."

He hands another beer to me, and I lay the second bottle beside the first. He has drunk a few of them himself. The man he calls Chris paddles over to us in his canoe. The rest of the party is strung out far down the river.

"We paddled to St. Louis once," Chris says.

"How long did it take you?"

"Three days, but we didn't work at it very hard. You can probably get there in two. Have you heard about the weather they're expecting tonight?"

It seems that everybody I meet wants to tell me about the weather.

"No."

"It's supposed to rain pretty hard and get cold. You might want to find yourself a warm place to stay."

"Sounds like a good idea. Do you know any places close to the river?"

He tells me the name of the town where the springfest is being held, but the bratwurst man is shouting to another of the party and I miss it. I understand, however, that it isn't far.

"A hotel room might become available if it rains like they say it will."

The rain is already beginning to fall, although it's soft and warm. I leave Chris and the bratwurst man and catch up and pass the others in the floating party. They all give me friendly waves. It must be a nice party where these people are going.

The rain is coming down hard as I pull into a protected lagoon at the little town where the springfest is in full swing. I tie Gloria to a dock with other boats. On land I discover that the party is far ahead of me and far younger than I and the group out on the river. Buses have brought college kids from St. Louis, and the buses are lined up on the street with their engines running. The beer tent is packed so full that I can't see the band playing inside. I can hear it, though. Most of the revelers have taken shelter in the beer tent, except for staggering young men on the sidewalks who don't seem to realize that it's raining. They remind me of how old I've become, and I keep out of their way as I walk the main street looking for a quieter spot. I wouldn't leave Gloria among this group overnight, and I don't want to be among it either. Wine from the surrounding hills is supposed to be the main attraction, but the Budweiser tent is where the action is.

Darkness will come early with this rain, which is no longer warm. I set off again—colder and wetter than when I arrived and disappointed that the party was not what I thought it would be. Before I stop, I want to get beyond the sound of the rock band.

Long after the music fades, I still haven't found a promising spot. Trees crowd the river on the left bank, and a built-up rock terrace forms a bed for the railroad tracks on the right. There is never a sandbar when you want one. Finally I see a clearing on the left bank. It's almost dark. I land Gloria and sink up to my ankles in mud as I walk toward a small bluff where there is enough flat ground for a camp. It's high enough to be out of the mud, at least the worst of it.

While I listen to the weather radio, I set up the tent beneath the bluff and hope it will give me shelter from the north wind that is predicted to become strong and cold during the night. The rain falls steadily and I do what I have to do, but I'm wondering why I'm doing it. I am more miserable than I have been on the whole trip, more miserable than I would have been if I had never stopped for the party where I didn't belong. While I wait for the water to boil, I squat beside the stove and hold my hands close to the flame.

The stove and cold hands remind me of a camping trip with Amleth in Colorado the summer he turned fourteen. It was his idea. I think Annie had told him about our honeymoon there. An outfitter in Estes Park provided all the gear and food we needed. Although we were spending only two nights in the woods, Amleth carried enough trail mix to last a week. Annie didn't go. She stayed in the lodge where there was a huge bed with a down comforter and late breakfast and all the books she wanted. No way was she going to hike through the woods and sleep on the ground. And that was fine with Amleth and me. At least he said it was.

It rained all the second day as we hiked along the trail. I expected Amleth to whine or complain, but he trudged stoically along, more stoically than I. He didn't seem to mind the rain, and I had to admire him. He was a different boy in the woods than the one on the ranch who didn't like working outside. We set up our tent on soggy ground and squatted beside the stove, which was the only fire we were going to get. Sometimes our hands touched as we turned them over for warmth, but neither of us drew them away.

"You're a pretty tough kid."

He looked at me with such surprise that it made my heart ache.

"You're a pretty tough dad," he said.

It was my turn to be surprised.

"Can you imagine what Mom would say if she was here?" he asked.

We laughed together as we each heard what Annie would be saying if she were with us. If she were with us, nobody would be laughing, but we laughed that night until we fell asleep. I remember that fire as if it were yesterday, his face glowing in the dark and his hands touching mine.

There is a flicker of light in the darkness where the river must be. It could be a house behind trees with the light appearing intermittently through the branches, or it could be a small fire like the one I have. Or it could be nothing, which is what I suspect. The night and the rain are playing tricks on me.

Before I crawl into the tent, I turn off the flashlight and look one more time across the dark void where the river must be. There is nothing—only darkness and the cold rain that continues to fall.

~~~

In the morning the sky is clear and the humidity has dropped. My skin feels dry for the first time in days. The cool crisp morning is more like fall than spring. I look across the river where I saw the light the night before. As I expected there are no houses, and nobody has set up a camp unless he set it up on the railroad tracks.

Once again a northwest wind twists Gloria to one side or another when we're on the water. I could surrender as I did coming down to Kansas City, but I've become so used to paddling that I feel unbalanced when I don't. Quite by accident I discover that if I tilt Gloria a little onto her side using the knee braces, she will turn the opposite way. This makes no sense until I think about the angle of the boards on the bottom of her hull. By tilting her some degrees I am substituting a chine, where two boards join together and curve inward toward the stern, for the straight keel at the bottom. Still it is the opposite of everything I understand. With the black horse all I had to do was lean a little to one side or the other, and the black would sense the change in my position and turn that way.

If I lean too much in Gloria, I'll be under water again. So the trick is to keep my body perpendicular to the water while tilting Gloria with my knees. And if I stroke a little deeper with the paddle on the side Gloria is tilting toward, she turns more. It doesn't happen right away, and that's also hard to learn. Nothing happens immediately after the stroke, but soon her bow shifts subtly as the delayed force works its way forward and straightens her in the current. So the trick is to tip Gloria on her side but to keep my body straight. The trick is to not overstroke with the paddle but to do it gently. The trick is to wait.

—I wish we had gotten lost in the woods.

I'm talking to Gloria again, but she's just righted herself and isn't inclined to turn back and listen to me.

After our two nights in the woods, Rosario called from Omaha. She had been out of college only a few months, working in our office that was next to Joe's, and learning our business from the man I'd hired before her. He didn't like her ideas, or maybe he didn't like that she had ideas. So he quit— dropped his keys on her desk in the one-room office they shared and walked out the door. It wasn't a complicated business back then. We raised beef on the ranch, and the Omaha office sold it to special accounts for higher prices than we could get if we sold the cattle in the auction arena. I flew back to Omaha to fill in for him. I should have known that Rosario could take over without my help. Maybe I did know or would know if I had just waited another day, but I flew back anyway. Annie and Amleth stayed one more day at the lodge and drove back to the ranch without me.

We never went hiking again. Someone in our business was always start- ing or quitting; something was always wrong or right; some part of the business was always changing, either on the ranch or in the office. And some change came over Amleth in his years of puberty that made him as strange to me as I was to him. Other boys called him gay to hurt his feelings, but that's just the way they made fun of someone who wasn't like them. Every generation has its mocking names. We had ours. It hurt him, though, and he stopped being the resilient little boy who liked me to wake him up if I got home late from a trip, or who would drive with Annie and me, and some- times just me, to Omaha if there was a chance of going to the zoo or watching a Star Wars movie in a big theater or listening to the orchestra, or who forgave me when our plans didn't quite work out. Sometimes I had to drop him off at the zoo and come back later and pick him up. He said he under- stood. He said he didn't mind being alone.

A noise startles me and makes me look up from the water where I've seen Amleth's face as he waits for me at the zoo entrance. A barge is edging slowly around the next curve. There are four barges in all, arranged two across and two deep with the towboat behind. The outside barges are so close to the right bank that I am sure they must be rubbing against the rocks. I move to the other side so that I, too, am nearly rubbing the bank. As the barges come closer, I turn Gloria to face them, and prepare myself for the mighty disturbance that I've been anticipating ever since reaching this big river. The barges, loaded with huge gray pipes and machines that look like turbines, pass peacefully with barely a ripple, but now comes the towboat whose propeller is churning the water behind it. Tensely I wait for the turbulence to reach us. Small waves spread across the river, strike the bank behind us, and ricochet back. And that's all.

It bothered me that Amleth was so isolated. He never had a friend come over and stay with him the way Joe used to stay with me. Maybe that was because of what the kids called him, but I don't know. I wonder what they would have called Joe and me. He was the first person I ever kissed who wasn't a woman in my family. We were only seven or eight then, maybe a little older. After we found out he was moving away, we kissed each other like the people we saw in the movies. When he came to visit me from Omaha, I'd be waiting outside the house for his grandfather to bring him to the ranch. I could see the dust for a mile before they arrived. We ran to each other and hugged like long-parted lovers. And we were, in a childlike way. It was a long time before I kissed a girl like that, but I did. We don't talk about those memories now. They embarrass us.

Amleth's first date was for the prom when he was a sophomore in high school. He was just a late bloomer, as my mother used to say, and maybe not even late. Before that age I didn't think much about girls either. I was happy to see that he was finally breaking out of his isolation. That's why I was so upset when Annie bought him the new piano for his birthday. It was a grand piano and took up half the living room. Why would she get him something like that when he was just beginning to bloom? He stayed in the house and practiced even more than before. I complained about the cost of the piano, but what really bothered me was the way it kept him inside.

Yet the piano sounded good. I had to admit that. Even I could hear how he was improving. He used to play a few notes at a time, but after he got the new piano there seemed to be a note under every finger. Sometimes the whole house vibrated when he leaned into the piano and his fingers struck the keys and the keys struck the strings beneath the raised lid. Someone had to come from North Platte every six months just to keep it in tune.

But I was right about the piano. He didn't have any more dates after he got it, and I almost gave up trying to get him outside to do any work. It was easier to get one of the Mexican kids to do it. He was never going to be a rancher anyway, Annie said.

By afternoon the wind dies down, and I'm glad for that. Otherwise I'd have to be fighting against it because the river has turned to the north as it's circling around St. Louis and getting ready to find the Mississippi. St. Louis must be close because we're in the flight path of an airport. Jets are constantly flying overhead, and I look up at them and wonder where they're all going. They seem strange and foreign to me now that I've become used to the pace of the river.

We pass the second power plant of the day, and huge houses stand on the bluffs south of the river. They dwarf the one I built for Annie where the grand piano sits and gathers dust. I have no idea what Consuelo will do with it. Sell it or give it to the school, I told her. She acts like she's afraid of it, and maybe she is. I couldn't touch it either.

Sparks are flying from a welding operation on a bridge under construction, and I move to the center of the river to get away from the falling sparks. They stop before I reach the bridge, and I look up through safety netting to the workers overhead. The welder flips back his mask and waves down to me.

Two huge gambling casinos sprawl across the west bank of the river—one on each side of a freeway bridge. I've reached St. Charles, Missouri, very nearly the end of the Missouri River, half-way to the ocean, and a thousand miles from where I began. The blue and white mileage signs will soon become single digits and soon I will reach the Mississippi, but that is yet to come. If I have learned anything about this river, it is to accept what is to come when it comes and not make up something before it happens. If I've learned anything, it is that sometimes you have to tilt opposite the direction you want to go, take a light stroke, and wait. But I'm not sure that I've learned anything, except that I can no longer imagine myself anywhere else.

～～～

"You should write a book about your trip," J. Morgan tells me at the breakfast table of the small inn I've found close to the river.

Gloria is out in the parking lot, and I couldn't very well make up stories about why she's there to J. Morgan Batteau, who is seventy-five years old and has a voice so rich that it makes me want to close my eyes in the middle of breakfast and listen. His nose is his other distinctive feature. It's the biggest nose I've ever seen. On a person with a less evocative voice, it might be considered unattractive.

"I'm going to do that someday," J. Morgan says. "Write a book, I mean. I've already written the first few lines and know them by heart. Do you want to hear them?"

"Sure."

"I was born in the Garden of Eden, which at that time was located in the Atchafalaya River Basin, an ecological system of such abundance as the world had never seen and may never see again. A mud lump rose to the surface of the waters, then submerged and rose again near the location of what, millennia later, became the hamlet of Krotz Springs, Louisiana. I was born with the caul, which in ancient times presaged the birth of great persons. There were no other such signs and portents of great events in that region that night, so we took it as an indication of things to be."

"That's really good. When are you going to write the rest of it?"

"I don't know. Better do it pretty soon, huh? If you ever write your book, make sure you put me in it, at least the part about the caul. That was the time before the oil rigs. We got everything we needed from the land and the water. If there is a prettier place, I want to see it before I die. You know about the Atchafalaya River, don't you?"

"I guess I don't."

"The Atchafalaya is the only distributary of the Mississippi—a distributary, you understand, is a river that runs out and not in. Look for it when you get down that way. They have a lock and dam that controls the flow because they're scared what will happen if the Mississippi decides to follow the Atchafalaya instead of that old winding route through New Orleans. New Orleans and Baton Rouge would be high and dry if the river changed its course. Can you imagine New Orleans without the Mississippi?"

I can't imagine New Orleans in any way yet.

"There is more concrete in the Old River Control on the Atchafalaya than it would take to build all the pyramids of Egypt, but if that old river decides it wants to go somewhere else, there is nothing in the vanity of man that will stop it. You know about the flood of '27."

I fear he will become dismayed by my ignorance.

"It's a good thing you're taking this trip. You don't seem to know anything about where you're going. They thought levees would hold it then just like they do now, but the river ran right over them. Covered practically the whole delta with water. Thousands of people were killed, and it took months for the water to disappear. Changed the whole region. Hundreds of thousands of people just got up and left. That old river," J. Morgan says, "he'll go wherever he wants to go."

During the winter when I was thinking about this trip, I saw St. Charles on the map and decided that it would be a natural place to stop for a day and get ready for the Mississippi. But if J. Morgan is right, and I suspect he is, there is nothing I can do in all my vanity that will make me ready.

Nevertheless my plan is fixed, and I have a list of chores that I want to accomplish. The first is to wash every piece of clothing I have, except for the shirt, pants, socks, and underwear I'm wearing. It is a fine warm day, and I'm sweating by the time I arrive at the laundry. I expect to do the washing myself, but I find that I can have it done for a modest fee. Some of them, I warn the woman who gathers the clothes, especially the socks that soak up mud like a sponge, are dirtier than she might be used to. She is undaunted, and I leave the mess with her. As I walk out the door, I expect her to call me back, but I escape into the fine morning without such a call.

My second chore is to get a haircut. The last one I had was from Consuelo a few days before I left. There is a barbershop two blocks from the laundry, and an old grumpy man gets up from the barber's chair to make room for me. He wraps a dirty cloth around my neck and asks me how short I want him to cut it. He makes me feel like I'm imposing upon him.

"I don't care. Just trim it up some."

His disposition is contagious. Consuelo always talked to me when she cut my hair, but the barber is silent and so am I.

As I walk along River Street, I look for a place where I can buy rope to replace the bow rope on Gloria, which has become frayed somehow. There must have been a flaw in it from the beginning. Although it wasn't on my list of chores, I buy a Nicaraguan cigar from a tobacco shop on River Street. A thousand miles ought to be worth a cigar. Then I buy a bottle of French wine, a wedge of Danish cheese, and a tin of mixed English tea crackers from a wine shop. Nowhere is there a hardware store that sells rope, but I could make the repair in a hurry if I could fashion a rope out of T-shirts, or jewelry, silver, china, Asian furniture, food or beer or ice cream, lithographs and fine prints, or original water color and oil paintings of Lewis and Clark and Sacagawea, especially Sacagawea, although she was never here. The others were, however, and the pictures and stories of their exploration are every-where, even in the window of the Asian furniture store.

In addition to rope I want to find a pair of simple comfortable tennis shoes that I can wear on land. I can't find them either, but I will settle for leather deck shoes that cost $125 if the shoe salesman is able to remove my kayak shoe. It's still damp from the day before and from the weeks before that. For all I know it is holding water from the first step into the Loup. I help him pull the right shoe from my foot. He wedges the deck shoe over my damp sock. He doesn't ask how my shoe and sock got wet, or what kind of shoe it is, and I don't tell. Maybe he thinks it's a new style from the East Coast or Hollywood. In addition to the shoes I buy a pair of socks and put them on inside the store. The wet kayak shoes and socks I stuff into the bag with the wine. It feels fine to have dry feet.

I give up on the rope and postpone all the other errands I had planned and head for the river, which draws me toward it as if I've already been away too long. In a grassy park I come across a plaque that says Lewis and Clark camped on this ground from 16-20 May 1804, nearly two hundred and one years ago from this very day. They crossed the Mississippi from their winter camp in Illinois and stopped at St. Charles for several days to make final preparations. They had all winter to prepare. You'd think they'd want to get going.

I'm glad I've arrived a year after the two hundred year anniversary because there would have been a mob of people here to celebrate that event. There is no mob now, just a replica of the keelboat the explorers sailed and dragged up the river that I've come down. It could hold any number of kayaks.

The keelboat reminds of my conversation with Thomas the fisherman far up this river that is so different from what it was two hundred years ago. The plover, sturgeon, and catfish didn't need any help then, and the Asian carp was still in Asia. Would the explorers recognize the river today? I suppose they would. But I wonder what they would think about the change that followed them. For Thomas's sake I address the spirits that might still be hiding inside the keelboat.

–Leave the river alone.

Across an asphalt parking lot is a newly built wooden dock, empty of boats. There I sit down and place my bag of French wine, English crackers, and Danish cheese beside me. My feet and new shoes dangle from the dock above the slow-flowing water. I don't know where the shoes came from— probably China. A huge paddlewheel boat, a gambling casino that has gone out of business, is tied up fifty yards downstream with a ramp leading up to it. Like the dock and river, it's deserted. Thousands of Lewis and Clark's keelboats would fit inside the sternwheeler, but it isn't big enough to hold all the gamblers that are in the new casinos upriver beside the freeway bridge.

With the corkscrew of my Swiss Army knife I uncork the wine and take a swig directly from the bottle. With another blade from the knife I cut a slice of the creamy blue cheese and wipe the cheese on a triangular-shaped cracker. There is a choice of square crackers, circles, or triangles, and I alter-nate shapes until the cheese is gone. Then I unwrap the plastic from the

Nicaraguan cigar, shield the match from the wind, and light it. I plan to ration the wine so that it will last through the cigar.

I feel like calling Joe and telling him I've gotten this far at least, that tomorrow Gloria and I will reach the Mississippi. The cell phone is in my pants pocket—turned off—but I feel it pressing against my thigh as I stare at the flowing water. I'll tell Joe what J. Morgan told me.

This old river, he'll go wherever he wants to go.

~ ~ ~

The hostess from the bed and breakfast inn describes the ham and egg casserole with great formality as if it were a work of art instead of some food that will give me energy to get down the river. J. Morgan is across the table from me. His voice, which only the day before made me wish that I could close my eyes and listen for hours, is drifting away, for my mind is already occupied with the distance I need to paddle before dark.

J. Morgan is talking again about the flood of '27: blacks pressed into work gangs, men shot on the levies, dynamite and flooding in the parish below New Orleans. Somehow the flood made Hoover president. I miss the connection. The pineapple slices and strawberries that compliment the casserole have no taste, and I bite off the stem of the last tasteless strawberry and place it on the rim of my plate. I'm ready to go. There is still the formality of rising at the appropriate time from the table, parting from J. Morgan and those in his party, and paying the hostess for the overly-expensive room and the overly-described breakfast.

I should have skipped breakfast altogether. I should have used the free time yesterday to take a taxi to a sporting goods store to buy another paddle, or at least get my gear organized better. Instead I spent the afternoon at the river, smoking a cigar, drinking wine, talking to Joe, napping in the sunshine, and now I regret that I have let the time slip away.

Past the idle and empty replica of Lewis and Clark's keelboat I carry Gloria across the empty parking lot of the abandoned casino to the long boat ramp where I landed two days before. As quickly as I can, I push the bags into the hatches and stow the water bags behind the seat and in front of my feet. I slip into the waist skirt and life jacket and shove off, feeling the urgency of the miles I must paddle to get through St. Louis.

Sometimes during the early years on the ranch, someone—Juan or Carlos maybe—had a last story to tell at breakfast, but I'd cut him off. Was I the only one who could see how much work we had to do? Was I the only one who saw the whole picture while they wanted to tell a story that had nothing to do with it? I would see it on their faces then—Juan, Carlos, Annie. The story would have taken only a minute. If you were in such a hurry, why didn't you say something earlier?

Once again I see the expression Annie reserved for those times when something was my own fault and I was too stubborn to admit it. All right, it was my fault, and I didn't like it then either, and the only way to get over it was to work hard enough that I would make up for the fault and the cutting off of the story and the late start.

So I paddle hard and barely look up from the water. If I learn one thing on this trip it will be how to explain the whole picture to someone early enough so that this feeling doesn't creep up on me without warning. I go back step by step through the morning to understand how this happened, through the previous day when I had plenty of time to pack and get ready and did neither, until I remember the new deck shoes that are still on the closet floor of the bed and breakfast inn where I put them the night before.

In disgust I shake my head at myself and slow my paddling to a sustainable pace. If I don't, I won't even make it to the Mississippi. The river has its own time, and I have to let go of mine. It is only then that I see where I am and discover that there is no city yet—no houses, no manufacturing plants, no docks or barges. Instead there are planted fields on the flat ground north of the river, hills in the distance, thick trees on the southern bank. If it were not for the resolutely descending numbers on the mileage markers, I could be anywhere.

I land on the north bank and piss the breakfast coffee away under a blue sign bolted to a tree that tells me there is one more mile left of the Missouri. To get ready for the Mississippi, I check the hatch straps to make sure they are secure, take a drink of water, and wedge the water bottle into place between the hip brace and hull. I consider looking for the bag where I have stored the Mississippi River maps, but I'm not even sure which hatch it's in. Besides, I tell myself, it will be like paddling through Kansas City—there will be nothing to it. Just watch out for the bridges. When I am sure that everything is secure, that everything is in its proper place, that I see the whole picture at last, I re-enter the cockpit and ease back into the current where I slowly and cautiously paddle toward the confluence.

The Missouri swings south to align itself with the flow of the Mississippi and widens in anticipation of it. I look for a grand monument to mark the meeting of the two great rivers. There is no monument, only a small flashing green light on the rock revetment that separates them. The revetment stretches into the rivers, narrows until there is a single rock showing above the water, and I enter the Mississippi without a ripple. I had heard that the Missouri was faster and more turbulent, but I can't see any difference between them. Except for the size. It's a big river now.

A green buoy, much larger than those in the Missouri, is anchored way out in the river. From it comes a deep resonant tone, a single continuous note of mystery and depth. This is the river Joe and I must have imagined when we made toy rafts and set them free in the Loup. This is the river I heard when I lay with Annie in the sand, my ear close to the ground. She never heard it the way I did. I wish Joe was with me, that he would forget his legal papers and remember the vow we made back on the Loup.

Although the Mississippi is a wide powerful river, it is only water and Gloria is at home in water. To Gloria there is no difference between the water of the Loup and the water of the Mississippi, except that here there will be no grounding on sandbars. A bridge looms ahead, and I move to the center so that I will pass between the giant concrete supports. With the river rushing past the concrete I feel its power, and my stomach lurches the way it did when I rode with older cousins on back roads in the sandhills when the car shot over the top of a hill and my stomach felt as if it remained on the other side.

No other boats are on the river, not even small boats. St. Louis, it now seems certain, is going to be another Kansas City. Gloria and I pass beneath a railroad bridge that is nearly as high as the freeway and, shortly after, a lower bridge with wood pilings supporting it. Instead of cars roaring past, people are walking. Some stop and point at Gloria and me. We must be a curious diversion.

Then I see something else: pilings cut off at the river level and abandoned or maybe a wing dike that is just above the surface. Whatever it is, it doesn't look good. I suspect the hand of the Army Corps of Engineers to be at work again, and I'm going to see the work much closer than I would like.

It's a bunch of damn rocks that stretches across the river. We're too far out to make a run for either bank, and I aim for the biggest gap in the rocks that I have a chance of reaching. Now I hear the roar of the water, louder and more threatening than any bridge support. Shit, I whisper involuntarily when I see the drop-off beyond the rocks. The current gathers speed and Gloria and me along with it. This is no place to be turning sideways, and I stick the paddle into the water to guide us. It doesn't have any effect. Gloria shoots through the gap in the rocks, drops with the cascading water, leaving my stomach way behind, and twists completely around in the swirling water below. We're still upright. I have no idea how. Desperately I paddle through the swirling water to get ready for what might come next, but only the restored calm of the river comes next. What kind of idiot would dump rocks all the way across the river?

A towboat pushing a single barge is heading toward us, toward a dock where other barges are tied up, toward warehouses that have replaced the trees. The two blasts from its horn must be directed at us, and I steer Gloria farther out into the river to get away from it. The wind is picking up as the river turns more directly south. We pass the towboat and barge but are now in the path of another. I paddle farther to the left, closer to the center of the river from where I see a towboat with four barges emerging from a canal on the left bank. There are barges everywhere, and the river has become a freeway. It is not like Kansas City at all.

As the wind gets stronger, waves build and whitecaps wash across Gloria's bow. Without the waist skirt to shed the water, the cockpit would soon be full. The entire river is boiling with energy—current, wind, waves, and the turmoil from the gigantic propellers that churn the water on my right and on my left, in front and behind. The famous arch of St. Louis curves like a silver rainbow behind a gigantic levy wall. The levy is a paved parking lot full of cars. Downriver is a Budweiser beer sign mounted on a huge brick building. I could use a beer right now. A towboat without barges is coming toward Gloria and me—not toward us, I understand, but toward the line of barges tied up along the Budweiser plant. I paddle away from it, away from the plant and the beer and even the thought of beer. Another towboat with an array of barges forces us farther to the left, and another forces us back to the right. A towboat behind gives a long single blast on its horn.

If I had time to swear at the boat and whoever is blowing that horn I would, but the wind is getting stronger, the whitecaps higher, and the waves are now breaking in every direction. When I see a wave that might swamp us, I turn into it, but I can't turn for long because I soon have to straighten course or change it altogether to avoid another barge. Gloria doesn't seem any more at home in this river than I am. This barge traffic can't last forever.

It lasts longer than I can, and I look for a place to land. I'm closer to the right bank than the left, but the right bank has a sheer bluff that rises precipitously from the river and is solidly lined with barges without a break between them. Far across the river the left bank looks like a massive junkyard. Finally I spot an opening between barges on the right at some kind of loading facility where the bank appears scalable. I don't care if it's scalable or not. I'm getting off this river.

When finally we reach slack water along the bank, I take a deep breath, then another. I point Gloria upriver and sidle toward the bank where I grab a willow that is growing out of the rock revetment. Gloria sits quietly as if nothing has happened, like the mare we had on the ranch that would buck two or three times for no reason, then stop and stand so quietly with her soft blinking eyes that you would have thought nothing had happened. We would have gotten rid of her, but she made such nice colts.

Gloria sits blinking quietly in the gentle water along the bank while I gather the energy to get out of her. Once I do, I'm not certain I'll get back in. When the buoy turned us over in the Missouri or when Gloria plowed through the rock dam, I didn't have time to think. But in this stretch of river where the boats came from all sides and the wind blew hard and the waves rose above me, I had plenty of time to think and I kept thinking: get out of here; this isn't the river you expected.

Twenty feet ahead there is a small platform of sand that has formed below the revetment, and there I pull Gloria out of the water. I climb over the rocks to a wooden stairway that scales the bluff and find myself in the grass yard of an industrial plant with tall silos rising into the sky. The grass is mowed, the sun is warm, and the wind isn't blowing as hard as it was on the river. Or maybe it wasn't as bad down there as I thought.

In the plant office a man is talking good-naturedly on the telephone. He is about my age, and the expression on his face makes me feel welcome despite the strange clothes I'm wearing. He points to a chair beside his desk, and I sit down and wait for his conversation to end. It goes on a long time. It has something to do with an order for cement the next day but branches out far beyond the order. I think about what I want to say, and I'd better decide because the telephone conversation is coming to an end. When he hangs up, he reaches across the desk and we shake hands.

"Phil Harrison," he says. "What can I do you out of?"

"I'm kayaking down the river and pulled in here to get out of the river for a while. Would you mind if I hung out down by your loading facility until the wind dies down a little?"

"Be my guest," he says.

"It's kind of rough out there today."

"You bet it is, but it can get a lot worse. In a twenty-five mile-an-hour wind, you get three/four-foot whitecaps."

"How high are they today?"

They had looked bigger than three feet to me.

"Oh, I don't know. A couple feet maybe. Where'd you start from?"

"Nebraska."

"No kidding. Down the Missouri then. Where were you last night?"

"St. Charles."

"Did you come through the lock and dam?"

"What dam?"

"The one that bypasses the chain of rocks. It's the last lock and dam on the Mississippi."

"No. I stayed on the river."

"What did you do at the chain of rocks? Carry your boat around them?"

"Went through them. Who the hell put them out there anyway?"

"A glacier about a million years ago. Then the Corps changed it some to make a low-water dam. This time of year the water is usually high enough to cover them up."

"They weren't covered."

"Oh shit, you took the express route. That must have been a ride. You better get yourself some navigation maps."

"I have maps. I just need to find them. Is the barge traffic always this heavy?"

"It'll lighten up when you get downriver a ways."

"I don't think the barges appreciate me out there. They're blowing their horns all the time."

"They're just giving you a signal. One blast means they're turning right; two blasts they're turning left."

"I thought they were telling me to get the hell out of the way."

Phil rocks back in his chair and laughs.

"They might be doing that, too. You hear five blasts from their horn, you'll want to be getting out of the way fast. Are you camping?"

"Most of the time."

"We're about ready to close up here," he says, "but you can stay in the weigh shack tonight if you want. It's got a coffee pot and a microwave, and it's a lot more comfortable than a tent."

"Thanks, but I wouldn't want to get in the way."

"Don't worry about that. You got your boat high enough out of the water? I got a barge coming in any minute, and it'll kick up a hell of a wake."

I rise from the chair.

"How high do I need to get it?"

"Oh, I don't know. Ten feet will be plenty."

Gloria isn't anywhere close to being ten feet above the bank, and I hurry back down the stairs and scramble over the rocks. The barge is coming in. The captain waves to me through the glass of the pilothouse as if he is expecting me to show up. He idles out from the dock while I move Gloria higher on the revetment; then he maneuvers the giant barge deftly into the dock.

His friendly wave adds to the feeling that I'm not an intruder after all, and now I understand what the horn signals mean. Either the waves are getting smaller out on the river, or it was my imagination that made them so big. It doesn't look half bad out there now. I'm probably through the worst of it, and it will be even better in the morning.

Phil is waiting for me outside the office when I return with my gear.

"Want a tour of the plant before you settle in?"

"Sure."

"Just put your stuff in the office. It'll be safe there."

Phil leads me to the base of a giant twin silo that reminds me of the grain silos in Nebraska. We ride to the top in an elevator from where I can see the Arch to the north and the river all the way back to the canal where I should have gone.

"How high are we?" I ask.

"Two hundred and twenty-seven feet," Phil says.

On the industrial road that runs past the cement distribution plant stands the largest billboard I've ever seen. It's in the parking lot of a bar that has a much smaller Budweiser sign blinking on and off in the window. The billboard, white letters on a bright green background, has a single word as its message: JESUS.

"Kind of a strange place for that billboard."

"You can see it from the freeway," he explains.

That explains it.

He and I walk across the giant silo to the railing on the south side. We lean into the wind that strikes us with its full force. From this height I can't get an accurate feel for the turbulence on the water, but I can see the river where I will begin paddling tomorrow clearly enough. And as far as I can see are towboats and barges, one after another, heading upriver and down.

–Jesus.

~ ~ ~

Gloria is on the river by the time the first rays of sunlight reach the top of the bluff above us. It would have reached the JESUS billboard even earlier. The billboard is bright enough without sunlight. Every time I woke up I saw the enormous sign through the window of the weigh shack. The letters must be stamped on my forehead now like an old computer monitor that has been left on too long. After all the beers Phil and I drank at the tavern across the street, I should have slept soundly, but I didn't. I kept waking up in that green haze.

Huge vacuums, which have been running all night, continue to suck the powdery cement from the covered barge and distribute it to the silos through steel pipes that run up the steep bluff beside the stairway. It is a marvel that so little powder escapes. A vacuum has to exhaust air. So how do they keep the filters from plugging with cement dust? I should have asked Phil when I had the chance.

I wish there was a vacuum that could suck away a hangover.

The towboat engine is running, but if the propeller shaft is engaged it is spinning so slowly that it creates no wake. A silhouette appears before the lighted window in the pilothouse, and the captain, a tall trim man with a crew cut, leans over the rail with a cup in his hand.

"You're getting an early start," he says.

"I'm hoping there won't be as many barges out there this early."

"There won't be. Just don't get caught between us and the bank and you'll be all right. It's probably safer out in the middle."

"I'll try to remember that."

"Phil told me you're heading for New Orleans."

"Heading there."

"I've thought about doing that myself," he says. "Start up at the beginning of the river in Minnesota and come all the way down in a little boat. A guy would really get a feel for the river then, wouldn't he?"

"You're on the river all the time."

"It's different up here. I'm on the river, like you said. But where you are, you're in the river. You must see and feel everything."

"I'm not sure what I feel."

"Understood. I'm taking a load down to Memphis in a few days. Maybe I'll see you on the way. Good luck to you."

I push Gloria away from the bank and paddle through the slack water behind the barge and towboat until once again the current takes hold of us. Maybe this is what the captain meant by the feel of the river, to be in it instead of on it. It is to see Gloria's nose turn downriver and know the precise moment the current grabs us. I look back to the towboat, which the sun will soon reach but hasn't yet. The captain is now on the river side of the pilot-house deck. Resting the paddle across Gloria's bow, I twist my body toward the barge and wave to him. He stands straight and raises his hand as high as it will go.

Unlike yesterday afternoon when I felt pressed from all sides with no place to escape, the river is quiet this morning with few barges and no wind to disturb it. The only pressure I feel is inside my head from drinking too much beer. I won't repeat that mistake. And if I paddle through St. Louis again, I'll do it at dawn.

Who am I kidding? There will never be another time.

The navigation charts I've inserted beneath the shock cords in front of the cockpit are distorted by the wrinkles in the plastic map case, and the small print is difficult to read. Nevertheless I can see them well enough to know that they have more information than I can use. Every light, dock, landing, island, and bend of the river seems to be accounted for, including the warning to avoid the low-water dam at the Chain of Rocks back upriver. It might have been helpful if I had seen that warning yesterday, but who knows where I would be now if I had.

A dashed line follows the course of the shipping lane as it crosses from one side of the river to the other. There are even arrows to show the direction of the current to eliminate any possible confusion about which way the river is flowing. Gloria seems to have a pretty good idea without the arrows.

As we leave St. Louis behind, the spaces between terminals and navigation buoys become farther apart on both map and river, and houses populate the tall bluffs on the Missouri side. Now and then through the trees I get a glimpse of the low-lying farm ground that stretches across the river valley into Illinois.

Stay in the middle and you'll be all right, the captain said, and I do. The river is so wide that it's easy to find a comfortable passage around the barges, unlike the chaos through St. Louis. Sometimes I paddle fifteen minutes without seeing one. The towboats, especially those pushing against the current, throw up a giant wake behind them, but most of the turbulence stays in a narrow path behind the propeller, while the barges in front are so flat that they create barely a ripple.

I can't help but wonder if Sam Clemens ever floated down the river like the captain wants to do, like Jim and Huckleberry, if he ever floated far enough on a raft so that he really got the feel of the river from down here. It would be so different from standing on the deck of a paddlewheel steamer— to be in it instead of on it, as the captain said.

The captain wants to start at the beginning of the river up in Minnesota and sail in a small boat all the way down to the end. I was at the headwaters once when I was a boy, and my brother and I climbed over the rocks of the little stream that was supposed to be the start of the river. The sign said it was, and I believed in signs back then. Now I doubt that anyone knows where this river begins.

～～～

—Come on, Gloria. Which way do you want to go?

We are headed straight for a green buoy. Although I made a pact with Gloria back in the Loup to give her the lead as much as possible, she pushes it sometimes. I press my knees against her hull as a signal to pull away just as George and I signaled the black horse. Reluctantly Gloria turns her nose toward the center of the river, and I paddle a little harder. The current pulls us toward the buoy anyway. It's surprising how quickly it comes.

—All right, then. The other way.

Gloria turns toward the left bank where she wanted to go from the first, and I paddle harder still. The river is three or four thousand feet wide, and we miss the buoy by ten feet. Maybe Gloria remembers the teenage buoy on the Missouri that caught us by surprise and now wants to tease its bigger siblings on the Mississippi. Or maybe she is teasing me.

The black horse would do that. If we let him out of the corral into the small pasture, we couldn't catch him until he wanted to be caught. We'd try to entice him with grain, but he'd stand outside the gate and watch us play our games. Then he'd run off, prancing and shaking his head from side to side as he laughed at us. I'm sure he was laughing. George would walk out into the pasture and sit down. Eventually the black would come up to him to find out what he was doing there, and George would reach up, take hold of his halter, and lead him back to the stable. I thought it was clever of George to figure that out, but Carlos said that any horse would do that if you had that much time to waste.

There is another green buoy far in the distance, so far away that it very nearly blends into the river. Beyond the buoy a barge is headed our way, but it's holding close to the left bank. I've been keeping track of a barge that is coming up behind us, and I look back over my shoulder to see how close it is. It takes a barge a half hour or more from the time I notice it behind us before it catches up, which is plenty of time to get out of the way as long as I can figure out which way to go. This one is getting closer. It's following the current across the river just as Gloria did.

The maps are not as helpful as I hoped they would be. The buoys aren't helpful at all. They give a general notion about how the shipping lane is changing from the right to the left, but the barges are not in general locations. They are coming together, and we're between them.

"It's safer out in the center," the captain said, and that's where I'm heading even if Gloria wants to slip in closer to the left bank where the current is stronger. Soon I can see that the barge behind will pass us well to the left, but what if its captain had decided to stay in the center of the river, too? Where would I go then?

The two barges pass each other within the space between the bank and a second green buoy, which is one in a series of widely-spaced green buoys that mean no more to me than the series of widely-spaced red buoys that we passed upriver. At some point these green buoys will stop, and the red buoys will begin again. But why? And why did both barges decide to sail on the left side of that one?

Because they have to, I realize in a moment of clarity. The shipping lane is on the left side of the green buoys. Upriver it was on the right side of the red buoys. Between them is the crossing. How simple it is when you finally see it. It has only taken me seven hundred miles on the Missouri and another hundred on the Mississippi to understand this concept. There's no telling what I might learn in the thousand miles remaining. Now we can slip out of the shipping lane and get out of the way of the barges anytime we want.

–Good news, Gloria. No stopping us now.

Except during the crossings. We still have to share the shipping lanes during the crossings.

The river is heading away from the sun. Two fishermen with their poles sticking over the sides of a small motorboat are heading upriver and wave as they pass us. Wooded bluffs rise from the right bank where railroad tracks follow a built-up levy of man-deposited boulders. The valley extends far to the left except up ahead where the river squeezes between two bluffs and turns south again.

According to the maps nearly everything has a name on this river— Potato Bend, Mclean Point, Red Rock Landing, Seventy-six Towhead. I could make up my own names: Two Fisherman Bend, Silo Landing, Bratwurst Point, Snake Hollow, Watch-out Confluence. There are few names on any map of the Loup, but I could add names there, too. Blood Oath Bend where Joe and I pricked our fingers, mixed our blood, and promised each other that we would build a raft of our own. Catfish Landing where somehow a five-pound catfish found its way onto the hook of one of our setlines. Dead Man's Back where we felt the slippery peat beneath our bare feet. First Love Beach. But there lies the problem with names. They might be sweet at first, but sweet names can sour with time.

Grand Tower Electric Plant is in an old brick building on the left bank with its name affixed to it. The plant has several tall smokestacks and cooling towers, but they don't look so grand. That's another problem with names.

Often they exaggerate. A common tower becomes a grand tower to the namer.

About a mile downriver from the electric plant, children are playing on a sandbar where an outcropping of rock pushes the current away from the east bank and creates a protected cove. Two small boys run out into the water, splash each other, and run back to land. I've missed the sight of children on this river, and their gleeful shouts are a pull more powerful than any river buoy. I turn Gloria toward the sandbar. The boys are upon her before I get out of the cockpit.

"What kind of a boat is this?" asks one of them. He has a crew cut and is wearing bathing trunks the color of the red buoys. Despite his short brown hair you can see the cowlick that curls his forelock.

"It's a kayak."

"Can you sleep in it?"

"I haven't tried."

The other boy inspects the cockpit that I exit. He's wearing a pair of frayed blue jeans cut off above his knees. His hair is blond and longer.

"Not enough room," he says.

"I'll bet you could cut a hole in that wall and stick your feet through it. Then you could lay down."

"You don't have to cut any holes in a canoe," the boy with the blond hair says.

The boys are not surprised that someone is paddling down the river, and their conversation about where to sleep in a boat didn't begin with me. They've been making plans before I ever arrived.

"What happened to your paddle?"

"I broke it."

"If you had a canoe, you could carve yourself a paddle out of wood," the other boy says. "That's what the Indians did."

A skinny little girl about ten years old with white-blond hair and big front teeth walks up quietly behind the more forward boys. I smile to her as I unzip the life jacket. Her mother with the same white-blond hair and fair skin is not far behind the little girl.

"My name is Erika, spelled with a k," the girl says. "Are you staying here?"

"I don't know, Erika. Is there a place to camp?"

"Sure," says the boy with blue shorts, "there are camping places all over. She stays in the trailer, but me and Rick got our own tent. Mom, he came here in this kayak."

The mother's fair cheeks are burned red by the sun.

"You don't touch his boat unless you ask him," she says to the boys. Erika has edged closer but not yet close enough to touch Gloria.

"It's all right. They can't hurt anything."

"Don't be so sure," the mother says. "How far have you come?"

"Quite a ways."

"How far is quite a ways?"

"Nebraska."

"In that little boat?"

I nod reluctantly.

"How many miles is that?"

"I'm not sure. More than a thousand, I guess."

"And you're not done yet, I suppose." She doesn't wait for me to answer. "You must be a crazy man."

"Probably, but few have put it so perfectly."

It's always risky to try humor with a stranger, but I think the mother of these boys and the little girl, Erika, will understand any humor I try.

"You're welcome to have supper with us," she says. "Nothing fancy. Grilled pork steaks and salad."

Her invitation surprises me.

"Thank you. My father taught me never to turn down a free meal."

"So you're not so crazy after all. The boys will help you carry your stuff up to the campground. You don't want to leave your boat down here. The older kids come here at night and drink. After you get settled, we'll come and get you."

Erika leaves with her mother, but the boys, Rick and Ben, stay behind to help. They're amazed by all the bags I pull out of Gloria's hatches. It still amazes me, too. The boys want to carry Gloria. Ben, who is the older brother, grabs the bow handle, and Rick grabs the one at the stern. They struggle to carry her up the steep bluff from the sandbar, but neither complains. They work out a technique between them and don't ask for my help or opinion.

"Maybe a kayak would be better than a canoe," Rick suggests to his brother. "If one of those barges knocked you over you could just roll up again."

"But it would take two kayaks," Ben replies. "That's why the Indians never made them."

The boys leave me alone to set up the tent. They have a lot to discuss—kayak versus canoe, single boat or a double. I think they'll stick with the canoe.

As far as I know Amleth never planned any trips with other boys. He didn't have a brother or a friend like Joe to make plans with. I wonder what he would have said if I suggested that we get into a canoe like the Indians and go down the river.

–I mean, way down the river. Just you and me.

Angela, Erika's mother, and Erika find me at the tent site, away from the sandbar and the older kids who will come to the river after dark. I'm looking at a peculiar rock formation on the other side of the river. It's in shadow and blends into the reddish background of the bluff behind it. The river divides around the rock. It had to be part of the bluff once before erosion isolated it.

"Tower Rock," Angela says when I point it out to her. "Or sometimes they call it Grand Tower. It's a famous landmark, I guess. You got to watch out for the current over there. People say that there's a big whirlpool on the back side. Lewis and Clark stopped there, and one of them is supposed to have climbed up to the top."

"Those guys were everywhere."

"Weren't they, though? Erika made you something. Give it to the man, Erika. He won't bite."

Erika smiles with her disproportionately large front teeth and hands me a crayon drawing of a kayak in the river and a man with a big black hat sitting in the kayak. The kayak is nearly as long as the river is wide, but that's how big her paper is. She couldn't very well draw a little speck and say it was me.

"It's a fine picture, Erika. Thank you."

She holds her arms out to receive a hug, and I awkwardly entangle my arms in hers and pull her wispy body into mine.

"That's you," Erika says and points to the man with the black hat.

"That's who I thought it was."

Angela and Erika guide me down the campground driveway past rows of camper trailers, grills, and picnic tables to their camper trailer, grill, and picnic table. Her husband, Ben Senior, is grilling pork steaks, and he offers me a beer from the ice chest. I take one and sit down at the end of the picnic table closest to him.

"It's really nice of you to invite me for supper."

"No trouble at all," he says. "We've got more food than we need."

"Do you live around here?"

"About fifty miles away," he says. "Over in Perryville on the Missouri side. Angela and I work at the Toyota plant there."

"I'll bet that's a good job."

"Steady anyway and good benefits. Weekends we take the camper out. The kids like it. We're going to leave it here all week. Next weekend, you can't find a place to camp anywhere."

"Why is that?"

"Memorial Day. Everybody and their dog is out camping that weekend. In a couple years we might get a bigger trailer with a slide-out living room."

"Not until this one is paid off," Angela says.

How kind they are to me, this crazy man, as Angela calls me. They make me feel at home in this home of theirs away from home. The boys eat quickly and disappear, but Erika stays at the picnic table and draws more pictures for me. Ben's mother and father join us after supper. Their camper trailer is at another campground a few miles away where they've brought their horses for a trail ride they will take in the morning. We talk horses together—about some horses anyway. I see no point in talking about the black horse. He's back in the high country where he belongs.

It's dark when I prepare to leave them. Erika reaches out for another hug, and I'm ready this time. I pull her tight and squeeze her with both arms. It's not so hard when you're ready for it. I thank Angela and Ben for the meal, tell Ben's parents what a pleasure it was to meet them, and head back down the road toward the tent. Behind me I hear Angela's voice.

"Be careful, crazy man."

~ ~ ~

The black horse paws the ground on top of the towering rock. The sides are so steep that I have to use my hands as well as my feet to scale it. Below me the river swirls around the rock and forms a deep whirlpool on the back side. Green buoys and red buoys float into the whirlpool and disappear. Plastic beer coolers, picnic tables, and silver camping trailers follow. An Indian canoe and two boys are coming down the river. I shout for them to paddle away, but they don't hear me. The canoe is caught in the current and rushes toward the whirlpool. The black horse jumps into the river, and I jump after him. The boys hold on to him as he swims away. Amleth is one of the boys, and I am the other.

I unzip the tent door and stick my head outside. The tent, the grass, the kayak and everything else are covered with dew. A log floats by in the river, twisting and rolling in the current.

The campground is quiet, the campers still sleeping in their trailers as I break down the tent and pack my gear. The broken rock of the driveway crunches beneath my feet as I carry Gloria past the quiet trailers. She feels heavy on my shoulder. I miss the help of the boys, but I have Erika's pictures, the first one she gave me and two more that she made after dinner, packed safely away among the unused maps.

Beside Ben and Angela's trailer, I have an idea that causes me to stop and lower Gloria to the crushed rock. There I unseal the map case and remove the river map that shows Tower Rock. After sealing up the case, I unzip the forward deck bag, rummage through the stuff inside, and find the waterproof binoculars that I seldom use.

On the picnic table I write a note in the lower margin of the map. *For Erika, Ben, and Rick to be used on your river journey. From Crazy Man.* I place the binoculars on top of the paper to hold it down. Then I hoist Gloria over my shoulder, lighter now without the binoculars, and continue on down to the sandbar.

In the center of the river Gloria finds the current. As I pass Tower Rock with its sheer walls of limestone facing the river, the water beneath me rises into a broad, smooth, spontaneous upwelling. Ripples break toward the rock and the nose of the kayak follows. I let her go. Among the trees on top of the rock I see something moving, but then conclude that it is only Gloria and I and the river that are moving. Gloria and I are far enough from the rock that the whirlpool Angela described won't grab us. But there is no whirlpool anyway—it's only in a dream.

The water feels light, offering little resistance to the paddle. It will get heavier as the hours go by or if the wind comes up. I like these quiet mornings best. Even on the ranch where it's hard to imagine that one time would be quieter than another, mornings were quieter as the sun came up and every living thing stood blinking silently in amazement.

The mileage marker at Tower Rock had the number eighty. The last one I saw was fifty-nine. Fifty-nine miles to the confluence with Ohio. By this point the Mississippi has gathered the continental drainage from all of the northern plains and the eastern slopes of the Rocky Mountains from Canada to Colorado. Still, that is only a third of the landmass it drains—and the driest part. It will continue gathering water as we head south, becoming deeper if not wider, but probably wider, too—wide enough that Gloria ought to find enough room to get around the buoys.

Downriver a barge is working around a bend, and it's not having an easy time. The towboat starts and stops repeatedly. I count five barges across and six deep as I cut across in front of it. When the towboat engine stops, the current moves the barges away from the bank. After the barges swivel out from the bank, the towboat pushes the barges forward until the front barge touches the bank again. I am far downriver before I hear the engines of the towboat maintain their solid upriver roar.

A new suspension bridge crosses the river at Cape Girardeau, and its steel cables hang gracefully from two sets of tall concrete columns that rise higher than anything else around, much higher. A concrete wall follows the top of a concrete levy, separating the town from the river except for an opening in the wall above the point where I land. I am reluctant to drag Gloria very far on the concrete, but I am less reluctant than I was at the start of the trip. There are long scratches on her hull now.

A Coast Guard boat is tied up to a concrete pier farther down. Tires affixed to the side of the pier prevent contact between boat and concrete, and rubber bumpers dangling from deck ropes act as secondary cushions. I take off my life jacket and spray skirt and walk down to the Coast Guard boat where a young man in a blue short-sleeve shirt and blue pants is on the deck coiling a long rope. I'm tired of eating crackers for lunch.

"Do you know if there is a good restaurant close by?"

The sailor shakes his head. He doesn't know of any. A second man comes on deck, and the sailor relays my question to him. From the deference of the rope coiler, I assume that the second man is an officer. He shakes his head, too. It is a dumb question to ask a sailor.

"How strong is the wind supposed to get today?"

It has been getting stronger as the day gets warmer.

The officer shakes his head about the wind, too. He probably can't feel it from his sheltered spot in front of the cabin.

"I didn't know the Coast Guard had boats on rivers."

"We have jurisdiction on every navigable waterway," the officer says with stiff formality as if he's said it many times. "We're usually on the Ohio, but we're covering this district while the regular crew is in training."

That would explain why he doesn't know if the wind is blowing. He's only here temporarily. I leave the Coast Guard boat and return to mine, where I wiggle Gloria a little higher on the levy. I expect that she will be safe under the watch of the Coast Guard.

In the levy wall there is an opening where a steel panel on huge steel hinges will swing shut and seal it off should the river rise above the levy. A mural begins at the opening on the street side of the wall and continues for several hundred feet downriver where there is another opening to the river. The history of the first people is depicted in one panel at the beginning before the story turns to the European explorers and developers. The information signs before the murals explain that local citizens and businesses paid for the murals.

I follow the mural to its end and cross the street to a bar on the corner. There I order the biggest hamburger on the menu and beer in the biggest glass on the back bar. When the bartender sets the beer before me, I ask him if he knows how deep the river is out there beyond the wall. Bartenders hear stories from everyone.

"In '93," he says, "it came half-way up the wall. Pretty deep then. It goes up and down all the time, but it's got to be at least nine feet for the barges. Deeper than that now, I'll bet."

I tell him I bet he's probably right.

When I return to the levy, the Coast Guard boat is gone. But Gloria is still there, waiting undisturbed where I left her. I wiggle her back down to the water and set off again.

There is a speck of red about as far down the river as I can see, so far away that I have to raise my sunglasses and squint to be sure that it is a buoy and not something else. A barge is just emerging from the bend behind us. Nothing to worry about. It will take a half hour or more to catch up with us.

The sun is getting warmer every day, and I unzip the life jacket so that the heat of my body can escape. The snow that fell up in the sandhills and the frozen kayak shoes don't seem real any longer.

Late in the afternoon I cross another imaginary line between a red buoy we just passed and the next one in line and head toward a small dock where a number of small boats are tied up. Downriver from the dock the silos of a grain elevator rise above the oak trees whose leaves are turning the deep green of summer.

A boy with a brown cap pulled low on his forehead that nearly but doesn't quite conceal his eyes is standing on the dock as if he were waiting for me to arrive, but no one can be waiting for me. He walks over to the spot where Gloria bumps against the wood dock. His pointed cowboy boots aim toward Gloria as he squats on the dock and reaches out for her.

He says something, but I don't hear him clearly. I cup my hand over my right ear so that he will know I didn't hear. He repeats what he said, at least I think he is repeating. All that I understand is the word help.

"Help. Sure, I'd appreciate some help. Just hold on to her while I get out."

I haven't had much practice getting out of Gloria on anything but a river-bank, but I manage to raise my butt out of the cockpit and slide onto the wood planks without turning her over. While I slide, the boy holds Gloria with both hands.

He says something again. I struggle to understand him. His voice is high-pitched and has a twang that I don't recognize.

"Say again."

"How far you come in that boat?"

It's the question just about everyone asks.

"From Nebraska."

An older man is heading toward us on a well-worn trail that I expect leads to the grain elevator. Like the boy the man is wearing a brown cap, but it's not pulled as low on his forehead. He is wearing the blue-jean overalls of a farmer. Sometimes you know that you're going to like someone as soon as you see him. The boy likes him, too.

"Grandpa, he come all the way from Nebraska in this boat."

I untie the ropes that I've looped together beneath the cockpit combing and hold on to the stern rope. Then I stand up straight to meet the grand-father.

"Now that's a long way," he says. "I have a cousin who lives in Scotia, Nebraska. Used to go up there pheasant hunting in the fall. Don't suppose you know where that is?"

"I sure do. I'm from a bit farther west. Out in the sandhills."

"That's pretty country," the grandfather says. "I've been there, too."

The boy asks me another question, and I want to understand. It's the way he accents his words that makes it so hard. I understand the grandfather easily, but this boy seems to be speaking another language.

"He wants to know where you sleep in that boat," the grandfather explains.

"I don't sleep in it. I have a tent."

"Where?" the boy asks.

One word I can understand. Maybe I'll have to get the boy to speak one word at a time. It's when he puts them together that I have difficulty.

"Here."

I bend down and unhook the straps on the front hatch cover. The boy kneels down beside me on the dock. I like the boy, too. When I remove the hatch covering, he leans over and looks into the compartment stuffed with my gear.

"Cut a hole in that board and you could stick your feet in 'er," he says, pointing to the bulkhead. "Then you could float all night and not have to stop and put up your tent."

Boys seem to have the same idea. They want to sleep in the boat.

He looks up at me, eyes gleaming with the same vision that Ben and Rick had that has sent them all down the river ahead of me. I understood the boy this time. All I had to do was get closer to him.

"That board keeps the kayak from filling up with water and sinking if I flip over."

"You flip over yet?"

"I have."

"Where?"

"I hit a buoy on the Missouri River."

"You don't wantta be hittin' them buoys, that's for sure. Grandpa, he hit one of them river buoys and turned over in this thing."

The boy is delighted to imagine my mishap and to repeat it to his grand-father. I understand the boy's enthusiasm for river stories.

"You plannin' on stayin' abit? You want me to tireup for you?"

I hand the boy the stern rope and straighten up beside his grandfather.

"My best friend lived in Chadron, Nebraska," the grandfather said. "How far is that from you?"

"Not far. Seventy-five, a hundred miles."

I don't explain to him that I don't live there anymore.

"Richard Catch the Clouds. He was a professor at the college there and well-known, I think. I wonder if you might have heard of him."

"I haven't."

"We met each other in the army. Both of us were in the Korean War. Finest man I ever knew. He died last month. He was a great-nephew of Crazy Horse. I expect you've heard of him."

"Yes, I have."

We are standing face to face, and I have the feeling that although the man in the blue overalls is looking at me, he is also looking beyond me, seeing his best friend somewhere in the clouds.

"Show him the prayer, Grandpa."

The man looks at his grandson with an expression of kindness and sadness, of love. The boy smiles under the gaze of the grandfather. I remember how that felt.

"The prayer that Richard wrote. It's got awfully pretty words, Grandpa."

"I don't expect this gentleman has got time to hear any such thing as that."

The boy looks at me. It's my turn to say whether I have time or not, and it's not time that causes me to pause. I don't want to impose myself between the man and his friend. That might be a place the grandfather wants to keep private. Nevertheless the boy is waiting for me to say whether I want to hear the words or not.

"I have plenty of time if you don't mind me hearing it."

"Read it out loud, Grandpa, so he can hear the way Richard said the words. Read it out loud."

Now it is the grandfather's turn to decide whether to read the words as the boy asked or to leave them the way they were between him and his friend. The boy is hard to turn down, and the grandfather unsnaps the breast pocket of his overalls and removes a folded wallet that is stuffed with all sorts of papers. He extracts the prayer from the rest. Then he puts his wallet away before carefully unfolding the many-times folded prayer. He offers it to me.

"I think we want you to read it."

I look at the boy for confirmation.

"Richard came to visit every year or two, and we always went up to the Trail of Tears State Park. You know about the Trail of Tears?"

"A little."

"Last time he came he was sick with leukemia. We knew he wouldn't be back. He said he had some words he wanted to say when we visited the park. We walked down the trail to the river. It was almost more than he could do, but he wanted to say these words. This is his writing."

The grandfather shows me the words in blue ink that cross back and forth over the deeply creased folds. I leave the paper in his hand, but I can see that the handwriting is clear and strong. The grandfather begins reading:

When the people listen again
to the Spirit of the earth and sky,
of the wolf and buffalo,
of the prairie flower in the never-ending grass
and the great oak tree in the forest,
there will be no strangers in this land,
and the grass will grow plentiful again,
and the trees will rise into the pure air,
and the people will plant the good corn,
and the buffalo will return as many as the stars,
and you, the sons and daughters of the earth and sky,
will cross this river again
and I will be with you.

He holds the paper for a moment after he finishes reading it. Then he allows it to fold in upon itself and puts it back into its place in his wallet.

"Those are beautiful words, all right."

"Richard was a thinker. He thought more about things than anybody I ever knew. It was an honor to know him."

"I'm sure it was."

"You must have time to think, sitting there all day in your boat."

"I have time, that's for sure."

"I don't want to interfere with your plans, but you would be welcome to come home with us for supper and stay the night. My wife, Velda, is a fine cook. We could put your boat in the pickup and bring you back in the morning. I'll bet my grandson, Richard, would like to hear about your travels."

"Your name is Richard?" I ask the boy.

"Richard Cloud Morton," the boy says proudly.

I understand him perfectly.

"If it wouldn't put you out, I'd be pleased to join you."

Velda passes the fried chicken platter for the third time, and I fork a golden brown thigh and use it to shove aside the bones on my plate. The mashed potatoes follow, and the pan gravy, and the creamed corn and fresh young peas still in the pods. No platter passes my plate without further diminishment.

"I haven't had such good food in all my life," I tell her.

We are sitting at the kitchen table: Velda and Horace, their grandson Richard who is staying the week while his parents are vacationing in Las Vegas, and I who had the good fortune to land in their kitchen. Velda is in her late sixties, I guess. She is wearing a dress with bright flowers stamped in the fabric. It is not the same dress that she was wearing when Horace drove into the farmyard with a kayak sticking out the back of his pickup truck.

"I steamed the peas a little too long," she says. "Fresh peas deserve to be a little crisper."

"I think they're perfect. I knew they must have been homegrown."

"Everything you're eating was grown right here," she says. "Sometimes I think we should just buy the chicken and corn at the Safeway in town like everybody else. Save a lot of work, that's for sure. Chicken is so cheap it's hardly worth the time it takes to cut off their heads."

"Wouldn't taste like your chicken, Velda," Horace says.

I agree with Horace.

"I'll bet your wife is smart enough not to go to all that bother," Velda says.

"I guess she doesn't."

"Well, she must be an understanding woman to let you go off by yourself on this long trip. If Horace tried to do that, I would . . . well, I'm not sure what I would do, but he wouldn't be going."

"I wouldn't even fit in that little boat of his," Horace says.

"Even if you would fit, don't you be getting any ideas. Or you either."

She points her fork at her grandson.

Richard smiles, but he doesn't say anything. He's been quiet all through supper, getting ideas, probably.

"I'm a bad influence is what you're saying."

"No, I'm not saying that," Velda says. "Everybody should do what they want to do, but you're not such a young man to be doing such a thing."

"You're right. I'll be fifty pretty soon. I should have done this a long time ago."

"Well," Velda says as though she wants to soften her judgment, "I'm not going to say anything about a mid-life crisis, but we start having strange ideas when we get to that age. I ought to know. Of course that was some time ago with me."

"I don't believe that."

She waves her fork at me, too.

"Never mind. What do your children say about this adventure of yours? Aren't they just worried sick?"

So here it comes: the pain in another person's eyes, the awkward moment when the other person doesn't know what to say, although Velda doesn't seem to be a woman who struggles to find words, then the new stab in my own heart with the flash of renewed remembrance, which is strange since Amleth's death is always before me, never forgotten. Or I could pass over it and spare them the truth.

"Our son died the first of the year, so I don't know what he's thinking."

"Oh, I'm so sorry."

"It was an accident."

"A car accident?" Velda asks.

"Velda, he might not want to talk about it, you know," Horace says.

"It was a riding accident. He was riding a horse that he shouldn't have been riding."

"Boys," Velda said. "They break our hearts. You tell them that something is going to hurt them, but they do it anyway. There's no accounting for it."

"He was angry at me. My son. That's why he did it. I would have done the same thing."

"But shouldn't you be home with your wife?" Velda asks. "Think how she must feel with her son dead and you out here on such a dangerous trip."

"This trip isn't dangerous."

"Don't tell me that. Richard said you hit something in the river and it knocked you over."

"It's just water, and Annie and I have been apart a long time now. After awhile she didn't like the ranch very much, or me, I suppose. It came to that, anyway."

Velda has learned all and maybe more than she wants to know about my family, and the conversation drifts back to the four of us at the kitchen table and to the third helping of bounteous food that is becoming harder to swallow with each mouthful.

"Don't force yourself to eat more than you want," Velda tells me.

"My mother taught me to always finish what I took. 'Think of all the starving children in India,' she used to say."

"As if what you eat will help them. I know Horace wants to show you the garden before it gets dark. Richard Catch the Clouds showed him how to do it the first time, and our Richard helped him plant it this year. You'll see that there's plenty out there, so leave your plate alone now. We'll have dessert later."

"I'll help with the dishes before we visit the garden."

"No, you won't," Velda says. "Horace, show him that garden you're so proud of. Richard will help me with the dishes."

She smiles at the boy who has been silent throughout the meal. He is still quiet after his grandmother volunteers him to take my place, but I see the disappointment in his face. He would like to be a part of showing me the garden. After all he helped plant it. Maybe he would have escaped the kitchen if I hadn't offered to help, then again maybe he wouldn't.

"If it's okay with your grandmother, you can paddle my kayak around in the pond after you finish the dishes."

There's a chance that she will say no and further disappoint the boy, but there's not much chance, especially after the change in the boy's expression. No grandmother I know could resist that face.

"You can wear my lifejacket."

It's a message to the grandmother through the boy.

"I guess you can," she says. "But no fooling around when you get in that boat. You get yourself wet, and you won't get any pie before you go to bed."

Horace's garden evokes a mysterious feeling like the hill where Joe and I found the pottery and arrowheads. Every seven or eight feet there is a mound of dirt with a half-dozen stalks of sweet corn growing together. Around the corn and using it for a trellis are beans, peas, and tomato plants. He is experimenting with the tomatoes, he says. Between the mounds are creeping vines of squash, zucchini, pumpkins, and cucumbers. Horace walks straight across the creeping vines without paying attention to where he is stepping.

"Don't worry about your feet," he says.

It's hard not to worry.

"I've given up trying to persuade people to try this. Everyone wants to put their gardens in neat rows, but look what you've got here. You hill the corn together and let in sunlight for the other plants. You don't have to put up string for the peas and beans. They wrap around the corn, and they don't hurt it none. The squash and cucumbers are good ground cover. They hold the moisture in the soil and keep out the weeds. There's hardly anything to do after I plant it. I fertilize it with a little manure and move the corn hill a few feet each year. By the time it's returned to the original hill, the soil is built back up.

"By the end of the summer, Velda says she'll hit me over the head if I bring in one more zucchini or squash. I give it away to all the neighbors until they don't want any more. I finally have to bring in the hogs to finish it off. My hogs love zucchini. All that from this garden. The Indians planted like this for thousands of years. We think we can improve what they did? I wish I could figure out how to make my whole farm this way."

"Have you ever heard of Hidatsa black beans?"

"I've heard about the Hidatsa, but I can't say that I know anything about their beans. You raise them up there where you're from?"

"No. It's just a variety I heard about once."

"Well, there are lots of different kinds, that's for sure."

"How do you keep the coons out of the sweet corn?"

"Put the dogs inside the fence. Come the end of June, I've got me some happy dogs. I just wish I could get them to like zucchini."

Horace Morton and I sit in the backyard watching his grandson, Richard, paddle Gloria in the fishpond behind the house. The boy is doing well, and Horace and I wave to him every several minutes. Richard wanted to wear the waist skirt, but I told him we would leave the cockpit open, just in case.

"The boy is crazy about that old river," Horace tells me. "That's why he was down there when you came in. I was seeing about soybean prices at the elevator, but Richard just wants to be down at the river."

"Your son and his wife must have thought a lot of your friend if they named their son after him."

"They did. They were going to name the boy after me, but I told them that Horace was no name to give a boy. If they wanted to do me any honor, they could name the boy after Richard. It meant a lot to him."

"I'll bet it did. I'm wondering if I'll run into that Trail of Tears Park soon."

"You already passed it," Horace says. "It's up north a bit. If you want I could take you up there tomorrow."

"You've already been too kind. I suppose I'd better get back in the river in the morning."

"Next time you come, I'll take you there," Horace says. "They've got some signs and so forth about what happened, but I don't think people pay any attention to them. They should. What happened there wasn't right. The Cherokee came here on their way to Oklahoma after the government forced them out of Georgia. It was winter when lots of them got here, and lots of them died that winter. Some of the people who lived along the trail charged the Cherokee for the right to bury their dead. Can you believe that? No sir, it wasn't right what we did. It just wasn't right."

"No."

"Richard told me that when Columbus first discovered America, there were millions of native people living in the Caribbean islands. Tainos, they called themselves. Ever hear that name?"

"No."

"Me neither until he told me. I read about them since. Do you know how many were left after a hundred years?"

I shake my head.

"None," he says. "Some discovery, huh?"

Horace waves again to Richard who is paddling our way. The boy raises the paddle out of the water and holds it over his head. He's a natural in Gloria.

"When the boy gets tired of paddling, we'll go in and have some of Velda's apple pie. You don't want to miss that."

It looks like it will be awhile before we have any pie. Richard Cloud Morton is paddling backward across the pond. He can paddle backward nearly as fast as forward. I know what he is thinking. He is thinking that someday he will get in a boat like Gloria and head down this river that he's so crazy about. I hope he does it before he's fifty. Horace's fishpond is way too small for the boy.

~ ~ ~

The last breakfast pancake on my plate is almost gone. It will certainly stick to my ribs as Velda proclaimed along with the homemade food she has set on the table beside me: a pint jar of canned tomatoes, a quart of chicken noodle soup, a pint of watermelon pickles, the two slices of apple pie that survived the night before, now wrapped in waxed paper and wedged carefully into a small cardboard box, and three thick sandwiches with homemade bread—one ham, one roast beef, and one chicken. Beside the food is a Xeroxed copy of Richard Catch the Clouds' prayer, a gift from Horace.

Richard is looking at the Mississippi River maps that I gave him. The maps cover the river from St. Louis to Cairo, except for the section I left Erika and the boys. Although I haven't reached Cairo, I expect to get there today. Horace is listening to the computer voices, male and female, of the weather radio. "There's no reason for me to listen to it," I told him as I put it beside his plate at the beginning of breakfast. "If I want to know about the weather, I'll just look up and see what it is. And you're supposed to be able to talk to the towboats, but I can't get it to work. I'll bet Richard can."

Horace didn't want to take it, but it feels good to get rid of the stuff that I don't need. I give Velda, who has given me so much, a package of freeze-dried chicken teriyaki.

"This is what I eat when I cook for myself. If you get tired of chopping the heads off chickens, make that. Then you'll understand how much I've enjoyed your cooking."

Velda lifts the package and turns it over to read the ingredient list.

"You can't survive on this," she says.

"You are so right."

We have Gloria loaded into the bed of the pickup, and Richard and Horace are waiting for me to join them in the cab. Velda is standing on the back step. Above the hood of the pickup I raise the plastic grocery bag where Velda has put all the food.

"I'll eat like a king."

"You just be careful," she says.

Horace and Richard take Gloria and me back to the river. We've run out of things to talk about. In the parking lot of the grain elevator, Horace hoists one of the portage bags over his shoulder and I pick up the other. Richard and I carry Gloria down the path back to the river, with Richard in the lead. Freshly filled water bags weigh down the cockpit.

"I'll be fine here. Richard had better get off to school."

Gloria is in the water, and Richard is holding the stern line to keep her from drifting away. The gear is piled on top of the dock.

"Who's goin to hold thiseer kayak so you can get in?"

The boy is becoming hard to understand again.

"I'll be fine."

Horace and I shake hands solemnly like mourners at a funeral.

"While I'm paddling down the river today, I'm going to read Richard Catch the Clouds' prayer."

"He'll like that," Horace says.

I take the rope from Richard's hand, and grandson follows grandfather back along the trail through the trees. Richard turns around once, but neither of us waves. Somehow all this gear has to fit in the kayak along with food from Velda. Somehow Richard Cloud Morton has to sit in the schoolroom all day when all he can think about is this river.

After I pack the gear away, I slip the poem into the map case in the place of the missing maps. Then I slip into the cockpit without upsetting Gloria and dip the paddle into the water.

When the people listen again to the Spirit of the earth and sky

The sky is absolutely clear, not a single cloud to catch. The river is so smooth that the moving reflection of the kayak is distinct in the blueness of the water. The hills to the west have taken on a darker green than just the day before, which doesn't seem possible.

there will be no strangers in this land

Neither Amleth nor the black horse came to me in dreams last night. Was it because I had talked about them? Shouldn't that bring more dreams instead of none? If Horace thought that his name shouldn't be passed on to his grandson, what would he think of the name Amleth? Amleth was no name to give a boy. It was a name that required an explanation whenever someone heard it the first time, and no boy wants to explain who he is. He was already different enough from the other boys that a strange name became unbearable, and he took his middle name, Peder, the one that had come directly from his grandfather. Even that was spelled strangely, and he spelled it in American form until high school when a slight variation became not only tolerated but desired.

And where are you, Black Horse? Do you ever dream about Amleth? About George or me? George saw me carry the rifle into the barn and didn't try to stop me. What was he thinking as he waited in the corral and there was only silence? You watched me with your black eyes as I stood outside your stall. What did you see? I know what I saw. If I was going to shoot something, it shouldn't be you.

I cut through the tall chain link fence of the wild horse preserve on the high desert where he belonged, spread the cut ends apart, and led him through. Even without the halter that would never burden him again, he stood still on the rocky ground and looked at me with his black eyes as no other horse ever did. There was no need to raise my hands or voice to chase him away. He knew what to do. He knew long before I did.

the sons and daughters of the earth and sky will cross this river again and I will be with you.

This river turns in all directions as it flows to Cairo—north, south, east, and west—less south than I expected, as if the Mississippi knows that the Ohio is ahead and wants to travel alone as long as possible. Maybe all the turning of the river confused Jim and Huck. They intended to reach Cairo at the southern tip of Illinois and paddle up the Ohio from there until they were beyond the reach of slave territory. They passed it during the night and never saw it. Maybe if they had one of the maps Richard Cloud Morton now has, they wouldn't have missed it.

I miss Cairo, too—don't see it all. It must be somewhere over on the Ohio River side. The Mississippi passes through low-lying farmland without a hill in sight. The sun is directly above me where it's least informative so that I can't tell from it which way I'm going. Ahead is a highway bridge where the channel crosses from right to left and we cross left to right and beyond that it's hard to see where the river ends and the sky begins.

In the middle of this water and sky, Gloria remains stable but I do not. I press my knees against her hull so that her balance will transfer to me. It's supposed to be the other way around, but every ripple and wave disturb my equilibrium so that I can't tell if my reaction will keep us upright or turn us over. When Huckleberry and Jim saw the size of this river after daylight, they would have known they had passed the confluence. Even if they wouldn't admit it to themselves, even if they held on to some hope, each would have known somewhere deep down that they had passed the point of no return.

Below the finger of Illinois, which points down the enormous river, the boundary lines of three states converge—Illinois, Missouri, and Kentucky. For all I know I might be there now. I read once that you could see a difference in the water of the two rivers. The Ohio, it was said, was green and clear, while the Mississippi was brown and muddy. Or was it the other way around? Whichever it is, I am supposed to see the line dividing the two rivers for miles after they meet. Perhaps that is the view from above, but I'm in the river and can't see anything. I feel like I've reached an inland sea, and I have difficulty summoning enough courage to look back over my shoulder toward the point of land where the two rivers meet. It's not land that I'm looking for anyway.

Below the confluence there are so many barges that I can't tell if they're coming or going. *Be careful*, murmur the voices of the women I've met along the way. Above the roar of the towboat engines, I hear them. *Be careful*, chant the Indian women in Richard Catch the Clouds' prayer. Among the barges, now fifty or sixty lashed together into a single entity, I hear them.

From this point south the mileage decreases on the single river. Nine hundred fifty is the first sign I see—nine hundred fifty miles to the Head of Passes where the river divides again. Far ahead on the left bank are the bluffs in Kentucky. Kentucky was the home of Daniel Boone, the hero I pretended to be when I was a boy on the Loup. I wonder why I picked him. A television show I suppose. Or maybe it was because my brother had already laid claim to Davy Crockett. I can't remember who Joe picked. Maybe if there had been a television show about Crazy Horse, one of us would have picked him. I wonder if the boy, Richard, ever pretends to be Crazy Horse. Richard's namesake, whose voice is becoming familiar to me with the repetition of his prayer, surely chose him.

After the confluence with the Ohio the banks on the right are strewn with parked barges. Some are empty; some are loaded with rock or scrap metal. There are no towns or factories, only mile after mile of parked barges with towboats moving them from one spot to another like a game of musical chairs. But I hear no music except the bass rhythm of the towboat engines.

The river holds me in its grip all afternoon. It seems too far to paddle to one bank or the other, and I stay in the river, maintaining a precarious balance that I expect will become more stable but doesn't. Late in the day I come to an island around which the river divides. The main channel with the buoys of the shipping lane veers off to the southwest. A towboat and barge are coming out of the channel and one behind me is turning in. I am far enough out in the river that if I want to follow the shipping lane, I will have to paddle hard toward the west. I don't want to paddle hard. The lethargic current of the back channel matches my disposition; the scale of its water provides relief to my senses.

The sun becomes hidden by trees on the right bank, but overhead the sky remains a deep cobalt blue. A bird calls from the trees on the island. It could be a dove. There is a similarity to the plaintive call of the mourning dove that we hear on the ranch at first light or at the end of the day. The bird seems to be following us because its call remains strong as I paddle slowly down the small channel on the east side of the island. Upon reaching the treeless sandy spit at the end of the island, I edge Gloria into the bank and let the current slowly swing her stern around. Here is where I'll camp. I'm not ready to get back into the main channel. That river is too big for me today.

I gather dead wood that has washed high onto the bank and more from inside the tree line and build a fire. It would be prudent to set up the tent before it gets dark, but I don't feel like it yet. I wedge a clothes bag beneath the hull of the kayak and lean back against Gloria.

I unwrap the intricate folds Velda has creased into the waxed paper surrounding a sandwich, which is cut into perfect diagonal halves. It is almost too perfect to eat, and my heart aches as I bite through the thick slices of homemade bread, through the butter and ham and cheese. When the sandwich is gone, I refold the waxed paper back into its intricate folds and reach for another. The breeze is cool and soothing; the fire is warm.

When the river is low, this island will become part of the mainland, part of Kentucky I suppose. However, since the boundary lines follow the old course of the river, who knows which course I'm on?

It will be dark soon. I pull up my shirtsleeve to see how late it is and accidentally touch a button that causes the stopwatch to begin running. There are too many buttons on this watch. I bought it for the trip because it was waterproof. It is so waterproof that it will tell time to a depth of three hundred feet. If I'm three hundred feet deep, I won't need the time. When I push a button to stop the spinning numbers, the watch switches to another setting that tells me what time it is in London. To hell with it. I'll figure it out in the morning. I'm too tired to fool with it now. There is no accounting for this weariness. I settle closer to the ground and look up at the evening sky. I'll close my eyes a moment, only a moment; then I'll get up. From inside the dark and ever darker forest, beyond the dancing fire, the bird continues to call—six notes like the mourning dove, calling and calling.

~~~

From the trees the Indian appears. He is chanting a song, six notes of an Indian dirge. Around and around the fire he dances in slow tempo, calling the sky, calling the river, calling the birds in the deep dark forest. A boy emerges from the trees carrying the maps of the river. His face is hidden from me, but I recognize the maps I have given him. The Indian man takes the maps from the boy and throws them into the fire. The fire shoots high into the air. The boy follows in the footsteps of the Indian man, stepping exactly and skillfully into his footprints.

The man beckons me to join them. I am so tired, so tired. The chanting stops; the Indian man is gone; only the boy remains on the opposite side of the fire. He is looking toward the forest where the man has gone. I look at my watch, but the hands of the hours and minutes are gone. The stopwatch is spinning madly beyond my control, the seconds and tenths of seconds only a blur. The watch begins to smoke and bursts into flame. I rip the burning watch from my wrist and throw it into the river just as the boy turns toward me and the fire illuminates his face.

The campfire has died down to coals. The dark uncertain outline of the trees stands against the night sky. The only sound is water lapping at the tip of the island. He would have talked to me if the watch hadn't started on fire.

I pull up the sleeve of my shirt. Glowing in the dark are the seconds of the stopwatch, spinning absurdly. I unbuckle the watch as if I'm still in a dream and throw it into the water.

These dreams with Amleth have become disconcertingly real. Even after waking I feel that he is close by, but he can't be. I am sitting beside the river, looking at the nearly full moon directly above me. Morning is still hours away. He's nowhere around here.

I'm not going to wait for morning. There's no rule about when I can paddle and when I can't, when to sleep and when to stay awake. That's why I'm on this river—to forget all those rules.

The remaining food from Velda I stuff into the rear hatch, drag Gloria down to the water, and feel the water's buoyancy lift her up. Far downriver a towboat works against the current in the channel. Its powerful spotlight sweeps the river before it but doesn't reach us.

Where disturbed, the river sparkles and reflects the moonlight, which is so bright that it hurts my eyes to look at it directly. Where the water is quiet, the light settles into it like the memory of a long dead chant.

Would Amleth have talked to me? In all my dreams he never speaks, but in this one his face was so clear, the expression so like Amleth, that it wasn't like a dream at all.

I try to be alert for the buoys that glisten in the moonlight, but I forget. Then from nowhere a ghostly figure appears, its shape and color indistinct, moaning as we pass. Behind me appear the lights of a small town up a chute of the river. Afterward the lights on land become farther apart. It is dark all around us except where the moonlight reflects on the water—a long line of light that follows us wherever we go.

The river gathers speed and I hear the sound of rushing water. I'm not sure what is causing the noise, but I remember the sound from the Chain of Rocks and steer Gloria away. A tall smokestack stands ahead of us and catches an edge of the moonlight. A beacon flashes on top, warning airplanes to stay away. Perhaps it's warning us, too, for we will soon be upon it. Then the river turns away, and the smokestack is left behind. Polaris comes into position over the tip of Gloria's bow. The river has turned from south to north before I understood what was happening. The current slows and the river becomes quiet again, leaving only the sound of the paddle dipping into the water.

We head north for a long time, although time is uncertain here in the river with no watch except the moon. The moon is just above the barely visible western horizon. So maybe the river is going to fool me after all and take me back to where I was. Finally there are a few lights ahead, then more as Polaris moves off to the right. Slowly, slowly as it always turns, the river turns away from the star. The lights come closer, revealing a road high on a levy, a parking lot and a park, and a long steep concrete boat ramp with an illuminated sign at the top. NEW MADRID

I've read stories about the New Madrid earthquake, which was so strong that some say it made the river flow backward. Would you feel an earthquake if you were in the water, or would you only hear it, like the sound of rushing water in the night?

Gloria slips quietly onto the incline of the boat ramp, and I stiffly lift myself out of the cockpit. There is not a person in sight. From the rear hatch I remove the plastic grocery bag and take out the last of Velda's sandwiches—chicken so full of flavor that I hear Velda's voice as I eat it. "You can't live on that," she told me when she saw the packages of freeze-dried food that I'd been living on. I pull the last slice of apple pie from the cardboard box and eat it with my fingers.

The town of New Madrid is at the top of the New Madrid Bend, the longest bend on the river. In a couple more hours of paddling I'll be a mile or two west of the point where the river turned north, and I will have spent the whole night getting nowhere. But that's only one way of looking at it. Another way is to see that it doesn't make any difference.

Back in Gloria I head down the river away from the lights of New Madrid and toward the smokestack, which is like a shadow far in the distance, its flashing red beacon still warning us to stay away.

Once we pass the smokestack, the eastern sky turns a dull gray and dims the stars above the low-lying flat horizon. The sky becomes rose-colored before switching to gold from the sun's aura. Seldom do I see such subtleties of color. I should be tired, but I can't tell if I'm tired or not. The paddle blade dips into the water and sweeps past the cockpit as if I have nothing to do with it.

When Amleth was a baby, he would fight sleep by trying to push it out of his eyes with his hands. Annie said that his hands and fingers were dexterous at an early age, but they weren't dexterous enough to push away sleep for long. I liked holding him then. Pressing my cheek or lips against his head, I would hum a song, any song, whisper words, any words, as long as the tone was right. He would settle into me and give up the struggle against sleep. I might ease gently into a chair so as not to startle him and sleep, too, for there is nothing as soothing as a soothed child. Sometimes before I fell asleep, he would smile at me from a dream.

My hands have stopped moving, and the paddle is resting across the cockpit combing. Somewhere out there is the river, but I see only my hands holding a paddle. I release the paddle and rub my eyes. Maybe I'm tired after all.

The cell phone rings from the deck bag, startles me, and the paddle slips off the deck into the water. As I retrieve the paddle, the phone rings a few more times and stops. I must have forgotten to turn it off. Joe is the only one who calls now. Reaching forward I unzip the deck bag and find the smaller dry bag with the phone inside it. Joe's number is still on the screen. His voice is not as soothing as the whispered breath of a sleeping child, but I would like to hear it anyway.

"Good morning," he says, after I press the send button and send the call back to him. "Where are you?"

"In the river."

"Getting an early start?"

"I guess so."

"Hey, I finished that little change Juan wanted to put in about the ranch house. I'd like you to look it over and sign it. He's been bugging me about it."

"You can sign it for me."

"Yeah, I know, but I thought you ought to at least take a look. How close are you to Memphis?"

"I don't know."

"Well I was thinking I could fly down there. We've always talked about going to Beale Street. Remember? We could eat a little barbeque, listen to some music, drink a beer. What do you say?"

"I could drink a beer."

"Good. I've got a map right here in front of me. Where are you?"

"I left New Madrid a couple hours ago."

"Geez, you must have started early. All right, here's New Madrid. Hey, you're almost there. It's a straight shot down to Memphis."

"The river doesn't go straight."

"I see that. Damn, that was a waste of time at New Madrid. If you had just cut across land you would have saved yourself a lot of work. Well, look, I'll fly down to Memphis tomorrow morning and scout it out. Whenever you get there is fine with me. I'll check in with you tomorrow and see where you are. Maybe you'll know by then."

"I will."

"Take care."

"You, too."

The phone battery is low, and I turn the phone off to save what's left and stuff it back into the dry bag. It was good to hear Joe's voice.

I point Gloria toward a giant sandbar on the inside curve of a wide bend where the channel sweeps, as it always sweeps, to the outside. The paddle hits bottom some distance from the bank, and I make the strokes shallower until Gloria grinds to a stop. I get out and pull her the remaining distance to the sandbar. The sand looks as if it's been washed clean. White and red granules form curving terraces that show the receding stages of the river.

Among the rolled-up maps, I find the one that shows where I am—mile 865 at Little Cyprus Bend. I sort forward through them until I find Memphis. Beale Street is beside the dot of mile 736. It's farther away than I thought. One hundred thirty miles is a long way to go if I want to get there tomorrow. And now I do.

If I paddle all day, set up the tent in the dark, and leave early in the morning, I might make it. That is, if the wind doesn't blow. The wind isn't blowing now, and the sun is warm—not hot but perfectly warm. I'm hungry again and look inside Velda's sack, spot the pint jar of watermelon pickles, and eat all the pickles and drink some of the juice. Now I'm only warm. A flutter of sound surrounds me. It's like wind blowing through trees, but there are no trees close by. A flock of pelicans, fifty, a hundred, even more, have landed in the gentle water out from the sandbar. They think I'm part of the topography and I will be. I recline slowly down to the warm sand and close my eyes. The flutter of wings, the peaceful circling of the pelicans soothes me as I once soothed Amleth, and his smile comes back to me.

~ ~ ~

With my cell phone beeping a low battery warning, Joe tells me he'll be waiting on an island just south of a bridge that looks like the M in Memphis.

"Don't worry. You can't miss it," he says just before the phone goes dead.

I always worry when he says something like that.

I need to change the maps in the map case so that I can find the island he's talking about. Each map covers about ten miles of river, and I've passed through the maps I started with in the morning. I paddle over to a bank cleared of trees where farm ground runs right up to the river and grain elevators stand beyond the revetment. It is a rare sight, for this river is circumscribed by levies and trees and penetrated only by occasional dirt roads leading to abandoned boat ramps. The land is so flat that it's amazing to me the river flows at all. It seems like it ought to stop right here and begin spreading out into a shallow sea. And maybe it has because stretched out as far as I can see are flat fields covered with water. Hundreds and hundreds of acres of rice fields.

Joe and the maps don't speak the same language. There are several bridges across the river at Memphis and any number of islands that aren't islands anymore, but there is nothing that looks like the image Joe left me—an island out in the middle of the river with a tram connecting it to the mainland. What does a tram look like anyway? Maybe it will become clear when I get there.

Back in the river sweat burns my eyes as it gathers beneath the brim of my hat and streams down my forehead. I scoop up water with my hand and splash it across the back of my neck. The water leaves brown streaks on my shirtsleeves from the wrists to the elbows and probably on my neck, too, but I'm too hot to care. It's so hot that I've stuffed the life jacket into the cockpit to allow the air to circulate around my chest, but the hot air doesn't help much. I wouldn't mind a little breeze right now, just enough to dry the sweat before it reaches my eyes.

Coming downriver is a clean white towboat with only two barges in front. Of the hundreds of towboats and barges I've seen, there is something familiar about this one, the gray dust on the barges in contrast to the starkly clean towboat.

As it rumbles past us, a man steps out on the bridge of the pilothouse and waves whole-heartedly with his arm moving back and forth over his head. It is the captain from the cement plant in St. Louis. I lay the paddle across the cockpit and wave back, putting my whole body into the wave as he has done. Gloria rocks back and forth in the water. We are too far apart for words to reach each other, but he is telling me something anyway. He is telling me that I know someone on the river, that I belong here after all. I never imagined how good that could make me feel.

Gradually the towboat leaves us behind, although I paddle with renewed vigor in its wake and delay the moment when I finally lose sight of it. By then, miles down the river, a bridge with a superstructure in the shape of an undulating M takes the place of the towboat in my thoughts. It is, I hope, the bridge that Joe told me to look for, but I can't be sure because there is no island beyond it and no tram. Aren't trams found only in mountains? There are no mountains here—only this flat land that stretches out to the horizon. Even if Joe were good at giving directions, which he isn't, and if I were good at following them, which I'm not, what he sees from land and what I see from the water might be completely different.

I've been worrying about the barge traffic in Memphis, suspecting it will be like St. Louis. But so far it isn't bad at all—a few barges coming up on the right bank, none behind, clear sailing as we pass beneath the M on the freeway bridge.

Someone is jumping up and down on a rocky knoll on the left bank, waving his arms over his head and shouting. It's not an island, but even at this distance I can see it's Joe. If he hadn't told me to look for an island, I wouldn't be so far out in the river. Now I have to paddle straight across to reach him, but you can't paddle straight across. The current carries you down. I point Gloria upriver and paddle against the current while Joe scrambles across the rocks down to the water's edge.

"Holy shit," he says when I'm close enough to the bank that it's clear I'm going to make it, "I thought you were going to float right on by."

Using my last reserve of energy I paddle the final few yards to the bank. I'm not sure that I will have enough strength to even get out of the kayak.

"Didn't you see the M on the bridge?"

He reaches out and grabs Gloria's bow.

"I saw the bridge, but I didn't see an island."

"This is the island."

He points to the rocks at his feet.

"It doesn't look like an island."

"Well, it is. I could see you way up the river. At first you were just a spot and I wasn't sure it was you, but then I saw the paddle flashing in the sun. Man, you look small out there. How you doing? You look like shit."

"Good to see you, too."

Joe laughs with the high-pitched squeak at the end that so annoyed his older brother but always makes me laugh. Gloria rotates into the bank and scrapes against the rocks. He inches forward on the revetment, careful not to slip in his new sandals. He's wearing blue shorts, a Hawaiian shirt, and a black Memphis ball cap. Like a tourist from the north his feet are winter white.

"I found a marina on the other side where you can dock the boat. They won't even charge you anything. You have to go down to the tip of the island and come back up. It's not far," he says. "Whatever you do, don't miss that turn."

I have a little energy in reserve after all. And it isn't far, another hundred yards or so, and I don't miss the inlet that separates one body of land from another. So maybe it is an island, or was.

There's a path up on the mainland levy where people are walking and jogging. Big new homes face the river on a bluff south of the inlet, far above the reach of high water. To the north a glass pyramid rises above the trees. Finally a city that knows from where it came. Finally a city that hasn't turned away from the river.

Joe has cut across the island and is waiting for me on the dock of the marina. He grabs the paddle that I extend to him and pulls Gloria in.

"Looks like you need a new paddle," he says.

"This one works fine."

Joe kneels on the wood planks, reaches down, and holds Gloria against the face of the dock.

"How did you break it?"

"Ran into a buoy."

"You're not supposed to do that. What about the other one? You had two when you started, didn't you."

"Lost it on the Loup."

"God, you're lucky you got this far. We'd better get you another paddle tomorrow in case you lose this one, too."

I pull the waist skirt free.

"I'm not going to lose this one. This dock is too high. I'll end up dumping over if I try to get out here."

Joe gets off his knees and looks around.

"Down here," he says and walks toward a section of dock that is lower. "Hey, it's perfect." He's not quite shouting and not quite laughing. "It's covered with duck shit."

I paddle over to him. This time he squats rather than kneels as he steadies the kayak, and I slide my butt onto a relatively clean spot. After all, everything is relative. A man walks out of the small marina store and extends his hand as soon as I stand up.

"James Monroe," he says of himself. "Been waiting for you all afternoon. That's some trip you're taking."

"James, here, runs the marina," Joe says.

James and I shake hands. His glasses are so thick that I can't really see his eyes, but I can hear friendliness in his voice that makes me glad I finally got here.

"Where do you want us to put the kayak, James?" Joe asks.

"She'll be fine right here. Don't you worry," he tells me. "We'll watch her. Won't anything happen to her here except the members are going to be real curious about looking her over."

Joe and James each grab a handle at the ends of the kayak. I take hold of the cockpit, and together we lift Gloria fully loaded out of the water. I'm concerned that the weight might be too much for her hull, and I watch the center for any sign of stress. There isn't any. Gloria is stronger than we are for it's all that we can do to lift her. I remove a clothes bag and a toiletries bag from the rear hatch and stretch the cockpit cover over the combing.

"That's it?" Joe asks.

"That's it."

James calls us a taxi and gives Joe and me a Coke while we wait. I've gotten used to drinking warm water, and the Coke is so cold that it hurts.

"Those barges must seem pretty big out there," James observes, tilting his head toward the river that is flowing out of sight on the other side of the island. "Any of 'em get in your way?"

"Not yet."

But I see what he means. Gloria looks small and vulnerable compared to the boats moored in the covered marina, but those boats don't amount to much either compared to the barges on the river.

"She's made for the ocean. Pretty much knifes right through any waves that the barges throw off."

"Oh, she's a fine boat, all right," James says. "I can see that."

A line of river mud runs the length of Gloria at the water line, and there are deep scratches in her hull that I haven't seen before. Nevertheless, she's a fine boat as James says, and I wouldn't trade her for any of the bigger boats moored at the Yacht Club or any of them out in the river.

"I got us rooms at the Peabody Hotel," Joe says as we ride in the taxi over a bridge that connects the island to the mainland. "They've got a fountain in the lobby that ducks swim in. Every morning they bring the ducks down from the roof. I'm not kidding. They come down on the elevator. It's supposed to be quite a show. We have to watch it tomorrow."

The taxi drops us off in front of the hotel, and I follow Joe through the door that a doorman opens for us and down a hallway where a security guard in a black suit is standing. Joe doesn't notice the security guard, but I have a feeling I wouldn't make it inside if I hadn't been with him. I haven't shaved since leaving Horace and Velda, and I'm wearing the same shirt and pants. Somehow, somewhere, I lost one of the two bags of clothes I had with me. It's getting so that there's plenty of room in the hatches now.

The ducks are gone by the time we arrive, but Joe points to the sign beside a large ornate fountain that announces DUCK CROSSING. They arrive at eleven and leave at five. The elevator door closes on the lobby and whisks us up to the floor whose number Joe has punched on the panel. It's high up. The unpleasant odor that rides up with us must be from me. I think it's my wet socks.

"What time is it?"

Yesterday morning I was among pelicans that soothed me to sleep. Today I'm in a luxury hotel where there's a duck show every day at eleven and five. It's hard to reconcile the two places. Joe looks at my hand. He's wondering if I've become too lazy to tell my own time. I raise it so that he can see my wrist is bare.

"Lost my watch, too."

He raises his eyebrows as he checks his watch.

"Six-thirty," he says.

The elevator door opens, and I follow him down the hall. The water in my waterproof socks squishes inside my shoes on the thick hallway carpet.

"What size shoes do you wear?"

He has grown since we were boys. I was a lot bigger than him then, but his feet now look as big as mine.

"Eleven," he says.

"Did you bring along an extra pair. I don't have anything except these kayak shoes. You're supposed to be able to wear these things in water and on land, but they don't work worth a damn on land. Always wet."

He looks at my feet and sees the impracticality of wearing wet shoes to Beale Street.

"I've got a pair of tennis shoes. You can borrow them if you want. We'd better get you some new shoes tomorrow."

"I'll just keep yours."

He thinks I'm kidding.

When he inserts the keycard into the door lock, a green light on the lock blinks like the lights that blink from some of the green buoys in the river at night. He pushes the door open and gives me the cardkey. He's not coming in.

"I got you a suite. Thought you might like a little extra room after being stuck in a tent all these nights. I'll bring you the shoes. I'm right across the hall."

"How about some clothes, too? A shirt and a pair of pants, underwear, socks, the whole deal. Most everything I have is dirty."

"I'll bring you whole deal," he says.

Joe lets the door close, and I walk over to the sheer curtains that cover the windows and pull the curtains apart. He has gotten me a suite that faces the river. With Joe I don't know if this is accidental or intentional, and I've known him all my life.

Across the river sunlight is coming in low over the flat Arkansas plain. From where I stand many stories above the ground, the water appears unmoving. But I know it's moving. I still feel its movement in my body, and it's enough to make me dizzy.

I'm still looking out the window when I hear a knock at the door. It is Joe bringing shoes and clothes. He will meet me down in the lobby, he says. "No hurry. Take your time."

In the next room on the king-size bed that is twice as big as my tent, I find a small box wrapped in gold paper with an envelope propped between the box and a pillow—one of four pillows. There is no inscription on the envelope, but I know it's for me and I know it isn't from Joe. I know him that well, at least.

> *I wish you a happy birthday, but what I wish most of all is that happiness comes back into your life, just as it has for Joe and me. You must finish this journey. We may be the only people who understand that. But when you are done, remember we are north by northwest on the compass. I know because I placed the compass on the map. You will see my mark. I pray that you will be safe.*

> *Joe has something to tell you. I hope it is good news.*

> *Love,*
Charo

Refolding the heavy stationery I lay it on the edge of the bed, pick up the box, which is heavy for its small size, pull away the wrapping paper and open the lid. Rosario has packed a brass compass in wads of cotton. I turn the compass until the N of North is in line with the needle. With a file or some tool like it, she has etched a notch in the brass case just to the left of the needle.

It is not like Rosario to be mysterious. If she has something to say, she usually says it right out. And if Joe had good news, he would have told it to me as soon as he saw me. Maybe they don't understand how far behind I've left the business that once so completely engaged us.

In the shower I let the water run off my body as I knead the socks on the bottom of the tub with my feet. Whenever I close my eyes, the river returns and my body sways with its motion.

Rosario might be right that she and Joe are the only ones who understand. There is this little river in the sandhills, fed from springs that percolate up from the aquifer beneath. There is this river that has always been a part of me along with the simple notion that I could build a raft of some sort and let the river take me wherever it is going. But if I've learned anything, it is that nothing is ever simple.

The shirt Joe loaned me is a little short in the sleeves, and the shoes crowd my toes a bit. I stuff my dirty clothes into a plastic bag that is hanging in the closet and call for laundry service. It is ridiculous to expect that tomorrow morning the clothes will come back clean, but it's no more ridiculous than the cost of the laundry service.

Beale Street is only a few blocks from the hotel, and we walk between the barricades that close it off to cars. Our first stop is a restaurant advertising gumbo that won first prize in the Memphis cook-off in 1988. The gumbo is good, and I wonder why it hasn't won since. A piano player is getting ready to play, and we sip beer from long-neck bottles and get ready to listen. Blues, Beale Street, gumbo. I look around the restaurant and see middle-aged white people, tourists like Joe and me who've come from Omaha. For some reason I expected something different—maybe that more black people would be here with us. After all, they made the blues, but they're not here in this restaurant except for the waitress, who brings us more beer, and the piano player. He begins playing, and Joe taps his fingers on the tabletop, which is covered with butcher paper. Our beer bottles sweat new rings on the paper every time we lift and set the bottles back down. The piano player inhales a cigarette and takes a long swig from a tumbler of amber liquid that he sets on top of the piano without stopping the song. We clap politely with the other tourists when he finishes the first song, but he is into the second without acknowledging our applause.

We leave the restaurant and enter another farther down the street whose specialty is a Southern Feast—catfish and ribs. The ribs are good, but they aren't as good as the ribs we used to get at The Three Pigs. The catfish is coated with cornmeal and deep fried and tastes like the river, although there is no river in this catfish. It comes from commercial ponds in Arkansas, the waiter tells us. The band has too much spirit to make anyone blue. Joe taps the tabletop again. He loves music of any kind, any kind except country. When the band takes a break and the taped music of the intermission fills the void, he turns toward me and leans across the table.

"Did you find the present from Rose?" he asks.

"Yes."

"What do you think of it?"

"It's really nice."

"Did she say anything about her and me?"

"She said you had some news to tell me."

"Nothing else?"

"She hoped it would be good news."

"Damn. I was hoping she would sort of break the ice."

Joe smiles with a nervous twitch that I never see unless he's going to tell me something about the business that I won't be happy to hear. But I don't care about business anymore. He ought to know that.

"It's ninety degrees down here, Joe. Any ice would have melted a long time ago."

"Okay, here's the deal. Rose and I are thinking about getting married."

"You're kidding."

He shakes his head. He's not kidding.

"When did this happen?"

"I don't know. Maybe since her divorce. At least for me."

"That was three years ago."

"I know."

"We told her that guy was bad news. She should have listened to us."

"You told her. Me—I keep out of that stuff."

"You're into more stuff than I can keep track of."

"Not anymore."

"Goddamn, Joe. I know she's smart and competent and all that, but she's just a kid."

"She's thirty-seven years old."

"That can't be."

But of course it is. All you have to do is add up the numbers. Where do all these numbers come from? She's told me about them herself, how they add up, how her biological clock is ticking. All those other babies on the ranch and none of her own.

Joe is tapping the tabletop in time to the recorded music, a nervous habit that has nothing to do with whether or not he likes it. I take a long drink from the bottle of beer and feel the cold liquid flow down my throat and into my gut.

"She wants a baby. Have you talked about that?"

"Well, you see, that's the second thing I wanted to tell you. Rose and I are going to have a baby."

"What?"

"Sort of a surprise, I guess."

"Sort of."

"Yeah, I know. We're hoping that you and Annie will be the godparents."

"Annie maybe, but I don't think I'm up to it."

"Think about it, at least."

"Have you told Annie?"

"Not yet."

"Better get us another beer."

Joe tries to flag down the waiter who is hurrying by with a tray of food. Failing that, he gets up and walks over to the bar. Like Rosario, he was married once before, but so long ago and for such a short time that it seems like it never happened. Since then he's been in love more times than I can remember but backed away every time it got serious. I thought he would keep on backing away.

And Rosario. Why didn't she tell me when I saw her at the river? She must have known then. Maybe that was why she wanted me go with her back to Omaha.

Joe returns with two more beers and puts mine in front of me. I finish what's in the other bottle and push it aside. Here I thought the whole world had stopped because I did, but it just kept right on going. Maybe that's the biggest shock of all. I raise my bottle so that it's pointed toward Joe, this friend I thought I knew all about.

"I wish you and Rosario all the happiness in the world."

"Appreciate that. We were a little worried about how you'd feel—you know, with Amleth and all."

"Doesn't have anything to do with Amleth."

The band begins playing again and drowns out any words that we might say. We've said enough anyway. This band plays more rhythm than blues, and it's blues that we've talked about coming all this way to hear. We leave the restaurant and walk farther down the street. Outside each place where there's music, we stop and listen to determine if we want to go in. It all sounds pretty good, but we keep walking until we run out of street and music. I buy two beers from a joint that is selling them out a window and give one to Joe. I'm tired and don't want to walk any farther. We sit down on the curb with our feet out in the street. His shoes are beginning to chafe my little toes.

"Happy birthday," he says.

"Thanks. Is it today or tomorrow?"

He looks at his watch.

"Tomorrow."

"I've sort of lost track of the days."

"I'll bet you have."

"I don't want to read any of that legal stuff you brought with you."

"I know. That was just the excuse to come down here."

"I've got an idea. Why don't you call the office and tell them to put everything on hold. Buy a kayak and a sleeping bag here in Memphis and come along with me. One last fling before you have to settle down."

"Me? I don't think Rose would like that just now. Besides, I got enough of that outdoor stuff when I was a kid. Dad was always dragging us off on a fishing trip somewhere."

"I never forgave him for taking you away. It broke my heart, you know. We were just kids, and there was nothing we could do about it. Never forgave him for that."

"He couldn't make it out there. He wasn't like your dad who had his own ranch. It wasn't his fault."

"So I'll forgive him."

I raise the beer bottle in a gesture of forgiveness. I'm too tired to hold old grudges.

"Do you remember our plan?" Joe asks.

"Which one?"

"You were going to marry my little sister so that you and I could stay together when we grew up."

"Whatever happened to that plan?"

"The same thing that happens to all of them," Joe says. "Or maybe Annie had something to do with it."

"Or your sister. We never told her about it, did we? That might have been the place to start."

"At least we made it to Beale Street. How long have we been talking about doing this? But here we are."

Here we are, two old men in the eyes of those boys who made plans beside the river—one fifty tomorrow and one soon to be—sitting on the curb of Beale Street with our feet in the gutter, watching the other tourists walk by on the street where it's hard to find real blues anymore.

"You want to go back up and listen to some more music?" he asks.

"Not really. How about you?"

"Nah, I've had enough. I'd better call Rose before it gets too late."

We start walking back to the hotel and come across an old man sitting on a park bench and playing a guitar that looks as old and worn-out as he does. A half-dozen people have formed a semi-circle around him. Joe and I extend the semi-circle by two. The old man's eyes are closed, and he doesn't see us arrive. He doesn't see anybody. From deep down in his belly or some-place deep down inside him comes a song about a woman who is making him cry the blues.

"She so pretty," he sings and slams out three chords on his worn-out guitar. "Make a dead man rise."

~~~

We're waiting for the ducks. Earlier we had an unobstructed view of the roped-off strip of red carpet that runs from the middle elevator to the ornate fountain in the center of the lobby, but spectators have since gathered along the rope line. Joe points up to the balcony, which is jammed with people.

"We're going to have to move if we want to see anything."

We will, but I'm not certain that the ducks are worth the effort.

An elderly couple is sitting on the couch next to the overstuffed chair in which I'm sitting. Like me, the husband is drinking coffee from a porcelain cup, but his wife has finished the Bloody Mary she ordered from the lobby bar in the corner and is looking around impatiently for more service. When she turns her head, her white hair turns along with her white face like a hat of frozen snow. A black man in a dark suit is walking toward us, and she extends her empty glass toward him. He passes without acknowledging her and joins a young woman and two children standing among the spectators. The woman in the white hair puts her glass on the table in front of her.

"This used to be such a nice place to stay," she tells me.

A voice broadcasts over the public address system that the ducks are about to arrive. Joe heads for the rope line. He's waited all morning and is not going to miss them now, and I'm right behind him.

While we jockey for a view, a man in a red suit and black top hat tells us that the ducks first appeared in the fountain in the 1930s after the general manager returned to the hotel from an unsuccessful duck hunting trip during which he'd enjoyed a little too much sipping whiskey. Back in those days they used live decoys, and he put his live decoys into the fountain as a whiskey-inspired joke. The ducks were such a hit with the guests that they stayed there. Then a former animal trainer from the ciYou are herercus offered to teach the ducks to march in and out instead of being carried, and ducks have been marching in and out to John Philip Souza's *King Cotton March* ever since. In their off-time the ducks live in a penthouse on the roof of the hotel.

The duckmaster steps onto the waiting elevator, promising to return shortly with the ducks. Soon a trumpet fanfare sounds over the loudspeakers, and the elevator doors open. Out comes the duckmaster with his brass duck-head cane and black top hat and behind him waddle the ducks on the red carpet, keeping duck time to the recorded music. At the marble fountain the ducks flap up the steps and glide into the water. Joe chuckles delightedly during the entire march. He loves all demonstrations of absurdity as long as they're done in style.

"Quite a show!" he says to me as the crowd disperses around us, but I can see that he's a little embarrassed by his own enthusiasm. "But that's not all. Wait until you see the replica of the river they have at the museum on Mud Island. You can't leave until you see it."

Although we haven't discussed when I'll be leaving, he must know that I'm ready. I thought the long days of paddling to get to Memphis would have made me feel like staying longer, but strangely it has done the opposite. Last night I had trouble sleeping, although the bed was soft and luxurious. The noise of the air conditioning bothered me, and I kept dreaming that a barge was coming up from behind. Then I would wake and see the glow of light through the sheer curtains and know that I wasn't in the river. But I didn't know where I was. For a few seconds I experienced what it is like to have amnesia. Now if we cross over to Mud Island where Gloria is waiting, I know I won't come back to this hotel.

"So let's go see it. I'll go up and get my stuff. What do you want me to do with your clothes?"

"Just leave them on the bed."

"What time is check-out?"

"I don't know," Joe says. "Don't worry about it."

My laundered and pressed clothes were hanging on the doorknob this morning, and they're lying on the bed now in a plastic cover. The clothes look brand new, so maybe it was worth the price after all. I stuff everything into the dry bag, except the clothes that I put on. On the bed I leave Joe's clothes. His shoes, which have pinched my toes all that I can tolerate, I leave on the floor. My shoes and socks are drying on the edge of the bathtub, and I pull them on.

My luggage and attire must look odd to the cleaning lady who rides down a few floors with me in the elevator because she glances first at my two yellow bags, then down to my shoes. She doesn't say anything, however. My socks don't smell as bad as they did yesterday, but there's a faint odor of something not quite dry that is trapped with us in the elevator car.

In the lobby I give Joe the keycard to my room and walk with him down the hallway past the security guard who no longer pays any attention to me. Joe wants to take the tram over to Mud Island. He has a city map and shows me how far we have to walk to reach the tram station.

"Or we can catch a cab," he says.

He likes being the tour director.

"A walk would do us good."

It's farther than it appears on the map, which Joe consults often. "A few more blocks," he tells me. He said something similar a few blocks back. At last we see the tram station ahead, and we cross Front Street to be on the river side.

"I have a dream today!"

The voice is coming from the park next to the station, and I'm thinking that it's a recording for the tourists.

"Let freedom ring from the snowcapped Rockies of Colorado!"

But it's not a recording. A small black man is standing alone in the park, gesturing out to the sidewalk. I want to keep walking, but Joe stops as if he has all the time in the world. I can smell the river now, that mixture of water and mud, the diesel exhaust of the towboats, the sun baking the banks of broken concrete, sand, dirt, and trees.

"Let freedom ring from every hill and every molehill of Mississippi. From every mountainside, let freedom ring.

"He's good," Joe says. "I thought it was a recording."

"I did too."

The small man is walking toward us, as real as you would ever want to be.

"Hey, that was good," Joe says to him. "You got it just right."

"I used to speak down at the Civil Rights Museum, but they won't let me do it anymore. Afraid I'm going to take away some of their donations. Put me in jail like Dr. King."

"Sorry to hear that," Joe says.

"Oh, I know every speech Dr. King ever gave. 'And so today, you do not walk alone. You gave to this world wonderful children. They didn't live long lives, but they lived meaningful lives. Their lives were distressingly small in quantity, but glowingly large in quality.' You tell me what you want to hear and I'll give it to you."

The man's teeth have worked loose and he pushes his plate back onto his gums. Joe looks at me, but he's the one who stopped and he's the one who has to decide what to do next.

"Maybe another time," he says. "My friend here has a date with the river over yonder."

"'I refuse to accept the idea that man is mere flotsam and jetsam in the river of life unable to influence the unfolding events which surround him. I refuse to accept the view that mankind is so tragically bound to the starless midnight of racism and war that the bright daybreak of peace and brotherhood can never become a reality.' Nobel Prize speech, December 10, 1964."

"I like that," Joe says. "The river and all."

"The last speech Dr. King ever made was right here in Memphis. I was there that night with my father. April 3, 1968. Maybe you would like to hear that one."

Joe looks at me again, but he doesn't have to. We're going to listen to the speech.

"Let's hear it," he says.

I can't decide if this man is a little crazy, if he's a con-man, or if he's someone carrying inside him a voice that he heard almost forty years ago and can't get rid of. Maybe he's some of all three. "You must be a crazy man," I remember Angela saying. I thought she was kidding, but maybe she wasn't.

The small man has to keep pushing his false teeth back on his gums, but oddly enough it doesn't detract from the intensity of his words. Most people walk around us on the sidewalk, but a few have stopped to listen with us. The man's voice is rising to a crescendo, and it is eerie how real it sounds.

"'I've been to the mountaintop. And I've seen the Promised Land. I may not get there with you. But I want you to know tonight, that we, as a people will get to the Promised Land.'"

Then it's quiet, and no one moves for a second. A young black man walks around from behind us and hands the speaker a bill. Joe is reaching for his wallet. So maybe he's decided that the man is a performer or a con man after all. I watch him sort through bills until he finds one that's just right. I'm not sure what it is, but the speaker is pleased with the offering.

"Thank you, brother."

He shakes Joe's hand, then mine.

"You have to admit," Joe says, after we are far enough away that the speaker won't hear him, "he was really good."

In the park on Mud Island we follow a miniature replica of the lower river, which begins at Cairo where the Ohio joins the Mississippi. Perhaps there wasn't room or money to extend the replica all the way up to Minnesota, or perhaps the interest of the builders was more regional, more southern. We stop at Memphis and look down at our feet, Joe in his sandals and I in my kayak shoes.

You are here, a sign says.

"You still have a long way to go."

I was thinking the same thing. We have walked only fifty feet or so from Cairo and have blocks yet to go.

"If it showed the Loup up in the sandhills, the beginning would be somewhere out there in the river."

Joe looks where I'm pointing to the real river that is flowing below and beyond the stone wall of the public park.

"While I was waiting for you yesterday," he says, "I sat down there by the river. Until you're right beside it, you don't know how big it is. It's not the same as being out there, but I started to understand what it must be like. Do you think any of those boats we made when we were kids ever made it this far?"

"I hope so."

We walk along the concrete replica, following every bend and turn. The river travels east, west, and north nearly as much as it flows south. There must be hydrological principles that govern or once governed its meandering course, but once again I can't help feeling that there is something else, some will of its own independent of scientific principles. Joe and I walk beside the water that is pumped in at the beginning of the replica and flows into a large pond at the end—the Gulf of Mexico, the ocean—where a fountain sprays water into the air and paddling ducks distort the replica's proportions. Now we have seen it all.

"Maybe after I retire, you and I can take a trip like this together. Imagine that, a couple of old geezers paddling down the river."

He laughs at the absurdity of his idea, maybe at the absurdity of all our ideas.

"We could look for the boats we launched up in the Loup and give them a push if they didn't make it."

"I wonder if any did," he says.

"I do, too."

We're already repeating ourselves.

A puff of wind brushes my face. I look up at the trees to see how strong it is there; then out to the river where it really matters. You don't have to be far from it before you can no longer see the first wind ripples on the water.

"Feels like the wind is coming up."

"You're wanting to get going, aren't you?" Joe asks.

"Maybe I should."

"I still think we ought to find you another paddle."

"I don't want another paddle."

"The paddle is an instrument of defiance, you know. Coming across the river yesterday, paddling the way you did, was an act of defiance."

"My defiance is a little damaged right now."

"I know, but you've still got some left."

"And you. Who would ever think you would get married again?"

"What about Rose and me? Think we have a chance?"

"Wrong guy to ask. Just listen to her when she says something or when she doesn't."

"I will. We're going to wait until you finish this trip to get married. Shouldn't be too long, should it?"

"I don't know. It's hard for me to think that far ahead. I think you ought to just go ahead and do it."

"It scares me to death to think that I'm going to become a father at this age. What the hell do I know about kids?"

"I know one thing. If it's a boy, give him a simple name."

"I'll let Rose pick the name."

"Good idea."

"Hey, you're going to miss the tour of Graceland. They say that Elvis's ghost is still walking around out there. They hear him singing late at night. But at least we saw those ducks. If I hadn't seen them with my own eyes, I would never have believed it."

He tilts his head back and laughs in his high-pitched cackle at the absurdity of ducks walking off an elevator. It's a laugh I've relied upon all my life, and already it's carrying me down the river.

~ ~ ~

My last sighting of Joe is of him standing on the southern tip of Mud Island, not up on the clean grass-covered hillside but down in the sand and mud next to the water. When we were boys, we would always find our way down to the river.

I wonder if he will decide to look for the ghost at Graceland or if he'll go back to the hotel to watch the ducks walk back on the elevator. Or maybe he'll catch an early flight back to Omaha. If so he'll soon be describing the duck march to Rosario and making her laugh. Laughter is supposed to be good for babies in the womb. That baby will hear lots of laughter.

After the freeway bridge the river turns west. It doesn't take long before Memphis is out of sight, but I still carry some of it with me. The hotel laundry starched and ironed my shirt so that there is a stiff crease on each sleeve from the shoulder down to the cuff. The cuffs are already wet with river water. It won't be long until the sleeves are wet, too, and lose their stiffness, but the starched collar aggravates my skin.

Who would have thought Joe would ever become a father? He has no idea what's waiting for him. After all these uncountable generations, evolution if not wisdom ought to give fathers and sons some way to get along better than we do.

When I was a boy, I had the ability to get under my father's skin, to strike a match that set off the temper of a normally placid man. I don't know why I did it or even how. My brother never did. Maybe I thought someone needed to shake things up a little. From my father I learned that a father's job is to put up with his son until the son is finally old enough to leave. Only then did he and I begin to see eye to eye, which I expected or at least hoped would happen between Amleth and me.

I remember his phone call like it was this morning. The voice didn't sound like Amleth at all but like an older man.

"Are you going to be at the ranch after New Year's? There's something I would like to talk to you about."

He was spending his Christmas vacation in Denver with Annie. I was at Joe's house in Omaha, but I drove back to the ranch on New Year's Day.

Juan and Consuelo made a big deal out of his coming. You would have thought it was their own son who was coming home from college. The first night he arrived, Consuelo cooked a meal that had no meat in it at all, and Juan didn't say a word about it as if this was the way they ate all the time. I didn't say anything either, except that the food was really good.

The next morning Amleth saddled Pecos, the horse I had given him when he was fifteen, and rode out to the west, which perplexed me because he had never been much interested in riding. He did the same thing the next morning, perplexing me even more. The piano stood unused in the living room even after I told him that I had gotten it tuned before his arrival. On the second afternoon Juan dropped by to talk about expanding the calving pasture on the Wilkins place. I made coffee, and we sat in the kitchen and talked about this pasture that neither of us was interested in.

"Where is your son?" Juan asked.

"He went out for a ride."

"Maybe he would like to go over to the Wilkins place with us to take a look."

"I don't think Amleth will be interested in a calving pasture."

"But you never know," Juan said, as if he did.

Was there something that everybody knew and I didn't?

Sometimes words run through my mind as if they are still being spoken. The same words, again and again, whether I'm on the ranch or a thousand and more miles away. It seems like they're outside of me, floating along with me no matter how far I paddle.

His face is different the third morning, wind-burned from the long cold rides, but different even from that—expectant, worried, hopeful. When is the last time I have seen him hopeful?

"Want to ride along with me today?" he asks. "I'd like to show you something and talk to you about an idea I have. Maybe you want to take the black. I think he needs some exercise."

It is a strange thing for him to say, but everything about him is different.

"I'm not sure that's a good idea."

"It's okay," Amleth says. "If he needs to take off, I won't mind. Neither will Pecos. He knows his place."

Surprisingly the black horse is content to walk beside Pecos along the river where Amleth is leading us. I am surprised, too, how well Amleth sits his horse, easily and comfortably as if he has done it all his life. When had he learned to do that? The two horses walk at a brisk pace, constantly checking with each other to make sure that the other isn't getting ahead. I didn't know Pecos had it in him.

There is still snow in the gullies from an earlier storm that hadn't amounted to much. The ground is firm but not frozen, and we listen to the crisp sound of the horse's hooves striking the firm soil. The sun is behind us and casts our shadows and the shadows of the horses ahead of us. Steam pours from the horses' nostrils and from ours when we breathe deeply. It feels good to feel the cold air go all the way down to the lungs.

When we reach Wamaduze Creek, Amleth turns and follows it to the beaver dam a mile north. Beyond the dam there is a culvert that directs the water under an earthen bridge that we built across the creek after we bought the land west of it. So this is where he has been riding. I should have guessed. Each of us picks a favorite place. Mine is the river below the barn. Annie's was the hill north of the house. But I understand why he likes it beside the beaver dam. There is a fine meadow in the low ground and cottonwood trees that follow the creek.

Once across the culvert he pulls Pecos to a stop and lets him nibble on the winter grass. The black bites off some grass, too, and eats it while he surveys the land. He would never relax enough to keep his head down like Pecos.

Amleth points to the field of alfalfa that we planted on the higher ground above the hay meadow.

"I'd like to try raising some Hidatsa beans over there as an experiment to see if we could get them to grow in with the alfalfa. I think we could still get two cuttings of alfalfa after harvesting them."

"What are Hidatsa beans?"

"It's a black bean that's native to this country. The Indians farmed them up in the Dakotas."

"I've never heard of them."

"I know. That's because the market isn't big right now, but it could be with the right ideas. And I'd be willing to help some with the cattle side of the business, too, if I need to do that to get this started. I've been working on recipes with the beans. I could make something for you tonight. We could invite Juan and Consuelo over for dinner and see what they think. Consuelo knows a lot about cooking with native produce."

"I guess we could do that."

"But you don't think it's a good idea. I mean the idea about growing beans."

The hopefulness begins to leave his face. I don't want it to leave, but I can't imagine a bean field over there. The soil isn't heavy enough for any beans that I know about. And I can't imagine Amleth working with the cattle either. I don't know if I want to imagine that.

"They grow a lot of beans out west by Alliance and some up north of the Niobrara, but we don't have much experience with them around here. Maybe we could contract with someone to grow them."

"I don't want to contract with anyone. I want to grow them myself so I know what's in them. It's just one field."

He's right. It's just one field, and by spring he will have forgotten all about it.

"All right, if you want to come back here after school gets out and plant some beans, it's okay with me."

"I'm not going back to school."

"What do you mean?"

"I'm not going back. There's no point to it anymore. I'll never be good enough to make a living playing the piano, and I'm not going to spend the rest of my life teaching a bunch of kids to do something I can't do myself. This is what I want to do."

Amleth sweeps his arm violently in front of him as if he wants to throw off all at once the futility of playing a piano for nearly twenty years and still not being good enough to make a living. The black horse jumps away from his arm. I'm caught off guard, lose my balance, and nearly tumble out of the saddle. For a second Amleth looks as if he will laugh, but he changes his mind when he looks at my face.

"You can't make a living off one field of beans either."

I've told him a hundred times not to make abrupt motions around the horses.

"Why not let me try? I'm not like you. I don't need much. I could build a little cabin here on the creek. George said he would help me."

"George? What does he know about building anything?"

"Plenty, if you give him a chance. A cabin here is something I've always wanted to do. Isn't there something that you've always wanted to do, something besides working all your life?"

"Sure, but sometimes you don't get to do those things."

"Why not?"

"I don't know, you just don't. This field will still be here after you've finished school."

"You never finished college either."

"Maybe I wish I had."

"So do it then, but leave me out of it."

"Jesus, Amleth, quitting school when you've only got one semester left, a cabin on the creek, beans in the alfalfa field. It sounds sort of crazy."

"If it was Rosario's idea, you wouldn't say it was crazy."

"Let's not get into that. Let's just forget about this whole thing until you finish school."

"I'm not going to finish school."

"Well, you're going to have to because we're not going to plant beans in that field until you do."

"Mom owns half this ranch, and she's got as much to say about it as you do. She's got more to say about it than Rosario does."

"No, she doesn't. If your mother wanted to have anything to say about this ranch or about these beans, she'd be here."

"You know why she's not here. She doesn't think there's anything for her to do. It was always your ranch, your cattle, your way—never ours. You pushed her away, but you're not going to do that to me."

"Keep your voice down. You're spooking my horse."

"What is it you want from me? Tell me. What is it?

"I want you to keep your voice down."

The black's ears are up, and I can feel his muscles tensing beneath me. I don't intend to be caught off guard again.

"You and that goddamn horse. Always talking about it like it's something special, like you're the only one good enough to ride it. It's not so special."

"If you knew anything at all about this ranch, you would know how special this horse is. He's made more money for this ranch than a hundred fields of beans would ever make."

"Maybe, maybe not, but I know one thing. You're not the only who can ride that horse."

"That's enough, Amleth."

"My name is Peder."

"Whoever you are, you leave this horse alone."

Amleth jerks Pecos's head up from the grass, kicks him in the flank, and speeds off across the culvert. The black takes it as a challenge. His nostrils flare, and he dances sideways against the tight rein I hold on him as Amleth and his horse cross the meadow and head up into the hills. For once I don't let the black horse go.

And so it ended like that—one sentence that stands between us like a river we'll never cross. I talked about money, but it wasn't money that made the black horse special. I don't know why I said that. Amleth's idea wasn't much different from the idea Rosario had to finish some of our cattle on the range and charge more for them than those we fed with corn. It was a lot like Horace's garden where he grows more than he knows what to do with. Most of all it was Amleth trying to find a place where he belonged. We all do that. I know I did. Hidatsa Black Beans, naturally grown in the pure soil of the Wamaduze Valley. It might have been a good idea if I had just let him finish, if he had left Rosario out of it, or Annie, if I had not felt that he was cursing me instead of the horse. It might have all been different if he had not saddled the black horse the next morning before anyone was awake. He never got up early on the ranch unless I made him.

Wind ripples disturb the water beneath Gloria. Farther ahead the full force of the wind is catching the current and backing it up into waves. Before I know it we reach the waves, and the wind pushes the brim of Juan's hat down over my face. The water feels heavier with each stroke of the paddle, and my body feels each stroke, each yard of progress. I am getting tired of this goddamn wind. It's beginning to blow earlier each day and harder.

I grip tighter this paddle of defiance, as Joe calls it, to prevent the wind from twisting it in my hands. Even so, a strong gust nearly rips it away, and I curse the wind as I used to curse the god of the prairie wind that never heard me either.

To hell with this wind, I say, either within the silence of my mind or out loud to the river. I'm losing track of the difference.

~ ~ ~

From the midst of green foliage on the right bank a movement like an arm in a white shirt beckons me. Immediately it disappears. I look away to clear my eyes. Now there is nothing—my imagination again or perhaps it was the egret taking flight. Then I distinguish among the trees a wood plank observation deck overlooking the river. There may have been a person after all, not a bird or a flight of imagination.

The map says Helena, Arkansas is to be found before the bridge that I see farther downriver, and I turn Gloria into an inlet just beyond the observation deck and paddle into the quiet water of a harbor. The sun beating down on me in the middle of the river makes me continually thirsty, and of the two water jugs I filled in Memphis yesterday, one is empty and the other half-empty. From my reading of the sun it is mid-afternoon—plenty of time to find water in the town and return to the river.

A single barge is tied up at the steep bank of the levy that protects the town from high water, and I land just beyond it. Two girls are running along the top of the levy and playing with a black and white spotted dog. They stop running when they see me. I wave to them. Cautiously they wave back. The dog isn't ready to stop playing, and it circles the girls and nips at their heels, distracting them momentarily, but I am a bigger distraction.

The dog has spotted me and bounds through the tall grass to greet me. It's a puppy and wants to play. When I put down the water containers to pet it, it nips at my hand and runs away, but it's beside me again as I climb the levy. The girls are still standing at the top.

"Your puppy likes to play."

"He's not ours," the smaller girl says. Like the older girl, she is wearing a white blouse and black skirt. "He's been here all week. Somebody dumped him."

"That's too bad."

"I want to take him home, but Natasha says we can't. Momma won't let us keep him."

Natasha is the older girl. Her black curly hair is pulled tight against her head and tied in back with a large white ribbon.

"What kind of boat is that?" Natasha asks. She is serious for her years, as Rosario was at that age.

"It's a kayak."

"Like the Eskimos have?"

"Yes."

"You going far in that kayak?"

"I hope so."

"How far?"

"To the ocean."

"Why don't you have yourself a big boat if you're going that far?"

"It's big enough for me."

"Not me," Natasha says. "I wouldn't go down that river unless I had a big boat. I'm going to get me a big boat someday."

"If I'm still out there, I hope you give me a ride."

Without laughing or even smiling at my joke, she takes her little sister's hand.

"Come on, Sissy," she says. "We got to do our homework."

A sidewalk follows the top of the levy and the girls stop at a bench a short distance away. Natasha helps her little sister hoist a book bag over her shoulders. She picks up her bag from the bench and slips her arms through the straps without assistance. The bags are heavy, and the slender girls lean forward to counterbalance the weight. The puppy runs after them, around them, but the girls can't run anymore.

"Go on, dog," Natasha says harshly. "Git!"

The puppy sits down on the sidewalk, scratches himself, and watches the girls leave. Then he remembers me and runs back to where I have been left on the sidewalk. He jumps up and tries to nip my hands again.

"All right, settle down."

Squatting down I scratch the puppy behind the ears. He sniffs my kayak shoes and licks them; sniffs my hand and licks it; puts his paws on top of my arm and tries to lick my face. I'll have none of that and stand up straight. His big paws mean that he will become a big dog someday, that he will lose his puppy charm and enthusiasm. He doesn't look like any distinguishable breed—a mongrel as far as I can tell.

The girls walk down the levy toward the commercial street below. The street and perhaps the town of Helena have hit hard times and there isn't much here—a record store, a radio station, a few empty storefronts, a burned-out warehouse farther down. A grain elevator at the mouth of the harbor is still in operation and is filling the barge. Dust rises from the chute conveying the grain. I can't tell what kind of grain it is.

The town may have hit hard times, but the levy has been made into a fine park with green grass and an overlook that surveys the inlet and the river. A huge music stage stands at the bottom of the levy. It has a gigantic roof sloping up toward the top of the levy. The levy could serve as the bleachers for thousands of people, but it's empty today now that the girls are gone—empty except for the puppy and me.

The nicest building in sight is at the end of the park, a renovated train station with the sign: DELTA MUSEUM—TOURIST INFORMATION. The puppy follows me down the steps toward the museum where I'm hoping I'll be able to refill the water jugs. He's behaving himself, and I don't have the heart to chase him away with a harsh voice like Natasha. I don't think Natasha had the heart for it either, but she did it anyway. She had to. I let him follow me to the door of the museum where he can't follow any farther. His sad eyes are the last I see of him as I close the door.

An elderly woman with a name tag that identifies her as Miss Sutherland greets me from behind an open window at the front office.

"Do you have a water fountain here where I can fill up my water jugs?"

"Let me do that for you," she says.

She takes the water jugs from me and disappears into a back room. A short time later she returns and places the two containers on top of the window counter.

"That's a big stage out there."

"That's for our Blues Festival in October," Miss Sutherland says. "We get a hundred thousand people who come and listen to the music. Oh, we have music all down the levy. You must come back for that if you like the blues, and who doesn't like the blues?"

"Yes. Who doesn't?"

"That weekend you can't find a place to stay anywhere close to here. But if you're looking for a nice place to stay tonight, we have some lovely bed and breakfasts just up the hill. You probably passed them when you came in."

She has a friendly smile and is attired in a light summer dress. For some reason I think of afternoon teas when I look at Miss Sutherland, or maybe mint juleps, although I don't know why. I've never been to an afternoon tea; never had a mint julep.

"I came in on the river, so I didn't see the bed and breakfasts."

"A towboat?" she asks.

"A canoe."

I'm thinking that a canoe will sound less strange than an Eskimo boat.

"In a canoe? Land's sake, are you telling me that you're going down that river in a canoe?"

"Not such a good idea?"

"It's a good idea if you want to get yourself killed. There are whirlpools out there that will suck you to China. I've heard of whole trees and barges getting sucked down, and nobody ever sees them again. I don't go anywhere near that river unless it's across the bridge, and I don't much like it then."

"You must have had a bad experience."

"I'm not foolish enough for that. I crossed the river once on a ferry when I was a young girl before they built the bridge, and that was enough for me. Here, you better sign our register. It might be the last record there is of you."

She doesn't look like she's kidding. I sign the register below other tourists, mostly from Arkansas and Mississippi, which is now just across the bridge that was built sometime after her girlhood.

"Nebraska?" she reads from the register. "You came all the way from up there in a canoe?"

"It's not a canoe actually. It's a sea kayak, and it's made to paddle through big waves and whirlpools and all that kind of stuff."

"So where do you sleep? Out in the wilderness, I suppose."

"Now and then I find civilization close to the river where I can spend the night in a bed."

"Hmmm," she murmurs as if she still doesn't believe any boat should be out in the river, but then she smiles. "Well, I hope you have a fine trip. It's too bad you can't stay in one of our lovely homes here, but I wouldn't recommend that you leave your boat unattended overnight. Not if you want to see it in the morning. You leave anything lying around here, and it's apt to just get up and walk off. I'm not supposed to say anything more about that, but there you have it."

"Thanks for warning me."

"We have a park across the harbor where you can camp, or there's a casino down by the bridge. They have nice rooms, and it's right on the river. They have good security, too. Your kayak would be fine there. Of course, that's in Mississippi, and I'm not supposed to tell you about that either."

Certainly she has forgiven me.

"But you do have to see this museum first. We're very proud of it."

Feeling that I've already gotten my money's worth of information before learning anything more, I put a few dollars in the collection box. But I do learn more. I always thought what was called the Mississippi Delta was at the end of the river, south of New Orleans where it enters the Gulf, but I'm in the delta already and have been for some time. The Delta Blues came from here, from the fields and towns along Highway 61, where the land is rich and the people are poor, as the inscription says beneath the enlarged black and white photograph of black slaves working a cotton field. Miss Sutherland is right. Given the state of my ignorance, I am lucky to have made it this far.

For millions of years the river flooded this land so that there is now a hundred feet of alluvial topsoil across the delta. It is a staggering depth compared to the few inches in the sandhills where I began, ground so fragile that it would become a desert with misuse or a slight change of climate so that it wouldn't be fit even for the buffalo and the wolf.

On one wall are photographs of the 1927 flood: people sitting on roofs of houses, whole towns under water, crops ruined, poverty deepened. Now I understand Miss Sutherland's apprehension, her sense of the river as an ominous threat, a looming disaster. I finish the loop through the museum, humbled by my ignorance. Miss Sutherland is waiting.

"So what did you think?" she asks.

"I think I now understand why you build your levies so tall."

"There's no levy we build that will hold that river. Someday we're going to find that out all over again. There are going to be rains up north and rains down here like the days of Noah, and this river is going to take back all that we've done to hold it in. You just wait and see."

"I hope those rains don't come this week."

"Not this week," Miss Sutherland says. "We're supposed to have dry weather all week. We need rain; we're praying for rain."

"Don't pray too hard."

"If it starts raining, you better get yourself off that river, especially if you see trees disappearing. You hear?"

Miss Sutherland smiles her most hospitable southern smile.

The moment I step outside the puppy is back at my feet. I had forgotten all about him. I am tempted to reach down and pet him, but that was a mistake I shouldn't repeat. Even without encouragement the puppy follows me up the stairs to the top of the levy and down through the grass on the other side, while I pretend to ignore him. If another child would come, he would forget me and my inattention. Where are they? All the children can't be home doing their homework like Sissy and Natasha.

The puppy watches me store the water jugs. He springs away as I push Gloria's bow into the water but is back as I settle into the cockpit. His eyes are on a plane with mine now. His wagging tail wiggles his whole body.

"Ah, puppy, I can't take you with me."

Amleth fed every stray dog that wandered onto the ranch, and they followed him around as if he were the Pied Piper. Bad luck for the puppy that Amleth isn't along. Against my good judgment, but according to Miss Sutherland I have none anyway, I rub the puppy behind his upraised ears, and he stretches forward so that his paws are pushing on the top of the waist skirt. Gloria slips away from the bank, and I let her go. I have to. The puppy's front paws splash into the water, but his hind legs remain on the bank.

Without looking back I paddle down the inlet toward the river. From the edge of my vision I watch the puppy bounding along on land keeping up with Gloria. Soon I'll reach the river and head out into deep water, and he'll run out of room. Sissy will be back tomorrow, and maybe she'll find a way to convince her mother to let her keep him.

There is a splash, and he's swimming toward me.

"No! Go back! Go back!"

He keeps swimming, and I raise the paddle over my head.

"Heeeah! Heeeah!"

The shout works with cattle and horses but apparently not with dogs. I could paddle out of his reach, but he's already losing steam. Amleth would never forgive me if I let the dog drown. His paws scrape Gloria's side. He's beginning to sense his folly and turns back toward the bank. Then he reverses course and comes back to me. He looks desperate now.

"You dumb dog."

I grab the skin on the back of his neck and lift his head and front paws onto the taut waist skirt in front of me. He's not content with that position and scratches for all he's worth to get his hind legs out of the water. If he doesn't tip us over, he'll rip the waist skirt to shreds, so I dump him back into the water. Then I pull the waist skirt free of the combing, lift him up, and stuff him into the cockpit between my legs. When he realizes that he's safe, he feels obliged to thank me with his tongue. I am not able to fend him off as well as I could on land, but land is where I need to get or we'll both get dumped into the water.

Despite his exuberance I find a way to paddle, and he settles down as he becomes interested in this new form of transportation. Soon his front paws are planted firmly on the deck the way the dogs on the ranch leaned out the bed of the pickup or out of the cab window when they were with Amleth. Now that we're not going to capsize, I begin to see the humor of the episode. If Miss Sutherland were watching, she would know for sure that I'm never going to make it.

Rather than paddling back to the levy, I head toward the park on the other side. He might realize his mistake and look for a safer companion once we get there. If so I can still make some progress before dark. But it doesn't look hopeful. Whenever the puppy turns to look at my face, which he does often, he doesn't look like he plans to go anywhere.

When Gloria noses onto the bank, the puppy jumps out. He doesn't take off running as I ought to hope he would. He is happy to be on land, but he's not going anywhere. His foolishness makes me smile. I can't help it. Fools love company, they say.

Since it doesn't look like I'm meant to get out of Helena today, I may as well camp here. The puppy follows me as I scout out a suitable place among the trees for the tent. I know I should leave the puppy alone, but it's hard to resist patting him on the head now and then. I find a clearing that opens out to the river where there's a breeze that might keep the mosquitoes at bay.

"What do you think? Is this good enough?"

It's hard not to talk to him, too, since he pays attention to everything I say.

After I set up the tent, roll out the sleeping bag, carry Gloria over to the campsite, I feed him a can of chicken I intended to have for tomorrow's lunch and some of the freeze-dried rice teriyaki I make for myself. Then reality sinks in. He's good company while I set up camp, and I can't help but enjoy him as we eat our dinners and watch the river flow by, but tomorrow I'll have to find a way to leave him behind. Nothing else makes sense.

At dusk the mosquitoes force me into the tent. The puppy is ready to follow me, but I zip him out, hoping he'll be gone by morning. Surely he'll be gone by then. As I lie in the sleeping bag with the flashlight propped on my forehead, I try to read *Huckleberry Finn*. He and Jim are also in Arkansas. Dreaded Mississippi and the cruelest of the slave traders are on the opposite bank. I do my best to concentrate on the story, but I find that I'm listening for the dog. Has he left yet? Will he make it easy for both of us and leave on his own?

A boy in a white long-sleeved shirt is running through a field of beans and corn. I have trouble keeping up with him. The bean pods are full and ready to pick, and the vines spiral up the corn stalks. A black dog with big white spots runs past me, catches up with the boy, and dances circles around him. You can't help but laugh at the dog's exuberance. I haven't heard the boy laugh for so long, but when he sees that I'm watching him, he stops laughing. "Git!" he shouts at the dog. The dog doesn't understand why he has to leave. He whimpers and scratches the dry corn stalk beside the boy.

The flashlight has fallen from my forehead onto the tent floor and is focusing a beam of light onto the tent wall. For a moment I am suspended between consciousnesses and sleep until I hear the dog whimpering and scratching the tent at the spot where the light is fixed.

–Ah, shit.

If I don't chase him away now, I'll never be able to do it. I kneel beside the tent door, unzip it along the bottom and up the semicircle to the top until it flops open, and in he bounds.

~ ~ ~

When I unzip the tent door in the morning, Horatio runs directly to Gloria and pees on her bow. At least he didn't do it inside the tent. Afterward he circles around the campsite, enjoying his freedom. I'm still holding on to the possibility that he will decide to leave. But the circumferences of his circles become increasingly smaller as I pack the gear into bags and take down the tent, and smaller still after I carry Gloria back to the water on the quiet harbor side of the peninsula and begin loading the hatches. When all is loaded, I sit down on the bank beside Gloria and wonder how I can leave with Horatio sitting on the bank beside me.

His name came to me in a dream. It is a pretentious name for a dog, but maybe dogs are the only creatures that should have pretentious names. Horatio drops the stick he has been chewing and edges closer so that his head is over my lap and his body is touching mine. He has a black spot that seems to cover one eye like a patch, except that neither eye is covered and both are watching me.

I reopen the rear hatch, reopen a waterproof bag, and take out a coiled nylon cord. From it I cut off a piece twenty feet long and tie one end around Horatio's neck with a loop and bowline that won't allow the rope to tighten around his neck and strangle him. The other I tie around a young sapling close to the water's edge. He puts up a big fuss when I walk away, but I can't have him following me into town. He's likely to get run over. What I should do is take him back to the levy and tie him up there for Sissy and Natasha. That's what I should do.

Instead I walk along the peninsula until I come to a dirt road that turns to asphalt and enters the main street of Helena. On the main street I find a small grocery store. There I buy the smallest bag of dry dog food they have, a few cans of dog food to supplement the dry pellets, a box of Milk Bones, and a flea collar. On the way back to my campsite I come across a discarded piece of plywood about two feet square, and a new idea comes to me.

Restraint of any kind is foreign to Horatio, and he doesn't understand that the rope will allow him to go only so far. When he sees me, he tests the length and strength of the rope again and again and knocks himself down each time. He will have to learn restraint if my plan is to work. If it doesn't, I'll be taking Horatio back to the levy or maybe farther into the town.

On the bow of the kayak where the maps have been, I lay the plywood over the elastic shock cords, cut two lengths from the nylon cord that no longer restrains Horatio, wrap each length around the hull of the kayak and over the plywood, and cinch it tight with tie-down knots. I cut down a sapling with the hatchet, make wedges from the soft green wood, and stuff two wedges under the plywood on each side of the curved bow. Then I pick up Horatio and place him on top of the plywood.

"Stay."

Horatio's ears, one black and one white, droop when I push him down on the plywood.

"Stay."

For additional emphasis I point my finger at him, and he stays until I move away. Then he jumps off the platform and wags his tail vigorously in enjoyment of the new game. I put him back on the plywood, repeat the commands with voice and finger, and continue to repeat them as I back away. He stays until I stop repeating.

After much pushing, nudging, and commanding from me, he settles down on the platform. It is barely large enough to accommodate him. With the bow rope I pull Gloria along the muddy bank of the inlet to test his reaction. He understands that the game has changed and eyes the water warily. Perhaps he remembers his narrow escape the day before.

It's time to move on to the next phase, and I pull Gloria into the bank and straddle the cockpit. Horatio stands up on his two-foot square platform, but I push him back down. Slowly I paddle along the bank of the quiet inlet. Horatio turns sideways so that he can watch me. His weight affects the balance of the kayak, and I'll have to learn to adjust along with Horatio if my plan is to work. When I reach forward and pat his head, he believes it is a sign to crawl into the cockpit with me. I push him back onto the platform before he can get more than his front paw into the opening.

We practice through the morning, my plan swinging from imbecilic to ingenious and back again. I jiggle the kayak with my braced knees to simulate turbulence, and Horatio stays on. We land, we shove off from the bank; land, shove off. Horatio even gets on the platform on his own and I think his training has turned the corner, but then he jumps headfirst into the water before we reach land. Nevertheless, little by little, Horatio is becoming more comfortable on the platform, and I am becoming more comfortable with him there. Finally I put on the waist skirt, stretch its elastic edge over the cockpit combing, and shove off from the bank. I hope Miss Sutherland isn't watching.

After entering the river I stay close to the right bank although this keeps us within the shipping lane. I'm hoping that the shipping lane will cross to the other side before a barge forces us out. We're going faster now, and Horatio lifts his head from where it had settled between his paws.

"It's okay, Horatio. Lie down."

Yes, I've called him his name, but that's not the reason he's looking at me. The change in the current, the expanse of the water concerns him. He wasn't planning on this when he got up in the morning and peed on the kayak. I don't suppose dogs plan on anything. And I have given him a name without his consent and have said it out loud. I'm tempted to reach forward and brush over the short fur on top of his head so that he will forgive me, but he might misinterpret the gesture. Instead I point to the platform.

"Down."

One thing is clear: I haven't thought this idea through very carefully. If a barge does come, I'll have to move out of the shipping lane. And if Horatio sees the strength of the water against one of those red buoys out there, if he hears the sound, sees the buoy swerving back and forth under the pressure of the current, there is no telling what he might do. I let him inside the tent during the night because I had a bad dream, but I didn't think about what would happen next or how he could complicate this trip. I had given up all responsibility for the ranch, for the business, put everything that I needed into this one skinny kayak—everything I need—and now Horatio is sitting in front of me, looking at me, wondering, surely, what I have done.

"I could live in an oyster shell and count myself king of the universe but that I have bad dreams."

Horatio raises his ears, and his head follows his ears. I reach forward and smooth down both with my hand as he licks my fingers.

We continue along the right bank, Arkansas rather than Mississippi. The shipping lane moves across to the left, and we have escaped calamity through the first stretch. To give Horatio a break and to check on the platform, I land on a sandbar where I cinch the two ropes a little tighter. Horatio is thrilled by the solid ground and races back and forth until his nose picks up something in the sand. For a moment he digs furiously, but soon he is off again. Whenever he slows, I clap my hands and pretend that I'm going to chase him. But I don't even try.

When it's time to leave, I call him. He thinks I'm still playing and won't come, or perhaps he's had enough of the river and the restraints of the platform. I push Gloria into the water. He stops running and looks at me from some distance down the sandbar.

"Come on."

He doesn't come, and I sit down in the cockpit. The bottom of the kayak lodges in the sand. I pat the top of the platform. Still he doesn't come. I call his name, and at the same time push Gloria free with my hands. Horatio dashes into the shallow water and jumps up onto the platform. He circles once and settles down with his black patch facing me.

"Did you think I was going to leave you?"

Horatio nips playfully at my fingers as I ruffle the short hair on the back of his head.

"Amleth would never forgive me."

Our luck of avoiding barges is about to end. Ahead where the shipping lane moves back to the right bank, a towboat pushing a huge array of barges is heading toward us. The bank is heavily defiled with concrete riprap and provides no possible landing. The shipping lane is wide, and perhaps the barge will move out from the bank toward the center. I hope it moves out. While waiting for the captain to decide where he will go, I paddle slowly and nervously sing a lullaby that I haven't sung for a long time. *You take a stick of bamboo, you take a stick of bamboo, you take a stick of bamboo, you throw it in the river.*

I watch for the left side of the left front barge, but I don't see it. The barge is not turning away from the bank. Humming the old song about bamboo, hoping that Horatio will find it as soothing as Amleth did, I edge farther out into the river.

Why am I clinging to the right bank? Should anything happen, I won't be able to get to it until after the barge passes, and the cement boat captain warned me not to get caught between the bank and a barge. I may as well head straight across the river and get out of the way. At the moment of decision I look back and see what I should have seen much earlier. Another barge is coming down the river. Probably there is time to cross before it catches up, except the shipping lane is unusually wide in this spot, and the approaching barge has taken a position on the far left side. Two blasts shout out from his horn. He will pass on the left. That was what Phil told me back at the cement plant. One blast, turn right; two, turn left. Or was it the other way around?

Horatio stands up on the platform when he hears the horn, and I command him to lie back down. He ignores my command. Although there is time to push him down before the passing of either barge, my hands are frozen to the paddle as I try to maneuver us between the two barges. There is room for all three of our vessels, but not enough room for comfort. Horatio barks at the unaccustomed noise of the engines. The lead barge heading upriver glides by with barely a ripple, but the towboat propeller behind is churning up a tremendous wake.

Horatio watches the wake of the upriver towboat coming toward us. I'm watching two wakes, one on each side. At the last moment I turn Gloria to face the bigger wake on the right. Again I command Horatio to lie down, again he doesn't, and now I don't have time to release the paddle. The wake that he doesn't see joins the wake coming from the right and violently churns the river beneath us. Horatio loses his balance, dances for a moment on the platform, and tumbles into the water. Waves splash up from the underside of the platform, which gives them a grip on the kayak that they wouldn't normally have. I flail the paddle across the water to keep Gloria from turning over. Horatio is swimming alongside, bumping against the hull but unable to get back on top.

The biggest waves pass us and the turmoil dissipates quickly in the deep channel of the wide river. Horatio and Gloria float along at the same speed, and for better or worse, he has decided to stay with Gloria and me rather than set off for land. When the danger of capsizing has passed, I pull the waist skirt free of the combing, reach down, grab the skin behind Horatio's neck, and hoist him into the cockpit. We're getting quite good at this. He doesn't even seem particularly worried. I push him farther into the cockpit and sternly command him to lie down. He would rather keep his head above the rim. I don't blame him. We've had enough of this foolishness in the shipping lanes, and I set off directly for the Mississippi bank as fast as I can paddle. Nevertheless the current sweeps us south for a long distance before we come to shallow water. One thing is certain: I haven't thought this through very well.

We land at a small clearing in the trees, and Horatio scrambles to get out. I give him the boost he needs, and he sets about exploring the boundaries of the clearing. Maybe he's had enough of the river and me and is looking for a way to escape. But he's back, sniffing Gloria and peeing on the same spot on her bow as he did earlier in the morning. I untie the ropes securing the platform and toss the plywood some distance from the kayak. Horatio runs over to it, smells the perimeter of the wood, and lies down on top of it.

I unfasten the straps that hold down the two hatches and pull off the covers. In particular I study the larger opening of the rear hatch where I remove the bags immediately below the opening and shove the rest of the gear as far back into the hatch as it will go.

"Come here."

I pat the top of the kayak.

Horatio plays along with me until he realizes that I intend to stuff him into the hatch. His rear legs go into motion as if he's climbing a ladder, but I maneuver him inside anyway. When he discovers he can look over the edge by sitting upright, he decides that it isn't so bad and licks my hand. It's better than the stupid platform and better than the front hatch, which would take in water from waves that wash across the bow. His weight will be lower, too, and he won't get dumped out if the kayak rocks a bit. And if he jumps, we've gotten pretty good at mid-river rescues. This time I'm going to think it through.

Some stuff has to go. With Horatio in the hatch there isn't enough room to put everything back. I lift Horatio out, empty both hatches, and lay the bags in a long line on the bank. First to go are two pairs of long underwear, three pairs of heavy socks, and a fleece jacket. I consolidate the remaining light-weight clothes into a single clothing bag and toss the other bag on top of the discarded clothing.

"Progress, Horatio. We're making progress."

I don't need the jar of instant coffee or the two packages of now-crumbled Ritz Crackers I've been carrying since I bought them somewhere on the Missouri or three melted chocolate bars. Nor do I need the metal food bowl or the metal cup. I can eat out of the pan and use the cup on the thermos. The foil packages of freeze dried food can be stuffed into small crevices rather than being packed in a bag, and another bag is dispensed with.

Eventually I find room in the hatches for the remaining stuff and for Horatio, who comes down to inspect the progress as I jam the last bag into the front hatch. He takes the opportunity to lick my face, and I scruff up the fur on his head.

All the discarded supplies I stuff into the discarded dry bags and loop the ends of the bags around a low-hanging branch of a willow tree.

"Okay, Horatio, last chance. If you don't want to go with me, this is the time to speak up."

With those words to an uncomprehending dog, I discover within myself how much I would hate to see him go. I haven't been attached to an animal since I was a boy, and Joe and I took Snafu along with us on our river explorations. After my idea with the platform, Horatio shouldn't trust me at all. But he does. He allows me to pick him up and put him in the rear hatch without a fuss and seems quite satisfied there.

We stay in the shallow slack water along the bank. It has a sand beach that stretches for miles. Miss Sutherland was right about the need for rain, for the river is low. I expected it to be higher in the spring. The topography on the Mississippi side is like the sandhills in Nebraska. Tall dunes have formed there, and some of the dunes must be fifty feet high.

Although our progress down the river is slow, Gloria feels lighter than she did before, lighter than the small reduction of weight can account for. Perhaps it's the improved balance of having Horatio in the rear hatch rather than on the platform in front of me. I feel his nose against my back as he stretches forward with his front paws upon the deck, and I strain to twist around enough in the cockpit to see him.

"How are you doing back there?"

It is absurd to talk to a dog, but Horatio doesn't mind. Besides I talked plenty to the black horse. Annie told me that if I would talk to Amleth with the same voice that I used with the black, I would get a lot farther with him. Her advice was always sound and sensible. Maybe if she had been wrong now and then, it would have been easier to accept.

From the maps that are once again in front of me, I see that the channel and the shipping lanes will be changing to our side of the river in a few miles. I don't want to try another crossing today. I like this place. I like the sand dunes and the open ground.

Horatio springs from the hatch as soon as we land and races up and down the dunes while I drag Gloria to higher ground. I pitch the tent among a patch of thorn trees from where we can see the river stretching out below us. The sand shimmers in the late afternoon sun.

I decide to call Joe and tell him about Horatio. He'll laugh when I describe the stupid platform I built. The cell phone isn't in the deck bag where I usually keep it. I could search the other bags, but it wouldn't do any good because I know where it is. It's back in Memphis, probably not on the desk beside the room phone where I was charging the battery, but somewhere there. We're getting rid of more stuff than I expected, but that's how it goes. Still I miss the sound of Joe's voice and his cackling laugh.

"So it's just you and me now."

Horatio cocks his head like the picture of the dog before the old phonograph. I swear he's listening.

When we settle down to eat, I open a can of dog food and dump it into the larger of the cooking pots that I never use. I eat the freeze-dried stew directly from the foil pouch and drink directly from the water bottle. It's more efficient all the way around.

Inside the tent I lie in my open sleeping bag with my head propped up against the last remaining clothes bag and the flashlight lying flat on my forehead. Huckleberry and Jim have met up with some bad actors across the river in Arkansas. Horatio looks up from his spot in the tent where he is chewing on a willow stick. Is that me laughing? It has to be.

When I turn off the light and settle deeper into the sleeping bag, I am reminded of a saying my father reserved for the end of long days when we worked hard but nothing went right.

"Well, Horatio," I say in the darkness of our tent, "didn't do much today, but we'll give her hell tomorrow."

~~~

As soon as I unzip the tent door, Horatio runs down the sand dune, takes a drink from the river, runs back up the sand dune, pees on Gloria, and is back with his nose in the tent waiting for me. I finish buttoning my shirt and reach for my pants that are in a roll at the end of the sleeping pad.

"Easy enough for you to get ready. You're a dog."

Horatio moves aside as I toss out all the bags from inside the tent. Now the tent is nearly empty except for me and all the sand that's scattered around the floor. There is more now with Horatio, and the sand gets into everything.

I try to sweep it out the door with my hand, but it's like herding fleas into a jar. With my feet outside and my butt inside, I pull the wet kayak shoes over wet socks, envying Horatio's simple self-sufficiency.

As I pull up the tent stakes, I discover than I can pick up the whole tent without it collapsing. I shake it out, and sand drops out the open door onto the sandbar where it belongs. These small efficiencies give me more pleasure than they probably should.

I remove three granola bars from the food bag and give one to Horatio who carries it down the sand dune in case I change my mind and want it back. I seal up the bag and stuff all the bags and gear into the hatches.

"Are you ready to go?"

Horatio looks at me and wags his tail. Who am I trying to kid? He's been ready for the last half hour.

Horatio trails behind us as I drag Gloria down to the water. No longer does he climb the invisible ladder to resist being placed inside the hatch. I pick up the paddle, push Gloria into the river until she floats, straddle the deck, lower myself into the cockpit, dangle my feet in the water to rinse off the sand and mud, bring them inside, stretch the waist skirt over the cockpit combing, and finally, finally dip paddle into water as we begin our day in the river.

The river turns so that we head directly into the sun, and in the glare of light on water I think I see something, a flash like a paddle reflecting the sun. But of course there is nothing—a mirage caused by water vapor rising from the river or a tin can or bottle reflecting the light.

"You didn't see anything, did you, Horatio?"

When I look back over my shoulder, Horatio raises his ears alertly. He perches his front paws on the deck and leans toward me. Gloria drifts sideways in the current.

"Down there."

I point toward the sun and pull off my sunglasses, which only makes the glare worse. Unexpectedly through the glare comes the vision of a small child laughing at Horatio's funny face, at the black and white spots surrounding his eyes that make him look as if he's wearing a mask of one color or the other.

When I was a child, my brother and I would sneak Snafu into the house when it was too cold to go outside and play. Dogs weren't allowed in the house. That was a ranch rule started by my grandfather, continued by my father, and finally me. Nevertheless when our father left the house on those cold days, my mother permitted my brother and me to bring Snafu inside as long we got him out before our father came back. Annie and Amleth continued the conspiracy and extended it even to warm weather. My father and I knew that the rule was being broken and we didn't much care, so why couldn't we just let it go? Dogs, like everything else on the ranch, were supposed to be useful. If a dog was no good for work, the father was supposed to take it out to a blowout away from the house and shoot it. I did, more than once, so how can I explain how this masked puppy sort of slipped into my tent and into the backseat? Even now I think I owe someone an explanation. Maybe I'll have to teach him to do something useful.

"Horatio, what do you suppose you can do?"

When I twist around to get Horatio's response, I discover that he has one of the hatch straps in his mouth.

"Hey! Let go of that thing!"

I tap his snout and pull the strap away. He has nearly chewed it through. What should I expect? The straps are dangling there beside him, too enticing to pass up. Besides it's only one. If I ever put the hatch cover back in place, there are still two more to hold it.

"The next time we stop, I'll find you a stick to chew on."

But I don't have to wait. There are plenty of sticks floating in the river. I fish one out that seems about the right size and hand it back to Horatio. He takes it in his mouth but doesn't know what to do with it. It's too big, more burden than toy, and I take it back and toss it away. Horatio rises on his hind legs and paws the deck as if he's going to jump into the water after the stick.

"Whoa, stay there! Stay!"

Horatio stretches his neck toward me and touches my hand. I have to stop giving him confusing signals. I've never been around an animal so eager to please.

The day is turning out to be another hot one. The river, at least, offers some relief as the breeze passes over it. Horatio rests his chin on top of the deck and watches the water go by. I watch it, too, for when I look too far downstream, it seems to take forever to get anywhere. It's better to paddle without thinking. Forget everything and just paddle.

About midday I paddle to the bank so that we can have a break. Horatio jumps out the moment Gloria bumps the sand, splashes ashore, and disappears from sight before I can even get out of the cockpit.

"Horatio!"

He races back past Gloria and me along the sandy bank, skids to a stop some distance beyond us, and retraces his footsteps back. Running gives him a simple joy that pleases me more than any useful work I can imagine him doing. When he slows his pace, I clap my hands and off he goes again. Because we are alone, I can laugh without reservation.

Finding a stick the right size for fetching, I wind up and throw it as far as I can. A sharp pain surges through my shoulder and reminds me that the simple joy of throwing something hard is no longer mine. Horatio makes me forget the pain as he races headlong for the stick. He overruns it, slides to a stop, and dashes back. He picks it up with his teeth and looks back at me.

"Bring it here."

When he doesn't move, I clap my hands. He drops the stick and runs back to me.

I bring out the lunch bag from the front hatch and remove the map case from under the shock cords. It's time to add new maps. Horatio chews on the Milk Bone I give him but is more interested in the peanut butter and crackers that I'm eating. When I give him a cracker loaded with peanut butter, he swallows it whole. Some of the peanut butter clings to the roof of his mouth. He stretches his neck as if that will help get it down his throat. It seems to work, and he steps onto my lap looking for more. I push him back but don't bother to scold him.

"Do you know that we're going to the ocean?"

Horatio cocks his ears to listen as the black horse did when George and I talked to him. In competitions George would talk the black through the entire routine. Maybe that was the reason they didn't win every time, given that it was an unfair advantage to have a horse that understood Lakota or a

Lakota who could speak horse. My conversations with the black were limited to English, but he listened anyway.

Are you ready?

We're beside the river, and there is not a single building or car or person in sight. His ears swivel back toward me, and I feel him gathering himself, his body rippling with energy. He blows air through his nostrils and prances sideways as I press my legs against his flanks. *Ready?* Then I give him the reins and let him go. He explodes like a racehorse leaving the gate, and I lean forward and grab his mane as he runs along the river. It feels like flying.

Horatio paws the river maps I have in my lap. Yes, Horatio, we're beside the river now. My days of flying are over. Horatio lays his head on the map on top of Scrubgrass Bend and closes his eyes as my hand strokes across them. It took a long time before the black trusted me enough to let me do that. It was the only way I could get him to stop looking at me. A horrible odor rises from the maps, and I know it's not me.

"Jesus, Horatio. No more peanut butter for you."

I push his head off my lap and stand up. My left knee pops, and my back is stiff. My shoulder hurts, and I'm not sure that I can lift my right arm above my head. I give it a try. It catches half way. I'll have to throw the damn sticks underhanded.

From the sandy beach I gather a couple chewable sticks and toss them into Horatio's hatch. Then I pull out bags looking for the one where I've stored repair supplies. Horatio joins me at the hatch and peers inside. It is the duct tape I want and finally find.

After rolling up the chewed strap I wrap duct tape around it, roll up the remaining straps and wrap them in tape, too. I tap the last taped strap and look at Horatio.

"Leave these alone if you don't want to swim to the ocean."

He licks my hand, but I've already forgiven him. I'm only pretending to sound stern in case someone might be listening.

Scrubgrass Bend accepts the force of the river and holds it on the right bank past the mouth of the White River, past the mouth of the Old White River where the prominence of Montgomery Point sends the current toward the opposite bank. We pass close to the last of the red buoys where the water surges noisily around it as we leave it behind. Far ahead, barely within sight, is the barrel shape of the first green buoy. The shipping lane seems interminably wide, but finally we reach the invisible line of green buoys that mark the left side of the channel. A tow and barge are heading toward us and preparing to navigate the corner.

"Hold on, Horatio. We've got a barge coming."

I turn around in the cockpit to make sure that Horatio has heard me. What I see makes my stomach turn sour, takes the air right out of my lungs, and leaves me without the will to bring more air back in. Horatio is gone. How could he jump out without me hearing it? Did I frighten him by passing too close to the red buoy? I turn Gloria around and paddle frantically into the current, hoping without hope that I will see him in time. The current is too strong, and I make little headway against it. He could have jumped miles back.

"Horatio!"

It's foolish to call for him, but I can't help it. I yell his name again as loud as I can.

Something causes me to look back, some sense of not being alone. Horatio's black and white spotted face rises above the open hatch where he blinks sleepily in the all too hot mid-day sun.

~ ~ ~

Horatio is getting used to the front hatch. Because the opening is smaller, he can't turn as freely as he could in the back hatch, but he's learned to turn below the deck and not within the elliptical opening. We stay farther away from the shipping lanes to avoid the barge wakes—except when the shipping lanes cross from one side of the river to the other, and we cross like a counterweight in opposition to the current.

Occasionally a wave washes across the bow, but it doesn't bother Horatio unless he's sleeping on the floor of the kayak. Then the splash of water is a rude awakening. I can't help but laugh when he pops his head out of the hatch after being doused with a wave. Sorry, I tell him, but I can't help laughing.

If Joe or Juan had told me that I should take a dog along for company, I would have thought they were crazy. But Horatio is good company, even better than Gloria. He gives me something to do at night besides reading *Huckleberry Finn*. I wonder if I will ever finish the book. Now when a dream wakes me, it's strangely comforting to feel Horatio tucked in against my feet or see his black and white face when I turn on the flashlight. I don't believe Amleth would mind if he knew I had found a companion—at least not a dog. He would like Horatio, too. I am more honest with Horatio than I was with people, than I am with myself.

"One time I went up to Minnesota where Amleth was going to college to hear him play in a concert. He didn't know I was coming, didn't tell me about it. Annie did."

Horatio swivels around in the hatch and looks at me. I swear he's listening.

"I rented a car at the airport and drove to a beautiful old concert hall in downtown St. Paul. My seat was at the very back of the balcony. At first I thought it was a poor seat, but I discovered that it wasn't. From there I could see the whole audience. When Amleth played Moonlight Sonata, there was a stillness that came over the hall as if no one dared to breathe. For once I understood all the work it took to play that one piece of music, to hold a crowd of people in silence, and I was proud of him. Annie was in the audience, probably close to the front. He would know where she was because everything he played was for her. She would know that, too.

"I called him the next morning, not early, because he never woke up early. I always had to wake him up on the ranch. He should have been able to set an alarm and get up by himself, but he slept through every alarm. How can you sleep through an alarm?"

Horatio rises up on his back legs and stretches toward me with his head and front paws. I rest the paddle across the cockpit and scratch him behind his upraised ears. He is tempted to nip my fingers but restrains himself. Instead he cocks his head to redirect the location of the scratching and licks the palm of my hand. I pick up the paddle again and stare over Horatio's head.

It should be an easy thing to pick up the telephone and call your son, but I didn't even know what name to call him. He wanted to be called Peder, but I always thought of him as Amleth. All right, I'll call him Peder. I didn't come up here to fight over a name. I came up here to listen to him play the piano, and now I want to tell him how proud I am. But I can't tell him about my pride because he will assume that I'm thinking about myself instead of him, about my reaction not his skill. I'll tell him that I listened to his music, and it was beautiful. Not that I thought it was beautiful, but simply that it was beautiful.

He was surprised when he heard my voice, surprised that I called him Peder, surprised that I was in town and wanted to see him.

Mom is here.

I know. She told me about the concert.

She told you?

Yes, I was there last night.

Why didn't you tell me you were coming?

I don't know. Why didn't you tell me?

I didn't think you would come. I didn't want you to feel that you had to come.

Why wouldn't I come? I went to every concert he played in grade school and high school, from the very first Christmas program in the country school when he was five years old and playing *Away in a Manger* on the school piano that was never in tune. Why would he think I wouldn't come now?

We are approaching a red buoy, and I tilt Gloria to the left with my right knee and paddle a few strokes on the left side. She edges off to the right, and we slip by with fifteen feet to spare. Horatio pricks up his ears, watches the buoy flop back and forth in the current, but lets it pass without comment.

What are you doing today? Do you want to have lunch or dinner?

Mom and I already made plans.

That's all right. Just because your mother and I don't live in the same place doesn't mean that we don't get along.

Mom and I are going to meet for lunch at a small restaurant close to the campus.

Good. I'll join you there.

Annie called me and told me that I should meet Amleth alone so that he and I could talk. 'We talk. Why don't all three of us get together like we used to?' She was glad I had come, but I should talk to Amleth alone.

"Amleth and I could talk. We just didn't agree with each other. If I said the horse was black, he would say that the color was more of an indigo. If I said the eyes were brown, he would say that they had some green in them, too. Maybe he was only trying to say, 'I'm different from you.' We're all different, Horatio. Just remember that."

Horatio responds to his name. It's a smart dog that knows his name within a few days. Once again he stretches his black and white face toward me across the maps, expecting me to put down the paddle and scratch him behind the ears. Not even Amleth could disagree with me about this dog's colors. They are as black and white as they can be.

"It was money that we disagreed about mostly, but I wonder now if that was just what came out. Annie and I paid his tuition, which was more than either of us got when we went to college. There was no reason I could see that he couldn't work and earn his board and room, but he didn't work much at college, unless you counted playing the piano. If he needed more money, he could come home in the summer and work on the ranch, but he didn't want to do that either. The dust aggravated his allergies, and he was afraid that the machines might damage his hands. Most importantly, as he told me last year, he refused to participate in work that contributed to the slaughter of animals. He didn't seem to mind taking the money from it, though. He couldn't understand why I was so stingy. He argued that my grandfather helped me get started with the ranch, so I wasn't as independent as I claimed. 'Someday,' he said, 'you'll be gone, and if you haven't sold the ranch by then I'm going to donate it to the Nature Conservancy.' 'Someday,' I told him, 'I'm giving the ranch to the Mexicans. They've worked for it.'"

But that was another time, and now I had heard him play, and I wasn't meeting him to talk about giving the ranch to the Mexicans or about money. Annie probably gave him all that he needed anyway.

Horatio, bored with my oration and no longer expecting me to put down the paddle, disappears into the hatch and emerges facing downriver. Or maybe it's the tone in my voice that turns him away. It often had that effect on Amleth.

Amleth was waiting for me in the restaurant, and this time I wasn't going to make him turn away. This time I was only going to tell him how well he played.

Last night was like watching George with the black horse, only it was you and the piano understanding each other, you knowing when to lean just a little to signal the piano what you wanted, and the piano responding. It was beautiful to watch, beautiful to hear.

A look of sadness comes across Amleth's face, and I know that it's happening again. One of us is just catching up with the other in time for the other to change direction or turn back. We can never get started at the same time or in the same place.

I'll never be as good as George is with the black horse.

He didn't call it indigo.

Why not? If you need to go somewhere else or take more time, your mother and I will help you.

He turns his hands over so that he is looking at the fingertips that touched the piano keys. I never noticed before that his hands are bigger than mine. His fingers are long and delicate like my father's fingers. My father should have been a piano player instead of a rancher.

I need more talent, not time.

You were so good last night, Amleth.

Amleth looks at me with another strange look, and I realize what I called him.

I meant to say Peder. You were so good last night, Peder.

I'm a good pianist in a good music department in a good university, but there are two others here who are better. They don't work as hard, but they're still better. And the difference between the best of them and me and what it takes to become one of the best of the best is more than these hands will ever understand. That's how good I was last night.

There was no point arguing with him. I was only trying to catch up, but already I was far behind. Annie said that the reason Amleth and I had so much trouble understanding each other was that we were too much alike. What the hell did she mean by that?

"What did she mean, Horatio?"

Horatio turns his head toward me, judging, I suspect, whether it is worth the effort to lower himself into the hatch and turn my way again. I see the white side of his face, and he looks at me with his left eye.

"I'm not trying to be the best paddler on this river. I'm just trying to get to the end of it."

Horatio looks ahead, and his ears prick up. If human ears were as responsive as a dog's ears or a horse's ears, we might understand a thing or two about each other. Our ears just sit there even when they hear the most beautiful music.

Like the metronome Annie set in motion on top of the piano when she sat beside Amleth on the piano bench, my paddle keeps time with the river. It is a very slow meter. I feel the time passing through the strokes of the paddle and watch the brief disturbance each stroke makes in the water. Sometimes I look up from the river and think hours have passed, but I see the same rock configuration ahead that I saw before. Other times I look up and am sure that only a minute or two has gone by in the water that divides around Gloria's hull, but I don't recognize anything around me.

Usually his lessons were over before I came into the house, but in the wintertime I might come in early. Then I would sit at the kitchen table where Rosario was studying with the other kids and listen to Amleth playing the piano in the next room. Sometimes, I remember, I found myself listening to the ticking of the metronome and not the music Amleth played.

~ ~ ~

Horatio is distracted by something he sees downriver. It's only a shadow that disappears where the river divides around an island. I have seen these shadows too often to take them seriously.

"Are you beginning to see ghosts, too, Horatio?"

Horatio looks back at me with the left side of his face as if to say that he knows well enough what he sees. The hulking form of a barge emerges some distance beyond the ghost, which was probably what attracted Horatio's attention. His hearing and eyesight are better than mine. Over my shoulder I see that no barge is behind us. I should edge back to the left side of the buoys and move out of the shipping lane, but instead I let Gloria slip farther to the right. Horatio looks back at me again.

"Don't worry. I see him. We have plenty of time to get out of the way."

A sandbar has formed on the island, and the brown water and brown sand and brown logs form an unbroken contour before the green depth of the island. Once again in front of the island, there is the same mirror-like reflection of light.

"Did you see it?"

Horatio doesn't confirm the reflection because his attention is on the approaching barge, and he's getting nervous. The captain of the towboat delivers two loud blasts of his horn. I raise the paddle over my head to acknowledge the signal, but still I linger in the channel and search the water on the right side of the island. Gloria turns sideways as we drift with the current. Then I catch another glimpse of the ghost ahead. This ghost is blue.

Even though I paddle straight across toward the right bank, the current carries us downriver toward the barge that is crossing with the channel from right to left. The barge does not slow and we don't either. We pass so closely in front of the lead barge that I hear, above the pounding noise of the towboat diesel engine, the hiss the barge makes as it slides through the water. The captain gives another long blast on his horn to show his displeasure. The horn frightens Horatio, and for a moment he looks like he might jump into the river. Instead he drops down below the hatch.

"Go to hell! We have as much right to this river as you."

The captain can't hear anything I yell. He remains in his pilothouse, thirty feet above the water. The volume and commotion of his engines and propeller drown out my words, even to myself. Horatio peeps above the rim of the hatch and looks at me.

"All right, maybe we got a little too close."

Gloria bounces in the wake of the towboat as I paddle away from it, and Horatio claws the deck to hold his balance. Together we ride out the turmoil of the too-close barge until we reach the head of the island where a back channel of the river turns into the glare of the late-afternoon sun.

Somewhere ahead of us is the blue shadow, but we'll never catch up with it. I have seen enough apparitions on this river that I ought to know. It was beyond foolish; it was reckless to charge across the path of the oncoming barge. We should just stay in the main channel, which is shorter and faster than the secondary channel that curves around the island.

"Where do you want to go, Horatio?"

Horatio is indifferent to our course; to him one route is the same as another. Gloria is holding to the stronger current, and I'm ready to go with her when a distinct movement, a flash in the glare of the sunlight draws my attention again. Horatio is not looking into the sun, and I can't use him for confirmation. But there it is, more distinct and more recognizable than a ghost. I lift my sunglasses and squint into the sun.

Some distance up this back channel, a half-mile or more ahead of us, is the outline of a small narrow boat. It could be a kayak like ours, but the movement of the paddle, the flash that I see in the sunlight, is different. Strangely, after taking such a foolish risk to finally get close to something real, I'm not sure that I want to follow it. Aren't there enough complications that come on their own without pursuing another? Horatio is proof of that. Just when I was learning to live simply, Horatio complicated everything.

"Oh, hell, let's see what it is."

We gain steadily on the blue canoe, for it is a canoe, and the paddler sits motionless in his boat facing us as we approach. Horatio sees the canoe and is eager now for distraction. He is impatient with our speed and claws the deck of the kayak. Perhaps we are both seeking distraction.

The paddler uses long oars to straighten his boat in the current as we approach it, and he is sitting on a seat that slides back and forth with his stroke. On the back end of his canoe is a flag with a white and red cross on a blue background that is similar to but not the same as the flag that used to be in my grandparents' house. Not until we are nearly abreast of the canoe do the delicate structure of the paddler's face become evident, her smile, her pleasure in seeing Horatio's eager greeting as he stretches toward her and the canoe. She takes hold of Gloria's bow as we glide in beside her and coos at Horatio. Her voice is all the encouragement he needs, and he flops out of the hatch into her canoe. She laughs at his intrusion, and now it is my turn to hold on to our boats.

"Horatio, behave yourself."

Horatio is trying to lick her face, and she puts down her oars and holds him.

"Oh, you're just a sweetheart, aren't you?"

Her voice has the soft rounding of vowels that my grandmother's had. I never considered it an accent. She holds Horatio's neck, roughens his hair, and places her face just beyond the reach of his tongue.

"Those barge captains think they own this river," she says.

"We got a little close crossing over."

"It wouldn't have hurt him to slow down a little."

"That's what I was thinking. Maybe we'd better paddle to shore before my dog tips you over or falls into the river. He's good at that."

"Maybe we'd better," she says.

There is a long sandbar on the island, and beyond the sand is a grove of fully-leafed cottonwood trees, taller and thinner than those back in the sand-hills. The woman rows with the left oar and holds Horatio with her right hand. Each stroke is long and smooth, but her canoe zigzags toward the bank as she allows the lazy current to correct the course that the single oar distorts. Eventually Horatio settles down into the bottom of her canoe, so that I can't see what mischief he's up to, and she's able to row with both hands. Her canoe glides through the water so smoothly that Gloria and I are not able to keep up with her. If she hadn't waited for us, we would have never caught up.

Horatio jumps out of the canoe as soon as it touches land and begins his race up and down the sandy beach. Partly he runs with the delight of being on solid ground; partly he's showing off.

"My name is Marta," she says to me and extends her hand.

Her hands are rough and strong, which doesn't surprise me. Her canoe with the strange sliding seat looks like it has come a long way. A line of river mud follows the hull just as it does on Gloria, and gear is packed before and after her seat and covered with canvas.

"Your flag looks a little familiar, a bit like the Danish flag my grandparents had."

"It's the Icelandic flag. Such luck to meet another Scandinavian in the middle of the river. You're the first person in a small boat that I've seen since passing through St. Louis."

"You didn't come from Iceland in your canoe, did you?"

"No. From the headwaters up in Minnesota. And you? Where did you start?"

"Nebraska."

"That's where cowboys live, isn't it."

"Some, I suppose."

"Are you a cowboy?"

"No."

"But you wear a cowboy hat."

"It's not my hat. Besides, a lot of people wear cowboy hats who aren't cowboys—all hat and no horse."

"Do you have a horse?"

"Not anymore."

"But you did? A horse and cows?"

"Yes."

"Then you must be a cowboy. I work for a travel magazine in Iceland," she says. "If you don't mind, I'd like to take your picture—you and Horatio. What a cute name for your puppy."

She is a tall woman with a straight back who looks like she would be as comfortable on the ranch as she is in the river. With a back like hers and those long legs she could sit a horse with ease.

She bends down to her canoe, removes a large camera from a waterproof bag, and steps back a few paces from the boats. She pushes her sunglasses to the top of her head and points the camera at me. I'm not sure I want her to take my picture.

"Do you mind?" she asks.

"How about I take your picture instead?"

"Sure."

She hands me her camera. It's heavier than I expected and there are so many buttons that I'm not certain which one to push.

"Just focus and shoot," she says. "What would you like me to do?"

Horatio is at her feet and answers the question for her. I'm the one who pulled him out of the river and feeds him, but he is standing on his back legs with his front paws pushing on Marta's legs, hoping that she will pet him. If that's how he feels, maybe I'll just pack him off with her.

Marta bends down and grabs him by the neck, roughing him up, talking to him, laughing as Horatio laps at her face and reaches it every now and then. I focus the camera and shoot. It's not as complicated as I thought. The film advances and I shoot another picture.

"Have you brought him all the way from Nebraska?" she asks.

"No. He hitched a ride in Helena."

"He's so cute sitting in your kayak, and he's very useful. I knew you couldn't be dangerous if you carried a puppy in your boat."

"I'm glad he's good for something."

"You will have to let me take a picture of you and Horatio in your kayak."

There are a few more hours of daylight left, but I feel tired now that I'm standing on land. I feel awkward, too, standing beside this woman. Before I plow across the river in front of an oncoming barge after a phantom that has gotten away from me every time, I should think these things through. Sooner or later I might actually catch up with something.

"I'm thinking that we might stay here tonight."

Marta stands with her straight back and loses the easy smile and laughter that she has with Horatio. She looks into the sun and shields her eyes with her hands. I would like to tell her that she can stay, too, but I'm afraid of the way that would sound. Horatio tries to jump up on her again.

"Horatio, stay down."

Horatio turns his head toward my sharp voice, and Marta winces from its tone. Horatio moves off to the kayak and sniffs the side of the boat. He shoots a brief stream of piss below his hatch and sniffs off down the beach. I didn't mean to speak so harshly, but the dog has to learn not to make himself a nuisance.

"You're welcome to camp with us if you'd like, if you don't mind Horatio bothering you all the time. He hasn't learned his manners yet."

"He doesn't bother me," Marta says. "Are you sure you wouldn't mind if I camped here with you? I was aiming for a campground a few miles down, but this is a lovely place."

"It is, isn't it?"

Often the river bottom turns to mud a few feet out from the bank. Here the sand stretches far out into the river, and the gentle current doesn't wash it away. A light cool breeze passes over the water. On the beach there is dry firewood and plenty of clear ground on which to pitch our tents.

There is room to pitch a thousand tents, and we space our two tents a discreet distance apart. Mine goes up first, and Horatio trots back and forth inspecting the two sites.

"You pee on my tent, and I'll feed you to the catfish."

Marta laughs and calls Horatio over to her. She reminds me of a line in a book I read once that said every woman reaches an unparalleled beauty in her 30s. I was a teenager then and such words were seductive. Maybe there was some truth to the line, but maybe there is none at all. Marta might be older than those women of unparalleled beauty, although it's hard to tell. Why can't I just set up my tent and talk to her about the river as I did with Horace and Tom Reeves instead of thinking such nonsense? She will see the river with different eyes—eyes so startlingly blue that they're hard to turn away from.

For supper we decide to share our food. From my food bag comes a package of fettuccine alfredo that I've kept passing over. She makes rice with sun-dried tomatoes, basil, and other spices that she stores in little plastic bottles in a canvas bag. For my contribution to the spices I dig out the bottle of hot sauce from Juan.

We have a nice fire before us and plenty of wood piled close by. Horatio has chosen a spot between us and is taking a nap. Marta and I have made backrests with our dry bags and are sipping the ginseng tea she has made. It tastes bitter, but I'm not complaining. The fire throws sparks into the air, and we watch the night shadow move east to west across the sky.

"Have you traveled to lots of places for your magazine?"

"Oh yes, to many places," she says. "My first trip was to Australia. I hiked for two months across the country. Then I went to Kenya on safari and to South Africa. Last year I took a boat up the Orinoco River, then went to the Andes in Peru, and finally to the pampas in Uruguay—I saw cowboys there, too—but none who were Scandinavian. They all had dark hair and sweet

Latin smiles. I also went to the Everglades last winter, but that was only two weeks. Oh, and I was in Tibet several years ago. I liked that very much. And of course I've been all over Europe, and now I'm here with you and Horatio, who is bored with our talk."

She scratches Horatio on the belly. He moves his legs as if he is running, but he's lying on his side and going nowhere.

"Why are you making this trip?" she asks.

"I guess I've wanted to do this since I was a boy. Thought I'd better do it now before I get too old."

"So you are leaving youth behind to make a trip on the river. Is that how you explain it? Nothing more than that?"

It is easier to talk to Horatio about these things.

"That about explains it."

"Okay. It's not my business to pry. I think we should tell only the stories we want to tell. We lie about the others anyway. We Scandinavian people like to roam. It's the Viking blood in us, don't you think? We have always been wanderers. So now you are following the custom of your ancestors."

"I've never thought about it that way."

"But you should. After all, Leif , whose father was an Icelander if I may remind you, was the first European to come to this continent, not that Columbus fellow who ruined everything he got his hands on."

"I thought Leif Ericson was Norwegian."

"Norwegian? Since when does a person born in Greenland who lived most of his life in Iceland become Norwegian? No, you have to get your history straight. He was an Icelander if he was anything."

Marta stands up, brushes the sand off the back of her pants, and walks over to her canoe next to Gloria. Her canoe has no name, or at least none that is painted on the hull. Her white shirt makes a striking contrast against the dark flow of the river. She returns with a bottle in her hand.

"Dump out the tea and try a little of this," she says. "Have you heard of *brennivin*?"

"No."

"We call it the black death. It's supposed to be served ice cold, but I'm afraid it will have to be as it is."

I dump out the remains of the tea, and she pours a shot of the *brennivin* into my cup and does the same for herself.

"*Skål*," she says and raises her cup up to mine.

It is one Danish or Icelandic word that I know, and I say it back to her. She touches my cup, and I follow what she does. If she swallows it in one gulp, I will do the same. But she doesn't. While watching my face, my eyes, she takes a small sip. Only then does she lower the cup into her lap.

"What do you think?" she asks.

I think I have never met a woman quite like her.

"It's good."

"Not too strong?"

"No."

The fire sinks in upon itself in the pit, and the half moon in the west casts a silver line across the river straight up the beach to our fire and to us. There is no other light except the moon and the stars and the dying glow of our fire—no beacons, no buildings, no antennas, no vehicles. The second cup of *brennivin* soothes me as does the quiet flow of the river, as does the sound of her voice. I would like to close my eyes and have her words become my dreams instead of the dreams I make alone.

Marta leans toward the fire, toward the silver line that is streaming across the river, so that I am able to see her face without moving my head. Everything is shadow and light, reflection—even her eyes that are looking at me. She reaches up to her head and unties the red bandanna that is knotted in the back. Her hair drops down, and she shakes it free. I didn't expect such long hair.

"If you don't mind, I'm going to take a bath in the river," she says.

She is up and moving toward the river before I can tell her that I don't mind at all. At her canoe she takes off her clothes and lays them on top of the canvas. I watch her outline against the river as she follows the silver line into the water. The moonlight is like a spotlight that casts Marta's shadow behind her. But of course that is an illusion. The moon illuminates the whole river equally, and the water that holds her shadow is already far down the river.

~ ~ ~

The slow current along the bank is disturbed by an obstruction, maybe a fallen tree or a rock embedded in the sand, and the river will not be silenced until the branch gives up its hold or the rock is smoothed away. As I listen from within my sleeping bag, Horatio gets up next to the wall of the tent, brushes the ceiling, and brings rain down upon himself from the condensation that has collected on the nylon fabric. If he sees that I am awake, there will be no peace. So I close my eyes and feel his breath on my face. When I peek, he is staring down at me. Marta is right. No one will see danger in Horatio's face.

"All right. We'll get up."

When I let Horatio outside, he closes in upon Marta's tent.

"Get away from there."

I wave him away. He wags his tail at my command but doesn't move. Marta unzips her tent and sticks her head outside. He's a lucky dog to receive such a smile in the morning.

"Good morning, cowboy," she says to me. Her voice is husky from sleep. She doesn't have the voice of an early riser.

Unlike Marta who bathed within sight of the camp, I walk upriver until the low growing brush that fills in the gaps between the cottonwood trees conceals me from her. There I take off my clothes and wade into the river. The water is warm and pleasant as I settle into it. Using soap as lather I shave the several days' growth of beard.

For the first time in many days I woke without memory of a dream. Did Amleth flee in the presence of this woman, a ghost afraid of her charms, or have I fled from him? I'm surprised how good it feels to have this woman close by.

Horatio is standing on the bank with a stick in his mouth. He has tracked me through the trees.

"What's the matter? Won't Marta throw the stick for you?"

He splashes into the river, swims out to me, adjusting his direction as necessary to accommodate the slow-moving current, and releases his stick beside me. I toss it back to the bank and follow as he goes after it. While I wait for the warm air to dry me, I throw Horatio's stick and laugh at his extraordinary energy.

Marta is heating water on her stove when Horatio and I come through the trees. She smiles at me, perhaps not with the same pleasure with which she smiled at Horatio when she looked out her tent, but it will do.

"Would you like some coffee?" she asks.

Marta's coffee has an aroma that is too good to pass up. I find my cup and bring it back to her stove with a half-dozen granola breakfast bars. She is making oatmeal and declines the breakfast bars. Marta's camp is the way it was the night before and gives no proof that she is eager to be on her way. This morning I am not eager either and find a comfortable spot close to her camp stove where I sip her freshly-brewed coffee.

"My map shows that the town of Vicksburg is not so far away," Marta says. "I believe Vicksburg is a famous town, isn't it?"

"There was a big battle there during the Civil War."

"I know about your war to free the slaves. I have heard that there are beautiful old plantations around Vicksburg that you can visit."

"I suppose there are."

"But old plantations don't interest you."

"I don't know. I've never seen one."

"So perhaps it interests you after all."

"It might, if you wouldn't mind our company today."

"I'd like your company," she says, "if you are not in a hurry. I don't like to hurry."

"I'm in no hurry."

"Good. And in Vicksburg, I am thinking about finding a nice place to stay for a few days."

"Do you suppose there are places to stay beside the river?"

"There must be. Don't you think?"

"Yes, there must be."

It is already hot by the middle of the morning when we leave our camp. Horatio has his head above the deck, but he is lethargic compared to the day before when we first met Marta. When we arrive at the main channel of the river a few miles downriver from our camp, Marta holds her course along the right bank. The red buoy is far out in the river, and I wonder if she has seen it.

"We're in the shipping lane here."

"I know, but I like to row close to land."

"What do you do if a barge comes along?"

"I pull ashore and get out. I don't like it out there. Sometimes the river lifts up the canoe for no reason, and then the oars miss the water. It scares me when it does that. So I stay on one side if I can. You cross over. I'll catch up with you in a little while."

"It doesn't matter to me. I'll stay on this side, too."

It doesn't matter today, but it would take forever to get down the river if I had to pull Gloria out of the water every time a barge came along.

Marta's oars and sliding seat are much more efficient than my paddle, and it is she who must wait for me. I understand how she feels about the water. The water is always tricky around the dikes and jetties, and I stay away from them, but it will also boil up in the middle of the river without warning and twist us around. Then the river seems sinister, but maybe it is only warning us not to relax, warning us that we don't understand what's below the surface.

After several miles the ever-turning course of the river moves the shipping lanes to the opposite bank. We meet no barge to interfere with us. Marta interrupts her stroke and points to a blue heron sitting on the last outcropping of rock revetment on the right bank.

"Why do you suppose they are always alone?" she asks me.

"I don't know."

"He won't like us getting so close."

The heron flexes its legs and lifts itself off the rock with slow ponderous strokes from its wings. It squawks its displeasure once or twice and heads downriver.

"Sourpuss," Marta says.

She resumes her stroke but at a slower pace than when we were exposed to the shipping lanes. Usually my focus is on the river: for changes on the surface—ripples, whirlpools, upwellings, for the first sign of wind, for barges ahead and behind, for buoys in the distance, for logs and debris to navigate around, for the far bank at the very end of my line-of-sight signaling a change of course—right to left, left to right. Then I know I will need to cross over once again. There will be a dozen or more changes of the channel before we reach Vicksburg, but we won't cross them today.

A submerged dike disturbs the water ahead and forces the current toward the center of the river. The water is high enough to pass over the top, but I don't trust it. Gloria doesn't either. She is already turning away from the dike.

"There's a dike up ahead. I think we should go around it."

Marta looks downriver and nods her agreement. She turns her canoe in line with Gloria although it will take her away from the bank.

"I don't like these dikes," she says.

There are three dikes, one after the other, a quarter mile or more apart. After the dikes a large sandbar forms on the inside curve of the bend. Marta and I agree that it is time for a break, and we paddle through nearly still water to the sandbar.

We land together, but Marta is out of her canoe before I release the waist skirt from the cockpit. Horatio jumps out of the hatch and follows her, but she shoos him away. For once he listens to me when I call him back. There is no shelter on the sandbar and Marta stops a distance away, pulls down her shorts, and squats in the sand. Looking away, I pull Gloria farther up the bank. So this is how we do it. I walk the opposite direction from Marta and unzip the fly of my trousers.

When I return to the boats, Marta is inspecting a willow branch that has been deposited by high water. New shoots have grown from the stripped waterlogged branch and are sinking their roots into the sand. Marta photographs the new growth.

"Isn't this wonderful?" she asks. "Five new trees growing from this dead branch. Life begins again in this barren place. No, Horatio. Keep your feet away until I finish photographing this nature."

Horatio does not disturb the ground around the willow branch until she has finished taking her pictures. Only then does he approach the branch, sniff it, and pee on it. Marta takes his picture, too, and he poses for her like the show-off that he is.

Without her I would have missed this willow branch. I would have been farther down the river looking for changes in the water, not on land. Marta walks down the sandbar with her camera, and I follow her. Horatio runs ahead of us and sniffs the ground in earnest. He begins to follow tracks that lead from the water toward the trees a hundred yards back from the river. I don't want him to go into the trees. He stops when he hears my sharp voice, and I hurry to catch up with him. When I see the tracks close up, I grab him and lift him off the ground.

"What are they?" Marta asks.

"I'm not sure."

"They're big. They can't be from a dog."

"They're not from a dog."

There are two sets of tracks. The larger are bigger than my hand and six feet or more apart from the front paw to the rear. And they're fresh. Sand has not yet blown into the depressions.

"I think they're bear tracks."

"Look," Marta says, pointing to the smaller tracks. "That must be a baby with her mother."

Marta follows their trail through the eye of her camera, snapping a picture every few feet. Horatio wiggles in my grasp, trying to get free, but I won't let him down. I watch the trees. Somebody needs to.

A baby with her mother, the most dangerous bear, I'm thinking. Long ago I read a Faulkner story about a bear hunt in Mississippi. It was a difficult story to understand, but they killed the bear. I thought all the bears here would have been hunted to extinction the way the wolves had been hunted on the prairies. Marta looks up from the tracks and surveys the woods without her camera lens interceding. We are as close to the line of trees as I want to go.

"I'd better get Horatio into the kayak. A mother bear will make quick work of him if she thinks he's threatening her cub. Maybe us, too."

"I wish we could at least get a peek at them," Marta says.

"The tracks are enough for me."

Marta laughs and takes my picture holding Horatio. I may paddle into deep water, she is thinking, but I am not so brave when it comes to a momma bear and her baby. It is foolish for me to think I know what this woman is thinking. Maybe I understand Horatio, and maybe I understood the black horse now and then, but I don't understand her at all.

"We won't get to Vicksburg today if I follow every track in the sand, will we?" Marta asks.

"That's just what I was thinking."

When we are back in our boats, Marta rows close to the bank and scans the woods for bears. Not trusting Horatio to stay in the hatch if he should see one, I paddle farther out, but I also watch the woods with Marta. Only Horatio has lost his interest in bears, and he settles down into the hatch. Perhaps he knows that we won't catch even a glimpse of them.

Marta's rowing style is much different from my paddling. Sometimes she shoots ahead with a spurt of energy; then she finds something floating in the water and slows down to observe it. Or she digs into a bag for a snack and offers some to me—a candy bar or nuts or fruit gelatin in a thin stick. She makes me realize how monotonously predictable I am, how I paddle with the same rhythm hour after hour. Somehow her irregular speed has allowed us to avoid all the barges in the shipping lane. We have not had to pull ashore a single time to get away from them.

The closer we get to Vicksburg, the more purposefully we paddle. Vicksburg lies only a few miles away. Once we complete the turn ahead, it should be in sight. Then we'll have to cross the river to the left bank. I wonder if Marta is ready for that. Hell, I whisper to the water, I wonder if I'm ready.

The size of the river deceives the eyes. The trees on the right bank lead all the way up to the bend in the river; then the more distant trees on the left bank curve beyond it. It looks like a sharp angle, but it's not. It turns and turns and there is no use looking for the end of it. I paddle up beside Marta.

"We'll have to cross the river to get to the Vicksburg side. It's just ahead of us."

"Are you worried that I won't go across?"

"Maybe."

Marta laughs at me and digs her oars deeply into the water. I paddle hard to keep up with her, but she leaves us behind. Horatio senses the change in our speed, and his head rises above the rim of the hatch to see what's going on. He sees Marta rowing some distance ahead and barks as if he doesn't like being left behind. Marta doesn't slow her pace until she is close to the opposite bank.

The river turns south before the face of the tall bluff at Vicksburg. There are huge mansions on the top of the bluff and huge gambling casinos below it next to the river. There is no good place to land. The bank is covered with rocks, and we will have to pull up on them if we want to stop. Marta has found an eddy formed from an outcropping and grabs one of the boulders on the bank to hold her in place. I paddle beside her and wedge her canoe into the bank with the side of Gloria.

"I'll hold you here while you get out."

She puts down her oars and scrambles onto the rocks. From there she grabs the bow rope of her canoe and ties it around a jagged boulder. Gloria drifts away and I look for a place for her. Gloria is less tolerant of the jagged rocks than Marta's heavy canoe. Marta picks her way along the rocks to stay with me. I pull the bow rope free from the shock cords and toss the end to her. She grabs it and holds Gloria close to the bank. Horatio stretches out toward her.

"Stay, Horatio," I say.

He rises higher and jumps anyway, slipping on a rock and bumping his nose.

"Oh, Horatio," Marta says. "Are you all right? Poor baby."

Horatio climbs across the rocks to where Marta is squatting and places his face in her lap. For a moment Marta forgets about me as she soothes Horatio. I pull the waist skirt free of the cockpit and straddle my legs over the hull, but I won't be able to put my left foot down. The bank drops away too sharply from the revetment.

"Pull me forward a little."

Marta lifts Horatio onto a flat rock and tells him to stay there. He does as she says. She pulls the kayak forward and grabs the bow with her hands.

"Shall I come farther down?" she asks.

"No, that's good. I'll see if I can get out without killing myself."

I experiment with my right foot until I find a rock that will hold me. Then I lift my weight gradually onto that foot until I can swing my left foot over the hull and onto the rocky bank.

"Tricky business," she says.

With Gloria still in the water, I open the hatches and unload the gear bags from each hatch into the large portage bags until she is light enough now for Marta and me to carry her above the rocks to a wooded area beneath a cyclone fence. Then we unload Marta's canoe and carry it above the rocks. It's a tricky business, as Marta says. We have to move one step, one rock at a time.

We've landed below a large casino, and hotel rooms with sliding doors face the river. I hadn't thought about how to get Horatio inside a hotel room, but Marta has.

"I'll go up and see if they have rooms there on the ground floor while you wait here with Horatio. They might not allow dogs, even a dog as cute as Horatio. We'll have to sneak him in."

"Maybe I should just tie him up down here or put him on a log and send him down the river."

"Oh, he won't do that," Marta says as she squats beside Horatio and looks into his eyes. "He's just telling stories."

Horatio licks her face and she laughs at him.

I give Marta my credit card to pay for my room. She finds a gate in the cyclone fence and scales the hill to the casino while Horatio and I wait beside the river. A mile or so downriver a freeway bridge connects Mississippi and Arkansas. On the Arkansas side, the land lies low and flat, but not on this side. These bluffs held great strategic military value during the Civil War. From here, or from upriver a way, the Confederacy controlled the Mississippi with cannon mounted on the bluffs, and Grant and his Union army fought a long slogging battle to take it from them. Grant even tried to build a canal to divert the river around the fortifications, but he failed. A few years later the river did the work on its own and moved away from the contested fortifications that are now miles from the river. It would be peaceful here now if it were not for the explosive sounds from giant trucks roaring by on the freeway. The noise rolls up the river like echoes of the long-silent cannon.

Marta waves from outside the sliding door of one of the ground level rooms. I carry Horatio up the path to the room and conceal him among the bags I carry, although it probably isn't necessary. There isn't a single person outside on the lawn, not a single person in the swimming pool, not a single person on any of the balconies above. Marta slides the door closed behind us as I slip into the room. I wonder what she's smiling about. Horatio? Me? Did I look that ridiculous scurrying like a thief across the grass and the empty cement patio beside the swimming pool? Then I see what is making her smile. The room is gaudy beyond all taste. It has a king-size bed with a purple velvet headboard fastened to the wall and a Jacuzzi tub next to it that is big enough for a party twice the size of ours. Horatio looks around with drooping ears when I put him down on the thick purple carpet. I wonder if he has ever been inside a building before. How will I prevent him from peeing on the rug, not that anyone would ever notice? What am I doing here with this woman? I should have thought this through a little better.

Steam swirls against the shower curtain as hot water rains down upon my shoulders. Perhaps I'll never get out. I'll set roots in the bathtub like the willow tree on the sandbar and stay until I fill the whole room with new branches.

"Do you plan to stay in there all afternoon, or are you waiting for some-body to wash your back?"

I pull the curtain aside and peek out. Marta is sitting on top of the gran-ite counter that runs the length of the bathroom wall. She is wearing a long-sleeved white shirt, which is like the shortest dress I've ever seen, and nothing more. Her hair is wet and combed straight.

"Or maybe cowboys are too shy," she says.

"I'm not a cowboy."

I pick up the bar of soap from the shower shelf and hold it out to her. She slides off the counter and takes it from me.

"You have to turn around if I'm to do your back."

She steps into the tub behind me as I turn around in the shower. I feel her slippery hands on my back.

"I want to take a Jacuzzi, but not by myself. Didn't you think about invit-ing me?"

"It crossed my mind."

"But you didn't say anything."

"I was building up my courage."

"It looks like you intended to take your Jacuzzi with Horatio and not me."

"Is he still in there?"

"Yes. Poor puppy."

"I didn't want him to pee on the carpet. Is he complaining?"

"Only with those sad eyes of his. I guess we'll have to use the Jacuzzi in my room. Turn around and I'll do the front."

I turn around and face Marta, who has no shyness and doesn't mind the water that sprays upon her. She reaches around me and rubs the soap off of my back.

"Your shirt is getting wet."

"It will dry."

Horatio thinks he will escape his prison of steep slippery walls when we walk out of the bathroom, Marta in her wet shirt and me with a towel around my waist. He stretches up the side of the Jacuzzi with his front paws and wags his tail. Marta pets his head and tells him that he must stay there a bit longer. He doesn't try to jump out or bark his displeasure as I open the sliding door and let Marta slide out in front of me. Maybe somewhere in his dog consciousness he knows that he shouldn't press his luck.

It takes a lot of water to fill the Jacuzzi tub. As we wait for it to rise above the jets so that we can start the circulating pumps, she sits in one end of the tub and I in the other. I have not known a woman so at ease with her body or with mine.

Her skin is brown. I have only brown hands and a brown face, like the cowboy she teases me about. She is brown from the waist up and from the thighs down. There must be times when she paddles without a shirt. That would be something to see. She is something to see right now. Sun wrinkles fan out from her blue eyes that have squinted into sunrises in the Andes and have watched the grass flow like waves on the plains of Uruguay and Kenya. When she moves her arms, her shoulder muscles ripple with energy and strength. She makes me feel young, which I have not felt since I was young, and that was before I can remember.

With her I imagine myself as another person—younger, stronger, confident that I know what I'm doing or don't care if I don't. I am foolish to feel this way, but I will be foolish again. It is not so difficult.

Marta turns on the switch for the Jacuzzi jets and the water swirls around us. It makes enough noise that I can't hear anything outside our room. I move to the center of the tub and pull her toward me. Her smile grows as she slips willingly into my arms. Now her smile is above mine, and I don't want to imagine anything else.

~ ~ ~

M y brother is riding for his life on the black horse across the bluffs. An uncountable number of cannon fire all at once. Shells explode around him but don't tear up the grass or rip down the trees. It is suicide to be out there alone. He falls from the horse and lies perfectly still on the perfectly mowed grass of the graveyard. As I dig his grave with my hands, the dirt is so soft that it flows out of the ground like water. Without looking at his face I lay him in the shallow grave. I'm afraid to look. I'm afraid he will ask me through his mask of death why he is lying there and I am not. The dirt that I push on top of him isn't soft any more. It's full of rocks and bottles, broken glass and beer cans, yellow softballs. After I remove the junk, there isn't enough dirt to fill the grave, and I have to pile the junk back on top. From the ground I hear the muffled notes of a piano rising up through the rubble —a child's song, not quite in tune. I have heard this song before, but I can't remember who played it. The music stops and among the thousands of white grave-stones standing in precise military rows, only one is lying flat on the ground. I pick it up and set it at the head of the grave. It has Amleth's name it.

Between the dream and morning are the hours I lie awake and know that nothing has changed, that only in dreams do I find the young and they are dead. This woman lying beside me cannot change me or them, for in the wake of our intimacy is the thing that does not change.

Marta's breathing is quiet, her body is curled beside mine, and her knees are pressed against my hip. If I turn toward her, I believe her body will conform to mine as it did before. You can't hope for more.

Quietly I rise from the bed and walk to the window where light enters from the edge of the heavy curtain. It is open just enough that I can look outside. Below is the river, and I feel as if I'm already there in Gloria, an abandoned but forgiving lover, flowing with the logs that drift silently in the current. If I were alone, I would pack up now and begin paddling. Time means nothing when you're alone except that at some point on every journey there comes a time when you just want it to end.

"Is the river still there?" she asks from the darkness inside the room.

"Yes. Did I wake you?"

"No, I'm still asleep."

"Sorry. I think a barge woke me up."

"Is there a barge out there?"

"Earlier."

"Open the curtain so that I can see you."

She sits up in the bed with her back against the velvet headboard and pulls the sheet up to her neck to cover her naked body. Horatio is on the bed with her, down at the foot, but he continues to sleep.

I slip into the bed beside her and cover myself, too.

"You were talking in your sleep," she says. "Don't worry. I couldn't understand anything, but I think you were having a bad dream. Understanding dreams is my special talent."

"One of many then."

"One of many. What was it about?"

I don't know why I hesitate to answer her. She never hesitates—no matter what I ask.

"It was about my son—my brother and my son."

The dream is already fading from my memory. How can something so real fade so quickly? Maybe I should just let it go. We had made a plan for the coming day—Marta and I. I can't remember the last time I planned a whole day. We planned to rent a car, visit the battlefield, a plantation if there was time. Then we would have dinner in the evening, watch the sunset over the river, wait for night together—one whole day and night according to a plan. Who knows what might happen after such a day? Another like it might come, but another won't come if I tell her about the dream—because you can't stop with a dream. Amleth has no grave. What I felt in my hand was not his gravestone. So why not let it go?

"Yellow softballs?" she asks after I finish telling her about the dream. Her voice is as soft as the yellow light that comes through the window.

"When I was coming down the Missouri, there were softballs floating in the river. I have no idea how they got there."

"So they came from something real."

"Yes, something real. Like the black horse. It was real, too."

"And the music from the grave? Where does that come from?"

"My son played the piano. He told me once when he was a little boy that he heard music when he woke up in the morning. 'Do you hear music, too?' he asked me. I never hear music when I wake up.

"I guess I expected him to grow out of all those dreams we have as children and take over the ranch like I did. But here's the strange part: even while I was trying to turn him into a rancher, a part of me wanted to be like him.

"My brother played the piano, too. He was never as good as Amleth, but maybe he would have been if he'd lived longer. They were the same age when they died—my brother and my son. Twenty-two years old. "

"Too young," she says.

"It was my fault that my son died, my fault that he rode that horse. I should have gotten rid of that horse a long time ago. Now I dream about them."

"Of course you do."

"The dreams remind me who I am in case I forget."

"Do you forget?"

"I did yesterday."

"Was it so bad to forget?"

"No."

"Perhaps these dreams are the way your subconscious mind is working through your grief."

"What bothers me most about these dreams is that I'm always watching, but I can't do anything. And whenever my son sees me, he turns away so that he won't have to talk to me."

"Maybe he'll talk to you when he's ready, or when you are."

"Do you believe in that stuff? Do you talk to ghosts? Do you take their pictures?"

"I've never seen one, but I think you have."

"No. These are just thoughts and memories that swirl around in my brain, mix themselves up, and come out in dreams."

"What is the difference?"

I don't have an answer.

"You should talk to him."

"I do, but he doesn't answer."

"He will. Some day he will."

Gloria holds reluctantly to the rocky bank while I close and seal the rear hatch. The sun has not yet risen above the bluff beyond the casino, but its orange light is already brighter than the lights in the parking lot. Farther down is the freeway bridge, a lighted shadow against the dark sky.

Marta crouches on the rocks beside Gloria, holding the handle at the stern. I am following a process that is beyond my control. Gloria is in the water, the gear is packed, and Horatio is leaning on the deck with his front paws, happy to be out of the hotel room. He doesn't understand yet that Marta isn't coming with us. A barge is approaching from downriver but is still beyond the bridge.

"You had better get away from here before that barge comes any closer," she says.

After slipping into the cockpit I fasten the waist skirt in place. Marta crawls forward on the rocks until she is beside me. She is smiling the way I feel. We met unexpectedly, embraced, believed foolishly or at least I did that an encounter between two people can be simple after all. But two people together are never simple.

"Be careful," she whispers.

I want to tell her how lucky I felt to meet her, how I wish that we could have stayed together longer, but before I can say anything she releases her hold on Gloria and pushes me out into the river. Gloria drifts away from the rocks. From behind me I hear her voice.

"I hope he talks to you."

I take up the paddle and steer toward the center of the river. How quickly it carries us away. Just before the oncoming barge blocks my view of the bank, I turn and wave to Marta, standing tall and straight on the boulders beside the river.

Water rises suddenly beneath the kayak like an eruption from forces that I can neither see nor understand. The water spreads out before Gloria, and a whirlpool forms as the flood of water settles back into the river. Gloria glides through in a straight line. Waves wash over the cockpit from the wake of the towboat, and I turn Gloria to meet the waves head on. By the time the barge completes the sharp turn at Vicksburg and clears the shoreline, we are too far down the river for me to see if Marta is still there or ever was.

~ ~ ~

The evening is so hot and muggy that I become dizzy when I forget to look up from the water. I feel tired right down to the bone; yet, strangely, I don't feel the exertion of paddling. It is as if the paddle is working apart from me. The rhythm of the paddle and the unconscious adjustments to the water affect me on land just as they do in the water, so I may as well stay in the river.

When I started up in the sandhills, I had no way to understand how far it would be, how the days would drag on, how monotonous the paddling would become. Maybe this is the best you can hope for: boredom, indifference, weariness such that you don't care what you find along the way. I just want to get to the end of this river, to get it over with.

If Horatio is suffering, he suffers in silence. If it were not for him, I might not stop at all. He has dropped below the deck where it is cooler. I've thought about doing that—cut a hole in the front bulkhead as the boys suggested, lie on the bottom of the kayak, and float with the current. It would be fine until a barge came along or Gloria decided to challenge another buoy.

An electric bulletin board, bigger than any highway billboard, flashes a warning to stay away from the dangerous currents that develop in the outflow on the right side of the slowly descending river. We have come to the Old River Control that J. Morgan told me about back in St. Charles, which has more concrete, he said, than it would take to build all the pyramids of Egypt. No concrete is visible anywhere around here except the heavy layer of riprap along the bank. The control structures, which are supposed to hold the river to this course come hell or high water, are hidden in the shadows beyond the trees like monsters with gaping concrete jaws. If J. Morgan is right, no amount of concrete, no amount of man's vanity will hold the river back if it decides to take the shortcut down the Atchafalaya, and someday it will.

But not today.

Horatio sticks his head above the rim of the hatch and blinks in the low angle of sunlight. I wonder if he hears something that I can't hear or senses something beyond my perception. It isn't much of an accomplishment if he can. Since leaving Vicksburg two days ago, the only noise I've heard is from the barges that pass. Sometimes they come six or seven in a row; then there will be none for hours.Last night I didn't even try to read. Huckleberry and Jim remain stranded somewhere up the river in Arkansas, and I'm leaving them there. The book no longer interests me, but it still has a purpose. The pages make adequate toilet paper.

Horatio looks sideways at me showing the white half of his face. Since leaving Vicksburg he's lost much of the enthusiasm that made me laugh despite myself. My lack of enthusiasm may have rubbed off on him, or maybe he misses Marta. He was the first to leap into her canoe. Somehow he knew that she would welcome him.

"Are you thinking about Marta?"

He turns the other way and looks at me with the black side of his face.

"I wonder if she's left Vicksburg. Do you wonder why we left her? I do. She was such good company, wasn't she? Now you're stuck with me."

The water is so still and calm that it is as if nothing has ever disturbed it. I watch the paddle enter the water, watch the stroke that pulls it past Horatio and me, watch the tiny whirlpool at the end of the stroke where the evening sun highlights the swirling particles of silt, and nothing more.

There isn't much time left to understand why I'm here. I told Rosario that I had to leave the ranch because I was dying up there. Everybody has to die. What's wrong with dying? You are seeking simplicity, Marta told me, a physical and emotional purging of all complication. That's one way to think, but it's not how I think. Since I was a boy, I have believed that I could join this river and make it to the ocean. That's all. I want to find out if I have been wrong about that, too.

Strange how reluctant I am to stop. But soon I'll have to stop and get more food. I've been eating raisins and peanuts since leaving Vicksburg. Mostly it's been too hot to eat. There are two packages of freeze-dried beef stew stuffed in the front hatch and enough peanuts and raisins to last one more day—maybe two. What if I stop and don't want to go any farther? What will I do with Horatio while I go to the store?

"You're a nuisance, do you know that? Marta was wrong. If I were looking for simplicity, I would never have picked you up."

Horatio rises up on his back legs and stretches toward me. He's heard the tone of my voice and thinks he can change my mind. I lay the paddle across the cockpit, reach forward, and scratch him behind the ears.

"What am I going to do with you?"

Some miles downriver a small ferry with a half-dozen cars on its flat deck crosses in front of us. It's an odd sight. It doesn't seem like it came from anywhere. There is no ferry landing on either side of the river. Since leaving Vicksburg I haven't bothered to update the map case, being content with the occasional sighting of a mileage marker. Therefore there is no map in front of me to explain what sort of civilization it portends. Not much of one, I suspect. From what I can see, there is only swampland on both sides of the river.

The river divides around an island up ahead. Islands are good places to camp—nobody to bother us and a chance, at least, that we'll escape the mosquitoes. A dike has been built to divert the water past the island, and we skirt the dike and follow the island until the island runs out. Then I paddle to the bank and laboriously get out of the cockpit.

Putting up the tent has become so routine that I could do it blindfolded, which is what I must have done when I packed up in the morning because I can't find the bag with the axe and extra rope I brought along to secure the tent in high wind. I suppose I might have left it behind a log. How else could I have overlooked the bright yellow bag? It doesn't matter. There hasn't been any wind for days. It feels like all the air has been sucked away from the river.

While I wait for the water to boil to make our supper, I open the front hatch and find the bag that holds the remaining maps. There aren't many left. When I started the trip, I couldn't encircle the cylinder of rolled-up maps with my fingers. Now only the inner core is left, and some of these maps from upriver are no longer useful.

Horatio watches me unroll the tight roll of paper and cast aside the maps where we've already been. The discarded maps curl back into their previous shapes. I flatten out the map that has a ferry crossing at the top and hold it up to catch the light from the flame of the gas stove.

"I'll be damned. Do you know where we are, Horatio? Over there is Angola, the prison farm. We've got Louisiana on both sides of the river now."

Horatio looks in the direction I point, but our location doesn't impress him. It's too dark to see anything except a shadow where there is land. To him it's just the river out there, the same as before. But to me, it's something else.

"Last state we have to get through."

~ ~ ~

The towers and cables of a suspension bridge rise above the trees on the right bank like a mirage floating among the clouds. It is an eerie sight that doesn't become clear until we enter the unusually sharp bend that reveals the straight stretch of river through Baton Rouge. Horatio sniffs the air, which is acrid from the exhaust of chemical plants and a huge oil refinery. Oil tanks cover acres of ground stripped bare of any living thing, and steel pipes twist around smokestacks and each other in a diabolical jumble. Horatio's tongue works over the roof of his mouth as if he tastes something that he doesn't like. I taste it, too.

Marta warned me about Baton Rouge. With all the river traffic it was no place for a canoe, and she was skipping it. She was skipping the entire industrial section between Baton Rouge and New Orleans to avoid the ocean-going ships that navigated upriver this far. She wanted nothing to do with them. Her warning sounded like another of those river stories that I've heard all along the way—whirlpools that will suck you to China, dikes just below the water's surface that will rip out the bottom of your boat, barges that would just as soon run right over you.

The ocean-going tankers and cargo ships are anchored and unmoving, but they dwarf the towboats and barges tied up beside them. There are towboats and barges everywhere—crisscrossing the river, tied up beside the ocean-going ships, tied to the docks on both sides, tied up to mid-channel moorings.

The frenetic activity ahead is enough to give me pause, but there is no pausing in the river. As I paddle into the turbid cauldron, a rogue wave catches me by surprise as it comes up from behind. It raises Gloria's bow out of the water, and twists us perpendicular to the current. Paddling deep and hard I realign Gloria with the wave so that she will not slide sideways into its trough. For a second we perch on the crest of the wave before it leaves us behind. Still we are carried forward in its draft toward a barge that is passing on the right. The towboat's propeller is throwing off an enormous wake, and the bastard steering it doesn't throttle down the engine to reduce it.

"Hold on, Horatio!"

I turn Gloria to meet the first wave from the towboat head on. She rises sharply before her bow slams down into the water. A second wave washes over her. Horatio drops into the hatch to escape it, then lifts his head above the deck and looks back at me with wet face and drooping ears. It's not funny this time. Waves are ricocheting from the banks and join the newly created waves from the towboats. Like a top in the water, we spin this way and that as the water washes over us. A deckhand standing outside the pilothouse waves to me as I turn into the wake thrown off from his towboat. It is smooth-riding from the deck where he stands undisturbed by the waves, but not where we are. I couldn't wave back if I wanted to, and I don't want to. Instead I curse him and the pilot inside the cabin who roars by with undiminished power. I didn't think this river could frighten me anymore, but it's not the first time I've been wrong. If we flip here, one of these barges will run right over us and grind us to pieces.

Refineries and chemical plants finally give way to tall buildings and gambling casinos, but still the river traffic comes on. There is a humming noise somewhere around us, and I realize it's coming from me—a chant to carry us through rough water. And it does, or something does. It's surprising how a person can adjust to almost anything. Another wave. Face it. Brace with the paddle. Lean into the surge. Dig deep again. Hum louder.

Miles down from the first bridge—how many miles, I don't know—we pass beneath a second bridge, after which the water becomes calmer. The bridge has nothing to do with calming the water. It is all a matter of the boat traffic, and we have finally escaped the worst of it.

I ease my knees from the braces and slow the rhythm of the strokes. Horatio sticks his head above the deck and looks around. His ears rise again as he senses that the worst is over. Gloria glides easily through the diminishing waves as she always does.

"That wasn't so bad, was it?"

Horatio stretches his nose toward me, but he's not ready to lift his paws out of the hatch. Beyond the last of a row of tied-up barges, I look for a place to land on the left bank where I can pump out the water in the forward hatch. The air smells fresher here, and of all the things that I never expected to see, a horse is staked out high on the levy, grazing contentedly on the lush grass. It raises its head and watches us float by.

"What are you doing here, fella?"

Horatio thinks I'm talking to him, which is rational, I suppose, for the horse is too far away to hear me. If we were a little closer to it, I might try to paddle against the current and land beneath it. For some reason I would like to touch that horse. I wonder if Horatio has ever seen one, and what he would do around it.

Downriver a tanker ship is rounding the bend that will take us away from Baton Rouge. The tanker is staying on the right side with the current. Even from a distance the tanker looks enormous, and I edge us a little closer to the security of the left bank. The tanker is not as far away as I first thought, and it seems to be heading in our direction.

–There's a whole river out there.

Expecting that the tanker will stay in deeper water, I move Gloria closer to the bank. The tanker's round nose is building a wall of water before it, and it keeps turning toward us. It's a big son-of-a-bitch.

–What the hell? There's no dock over here.

Against all logic the ship is heading toward the left bank, closing the distance more quickly than any barge ever has. Abandoning logic I steer Gloria toward the center of the river. The tanker follows us. I paddle harder, gauge the direction of the ship, and paddle harder still. Finally I turn Gloria away from the ship at a right angle and paddle for all I'm worth, and still the ship comes on. We're too close, way too close. The hum I hear now is not from me. It's from the hidden engines of the huge ship that slips by so closely that I feel the breeze it makes. Immediately I turn Gloria toward the tanker and prepare for the wave that will follow. On the side of the ship is a name in foreign letters. I watch it go by, resigned almost, for the wave that will finally overwhelm us. Long after the ship passes, I am still waiting.

~ ~ ~

On a sandspit that points downriver from the end of the island where I have pitched the tent, a breeze gives relief from the heat. Horatio rests on the sand close to my feet and chews the willow stick he found. I'm tired of throwing it. A clump of willow trees shades the log on which I'm sitting as I eat the last of the peanuts and wait for the sun to go down.

An aluminum canoe is wedged tightly against the log. When I first saw it, I thought that someone else must have landed on the island. But there were no footprints that led away from the canoe. It must have washed up earlier in the spring when the river was higher. Someone is missing a good canoe.

Gloria is among the trees on the other side of the island where I landed, and I've tied her bow rope to a tree trunk so that a rogue wave from one of the tankers that frequently sail by in the channel won't wash her away. The ocean-going ships make little disturbance out in the river, but their waves gather height in shallow water, break close to shore like waves in the ocean, and run up the bank. To get away from them I've set up camp on the quiet side of the island that faces east across a backwater.

The last mileage marker I saw was 201, so now I am less than two hundred miles from the Head of Passes. From there it's another ten miles to the ocean. At the pace I'm going, I ought to make it in three days. That's what I'm thinking. Three more days.

It's strange how I hardly look around to see where I am anymore. I just want to keep going until I get there. If I hadn't come this far, I might stop now because what I'm doing makes no sense. Nor is it clear to me what I will do when I reach the end. Turn around, I guess.

Tomorrow for sure I'll have to stop and get food and water. Maybe I can find a shirt, too. Somehow I managed to leave behind my last bag of clothes in Vicksburg. Now I'm down to the clothes I'm wearing, the long-sleeve shirt that has lost its mosquito repellant if it ever had any and the expensive pants from Switzerland that look like they've come from a Goodwill store.

I ought to take a bath and shave, but I need a new razor blade to get through this beard, and there are no more blades. Tomorrow I'll get razor blades when I stop for food for Horatio and me.

The whine of an outboard motor spreads across the water as a small boat passes downriver in the quiet channel. There are two men in the boat, one holding the tiller and another hunched forward in the bow. The man at the tiller points toward the island, toward Horatio and me I suppose, and slows the boat. They are a distance away, and I don't acknowledge them. I don't want company. Nevertheless the boat turns sharply toward the island. When the boat is close enough that I can see their faces, the man at the tiller raises his hand in a perfunctory wave. The other man remains slumped in the bottom of the boat and stares at me without expression from dead vacant eyes. Or maybe he is staring at Horatio. A low growl is coming from his throat. I've never heard him do that before.

"Evening," the man at the tiller says after he wedges his boat up onto the bank beside the canoe. He is a big man, and the coldness of his voice and his eyes sends a shiver down my spine. "You come down the river in that?"

He points toward the canoe. I nod that I have. I see no reason to tell him the truth. The man turns off the switch to the outboard motor and suddenly it's very quiet.

"You from up north?"

"A ways."

"Got anything to drink?"

"Water."

"Want a beer?"

With his foot he nudges the slumped-over man who makes me think of the prison farm upriver at Angola. They both do, although the big man at the motor goes through the motions of sociability while the other one doesn't bother.

"Give him a beer."

The man with dead eyes looks back at the other one. I don't want a beer from these men.

"Give him a beer," the man repeats.

The passenger is wearing a bright yellow rain hat although it isn't raining. It hasn't rained for weeks. He opens a cooler and holds out a can of beer for me to take. I rise from the log, walk over to the water, and take the beer from his hand. Horatio has gotten up, too, and is watching us alertly with his ears turned toward the back of his head.

"Thanks."

"Somebody's been messing with our lines," says the big man from the rear of the boat. "Got three or four missing. That ain't you, is it?"

"It's not me. I came down the other side of this island."

"You take that dog with you in the boat?"

"Yes."

Horatio has dropped his stick and is studying us the way the big man is studying me, the way I'm studying him. There is nothing to study in the man with dead eyes. I look in their boat to see what kind of weapons they have. There is a broken oar and a closed tackle box with blood smeared on the lid. I have a knife back in the tent. It won't do me any good.

"You want to buy you a nice catfish? Open up the lid so that the man can see what we got."

The other man doesn't seem to do anything on the first command.

"Open it up," the big man says again.

"Don't bother. I don't have a pan big enough to cook it in."

The big man opens his tackle box and pulls out a long fillet knife. Behind me I hear Horatio's growl getting louder.

"I'll slice it up for you."

"No thanks. I already ate."

"You sure you ain't the one been messin' with our lines? You can just give us fifty dollars and we'll call it square."

"It wasn't me."

I return the beer to the front seat of the boat in front of the man who doesn't bother to look up. Why is he sitting on the bottom of the boat instead of on the empty seat? His shirt is buttoned tight around his skinny neck. The other man is powerfully built across the shoulders and arms, but he's going soft in the gut. He might be forty years old. He might be older than that. If I thought he would leave us alone I would give him fifty dollars, but I have no confidence that he would. When I first saw the two men, I thought the man sitting on the bottom of the boat was the dangerous one. Now I suspect I was wrong.

But then I might be wrong about everything. Almost everybody on this river has tried, in one way or another, to help us get down it. Maybe these two men just take a little time to warm up. I might be the one who started us off wrong by wanting to be left alone.

"So now you won't drink our beer," the big man says. "You got a problem with us coming here? Maybe you think you own this island?"

"I don't own anything around here."

"How about that dog? He yours?"

"Yes. That's my dog."

"You ought to teach him some manners. It ain't polite to growl at company. I'll give you five dollars for him. He'll be good catfish bait if nothing else."

The man smiles, showing tobacco-stained teeth but no heart. I wasn't wrong after all.

"The dog's not for sale."

"Everything on this river is for sale," the big man says, "one way or another."

He puts the knife on top of the tackle box and steps out of the boat into the river. He is wearing tall rubber boots.

"Come here, boy," he calls to Horatio.

He bends over to attract Horatio to him, but Horatio doesn't want anything to do with him. "Let's just leave the dog alone."

The man slowly straightens himself and puffs up his chest as big as he can. I haven't been in a fight since I was a teenager, but I puff myself up the same way. Now we're face-to-face, two puffed-up men who ought to know better. I don't want this. I might very well lose a fight with this man. Maybe he'll decide that Horatio and I aren't worth the effort.

"You don't want us here, we'll pack up and leave. I got no problem with that."

"You got no problem," the man says, "then I'll just take the dog."

He means to walk by me and get Horatio, and I put out my hand to stop him. He swings at me, but he's slow and I'm able to duck enough that his fist glances off the side of my head without effect. My fist goes deep into his soft gut and catches him off-guard. Then I hit him again, a little higher, and knock the wind out of him. Horatio leaps at the man and grabs his arm. His growl rises to a high pitch, and he won't let go even as the man swings his arm around. I hit the man in the face with an anger that has increased with the fury of Horatio's growl. It's frightening how fast it comes, but it's here and I use it on this man.

My head seems to explode, and now I'm swinging at the man with dead eyes who has the club in his hand, but I'm not hitting anything anymore. I'm not angry, either. All the anger is far away now. I hear Horatio barking, screaming far away. Then everything becomes quiet. I'm not swinging anymore but someone is. Someone far away.

It must be dark, but I see my hand when I lift it up to my eyes. It can't be dark if I see my hand. And the other hand. I see it, too. The river is so close that I must be in it, but I feel dry sand beneath me.

Everything hurts as I raise myself up from the sand. I can't tell where it hurts or why, but it hurts to sit up. I shake my head to clear my mind, but that's a mistake I won't make again. To shut out the pain that rattles through my skull, I close my eyes again. Now it is dark. Slowly I open them and start over.

There is enough light to see the river and the trees behind me. I am on the island where the men came in the boat, where I fought with a man and must have lost. What is there to fight about on this island?

Horatio. There is a voice somewhere calling Horatio.

A dog is lying in the sand, but it's too still to be Horatio. Horatio would be running back and forth on the beach, bringing his stick so that I will throw it for him. He would be dancing around me, this Horatio I know. I walk over to the dog and kneel down beside it. Blood has dried in the socket of his eye where I whisk away the flies that are already gathering.

Something dies within us, within me, bearing witness to cruel untimely death. I'm losing my ability to shut it out. All death was this way for Amleth, whether it was a person or a cow or a spider. He should have built his cabin in some far-off land instead of returning to the sandhills where we kill for our livelihoods. In some distant way I understood how he felt, but I never told him. Instead I pointed out the weakness in his logic. The spider was a predator; so was the wolf. The cattle he wouldn't eat wouldn't be raised if we couldn't kill them. But when I rode out on Geronimo and found Amleth on the side of the hill that led down to the river, where there used to be a fence that I had to straighten and he had to remove, I wanted only to tell him that at last I understood. At first I was afraid to touch him for fear of doing more harm, but I had to see that no one, not even I, could bring more harm to him. His face was swollen and dried blood gathered around his mouth where he had bitten his tongue from the impact of his fall. It was all very clear, from the depression in the blowout where his head had struck the ground to the stiffening of his body. I knelt and cradled him, holding his cheek against mine the way I did when he was a baby fighting sleep. Why can't we hold on to them longer? What is it that makes them push us away or we them? When my knees couldn't tolerate bending any longer, I sat down with Amleth still within my grasp.

—You see, it's not so bad. You'll be all right. It's all right.

George finds me with Amleth and races back on his horse to get Juan. Then they come together in Juan's pickup. Juan looks white as death. But death isn't white; it is multicolored and warm. I get into the back of the pickup with Amleth because I don't want to leave him and I don't want to be inside the cab. Juan drives slowly over the rough ground of the pasture, agonizing over every bump.

"I'm sorry," he says out his open window. "I'm so sorry."

—It's all right, Juan. It's all right.

With my back to the pickup cab I hold Amleth's head against my chest so that the bumps will not hurt him anymore. George rides behind on Geronimo. Geronimo is an old horse now, but still strong and steady. Geronimo watches the truck and follows us where we go, but George never looks up from the ground.

At the house I carry Amleth inside and lay him on his bed. The bed is so small. When he was a boy there was room for me or Annie to sit beside him, but now the bed is too small. I get a chair. Juan brings another chair and sits beside me. He is crying but I am not—not because I'm strong. No, it is nothing like that.

I wipe tears and blood on my shirtsleeve as I pick up Horatio and carry him down to the river. The flies smell blood and circle my head while I kneel beside Horatio and brush them away from his horrible eye.

It doesn't make any sense. Why did they want Horatio? Why did they have to kill him? What am I doing here on this river?

With a board that has floated onto the bank I scrape out a shallow grave and ease Horatio into it as it fills with water. I cover him with sand and rocks so that at least the flies won't be able to get to him. His grave is below the line in the sand where the river has been and where it will come again.

Then I realize that the aluminum canoe is gone. They killed Horatio and took the canoe. Gloria, I think, even though it hurts to think. It hurts to move my feet, too, but I walk across the sandspit where Gloria is still waiting among the trees. I try to pull her down to the water. First I have to untie the rope; then I can pull her to the water.

Now I am standing beside Gloria. Horatio's grave is on the other side of the island, the tent is back in the trees, or at least it was. Maybe they took it, too. I don't want to go back and look. I should get help, but nothing can help Horatio now. When I pull away the cockpit cover from the kayak and drop it on the sand, it's as dark inside the kayak as Horatio's grave. Gloria floats away from the island, but I follow her and lower myself into the seat. The waist skirt and life jacket are in the cockpit beneath my legs. It's too much effort to dig them out, too much effort to lift my hands over my head or reach behind me, so I leave them where they are. The paddle is in my hand. It

reaches for the water, and soon I can no longer see the island. Soon everything is as dark as Horatio's grave.

~ ~ ~

Unlike daylight when there is no hiding from the sun, the night is cool.
If I hold my head still, I am able to keep from getting dizzy. The
paddle moves so slowly that the languid current is almost faster than the
stroke. Sometimes the paddle stroke sends sharp flashes of pain into my
stomach and ribs, into my skull. It keeps my mind from wandering.

On the left side of the river are acres of lights from a chemical plant; on
the right, a few beacons from a river plantation. A cargo ship is coming
upriver, its deck and superstructure aflame in light. A barge close to the plantation is moving more slowly. Its powerful spotlight sweeps across the water,
but Gloria stays out of the spotlight. Beyond the industrial site are the lights
of a town.

Juan said he would come for me in the pickup no matter where I am, but
I am eighteen hundred miles from the ranch. I would have to wait in a hotel
room for two or three days with myself for company until he arrived. By then
I could be at the end of the river.

So far I haven't imagined what will happen if I get there. The end has
been like the curtain that drops after the last lines of a play and hides all
the actors. Horatio stuck his nose under that curtain, but now he's gone.
Or maybe it's not a curtain that is blocking my vision. Maybe there is
simply nothing there. Nothing is no worse now that it's close than when it
was far away.

A shadow passes closely to the right, and I look over my shoulder at the
faint cone-shaped outline of a buoy. The night takes away all perception of
distance. Maybe Gloria is able to see them. I let her decide if she wants to
head across the river toward the town and drop me off or stay here in the
river. If I stop, Gloria will have to finish alone. I can't drag her on land and
hold her back now that she's so close. She is made for the ocean, and I'd have
to let her go.

The rhythm of the paddle is as automatic as breathing, and I paddle whether I think about it or not. Even when I forget I'm in the river, the paddle continues to enter the water, to pull past my body, and to enter again on the opposite side. If I want to stop, I will have to concentrate long enough to do so. It is too hard to concentrate—easier to look ahead, to watch even if there will be nothing when I get there, to fix on a light ahead, better if it is a single light, then another.

Close to daybreak I find that we have entered the nearly still water of the inside corner of a sharp bend. How did we get here? Gloria always stays with the current unless the wind is up. There is no wind.

A few paddle strokes lodges us in the sand. The contact with land makes me feel old and stiff. Gradually I lift one leg out of the cockpit, then the other, stand in the shallow water, and straighten my body. There is a red glow in the east, and a haze is upon the river and beyond it. It will be hot again. It is warm enough already to make me dizzy.

Something is missing when I get out of the kayak. Horatio is not running free and joyous on the sandbar. There is only Gloria and I, as it was when we began.

From the open front hatch I retrieve the last bottle of water. Beneath the bottle are the paddle jacket and pants I haven't worn for weeks. I pull them out and toss them onto the sandbar. The stove was in the tent, and without a stove I don't need the bag with extra fuel. In another bag is the epoxy to repair damage to Gloria, rubber gloves, tools, and duct tape. You never know when you might need some duct tape, but I close the bag without knowing. There is no need to look at what's in the rest of them. I toss all of the bags onto the sand-bar so that when the river rises it will carry them away. What difference does it make if I give them up now or the river takes them later? Lying on the bottom is the hatch cover that I fasten back in its place now that Horatio is gone.

As I push Gloria back into the water, she rises easily in the wake of a passing barge, glides lightly and softly through the turmoil caused by its propeller.

There are more ships now, more oil and chemical plants, more docks where goods are transferred from ocean-going ships to river barges or the other way around, but I'm not interested in any of them. Gloria stays in the middle of the river and moves only enough to avoid the barges and ships ahead and behind. I don't look at them as they pass.

One time when I was a boy, my father and I were driving back to the ranch late at night from someplace far away. It was my job to stay awake and keep him company, but my eyelids were so heavy. If I just closed them until we came to the highway sign illuminated at the far reach of the headlights, I would still be able to stay awake afterward. I opened my eyes in time to watch the sign disappear into the darkness behind us. For a little while I felt refreshed, but the eyelids became heavy again. Another marker appears in the water. I'll close my eyes until we reach it.

Amleth is running through the tall grass of the spring pasture. His dog is with him, but the grass is so tall that only the dog's black tail can be seen above it. The dog is happy and Amleth is laughing. I want to run with them, to laugh with Amleth and play with the dog. Light as the air, I lean into the wind and begin to fly. When I call to Amleth, he doesn't hear me. So I call Horatio, but the dog doesn't stop. An explosion rips up the ground beside Amleth and hurls Horatio twisting and turning through the air. The grass turns yellow and freezes solid as winter. Amleth screams but his voice is frozen like the grass. I've become heavy and am falling. Run Amleth! Get out of the way!

    –Run!

There is another loud crash, and I feel pain shooting through my body. Another crash and the noise is not a dream anymore. Gloria is floating sideways in the current, and my body is wedged down into the cockpit too stiff to move. Two barges, tied up side-by-side, are anchored downriver. Their bows project over the water like the upper jaws of half-submerged traps. I ought to do something to get away from those barges, but I feel like closing my eyes instead—just a few seconds, no more.

A bolt of lightning rips the air over us, and the explosion that follows nearly knocks me over. Or something does. The paddle is dipping into the water, and Gloria is moving away from the jaws of the barges.

Clouds now surround this flat land, swirling and reshaping themselves, dropping down, rising up, and rolling into each other. A wall of rain advances up the river and washes over Gloria and me. It's warm and cool at the same time—cooler than the hot moist air but warm like the river. I could sponge up the water in the cockpit and squeeze it out, but why bother? The water will have to rise high in the cockpit before it makes any difference. I let it rise.

Rain of such volume can't last long. It turns the surface of the river white where I cup my hand above the water and try to catch the drops. They dissolve as soon as they touch my skin. I can't see the clouds anymore, or either bank, or the barges and ships in the river.

The rain washes the mud from Gloria. She becomes as clean as she was before she ever entered the river. No bags stuffed with gear are on her deck, no maps, no bottles or trash to diminish her beauty. She is as sleek and beautiful as the day I painted her gold name on the bow.

I unbutton my shirt, pull it away from body, and drop it into the cockpit at my feet. Now the rain washes me, too. It may rain this hard for days and days, but I will never be as clean as Gloria.

A harsh sound booms across the river like thunder except that it doesn't go away. It is insistent and artificial like the rock walls that interfere with the course of the river. The tempo of the paddle speeds up to take us away from it. In the river everything will pass—wind and rain, ships and barges, rough water and smooth. Everything passes.

The sound becomes words and I look back and see a boat close behind with its bow pointed at us. I've begun to hate these boats with big engines and curved hulls that throw off such wakes. It has the whole river but still wants our narrow passage.

The boat follows us as we move to the side. A man in uniform comes out onto the deck bearing a long-barreled gun. The word Police is written in bold letters on the bow. The loudspeaker is talking to me. I sweep the paddle wide and Gloria turns sideways in the current as the engines of the police boat throttle down. Another man steps out of the cabin and stands at the rail beside the one with the gun. I see, now, that it's a shotgun.

"Didn't you hear me back there?" he shouts.

The large wake thrown off from the steep bow of the police boat catches up to Gloria, and I turn her into the face of the wake so that she won't be thrown over.

"Didn't you hear us?" he shouts again.

The series of waves passes, as everything passes, and the river is calm again.

"What do you want?"

He says something, but I can't understand him. The police boat has more momentum than Gloria and drifts past us so that the two policemen walk on the deck toward the back of their boat to remain even with Gloria and me. I rest the paddle across the open cockpit. The talking policeman is a short man with black hair and a large mustache that covers his mouth. He would be easier to understand if I could see his mouth. We are drifting farther apart. Perhaps that is the reason for his irritation, that and the rain that is falling. The rain feels good to me.

"Didn't you see that Navy frigate back there?" the policeman shouts.

"No."

"You have to follow us back where the Coast Guard is waiting."

"Why?"

The policeman shouts something over his shoulder, but I can't hear what he says. The police boat propeller reverses and shrinks the gap between us.

"You're supposed to stay a hundred yards away from a military ship. You're lucky they didn't blow you out of the water."

"How far is a hundred yards?"

"What?"

He turns again and shouts at the cabin for the driver to shut down the engine. I paddle backward to move out of the way, for the boat will soon overtake Gloria and me. I could compensate for the stop and go of the propeller, but I don't want to. The policeman retraces his steps to the front of the deck.

"What did you say?" he shouts.

"How far is a hundred yards?"

We're in the middle of this wide river approaching a bend that a towboat is negotiating with a dozen empty barges in front of it. A tanker is coming downriver. Barges are tied up on the right bank, one after another along the bank and side by side out into the river. Docks, machines, factories, and warehouses take up all the space. The river might be a mile wide here, but who can say for sure? We drift apart once again.

"Come over here," he yells at me. He gestures brusquely with his hand as if he's directing traffic in the middle of a street.

I paddle a few strokes until he raises his hand to stop me.

"That's close enough. I'm not going to talk to you out here. You understand? You're going to follow us back up the river where the Coast Guard is waiting, and then we'll talk. You got that?"

He wipes his bushy moustache that is getting wet in the rain. I raise my paddle in case he hasn't seen it.

"I can't paddle back against the current."

He glares at the paddle. The man with the shotgun inclines his head toward the policeman who is doing all the talking and says something in his ear.

"There's a place where you can land a little farther down," the policeman yells. "I want you to follow us there."

The policemen return to the cabin, and the loudspeaker broadcasts an order, "Stay fifty yards behind us."

He continues to use distances that don't mean anything to me, but I paddle after the police boat anyway. The police boat begins to pull away, but I continue with a rhythm that is beyond my control. Gloria stays within the V of the boat's wake, but we drop farther behind until the police boat slows down.

The policeman is broadcasting again from his loudspeaker. He will land in front of those trees up ahead. How green those trees look. Is there a park beyond them, an oasis in this industrial desert? The loudspeaker is giving more instructions, telling me where to land. Do they think I'm dangerous? Do they think that I carry a bomb inside Gloria? I suppose absurdity can reach that far.

Gloria and I land beyond the police boat, which is not handling the shallow water as easily as Gloria. I lift Gloria over the rocks that line the bank and set her down on the flat sandy ground. Over the loudspeaker the policeman tells me to remain beside my boat, and I stand beside Gloria and watch the police boat backing toward the beach. The policeman who had the shotgun doesn't have it any longer. He has put on a rubber rain slicker and is using a long pole to measure the depth of the water over the stern. He signals for the boat to stop.

I pull my shirt out of the cockpit, wring out the water, and put it on. The pocket has been ripped and hangs uselessly from the bottom seam.

Turning away from the police boat I look through an opening in the willow trees that grow next to the water. It doesn't matter where I am, where there is water, there are willows. Beyond the trees there is a house built on stilts, and it's not alone. We have landed among a row of houses standing in front of the levy.

The police boat drops anchor out from the bank, and a hoist lowers a rubber dinghy into the river. The policeman who talks and the other who had the shotgun climb down the ladder into the dinghy. Neither man makes a graceful entry. The policeman starts the outboard motor on the dinghy, and they buzz the short distance to shore. The policeman who talks is now also wearing a rain slicker. It has the stripes of a sergeant on the side of it. The other man is much bigger than the sergeant, taller and wider with sunburned cheeks in contrast to his dark glasses that he wears even in the rain. Beneath the tan are red splotches on the fleshy surface of his face.

Without saying anything the sergeant looks into the cockpit of the kayak.

"You're supposed to wear your life jacket," he says, pointing to the life jacket on the floor of the cockpit. "It won't do you any good in there."

"It's too hot to wear it."

"What do you have in here?" he asks. His finger is now pointing to the front hatch.

"Nothing."

"Do you want to open it up for us?"

It doesn't sound like a question, and I open the hatch and stand back. The sergeant bends down and shines a flashlight into the narrow void. While he looks at nothing, I notice that a woman is walking toward us through the trees, a woman with long red hair and a bright yellow blouse, a colorful woman. The policemen are intent upon searching Gloria and don't notice her coming up behind them.

"Going too fast?" she asks.

I'm surprised that she talks to me and not the policemen. The policemen are surprised, too, and whirl around to face her.

"We'll just have you stand back a bit, ma'am," the sergeant says.

She takes an exaggerated step backward and smiles pleasantly to the sergeant.

"A woman has a natural curiosity about people who come onto her property."

"We won't be here long," the sergeant tells her. "Open up the back of your boat," he tells me. He is no longer framing his orders with a question.

I unbuckle the straps over the rear hatch cover except for the one that Horatio chewed through and am reminded again that he is not with me. He wouldn't like these men either. The sergeant peers into another empty void.

"Where did you get this boat?"

"I made it."

"You made this?"

He doesn't believe me.

"Yes, I made it."

"You from up north?" the sergeant asks.

The other men asked this question, too, and I don't like it.

"I'm from Nebraska."

"Are you telling me that you came all the way from Nebraska in this?"

He points down to Gloria. She doesn't look like she has come that far. The scars from sand and rock are beneath her, and her deck is as sleek and clean as when she started.

"The Mississippi doesn't run through Nebraska," the other policeman says.

"You got some ID on you?" the sergeant asks.

I reach for my wallet. It should be in my pants pocket in a waterproof plastic case, but it's not there. I touch my front pockets, although I know the wallet won't be there either.

"I think it was stolen."

They don't believe that either.

"Who stole it?" the sergeant asks.

"Two men."

It's hard to separate the men upriver from these two, but I have to try. I wonder where I am now.

"I was camping last night on an island, and two men came in a boat. It wasn't as big as yours. They wanted to take my dog from me. I wouldn't let them, and one of them hit me with a club and knocked me out. They killed my dog. Here."

I tilt my head toward them and pull my hair away from the spot on top of my head where I know there is some kind of cut. It leaves blood on my finger. They will have to believe the blood.

"My God," the woman says, "let me see that."

Neither policeman stops her from coming toward me. The blur of colors—red and yellow—makes me dizzy. Or maybe it's the solid land. The woman touches my head and gently pulls it down. I reach out and hold on to her arm to steady myself.

"You'll need stitches in this, and you've probably got a concussion. Either you get this man medical attention right now or I'm going to do it."

She's not talking to me now. I raise my head so that the dizziness will pass.

"If you came down in this boat, where's all your gear?"

"Lost some of it on the way, some is back on the island or they stole it, threw the rest away. I'm about done with this trip."

"You bet you are," the sergeant says. "You're a hazard out there. A big ship loses control, you wouldn't be able to get out of its way. Besides, we got a big storm coming, and that little boat of yours isn't what you want to be in when it arrives. And getting that close to a Navy frigate is crazy. They're extra touchy about security after 9-11."

He's getting rid of me, so he can say what he wants. I won't argue.

"Bullshit, sergeant," the woman says. "I'm tired of 9-11 being an excuse for every idiot on the planet. You know as well as I do that if the Navy were concerned about security, they wouldn't be docking their ship here. What are they doing in New Orleans anyway? Protecting the strippers in the French Quarter? They're the hazards, not this man in his little boat."

I think she's on my side. She's still holding my arm although I've released hers. I feel myself weaving back and forth within her grasp. The two policemen have joined together on the other side of Gloria, so it's two facing two. They're tired of me, tired of standing in the rain, and will just let me go if she will let them.

"And if you want to do your duty, you will find the men who assaulted and robbed him and not bother him about paddling too close to our precious Navy."

"Where did this happen?" the sergeant asks.

"I'm not sure. Upriver, somewhere."

"More than a mile?"

"More than that."

"He'll have to report it to the sheriff in whatever parish he was in," the sergeant tells the woman beside me.

"That's what we'll do," she says.

Now they will leave if she will let them. The policemen are hoping she will.

"I'll see that he gets medical treatment," she says. "If we need anything from you, we'll call you."

She leads me through the gate of a wire fence that runs along the river. As we reach the bottom of the stairway that leads up to the deck of the house built on stilts, the engine of the police boat starts up and the noise heads back up the river.

"Did you really throw away your gear?" she asks.

"Yes."

"Why?"

"It's a long story."

"I'll bet it is."

～～～

Her name is Gloria. When she walked through the gate and saw Gloria in gold letters on the kayak, she thought it was some sort of magic that brought us here. She believes in magic.

"Why not?" she asks. "It's as good as anything."

We're sitting in metal chairs on the deck of her batture camp, as she calls the house on stilts. The chair arms of sprung steel curve down to form the base, which rocks back and forth every time I move. Before us is a plank table where Gloria has placed a glass pitcher of ice water. Condensation runs down the side of the pitcher and puddles on the table. I have a thirst that I can't quench and am already drinking my third glass of water. Gloria has carried Gloria inside the fence where she will be safe from scavengers prowling the bank or from any sudden rise in the river. If it were earlier in the spring, she would carry Gloria all the way up to the deck because the river sometimes rises high enough on the levy that a wake from a passing ship washes water up through the floorboards.

The rain has stopped. More than that, the sky has become cloudless for all that I can see through the tall sycamore trees that shade the deck where we sit. I'm holding a wet towel on my head. Wrapped inside the towel is a bag of ice cubes. We're waiting for a doctor she called to come and look at the cut. I'm surprised there are still doctors who make house calls.

Gloria makes me feel that I haven't imposed upon her at all, that it's as natural as anything to have someone land on her beach with the police behind him. Instead of asking me to give an account of myself, she feels obliged to explain where I've landed.

"There are only fourteen left," she says, talking about the row of stilt-supported houses on the river side of the levy. "The Corps of Engineers wanted them all torn down, but even the Corps will listen to a bunch of rednecks with shotguns. So the camps stayed. Some of them are fancy places now, but most of them are like mine, pieced together with salvage that floated down the river."

"That's a lot of salvage."

"Oh sometimes we have to help it along."

Her smile holds back the rest of the story. I switch hands holding the towel and ice and wait for her to go on, but she doesn't. Chickens are squawking through the intermittent crowing of roosters from the camp next door, and a jackhammer is breaking up concrete a distance away. From where we sit among the trees, it sounds like a very determined woodpecker.

"So how do you help it along?"

I don't have any right to pry, but Gloria doesn't seem to mind.

"Six or seven years ago I decided to replace those two pilings at the end of the deck. The old ones were rotten. I knew there were plenty of pilings at the salvage yard up there at the bend."

She points toward the bend in the river visible through the willow trees that grow close to the water. The sun is headed that way.

"Maybe you noticed it coming down."

I didn't notice it.

"Anyway, I rationalized that the salvage yard owner had stolen them from somebody else, and stealing them from him wasn't like stealing them from the rightful owner. You should see what happens when there's a wreck out there. Everybody becomes a salvage operator, grabbing and laying claim to whatever he can get his hands on. Besides, I needed the pilings and didn't have any money.

"So I paddled upriver in my canoe in the middle of the night, pulled two of the smaller pilings loose from the jam, and tied them to the canoe. The current got me, and we started heading for a moored barge. Somehow my rope got twisted around the canoe and I couldn't get it untangled. Just before the pilings went under the barge, I cut loose and escaped. If I hadn't, they would have dragged me under with them. I suppose I would have had it coming.

"The next day, Mr. Buglosi, the owner of the salvage yard came down here and told me that he would bring me whatever I needed. He didn't want me to kill myself trying to steal from him. So you see there are no secrets here on this river."

Maybe this camp is what Amleth had in mind for the cabin he wanted to build. I'd imagined something more substantial, something more expensive, but maybe it was like this, although you could wait a long time beside that river in the sandhills and there wouldn't be enough salvage to build anything. But we had piles of lumber on the ranch that we saved with only a vague use in mind. Juan was like my father and grandfather. He could never throw anything away. In the tool shed we had buckets of mismatched rusty nails that my brother and I had pulled from old boards and straightened on a concrete block. Many times I thought about bulldozing all the junk together, setting fire to what would burn, and burying the rest, but I could never gather the will to overcome the generational inertia or Juan's religious attachment to old junk. All together there was probably enough scrap for several cabins, for a deck like this one and the little shed at the far end, which like the rest of her camp only more so is a combination of mismatched boards, doors, and windows—lots of windows for light where he could put the piano if he wanted to.

"Did the windows float down the river, too?"

I point to the little shed where I imagine Amleth's piano.

"They might have come from an abandoned house, if I remember right."

Her cheekbones rise up in front of her eyes when she laughs so that she has to look over them to see above her humor.

"It's a cozy little room. What do you use it for?"

"It used to be my painting studio, but I'm thinking about tearing it down to open up the view. I don't paint anymore. When I was in law school, I discovered that I could always sell a painting in the French Quarter of a naked woman with fair skin and red hair."

She has a way of bringing me along to a certain point, then stopping. I'm having trouble reconciling the different parts of her story—law school, stolen pilings, appropriated windows, paintings of a naked woman with red hair and fair skin—although they are not as difficult to reconcile as they might once have been.

"I miss it sometimes," she says.

"What?"

"The river. This old shack. The people here. Their stories. Sometimes I think I shouldn't have moved away. I don't live here anymore, you see, but I can't bear to sell the place. I keep coming back to make sure that everything is okay, to make sure that I'm the same person who used to live here. But that wasn't the reason I came today. Today I just came here to batten down the hatches before the storm arrives."

"What storm?"

"Tropical storm Arlene. The policeman told you about it."

"That's right. Now I remember."

"It's out in the Gulf right now and is headed toward the delta. They say it's gaining strength and might turn into a hurricane. It's too early for hurricanes, but that's what they say. They've already begun evacuating workers from the oil platforms."

The doctor we've been waiting for walks out onto the deck with a backpack full of supplies. He must know the way through the house because I never heard him arrive and she calls him sweetie. He shaves the hair away from the cut and prepares to stitch up the wound. Gloria stands beside him to watch what he's doing. The doctor tells me that I am not to move my head, but it is difficult not to look up when Gloria is standing so close. I feel like I have to adjust my balance as I must do when Gloria and I are in the river. When the doctor finishes the stitches, he gives me a tetanus shot in the arm and tells me that I should rest for a few days.

He smiles at me strangely when I tell him that I'll give Gloria my address so that he can send me a bill. When he walks back into the house, Gloria follows him inside. I pick up the water glass and take another drink. Through the screen door I hear her talking to him in soft intimate tones.

A tanker ship is heading upriver. Part of the name is visible on its hull through the window of willows before it passes from sight. I hear a train whistle not far away, hear the engine and the heavy steel wheels on the tracks.

"Listen, I can't let you walk around like that," Gloria says when she comes back. "Your hair looks pretty bad with that shaved spot in the middle of your head. Let me give you a haircut."

"I'd appreciate that."

"How short would you like it?" she asks.

"As short as you can cut it."

"I have electric clippers that I used to use on my dog."

"That ought to work."

When she returns to the deck, she puts on the attachment that will give the shortest cut and runs it across my scalp, avoiding the patch the doctor has already shaved. The hair falls onto the boards of the deck and through the cracks to the ground below. It feels good to have it gone, cooler and simpler. Gloria runs her hand across the short stubble, feeling for uneven spots. She blows on my head to dislodge stranded clippings. Her breath is sweet and cool compared to the air.

After the haircut I stand in the shower and let the warm water soften my week's beard before shaving it away with the razor Gloria has given me. On the toilet seat is a set of clothes to wear until she washes mine. Who they belong to is another mystery from Gloria. From a tube of toothpaste in her medicine cabinet, I spread paste on my finger and use the finger as a toothbrush. In the strange clothes Gloria has loaned me, I feel like a stranger to myself as I walk out to the deck where Gloria is waiting.

"Feel better?" she asks.

"You have no idea."

"I hope those men who killed your puppy haven't ruined your trip. There are a lot of good people here."

"Good people all the way. It was just bad luck to run into those guys."

"You can use the phone whenever you want and cancel your credit cards before they use them or sell them."

I hadn't thought about the credit cards, and I don't want to think about them now. It will be complicated to find the telephone number for the credit card companies, to push all the buttons until someone will talk to me. I don't have the numbers of the credit cards anyway. That would take another phone call, either to Joe or Rosario, and I don't want to make that call either. Not yet. Most likely my wallet and credit cards are at the bottom of the river.

"Do you help every stranger who comes floating by?"

"Everyone who lands on my beach."

"Are there a lot of us?"

"You're the first."

"Lucky for me."

"Luck has nothing to do with it."

Gloria looks at me with an expression of kindness that I can't begin to understand. If someone had come in on the river below the ranch house, I wouldn't be looking at him like that.

"You look awfully tired. Maybe you'd like to lie down inside while I make us something to eat."

"Oh, don't do that. I'm not at all hungry. I'll be fine right here."

Gloria pushes her chair away from the plank table, stands up, and looks at me again. It makes me dizzy to look up at her.

"Are you always so thin?"

"I might have lost some weight on this trip."

"That would be one reason to take a trip like yours. Looks like you've found a diet plan that works."

Gloria has a pleasing figure to go along with her pleasing smile. Neither will benefit from a trip like mine.

"I have some homemade spaghetti sauce in the cupboard. You don't dare turn me down."

She walks inside before I can. I notice a buzzing sound coming from the sycamore trees around the batture camp. The sound must have been there all along or at least awhile, but it seems louder after she leaves. Cicadas in the trees. Must be a lot of them.

A hand is on my shoulder, and I look up at Gloria's red hair that is darker than it was before. It is not her hair that is darker. It's the sky beyond it.

"I think I fell asleep. Sorry. I didn't mean to do that."

"It's all right. Do you feel okay?"

"Yes. Fine. Just a little groggy, that's all."

"Spaghetti is ready if you're hungry."

I'm hungrier than I thought I would be, and her spaghetti sauce is the best I've ever tasted. I tell Gloria this several times, and each time she dishes more of it onto my plate. The cicadas are loud enough now that they drown out any noise except for the ships and barges that pass by on the river. Gloria has placed a candle on the table. The night is so still that the flame is seldom disturbed. With the way the night has closed down around us, I have the feeling that we are the last two people beside the river.

"To most people," Gloria says, "New Orleans is the end of the river. Maybe this is as far as you want to go."

"I don't think it's the end."

"I don't think so either. You have to be careful when you get down there. A few weeks ago there was a story in the *Times-Picayune* about a fisherman who lost power in his boat. The river carried him out into the Gulf twenty miles before a shrimper found him."

"I've heard a lot of stories about that river."

"I have, too. Someday I'm going to do what you're doing, start way up the river and paddle down here. I thought I would use a canoe, but a kayak like Gloria might be better."

"You can use Gloria after I finish. You start something like this, and you find that you don't know how to do it until you're almost done. But Gloria already knows the way, and she'll take good care of you. You won't even have to change her name."

"A kayak like Gloria would be a sweet way to come down the river."

The river-longing in her eyes is different from the others I've seen. Every longing is different, I remind myself, different and the same—different in why it comes but always with the same hope. You hope the river knows something you don't.

"Would you draw me a map and show me where you've come from? Maybe give me an idea what I could expect if I ever get up the nerve to do it myself?"

"I could draw you a map."

Gloria gathers the dishes from the table and disappears through the door into the cabin. I think I'll wake up any moment now and learn that this has all been a dream or that this person in these strange clothes isn't really me. But Gloria comes back outside before I wake up and places a sheet of paper and a pencil on the plank table. She slides the candle closer to the paper and moves her chair closer to mine.

I begin by drawing Nebraska. It's the easiest state for me to draw. From there I add Iowa, or as much as I can remember of it, and keep on going south.

"You might have to help me down here. I'm trying to figure out how Louisiana and Mississippi are arranged."

"Like this," she says and takes the pencil from my fingers.

She draws Louisiana as it cuts across Mississippi and finishes the state down to the delta where I haven't yet been. Then she hands the pencil back to me.

"Wait," she says. "I'll get a blue pen for the river."

Now she's gone again, and I put the pencil down on the table. I rub my fingers over my scalp and feel the short hair that must be mine. Gloria returns with a pen in her hand.

"I started up here on the Loup River. It's just a little river in the sandhills."

"Sand hills?" she asks.

"That's right, sand with a little dirt on top—enough for grass to grow and not much else. But from there you can see about as far as you'd ever want to see."

"It sounds beautiful," she says.

She must have heard something that didn't come from me, but I guess she's right. It is beautiful country. As I draw the blue river on the map, I see Juan at my first campsite, Joe as a boy, Joe as a man. Rebecca and her children. Bob Morrison and his airboat. The goose hunters. Rosario. Tom Reeves on the Missouri. The fisherman and his son. Erika, Angela, and her two boys. Horace and Velda and Richard Catch the Clouds. Horatio—his black and white face that made me laugh. Marta before Vicksburg. And Amleth, always Amleth.

"From here I'm not sure I know how it goes."

Gloria takes the pen and draws the river from the middle of Louisiana all the way down to the Gulf.

"You're here," she says, "and this is the ocean at last."

"At last."

Drawing the river has made me feel as if I'm in Gloria again. The constant sensation of motion is disorienting in the dim light of the candle, and I hold on to the arm of the metal chair to steady myself. Gloria places her hand on top of mine.

"Ken said you need to rest awhile. Please stay here as long as you want. It will be good to have someone living here again."

I'm tempted to tell this Gloria that I will stay awhile, but I can't. The river flowing in the darkness beyond her deck has accumulated thousands of miles of momentum by this point, and there's no way to stop it now.

~ ~ ~

Gloria rolls onto her side, and I shove the paddle out to brace us, striking something more substantial than water as I rise into a dark place.

I am not in the river.

My feet touch the wood floor, and I remember Gloria and her batture camp beside the river where waves wash through the floorboards in high water. When I went to bed I thought I might sleep forever, through the night and through the storm that is coming but hasn't come yet.

I walk into the next room where a door leads to the footbridge that connects the batture camp to the levy. From the other end comes the deep rumble of a towboat's engine as a barge makes the turn and heads upriver.

Outside on the deck I look for a sign of morning. There is a general glow from the lights all around the camp, and it reminds me of viewing a town from a distance in the sandhills—except there are no hills here unless you count the steep mound of the levy. The surface of the river is a few feet above sea level, but the rest of the river, two hundred feet or more, is below. It pushes on with the momentum of a continent behind it and all the ghosts and dreams that have drowned in its mighty flow. It should have washed them all away by now, but still they come.

If I wait longer, I might never finish. Arlene is out in the Gulf, gathering strength. I could wait for her at the batture camp and gather my own strength, but it is not my strength that has brought me here. The river will carry me if I'm too tired to paddle. It has no choice.

Inside the batture camp I pull the chain on the hanging light above the counter that separates the kitchen from the rest of the room. One of the three light bulbs comes on and illuminates the counter, the old gas stove, and the refrigerator, topped by a clock that no longer works. On the counter are my clothes that Gloria washed for me. She has sewn up my shirt pocket. On top of the shirt is the compass she found in my pants pocket and a twenty-dollar bill, still soggy from the day before. So I'm not broke after all.

I pick up the compass and turn it in my hand. The needle continues to point toward the door that leads out to the levy. Beside the pile of clothes is the map Gloria and I drew. I find a pencil and turn the map over to the blank side of the page.

> *Dear Gloria,*
> *Thank you for your kindness. The weather is fair, and*
> *I've decided to take off before the storm comes. Thank*

you for washing my clothes and for the wonderful dinner. I may never be hungry again.

I am leaving you my compass as an offering of gratitude. You will notice a mark scratched on the rim that shows where I'm from. I'll be going the other way awhile yet.

I'll try to get Gloria back to you so that you can take her on your own trip, but I can't think that far ahead right now. It's the strangest thing. I don't know how to explain it. All I know is that I'm so close to the ocean I can almost taste it.

Don't worry about the weather or the river. Gloria is a truer partner than any man has a right to hope for, but she will never forgive me if I stop now.

John

It's strange to see Gloria's name on paper rather than on the side of the kayak. I rub my finger over Rosario's mark and place the compass below my name. Now I'm free to leave.

At the sink I bend down to drink water from the faucet and straighten back up to fill the large plastic water bottle I carry with me. It is all that I need. Gloria is waiting beside the pilings at the bottom of the steps. In the dim light that glows over the levy, I hoist her up to my shoulder and carry her through the gate, through the trees to the river. She is as light as she was back in the barn in the sandhills before I loaded her down with gear and supplies. When her bow touches the water, she turns lightly and eagerly downriver.

"Are you ready, Gloria?"

She is always ready.

The river shimmers from the lights on either bank, taking what light there is and increasing the luminance. The last waves from a passing barge wash up the rocks on the bank and dislodge Gloria's stern. I lodge it again when I sit in the cockpit.

When I push off from the bank, the river takes us away. I look back to the dark void on the bank where I think the batture camp should be, but already I can't be certain that I'm looking at the right place, for the river changes everything.

My body hurts when I stretch forward with the paddle, but I must stretch if I am to reach the end of the river before Arlene arrives. My ribs are not broken, the doctor said; they are only sore from the boots of the men who killed Horatio.

Skyscrapers rise above the shimmering water. They are as out of place as the revetment that confines the river, as the jetty walls and dikes that block its current, as the casinos in the wilderness that line its banks. There are casinos here, too—bigger and brighter than any I have seen so far. But they pass away, too, and beyond the sharp right bend ahead the sky is hinting of light that is not artificial. Even here you can tell the difference.

Warily I watch the tall lighted buildings pass behind us as we slip silently through the city of New Orleans. The policeman said that I have no right to be in this river, but I am here and he is not. Rules in the river are different from those on land. That must have been how Gloria felt when she stole the pilings from the salvage yard. Certainly, surely, this river and this time are good for stealing away.

The steep enormous bow of a big ship emerges from the sharp bend and turns toward the skyscrapers we have left behind. It, too, steals quietly through the city. Its propellers are far below the surface of the river, and its engine is buried deep within its steel walls. As it passes, Gloria glides easily through its forward wake.

When the sun rises over the left bank, there is not even a hint of breeze from the south. Arlene must have turned away and taken all the wind with her. Wispy clouds float high in the sky, gold from the morning sun. Here the river is easier to navigate than it was above New Orleans where barges and ships lined the banks and crisscrossed unpredictably. Here are more ocean-going ships than barges, but for long stretches Gloria and I have the river to ourselves.

The river current has slowed almost to a standstill, as if the ocean is pushing against it with a force nearly its equal. With the paddle I push the other way at a steady pace. I don't know how to do anything else.

By now I ought to know why I'm here, but I know less than when I started. From the beginning people have asked how far I was going, and in the beginning I was foolish enough to answer that I was going to the end of the river. It sounded like an accomplishment of some importance. There is nothing important about the accomplishment. The river has taught me that much, at least.

Overhead the thumping sound of a helicopter draws my attention. It's not the first helicopter I've heard. Maybe they're still bringing in workers from the oil platforms, or maybe they're taking them back out. It has become hot, and the sun hurts my eyes if I look up from the river too long. It's burning the top of my head where Gloria has cut my hair short. I should have at least looked for Juan's hat before I left the island. I take off my shirt, soak it in the water, and wrap it around my head. I conserve drinking water so I won't have to go ashore and talk to anyone.

I wonder what Gloria is cooking today. If she can make a tomato sauce so good that you can smell the green vines, she can make anything. Maybe not the red cabbage my grandmother made at Christmas. Or the goose gravy on mashed potatoes. Or my mother's sour cream raisin pie with a crust so tender that you could cut it with a wish. Or Annie's clam chowder on the night of the year's first snow with Amleth and me sitting at the kitchen table, wondering if the chowder isn't ready, but happy that it isn't because it's almost as good to wait and think about as it is to eat. Where did a young woman from the sandhills learn about clams? Or Consuelo's tamales. A dozen of them with Juan's hot sauce and a bottle of tequila would be good right now. I haven't been hungry for weeks, so where is this hunger coming from?

–Horatio, we should have packed in a little food.

When I look up from the water, the front hatch is fastened tight, and Horatio is not there. Was that me who said his name? I look around the kayak, and there is no one else. It was a slip of the mind—How this water transfixes me. If the sun didn't hurt my eyes, I could look up and keep my mind from wandering.

—Are we making any progress, Gloria?

The trees on the left bank appear to be moving against clouds on the horizon, but the trees are rooted in the soil and we are the ones moving. It's all the same, except that something has happened to the horizon. Beyond the low rise of the grassy levy, beyond the narrow band of trees, the ethereal color of the azure sky reflects from water. Gone is the heavy weight of land.

When the sky darkens, I know that I can't stay awake any longer. Entering a small inlet on the left bank I discover a bayou that runs parallel to the river. Beneath overhanging tree limbs I paddle slowly forward, ducking under the lowest branches. A red flower from a vine dangles from a willow branch just ahead, a lonely spot of bright color among the deep green of the leaves, the brown of the water, and the fading light that sifts through the narrow opening of the bayou.

Gloria stops beneath the flower. We are close enough that I can touch it, but I don't. It is so fragile and delicate that the slightest touch could break it apart. There has been enough debauchment on this river.

From the straps in front of the cockpit I pull the bow rope free and tie it to the same tree limb as the flower. The slight current of the bayou takes up the slack in the rope. I release the elastic band of the waist skirt from the combing, lift my feet out of the cockpit, and dangle them over Gloria's hull. I slip out of the life jacket, wedge it behind me as a pillow, and sink lower and lower until I'm no higher than the water.

Snowflakes fall on the red flower. The flower is as light as the air, but the snowflakes are not. Each flake adds weight to the flower and pushes it down toward the river. Amleth wants to save the flower, but there is nothing we can do. If we try to lift it up, it will be ruined. The flower is going to freeze anyway. Then the red petals will turn brown like the dead grass in the sandhills. -Let the river have it. But he won't. He rides into the river on the black horse and plucks the flower from the air. He shouldn't be on the black horse. Horatio runs into the water after him. I try to follow them in Gloria, but she is spinning around and around in the current.

I hear him laughing, but I can't see him anymore, can't see anything. My hand touches the river, and it's warm like summer. A mosquito buzzes in my ear and lands on my face. I slap it so hard that it makes us tremble in the water. Which river are we on? We can't be in the sandhills any longer.

The paddle brushes against my hand, and the ridges of the duct tape guide my fingers along the shaft to the familiar thickening of the tape. The kayak is turning, and I'm afraid I'll begin spinning again.

–Straight, Gloria. Go straight.

The paddle propels us forward, but we become entangled in rope. Blindly I reach forward and touch the branch where the rope is tied. By feel I untie the rope and drop the end into the water. Leaves brush my face as Gloria floats with the imperceptible current. Electric lights form an irregular line far away. A red light on a buoy disappears off to the right. The current becomes stronger, and we are in the river again.

This time the dream was so close that I almost touched him with my hands. This time I heard his voice. I don't want to let him go.

The wind comes up and waves begin washing over the bow. Gloria rocks with them and faces the wind head on. I think I hear hoofbeats, but it's only the wind crossing the water. The water bottle rolls against my feet, and I reach forward in the cockpit and grab it. In one gulp I drink all that's left. From now on I'll have to drink from the river if I'm thirsty.

There are no stars to orient us. Lights of a town appear on the right bank. Perhaps it's the town of Venice that Gloria showed me on the map; perhaps it's not. I left the map back at the batture camp, but it doesn't matter. Even if I had a map, it would be too dark to read it. A map wouldn't show me the wind. A map couldn't follow the black horse. A map wouldn't prevent me from getting lost. Gloria turns with the wind and follows the current. You can't get lost in a river.

It becomes completely dark again, except for a faint light far ahead. It appears, disappears, appears again. It must be a light from a buoy anchored out in the river. I can't tell if it is a mile ahead or a few yards. I can't tell if hours have passed since I left the bayou or a few minutes. When I stop paddling, I'm not sure that we're moving. We must be, but I have no sense of movement except for the waves that rock us back and forth and wash into the cockpit. The water feels cool on my legs, soothing. Maybe I should stretch the waist skirt out over the cockpit combing, but I'm too tired to bother. I'll just close my eyes until we reach the lighted buoy.

I hear piano music and think it must be coming from a radio, but it's too gentle to be radio music. It is like a child touching the keys of a piano for the first time.

"You shouldn't ride when you're tired."

He's making a joke, this fine-looking boy riding the black horse bareback in the river. The boy and horse make a handsome pair.

–Don't they look fine, Gloria?

She picks up her pace to keep up with them. Maybe she's jealous, or maybe she wants to show off a little. We all like to show off now and then. I would help her if I could, but the paddle is floating in the water just beyond my reach. I let the paddle be and give Gloria the lead.

"I wasn't sure you would make it," the boy says.

"Is that really you, Amleth?"

"Is that really you, Dad?"

"I think so. You look fine on the black. I should have let you ride him a long time ago."

"I've been riding him all the time."

The black tosses his head, turns sideways, and prances beside Gloria. He's listening to every word Amleth speaks, waiting for Amleth to give the signal—a light pressure from his legs or a whispered command and the black horse will explode with the force of everything wild within him.

"Have you ridden the black all the way down here?"

"All the way."

The current carries us beyond the last rocks of the jetty where waves collide with the rocks and splash into the air. I thought I would know when we reached the ocean and maybe we have. But there's no difference in the water between river and ocean any more than there was when one river ended and another began. If we have reached the ocean, Gloria is finally home.

"What's it like, this trip you're taking?"

"It's long, Dad. Why are you here? Why are you taking this trip?"

"To find you. Somehow we got separated from each other. Somehow we got lost."

"I've heard that you can't get lost in a river."

The black throws his head again, impatient to be off. Our words mean nothing to him, except that they're holding him back. There's a burning light in his eye that is like the fiery eye of the sun as it burns through a brow of heavy clouds on the horizon.

"I'd like to ride that black horse one more time."

"He's your horse," Amleth says. "You can do whatever you want."

"He's your horse now."

Amleth grasps the black's mane with one hand and slowly reaches down with the other. I expect that he will take my outstretched hand and pull me up onto the horse behind him. Instead he reaches all the way down to the river, picks up the paddle, and holds it out for me. I'm afraid he'll leave if I take it from him, but I have to accept it. There is nothing else I can do. My hand touches his on the paddle, and he smiles at me. Then he leans forward on the black horse, whispers in the black's ear, and they're flying. Amleth bends so low over the black's outstretched neck and his body moves so perfectly with the black's enormous stride that I can't tell the difference between them. They have become one.